PRAISE FO
WALL S'
BESTSELL

MORAN

Seabreeze Inn and *Coral Cottage* series

"A wonderful story… Will make you feel like the sea breeze is streaming through your hair." – Laura Bradbury, Bestselling Author

"A novel that gives fans of romantic sagas a compelling voice to follow." – *Booklist*

"An entertaining beach read with multi-generational context and humor." – *InD'Tale* Magazine

"Wonderful characters and a sweet story." – Kellie Coates Gilbert, Bestselling Author

"A fun read that grabs you at the start." – Tina Sloan, Author and Award-Winning Actress

"Jan Moran is the queen of the epic romance." — Rebecca Forster, *USA Today* Bestselling Author

"The women are intelligent and strong. At the

core is a strong, close-knit family." — Betty's Reviews

The Chocolatier

"A delicious novel, makes you long for chocolate."
– *Ciao Tutti*

"Smoothly written...full of intrigue, love, secrets, and romance." – *Lekker Lezen*

The Winemakers

"Readers will devour this page-turner as the mystery and passions spin out." – *Library Journal*

"As she did in *Scent of Triumph*, Moran weaves knowledge of wine and winemaking into this intense family drama." – *Booklist*

The Perfumer: Scent of Triumph

"Heartbreaking, evocative, and inspiring, this book is a powerful journey." – Allison Pataki, *NYT* Bestselling Author of *The Accidental Empress*

"A sweeping saga of one woman's journey through World War II and her unwillingness to give up even when faced with the toughest challenges." — Anita Abriel, Author of *The Light After the War*

"A captivating tale of love, determination and reinvention." — Karen Marin, Givenchy Paris

"A stylish, compelling story of a family. What sets this apart is the backdrop of perfumery that suffuses the story with the delicious aromas – a remarkable feat!" — Liz Trenow, *NYT* Bestselling Author of *The Forgotten Seamstress*

"Courageous heroine, star-crossed lovers, splendid sense of time and place capturing the unease and turmoil of the 1940s; HEA." — *Heroes and Heartbreakers*

BOOKS BY JAN MORAN

Summer Beach Series

Seabreeze Inn

Seabreeze Summer

Seabreeze Sunset

Seabreeze Christmas

Seabreeze Wedding

Seabreeze Book Club

Seabreeze Shores

Seabreeze Reunion

Coral Cottage

Coral Cafe

Coral Holiday

Coral Weddings

Coral Celebration

Beach View Lane

Sunshine Avenue

The Love, California Series

Flawless

Beauty Mark

Runway

Essence

Style

Sparkle

20th-Century Historical

Hepburn's Necklace

The Chocolatier

The Winemakers: A Novel of Wine and Secrets

The Perfumer: Scent of Triumph

Seabreeze Summer

USA TODAY BESTSELLING AUTHOR
JAN MORAN

SEABREEZE SUMMER

SUMMER BEACH, BOOK 2

JAN MORAN

SUNNY PALMS

PRESS

Library of Congress Cataloging-in-Publication Data
Moran, Jan.
/ by Jan Moran

ISBN 978-1-951314-00-2 (softcover)
ISBN 978-1-64778-008-1 (epub)
ISBN 978-1-951314-08-8 (audiobook)
ISBN 978-1-64778-012-8 (hardcover)
ISBN 978-1-64778-013-5 (large print)
ISBN 978-1-64778-092-0 (large print)

Published by Sunny Palms Press. Cover design by Silver Starlight Designs. Cover images copyright Deposit Photos.

Sunny Palms Press

9663 Santa Monica Blvd STE 1158

Beverly Hills, CA 90210 USA

www.sunnypalmspress.com

www.JanMoran.com

*For my all my beach-loving readers,
and to my daughter-in-law Ginna Moran, who is
immensely talented, creative, and one of my best friends.*

1

Summer Beach, California

*I*vy could smell smoke even before she opened her eyes. Though it wasn't yet dawn, she rose and padded downstairs in the grand old beach house, which was still silent. In the quiet of the morning, she could hear the constant, low roar of waves crashing onto the shores of Summer Beach just steps from where the sprawling property ended.

In the parlor, Ivy glanced outside through a glass, arched palladium door that opened onto the terrace. Swinging the door open, she stepped outside and scanned the skyline over the ridgetop. *Had the fire reignited during the night?*

A thin layer of moisture coated the smooth stone, but the knitted wool slippers her mother had brought back from a buying trip to Peru kept her feet warm and dry. Through dim morning light, she saw thin, leftover smudges above the ridgeline, but no active plumes of smoke. Not like last night. She shivered as she thought about it. Turning back to the ocean, she saw a few early surfers bobbing on boards in the distance waiting for sunrise.

Yesterday's oven-hot, offshore wind blasts had mercifully given way to cool onshore flows. Ivy lifted her face to the fresh breeze, though smoke still edged the air. In her soft, clingy cotton sleep tee and shorts, her bare arms and legs quickly chilled with goosebumps, but it felt good after the dry, scorching Santa Ana winds that had roared in from the parched inland deserts. Infrequent yet dangerous, the winds had sparked the fire and whipped it into a frenzy on the hilltops above them.

She left the door open to cool the house and went back inside. She and her sister Shelly had only just opened their doors to guests, and now, due to last night's fire on the ridgetop above them, they had gone from a single occupied guestroom to full occupancy overnight. And these new guests weren't vacationers, but evacuees who'd lost their homes or couldn't return due to fire and smoke damage.

Like Bennett.

The thought of the Summer Beach mayor quickened her pulse. Also evacuated, he'd slept in the room next to hers, and she'd tossed all night thinking about him.

Ivy wove through the grand ballroom, where her industrious niece Poppy had stayed up late tending to new guests and clearing glasses and dishware after the open house earlier in the day. As newcomers to Summer Beach, Ivy and Shelly had welcomed close to a hundred of their new neighbors for an open house—before the fire had broken up the party and sent guests scattering to check on neighbors, loved ones, and pets.

At the open house, Ivy and Shelly had spoken at length, attempting to persuade their fellow Summer Beach residents to support their quest for a zoning change—from residential to neighborhood commercial zoning—for the old beach house so that they could operate as an inn. While they could rent rooms online through iBnB for a while, Ivy needed the status to expand operations and secure future income.

Since Ivy's late husband Jeremy had spent all their retirement savings on the old beach house —*without* her knowledge—she had to hustle to avoid foreclosure for back property taxes.

And she had just one summer to do it.

Ivy glanced around, taking in the lingering disarray from last night. There was only so much that even Poppy could do after the electricity had been knocked out by the raging Santa Ana winds.

Ivy and Shelly, along with their father and brothers, had kept vigil outside, hosing down the trees and rafters and roof to keep windswept embers from sparking fires. Once the winds died after midnight, her parents and brothers had left for their homes. She'd been grateful for their help, and fortunately, she'd heard the electricity hum to life during the night. Her phone charger beside her bed had blinked on, recharging her phone.

A soft snore rose from one of the antique divans they had found stored on the lower level, along with other antique furniture. Ivy peered past a palm tree that Shelly had arranged in a marine blue clay pot on a weathered stand. Poppy was asleep, nestled into the silk brocade, her head cradled in one of the new, sky blue pillows they had bought.

Ivy tiptoed past her.

As the first one awake, Ivy needed to start brewing coffee for their guests. She wondered how many people there were. Entire families forced to evacuate had crowded into the bedrooms on the second floor. They hadn't turned anyone away. Already she had a long to-do list in her mind, including shopping for supplies of every sort for their guests.

With a great yawn, Ivy pushed through the door to the kitchen.

"Morning," Bennett said, glancing over his shoulder.

"Oh," Ivy cried out, pressing her hand to her gaping mouth. "You're up." Instantly, she felt a flush creep up her neck. Aside from his role as mayor of Summer Beach, Bennett had also been her summer crush before college. That was more than twenty-five years ago, and now here she was, acting like a teenager again.

All because of that kiss last night. *Oh, that kiss.* The flush raced to her cheeks.

"Couldn't sleep." Bennett motioned to the coffee maker. "I foraged around and found the coffee. Figured I should get a pot going. Care for a cup?"

"Sure," Ivy said, hastily trying to recover her equilibrium. Bennett's hair was damp, as though he'd just showered, but he still wore his sooty clothes from the night before, when he and Mitch, the owner of Java Beach, had bolted from the meeting to assist in firefighting efforts. It didn't help that Bennett's shirt hung open, revealing his lean torso. She tried not to stare.

"A lot to do today," Bennett said, pouring coffee. "I've got to meet with Chief Hildegard. Start sorting out the mess up on the ridge and figure out how we can help our displaced residents."

He handed her the cup, his fingers brushing hers when she reached for it. Catching her gaze after she pulled away, he curved up a corner of his mouth and began buttoning his shirt.

"Ivy, about last night," he began, his deep voice sounding even more gravelly than usual.

And downright sexy. Ivy felt another flush whip through her chest, no doubt reddening her face even more. She'd lain awake half the night, replaying what had transpired between them. A mere forty-eight hours ago, this was a man she'd never wanted to see again after their disagreement over her sister.

"There's cream in Gertie. Need some?" Feeling flustered, she opened one of the twin vintage turquoise refrigerators—circa the 1960s—that Shelly had nicknamed Gert and Gertie. The sizeable, well-appointed kitchen had been designed to accommodate a large staff and caterers, but it hadn't been updated in decades.

"Don't need it." Bennett's eyes crinkled at the corners. "With all these folks here, it might be time for Gert to start pulling his weight."

"We have to plug him in first." She poured the cream into her mug. As she stirred her coffee, she thought about how right it had felt to hold him in her arms late last night. And yet, had they merely been seeking solace, overwhelmed by their efforts to keep the fire at bay, or had their protective emotional layers been peeled back enough for them to finally share their feelings? If the latter were true, then why did she feel so self-conscious now?

She was too old to second-guess her emotional decisions, and yet, here she was. But she'd long forgotten how to act in the new throes of a relationship.

Watching Bennett move around the kitchen, she remembered what it was like to have a man around. There was companionship, and she liked that. But in a relationship, there had to be more. Love and trust, of course, but also a commonality of purpose.

Ivy opened the old refrigerator and wrinkled her nose. "Needs a good cleaning."

"Let's see if it works first." He set his cup on the counter.

What did she and Bennett really have in common? She and Jeremy had their children—the glue that binds most married couples, even after the fireworks wane. But what about this man? Did she dare waver her focus on earning a living to appease her heart? And yet, going through life with another person by your side was satisfying. She hadn't expected to be on her own again quite so soon.

She pressed a hand to her forehead. *Too much thinking, too early.* This is what Bennett did to her. Exactly what she didn't need.

"Should be a plug behind it." Bennett shoved the refrigerator from the wall and tore away the cobwebs, then knelt and inserted the appliance's plug into the wall. The motor growled to life, surging before leveling out to a low hum.

"Sounds alive," Ivy said, taking a broom and dustpan from a narrow broom closet. "These old appliances were real workhorses." Ivy wedged behind the refrigerator to sweep out dust and cobwebs, taking care to keep her hair clear this time.

Bennett brushed off his hands. "We'll see how the old boy goes."

Re-emerging, she emptied the dustpan before shoving that and the broom back into the closet.

Bennett took a step toward her and ran his fingers along her bare arm. "You okay this morning?"

Still feeling self-conscious, Ivy swept her tangled hair from her face. Why hadn't she taken a moment to brush her hair? She ran her tongue over her teeth. *That, too.* She wasn't used to facing people this early, and especially not Bennett Dylan, who was disrupting her heart, her mind, and her carefully made plans.

"I'm alright," she replied, realizing her clingy, pale pink sleep tee and shorts revealed more than she'd planned, which he seemed to be appreciating, although, to his credit, he was at least trying to keep his eyes focused on her face.

"You seem flustered."

"You have to understand, Bennett, I don't usu-

ally *do that*. I mean, I haven't, not in a long time."
Right. That made her sound ancient. Or prudish.

"Relax, it was just a kiss," he said in a soothing voice. "Although it meant an awful lot to me."

His touch was warm and reassuring. "Me, too," she said, giving him a shy smile.

Jeremy was the only man she'd ever been with, which now seemed hopelessly old-fashioned to her. But he'd been the first guy she'd dated in college, and they'd stuck. And it had barely been a year since his brain aneurysm. Was it too soon for her to be looking at another man like this?

And yet, the man who stood before her now had been her first love, her summer crush right before she'd left for school in Boston, though she hadn't really known him or exchanged more than a few shy words. What were the chances that he would have come back into her life, especially like this?

"I'm just not sure," Ivy began. *Sure of what?* Of him, or herself? Bennett's wife had died ten years ago, which was plenty of time for him to come to terms with her death.

Ivy thought about her daughters, Sunny and Misty. *What will they think?* Especially Sunny, her mercurial daughter, who was backpacking in Europe. When Ivy told her that she had moved to Summer Beach, Sunny had taken it as a personal affront. The thought of her mother dating would be more than Sunny could handle.

Bennett took another step toward her and drew her closer with a hand on her waist. "I meant everything I said last night." He hesitated as though searching for confirmation in her eyes. "Could you sleep?"

She paused and then shook her head. *No.*

"I'm usually not that forward," he said. "And I'm not here to take advantage of you. I mean, I *am* the mayor, so I have to be careful."

"Why? Do you think I'm going to file a complaint against you?" Ivy stepped back and sipped her coffee, meeting his gaze over the rim of her cup—and grateful for the caffeine effect that was beginning to flood her system.

Bennett chuckled. "No, but—"

Just then, Shelly pushed the kitchen door open. "Why would you file a complaint against Bennett?"

Ivy sputtered in her coffee. "You shouldn't be eavesdropping," she said, reaching for a napkin to dab her top. She shot a sideways glance at Bennett, acutely embarrassed.

A slight grin played on Bennett's lips, those lips she'd kissed and tasted last night. He raised his cup.

"Well, you don't have to get so *salty* about it." Shelly stared at them for a moment before tossing her hair over her shoulder. "I sure hope there's more coffee." Wearing charcoal gray and violet yoga gear, she looked like she'd been up for a while—except for her slightly puffy eyes.

Ivy put her cup down. "There is," she said, reaching for another cup. She frowned as the dark liquid swirled in a cup. "We have to figure out how to take care of our guests today."

"Wasn't that the plan?" Shelly asked, stretching her arms overhead.

"It's just so many, so suddenly," Ivy said.

"At least we have the room." Shelly turned to Bennett. "You're staying for a while, right?"

"If that's not a problem," he replied, darting a look toward Ivy.

"Why would it be?" Ivy shot her words back, perhaps a little too sharply, as the feelings she had for him surged through her again.

Just a kiss, that's all it was. Yet that kiss had sparked feelings in Ivy that she hadn't known in years. Even with Jeremy—they'd been married so long that they'd developed a comfortable routine. He'd been physically attentive, of course, but they'd never been swinging-from-the-chandeliers people in *that* department. Her husband had been an intellectual, who was often more passionate about ideas and technology than people.

After handing the cup to Shelly, Ivy shoved back her tousled hair. Why hadn't she at least glanced in the mirror before coming downstairs? Her face was so hot it was probably as red as the tomatoes in the bowl on the counter. She gave it a spin.

Bennett and Shelly were staring at her. Bennett's lips curved up slightly at the edges, while Shelly's mouth opened in confusion.

Ivy stopped the spinning bowl and scooped up her coffee mug. "I'll make a list of supplies we'll need. Laundry detergent, tissues, toilet paper, soap…"

Bennett pushed back from the counter. "I've got to get to the office right away. And see if any more of my house has burned down."

"Then I'll see you later," Ivy said, hurrying from the kitchen.

As Bennett followed her, Ivy saw Poppy's head emerge around the edge of the divan.

"Hey," Bennett called out, catching up to her in the foyer. "If I didn't know better, I'd think you were running away from me. Talk to me, will you? This is new territory for me, too."

Stalling for a moment to sort out her feelings, Ivy drew a breath. On a round table in the foyer, the calming aroma from the roses and ginger flowers she'd picked from Shelly's garden filled the air.

Yet facing Bennett—and his dark-lashed hazel eyes—brought forth another torrent of emotions. Where did they fit in each other's lives? She'd have to manage these strange new sensations if she expected to rise to the task of tending to their new guests. Flushing and fumbling for words like a teenager in front of townspeople would be a disaster. With the zoning status pending, the last thing she needed was a public relationship with the mayor. Her crotchety neighbor Darla would surely seize on that, too.

"Bennett, I have so much work to do here," Ivy said, shifting from him as she clung to her familiar plan. An organized life was a safe life. *A mature life.* Falling into a new relationship right after arriving in the small town of Summer Beach? Sheer craziness. Like something Shelly would do —not Ivy, the sane sister.

Steeling herself against her emotional draw to him, she said, "You have no idea how dire my situation is."

"Actually, I do. The city has been considering this property for a community center."

Ivy was taken aback. "Is that what you want to see here?"

Bennett rubbed the back of his neck. "I want what's best for Summer Beach. If you can run this successfully, make it pay its way…"

"You don't think I can?"

"I didn't say that. But you need a zoning change."

"And I'm applying for that." She paused. "Can't you help?"

"As I said before, that decision is up to Summer Beach residents." He jerked a thumb in the direction of her neighbor. "Including Darla. You need to make nice on her."

She stared at him with an incredulous look. "We saved her house last night. If we hadn't hosed down the giant eucalyptus trees in her yard, any ember would have sent those up like flaming torches—and her house along with them. She can't complain about that."

Bennett glanced out the window. "Then why is she storming across the lawn right now?"

Ivy closed her eyes. The sun had just risen, and already the day was going sideways.

Seconds later, Darla pounded on the front door.

"Want me to handle this?" Bennett asked.

Ivy caught a glimpse of herself in an ornate mirror by the door. Skimpy sleepwear, tangled hair. She sighed. "I'll deal with her." She started for the door, but Bennett touched her shoulder, and she paused.

"I don't know where we stand with each other," he said. "But I do know that what we shared last night was special. Things like that don't happen every day, at least, not in my life. We both have a lot to deal with right now, but please promise you won't shut me out?"

She gazed up at him, knowing how hard it would be to deny her feelings. "We'll talk later. But go—you have a full day ahead of you. You don't need Darla to slow you down."

"Thanks," Bennett said. He kissed her on the cheek before hurrying up the staircase.

Darla banged on the door again.

Fortifying herself with a large gulp of coffee, Ivy reached for the doorknob. She braced herself and swung open the door.

"Good morning, Darla." Ivy blinked. The woman's blazing, multi-color rhinestone sun-visor and her shocking, ultramarine blue hair were even brighter in the morning light.

"My lawn is a soggy mess this morning," Darla said, huffing. "And those two you sent over trampled the flowers I'd just planted. They were so rude. They refused to leave when I told them to."

"No ma'am," Ivy said, folding her arms. "That young couple stayed there to make sure your house or trees didn't ignite from blowing embers. You should be thankful we cared enough to help you."

Darla scowled. "My house has stood for years. It's not going anywhere."

"Some of those houses on the ridgetop were older than yours, and now they're a heap of smoldering rubble."

"I didn't ask for help, and I don't need any," Darla shot back. "Could've done that myself."

"But you didn't." Ivy softened her tone. "You know, it's okay to accept neighborly assistance."

Over Darla's shoulder, Ivy spied Mitch am-

15

bling toward the door. He had a gym bag slung over a shoulder, and he carried a cardboard box. His wet hair was slicked back.

"Hey, what's going on here?" Mitch shifted his armload and gave Darla a hug. The scent of coffee and pastries wafted from the carton.

"Morning," Darla muttered, her deeply furrowed forehead relaxing a little. "These people destroyed my flower gardens last night."

Though Darla's words were still harsh, Ivy watched as she melted under Mitch's attention. *How does he do it?*

"That so?" Mitch grinned. "Bet Shelly would be happy to replace those for you. She's an expert horticulturist. I'll help, too." To Ivy, he added, "With all the folks that landed here last night, I figured you might like help with breakfast."

"You have no idea." Ivy waved him in. "We have a full house of guests."

"Come on in for coffee, sweetheart," Mitch said to Darla as he stepped inside. "Save you a trip to Java Beach today."

"I'll still be there to read my paper," the older woman said. Narrowing her eyes, she added, "But I have somewhere else to go first."

Mitch dropped his gym bag in the foyer. "Ivy, could you take this bag up to Bennett? Thought he might need some clean clothes this morning." He planted a kiss on Darla's cheek before she left, and then he headed toward the kitchen.

Ivy watched him go. Mitch was thoughtful, but she wondered how Shelly would react to his arrival. Even though he was easily ten years younger than her sister, Shelly was still attracted to him.

Or she had been until they'd found out Mitch had served time in prison. The FBI agents who'd come to collect the stolen paintings she and Shelly had found in the lower level had mentioned it. She and Shelly didn't know why he'd been imprisoned, which made Ivy uncomfortable.

Poppy raised herself up to a seated position on the divan, where she'd been watching the scene unfold. She'd slept in her clothes from yesterday, as their guests probably had, too. "Need any help, Aunt Ivy?"

"Shelly might need some support in the kitchen. Get some breakfast, too."

As Poppy hurried toward the kitchen, Ivy pinched the bridge of her nose and sighed. They'd only been in the house a few short weeks, but so much had happened. She gazed around the house, taking in the worn parquet floor with its honey patina, the sparkling chandeliers, and soaring windows that faced the sea. With her family's help, they'd come a long way in making the tired old house shine again.

Ivy picked up Mitch's gym bag and started up the staircase. Between each step were vibrant, hand-painted tile risers. The exquisite details in this house that had been designed by architect Julia Morgan still amazed her. The historic designation ensured that the house would not be torn down and replaced, as Jeremy had intended.

This was Ivy's chance to bring the house back to serve the community of Summer Beach, though she hadn't expected it would be quite so soon. As she made her way through the long hallway, she could hear people stirring in their rooms. The old house hadn't seen this much life in decades.

She wondered what the former owner, Amelia Erickson, would think. The mysterious woman had hidden more than a hundred paintings stolen during the Second World War in the lower level. It was only by accident that Ivy and Shelly had discovered them on the bricked-up lower level.

Though the FBI had collected the masterpieces, no one knew how the artwork had arrived there, or if Mrs. Erickson had truly concealed the priceless pieces for safekeeping, as Ivy believed. After all, the woman had opened her house to recovering military personnel during the war. Las Brisas del Mar—as the house was known then—had served as a center for physical therapy and rehabilitation. The house had been a haven for people in need, just as it was again now.

As she wove through the hallways, Ivy wondered if the house still harbored secrets.

When she reached Bennett's room, she tapped

on the door. When there was no answer, she cracked the door. "Are you decent? Mitch sent some clothes for you."

"Come in," Bennett called out.

Feeling awkward, Ivy slipped in, leaving the door a little ajar and wondering what the innkeeper protocol was in such a situation. She'd have to learn fast.

Bennett stepped from the bathroom holding a rolled-up towel in his hands.

He wasn't wearing his shirt anymore, and Ivy felt her heart hammer once more. For his age— mid-forties like her, or *any* age for that matter—his physique was gorgeous. Quickly glancing at the bag in her hand, she said, "Mitch brought this for you. He also brought breakfast for everyone."

"He's a good guy." Bennett unfurled the towel. Inside was his shirt. "I couldn't stand the smell of smoke on it. I figured it was better damp than smoky. The shops don't open for another three hours." He jerked his chin toward the bag. "What's in there?"

"I, uh…"

Bennett grinned at her. "Open it. Don't be afraid. It's not like it's drugs or something."

"Was that what Mitch—?" She stopped herself. It wasn't any of her business, but she *was* curious.

"No," he replied pointedly.

"Oh. Well, okay." If he wasn't going to offer

any explanation, she might as well open the bag. She unzipped it and looked inside. "T-shirts, jeans, flip-flops." She held up a faded T-shirt. "Grateful Dead?"

Bennett laughed. "That looks familiar."

"How come?"

"I gave that T-shirt to him years ago."

She tossed it to him, though she was actually enjoying the view. He pulled it over his head. "Ah, that's better. Still fits, too. Toss me the jeans."

"You are not changing in front of me."

"I won't." Chuckling, Bennett stepped toward her. "We'll take it slowly."

Outside the open door, Ivy could hear people emerging from their rooms. Although she'd had a crush on him years ago, she was a grown woman now. She knew the difference between infatuation and love that lasted years. Ivy pressed a hand against his chest.

"Bennett, I can't."

"I understand what you're going through."

Does he? Jeremy's unexpected death was one thing, but after she'd heard he had a girlfriend with him here in Summer Beach, her trust had been shattered as well. She shook her head.

He took her hand in his and traced circles on the back of her hand with his thumb. Shivers coursed through her.

"Slowly," he repeated. "I promise."

"Your recovery has been years in the making,"

Ivy said, referring to his wife's death. "But for me, it's only been a year." She shook her head, though her heart was splintering. *Would she regret this?*

She watched the rise and fall of his chest. He was close, too close now. Her heart had been broken—not once, but twice—and the wounds were still fresh.

"I have too much to do, Bennett. All these guests, and the things they need…we haven't even decided on a bookkeeping system yet."

He gazed at her. "That's not the real reason, is it?"

After trying to decipher Jeremy's actions and possible motives over the last year, she was tired, so tired, of lies. She wouldn't do that to another person.

"I'm just not ready for this," she said. Without giving Bennett a chance to argue or persuade her, she pressed her lips together and hurried out the door.

2

*I*vy padded around in her closet in her knitted slippers. She rummaged through the clothes she'd brought from Boston—most of which were entirely wrong for the mild California climate or were too conservative for casual Summer Beach. The only ones that worked were those she'd bought for their Nantucket holidays.

As she was searching for something clean and presentable that fit—which edged out much of her wardrobe—her slipper snagged on a wooden slat. Most of the wood floors in the house had been worn smooth over time, but then, a closet wouldn't have had as much traffic, she mused.

Ivy bent to dislodge the yarn with care. As she did, the piece of wood rocked to one side, as if it hadn't been adequately secured.

Anxious to be downstairs when the guests rose,

she found jeans and a flowing turquoise top her mother had also given her that concealed her muffin-top middle. Recalling the *T-Shirt & Jeans Handbook* on her dresser, she quickly dressed up her simple ensemble with earrings, a scarf, and a short white denim jacket. And just like that, she'd gone from simple to chic. She checked out her reflection, satisfied with the transformation.

As she finished dressing, she glanced back at the closet and made a mental note to secure the wooden piece. *One more item on my I've-Got-Too-Much-To-Do list.* Jen and George at Nailed It probably had the right supplies for that. With its endless dripping faucets and other minor maladies, this house was as needy as a toddler.

And she was growing to love it like one, too.

At the antique vanity, Ivy perched on the stool in front of the large oval mirror. She ran a brush through her hair and added a quick swipe of gloss on her lips.

Opening the door to leave, another thought struck her about the loose floorboard. *The closet.* Amelia Erickson had hidden a journal in the rear closet. But she had no time to investigate now. She hurried down the old servant's staircase into the kitchen.

"Shelly, we've got to—"

Her sister whirled around, her brow crinkled in annoyance. "You *knew* Mitch was coming here, and you left me here alone with him?"

Ivy held up her hands to deflect her sister's sudden wrath. "What are you talking about? You're the one who was making goo-goo eyes at him yesterday." After having just dealt with Bennett, she wasn't ready for Shelly's mood. And it wasn't even eight o'clock yet.

"Was not."

"Is that the best you can do? What are you, ten years old?"

"Okay, so maybe I had a moment of weakness," Shelly said. "But I'm not going there again. And don't surprise me like that."

"I sent Poppy in, too."

"That helped for about a minute."

Ivy knew the heartache Shelly was suffering over Ezzra, her on-again, off-again, hipster boyfriend in New York. The one who couldn't commit to lunch on Friday, let alone to a woman who had slapped the snooze button on her biological clock far too many times. "Have you spoken to Ezzra lately?"

"He called last night. He saw the fire online."

"Summer Beach is a small town," Ivy said. "I doubt we made the national news. He's stalking you."

Shelly threw her hand up. "It's over. And it hurts more than I thought it would." She glanced around and sighed. "*This* is my life now."

"And there's a good-looking man who just— wait, where's Mitch?"

"Getting another carton of coffee and pastries from his car."

Ivy reached for the coffee pot and drained it into Shelly's cup. "Bringing breakfast for our guests was really thoughtful. But our guests are his friends and neighbors, so what he's doing has nothing to do with you." Reverse psychology had worked when they were kids. Ivy hoped it still would.

"But I have no idea why he was in prison."

"Ask him."

"I can't ask him that."

"Why not?"

"It's rude."

"It's called being clear-sighted. Don't fall for someone and wish you'd asked them the hard questions in the beginning."

Shelly quirked her lips to one side in thought.

Ivy curled her arm around her sister's shoulder and hugged her. "I love you, Shells, and your heart-shaped, rose-tinted glasses. But lower them for just a minute to ask the tough questions."

Even though Mitch was young, Ivy had a good feeling about him. Maybe it was because he and Bennett were good friends. And between running Java Beach and the whale-watching tours, Mitch still found time to be active in the community.

And he cared about people.

Suddenly, Ivy realized what had been missing in Jeremy. All those years, he professed to care about her and their family—though she knew he'd loved Misty and Sunny—he'd never reached out a hand to others. He'd once said he *didn't do charity work* when she'd tried to get him to hand out baskets of food and toys during the holidays.

Mitch did it without even being asked.

So did Bennett.

Ivy glanced out the window and saw Mitch returning with another carton. She nudged Shelly. "Drink up and pull yourself together. He's coming back. And we have a lot to do."

Nodding, Shelly gulped her coffee.

A tap sounded at the kitchen door, and the young couple from Seattle poked their heads inside. "May we come in? Smells like coffee."

"Sure, have a seat," Ivy said, motioning to the stools around the large center prep island. As Shelly opened a thermos of Mitch's fresh coffee, Ivy opened a box of pastries. "Raspberry, blueberry, apple, or cream cheese?"

"And yogurt and granola parfaits are on their way," Shelly added.

"I'll wait then," Megan said, tucking her short blond hair behind an ear as her husband Josh dug into a flaky apple pastry.

Ivy folded her arms and leaned against the counter. "We appreciate what you did for Darla last night. By hosing down her trees and rooftop, you probably saved her house, and this one as well."

"Didn't sound like she appreciated it," Josh said between bites.

"We heard her through our window," Megan said. "We opened it to catch the cool ocean breezes. Is she always like that?"

Their room was right above the front door, Ivy remembered. "As long as we've known her. Which has only been about a month."

Just then, Mitch pushed through the door with another armload and slid it onto the counter.

Megan peered into the box. "Heard you have parfaits in there."

"On the bottom, I'll have one out in a minute," Mitch said.

Ivy grinned at him. "Mitch is the resident Darla-tamer."

"Well, that old eucalyptus tree has to be trimmed," Shelly said. "Though it really should come down. Too much of a fire hazard, and too close to the house."

"I love the smell," Megan said. "We have them in Seattle, but then, fire hardly has a chance against our never-ending rain."

"Neither do we," Josh said with a frown. He pulled his straw hat forward as if ducking a downpour.

"You should stay here," Mitch said. "Life is better in Summer Beach."

Ivy had to smile. She'd seen that slogan in City Hall. "Mitch, would you mind putting what you brought on the table in the ballroom? Once everyone comes downstairs, the kitchen will be awfully crowded. Poppy can give you a hand." Ivy glanced around. "Where'd she go?"

"She'll be right back," Shelly added. "She's raiding my closet."

Mitch caught Shelly's eye. "I'll set up for you." He picked up the carton and made his way to where he'd set up yesterday at the open hour.

Josh glanced outside and sighed. "Wouldn't mind spending more time here." He waggled his brows at Megan. "You going to tell them your idea?"

Megan's face brightened. "I've been thinking about Amelia Erickson and the paintings you found. It's a great story, and someone should cover it."

"Oh, they are," Ivy said. "We've gotten calls and emails."

"And?" Megan drummed her nails on the tile.

Ivy shrugged. "Bennett and the FBI both gave statements to the press, but I don't have time to talk to media. We've got a lot of work to do here."

"I made a video for my blog that explains what happened," Shelly added.

Megan smiled. "I've seen it."

"Besides, we have a deadline to get this inn launched and running at full occupancy this summer," Ivy said.

"Looks full now," Josh said.

"This is different," Ivy said. "These are our new neighbors, and we're happy to offer shelter." She wouldn't ask someone who'd just lost their home for their credit card—or cash—to pay for a room. Besides, they didn't have a bookkeeping system or a way to take payment, except through the iBnB website. "I'm glad we're in a position to offer local residents a close place to stay."

Josh lifted a brow in surprise. "No way that would happen in most hotels."

"We're different," Ivy said. *Was she too soft?* Probably. She imagined their guests had family or friends they'd go to stay with soon. As long as they would recommend the Seabreeze Inn, she'd consider that payment enough. What were a few nights, anyway?

"Do you know if anyone has ever told the story of Amelia Erickson?" Megan asked.

"Not that I know of," Ivy said. "I have a book —a collection of articles really—that Nan and Arthur at Antique Times compiled on the house. They'd know if anyone had ever written about the Ericksons. Why do you ask?"

"I'd like to film a documentary about Amelia Erickson," Megan said. "With the media attention, I'm sure I can raise funds to make it." She traded looks with Josh. "I'd like to film it here. I'm going to stay on to write it, too."

"We've decided to make some changes," Josh said. "Megan and I think this would be a good place to start a family. I'm pretty confident I can work remotely, or start my own company."

"Woo-hoo," Shelly said, coming to life. "That would be so cool! When do you want to start, Megan?"

"I've just started outlining the script," Megan said. "The story can begin with the discovery of the stolen paintings. But I've got a lot of holes in the story about Amelia's history and how she received the artwork."

"We do, too," Ivy said.

Shelly's eyes blazed with interest. "Would you want to interview us on camera?"

"I was hoping you'd both agree," Megan said, growing even more excited. To Shelly, she added, "I've been watching your vlog forever."

Ivy shook her head. "Count me out. I'm not camera-ready, not like Shelly." Her sister was used to filming her floral design, entertaining, and lifestyle projects. Now, Shelly was shooting the garden and renovations they were making to the house.

"Viewers would love to hear Ivy, too," Megan said, turning back to Ivy. "Since you're an artist, people would appreciate your point of view. Besides, if you hadn't studied art history, you wouldn't have known that those paintings were lost masterpieces. That's an important part of the story."

"Which Shelly can handle. I have enough to think about with this place."

Shelly and Megan traded conspiratorial looks, and Ivy knew she hadn't heard the last of this. But a documentary on Amelia Erickson would be fascinating, and she wondered what Megan would find.

Mitch returned to the kitchen with a berry, yogurt, and granola parfait for Megan. "Here you go. Anyone else?"

"Thanks, I'll get one," Ivy said.

"Me, too," Shelly said, following him out. Glancing over her shoulder at Ivy, she shrugged and grinned.

Ivy was pleased Shelly was giving him another chance. She liked Mitch, who seemed good for her sister. Whatever had happened in his past, he'd clearly reformed. Wasn't that all that mattered?

Ivy turned back to Megan and Josh. "The documentary is a wonderful idea, and I appreciate that you're interested in Amelia Erickson. I am, too."

"Have you found anything else around here?" Megan asked.

"Just what I gave to the FBI. A single page of a journal and an old letter."

Megan's eyebrows shot up. "Did you make copies?"

"I snapped photos with my phone," Ivy said. "I'll

show you later, but right now, it looks like breakfast is ready." Footsteps echoed above them on the old wooden floors. "I hear people coming downstairs."

While Megan and Josh joined Shelly to continue talking about the documentary, Ivy slipped into the butler's pantry to get serving platters and dishes. She was thankful that her mother Carlotta and her sister Honey had washed all the vintage dishes the day the family had come to help. Normally, she would ask Shelly for help, but watching her sister's lively interest in Megan's project—and Mitch—she let it go.

As she was laying out plates, Ivy saw Bennett speaking to Mitch. The two men were chuckling over the clothes Mitch had given him. Bennett gave him a bro-hug, and then he was off, but not before he cast a glance in her direction.

Though Ivy felt ill at ease with him here, there wasn't much she could do about it. She couldn't very well ask the popular mayor of Summer Beach to leave. She needed all the community support she could get for their rezoning request. For now, Ivy would have to deal with Mayor Dylan sleeping in the room next to hers.

She placed stacks of cloth napkins on the table, dreading having to launder and press linen napkins for fifty—besides bed linens and towels—but there wasn't anything else in the house. Again, shopping. *Paper napkins, stat.* Her environmental devotion to reusables would have to wait a few weeks until she could afford more help.

Poppy had reemerged, dressed in one of Shelly's sleek yoga outfits, and was helping Mitch direct sleepy, worn-out guests into the room.

"Good morning," Ivy called out as she arranged blueberry muffins on a platter. "I hope you all got some rest. Mitch was kind enough to bring breakfast for you, so please help yourselves."

Ivy didn't know most of the bedraggled people who were making their way downstairs, but she recognized Imani, the woman who owned Blossoms, the flower stall on Main Street. A tall, lanky young man followed her, and both of them looked bleary-eyed and dazed. Ivy crossed to greet her.

"Good morning, Imani. I'm glad you stayed over."

"We appreciate your hospitality," Imani said, running a hand over her long sisterlocks, which swung around her shoulders. "This is my son, Jamir. He's starting school at the University of California in the fall."

"Ma'am. Nice to meet you," Jamir said, extending his hand.

Shaking his hand, Ivy said, "Which campus?"

"San Diego," he replied with evident pride.

"Beautiful oceanview campus," Ivy said. "What do you plan to study?"

"Pre-med," Jamir said. "Even though my mom says it's too early to decide."

"Thank goodness he has a full scholarship," Imani said. "I appreciate that more than ever now." She heaved a sigh.

Ivy picked up on her meaning. "Your home?"

"It was the first one that went up. A total loss." Imani's eyes rimmed with tears while her son put his arm around her. "We weren't home, so we didn't have a chance to save anything."

Jamir kissed his mother on the cheek. "It's just stuff, Mom. You're insured, and we'll get it all back."

"I know, but it's overwhelming," Imani said. "And all your sweet baby things I saved for your little ones are gone."

Jamir hugged his mother.

The magnitude of their loss hit Ivy. She recalled parting with her possessions after Jeremy's death. Even though it had been her choice, it was also by painful necessity in order to fit into her rented room after she sold the condo. She couldn't imagine the devastating loss they must be suffering. She clasped Imani's hands. "You're welcome to stay here as long as you need to."

"I appreciate that." Imani sniffed. "I've already called my insurance agent. She said there should be coverage for housing, so don't worry about us."

"Even if there isn't," Ivy began, but Imani interrupted her.

"You're running a business." Imani leaned in.

"As kind as you seem, you have overhead, too. Feeding this many people, cleaning up after them. Most of these folks should have insurance coverage, so you make sure you get a credit card from them for their rooms. Some of their claims might be delayed, but emergency housing is generally covered."

"Mom's an attorney," Jamir said.

"Common sense, that's all," Imani said.

"Do you still practice?" Ivy asked.

Imani shook her head. "Decided to spend my life peddling flowers outdoors in the sunshine instead. Someone has to represent others, but I did my time. Got compensated well for it, too. Doing what I love now is my reward. Just like you and your sister are doing."

Ivy inclined her head. "That was forced on me, I'm afraid."

"So I heard. Word gets around in Summer Beach."

"I appreciate your advice." Grateful for Imani's advice, Ivy smiled. "Is there anything you need? We're about the same size. I have some clothes if you'd like to change."

"Thanks, but we'll pick up a few necessities in town this morning. My sister is driving down from Los Angeles to bring us supplies." Imani nodded toward the crowd. "You have a lot of folks to take care of. We'll have a bite and be on our way. But may I give you a credit card for the room?"

"You could, but I'd have no idea what to do with it. Give me a couple of days?" Ivy had yet to set up a merchant account. Another critical point to take care of—and fast.

Imani nodded. "Not like we're going anywhere."

Ivy moved on to another couple she had met yesterday at the open house—Celia and Tyler, the young tech retirees and investors. "Good morning, how you doing today?"

Celia swung around, her long black hair fanning around her shoulders. "I haven't slept so well in ages. You'll tell me where you found that mattress, won't you?"

"Of course, I—"

"You need black-out drapes," Tyler cut in. "Damn cheery sunshine came blazing through at 7 a.m."

"So noted," Ivy said. "I'll see what we can do about that for you."

Celia shrugged. "Don't mind him. He's spoiled. My fault."

Ivy didn't like the way Celia apologized for her husband's rudeness, but she said nothing. They'd both been through a lot. "Have you heard anything about your house?" Ivy asked.

"It's not too bad," Celia said. "Like Bennett next door, we sustained a lot of smoke damage. Lost our gazebo, but that's easy to replace."

Tyler looked irritated. "We should sleep on the boat."

"I need a bathtub," Celia said, folding her arms. "I'm staying here, but you can go if you want."

Tyler stalked off toward the coffee, while Celia flipped her hair back in annoyance.

"Don't mind him," Celia said. "He thinks we'll be back in the house in a day or two, but I'm not going back in until the house is clean and habitable. I can't breathe in smoke due to my asthma. And the smoke probably ruined my wardrobe."

"You're welcome to stay as long as you like."

Ivy made her way through the crowd to welcome guests and make notes of requests. Her head was spinning by the time she spied Shelly, who waved her toward the kitchen. Ivy followed her.

Shelly drew her hands over her face. "I wish we'd had time to build up to this."

"Full occupancy is a beautiful thing," Ivy said. "We need this."

"I know, but I had no idea how needy people are."

"What about your customers in New York?"

"Bridezillas aside, my corporate customers were fairly easy to manage."

"So what's the problem?"

"One needs hypoallergenic sheets and soap. Another wants a coffeemaker in the room. That woman in the lavender tracksuit has cats in her room, and that's setting off Pixie over there, who wants vegan food, while that guy is asking if he can get breakfast sent up to the room—all day because that's all he eats. Waffles, eggs, bacon, and hash browns. And he complained about the baby who cried most of the night." She pressed a hand against her forehead. "What have we gotten ourselves into?"

Ivy placed her hands on her sister's shoulders. "Wait? Which one is Pixie?"

"The Chihuahua."

"And she wants a vegan menu?"

Shelly rolled her eyes. "Not the dog. Her guardian."

Glancing back at their guests, Ivy felt a rush of empathy. This was a daunting task, yet as a mother, she understood what it took to address a family's needs and run a home. This wasn't so different.

"Look, Shelly, these people are traumatized, and they need care right now. They've all been yanked out of their homes and familiar routines. Some have even lost their homes, like Imani and her son Jamir. They need help and a sympathetic ear." Ivy thought of her two daughters, who seldom needed her assistance anymore. "These people need help, so we should help any way we can."

"I get it," Shelly replied, nodding. "And they

38

have no idea what to expect. Kind of like us. So what do we tell them?"

"Let's take them one at a time. First, we're not equipped to serve meals. There's probably a food service permit we'd need anyway. Mitch would know more about that. In the meantime, we can buy coffee and muffins to serve in the morning." Ivy paused, reconsidering. She thought not about regulations, but of human decency. This was still her personal home.

"On second thought," Ivy began, thinking quickly. "This is an emergency for these people. We need to care for their needs. We can make a simple vegetable stew, or beans and rice and tortillas, and add fruit and salad on the side. It's simple fare, but no one goes hungry. I'll worry about food service regulations after we're licensed. But for now, they're our guests. Let's make them comfortable."

"They caught me off guard, that's all." Shelly jerked her head toward the guests. "Do you want Pixie and her mom or the hypoallergenic woman?"

"Where's cat woman? I'll make sure Pixie and the cats are separated. And ask the hypoallergenic woman what she needs, or if she wants to bring in her own bedding and laundry detergent, we'll be happy to oblige."

"What about breakfast man?"

Ivy rubbed her forehead. "He can walk to the

village anytime he wants. Send him to Java Beach." She paused to collect her thoughts. "We can't call our guests by these silly names. It's disrespectful."

"I'll find out their names," Shelly said, nodding sheepishly. "I think Pixie's mom is named Gilda or Gretchen. She had short pink hair."

"Gilda. I remember seeing her in town last week. Nan told me that Gilda writes for magazines. I think Gilda just adopted the dog." Ivy glanced up and saw Poppy frantically wedging her way through the guests who were devouring coffee, pastries, and yogurt.

"Aunt Ivy, we have trouble." Poppy gestured over her shoulder. "There's a man named Jim Boz at the door. I saw him here yesterday at the open house. He said something about a complaint against us, and how we can't be operating as an inn." Her eyes widened. "What if he wants to shut us down? How can we turn these people away?"

"Boz works at City Hall in the zoning department."

Shelly narrowed her eyes. "I'll bet Darla complained."

"You're probably right." Ivy pursed her lips. Between guest issues and her pressing to-do list, she didn't need this. But she would deal with it.

3

As soon as Bennett walked into City Hall, Nan rushed to him with a handful of messages. "Morning, Mayor. Clark—Chief Clarkson just called. He told me about your home. I'm so sorry."

"Lot of people are worse off than I am," Bennett said, brushing ash from his shirt. As he'd walked through the parking lot, he'd kicked up a layer of white ash covering the asphalt. More ash had rained down on him from the awning over the front door. "The way I look at it, it's an inconvenience. But we have to get those other folks settled."

"Are you staying at your sister's house?"

He'd thought about calling Kendra this morning after Ivy had rebuffed him, but his sister and her husband lived in a small two-bedroom cottage. With their ten-year-old son, Logan, and two Labrador retriever mixes from the animal rescue they couldn't bear to separate, Kendra and Dave had a full house. Logan often had friends over, and their games, toy cars, and Legos were often strewn around the house. While he loved his sister and her family, he also needed a respite.

So despite the intense feelings he'd developed for Ivy—and the fact that she'd pushed him away this morning, it still seemed logical to stay at her house.

"Kendra's house is pretty small," he said. "I'm sure I could sleep on the couch, but I'd feel like I was intruding."

"Nice shirt," Nan said, smiling.

He pinched the Grateful Dead T-shirt he'd given Mitch years ago when he'd found him sleeping in his pick-up at the beach. Mitch had just been released from prison, and Jackie hadn't been gone long. Funny how the shirt had come full circle back to him. Only he needed it this time. "Got a lot of work to do today, and I need to pick up some clothes." He started for his office.

"You didn't say where you were staying," Nan said, trailing him. "We have an extra room you can use."

Bennett hadn't meant to advertise where he was staying, but the news would travel fast in Summer Beach. And why shouldn't he let her know? "I'm staying at Las Brisas."

"You mean the Seabreeze Inn." Nan's eyes widened. "With Ivy?"

"You know we can't call it that," he said, skirting her comment about Ivy. He had too much work to do today to let Ivy fill his mind.

"Only a matter of time, I'm sure," Nan said, shaking her curly red hair.

He wasn't sure if she meant the inn or Ivy, but he didn't ask. A thought crossed his mind. "You said Ivy was renting rooms through iBnB?"

"That's right."

"Would you go online and book me in for a week?"

"Probably going to take longer than that to clean up your place."

She was right. With what damage Bennett could make out last night, he had a lot of clean-up to do. He couldn't think much about his own house, not with others in the community suffering so much more.

"Use your judgment," Bennett told her. "Is Boz in yet?

"He went to Ivy's this morning. You must have just missed him."

"Suppose I did." He wondered why Boz had seen fit to pay Ivy and Shelly a visit on such a busy morning. "Giving them a hand, is he?"

"Darla was waiting when I unlocked the door." Nan's eyes widened. "I overheard some talk about the zoning."

A wave of guilt washed through him. A couple of weeks ago, Bennett had told Boz to take whatever steps he needed to ensure that Ivy was not operating outside the residential zoning restrictions. Yet, this was a different situation. His lodging there until he could return to his home had nothing to do with his stance, either. The people who had been displaced lived and worked in Summer Beach. It made sense for them to stay in the community.

"If anyone who suffered in the fire needs help, put them through to me," Bennett said as he entered his office. His cell phone buzzed.

"Will do." Nan hurried back to her post in the reception area.

Bennett sat at his desk and answered the call. "Clark, what's the latest?"

Chief Clarkson's voice boomed through his phone. "Are you available for a press conference at thirteen-hundred hours today?"

"You're on. The fire chief will be joining us, I assume?"

"Affirmative."

"And the fire? Still under control?" He hadn't seen any signs of fire on his short drive to the office.

"As far as I know, Chief Stark and her team got it under control early this morning. But they're still working up there to make sure all the embers are out."

"That's a relief." Bennett gazed out the expanse of glass in his office. Charcoal smoke still smudged the sky over Summer Beach and formed a haze over the community. Wildfires in California were serious, and Bennett slept better with Paula Stark as chief of the Summer Beach Fire Department. "See you at one."

Bennett flipped through the messages Nan had given him, and saw that he could delegate most of the requests to his small staff. He tapped the phone on his desk. "Nan, could you ask everyone to gather in the meeting room?"

Half an hour later, after Bennett had organized his team and given out instructions in the meeting, he asked if there were any other questions.

Nan leaned forward. "What are your clothing and shoe sizes, Mr. Mayor?"

"What for?"

"You want to handle a press conference in a Grateful Dead T-shirt? We're pretty casual, but that might be taking it too far. You need a change of clothes."

His aides around the table chuckled.

"I did change," Bennett said, grinning. "But there's no time for that. I've got to head up to the ridgetop neighborhood and check in with the fire chief."

"That's why I'm going to call Jeffrey," Nan

said. "I'll have him bring some clothes from the shop."

"Good idea, thanks." Nan was on top of things, as always. She might have her faults—sometimes she gossiped—but they all did. Still, she was a loyal member of his team. "I'll text you," he said as he gathered his papers.

Ten minutes later, Bennett neared the ridgetop area of Summer Beach. In daylight, the damage was worse than he'd expected. Almost every home on the ridgetop block had suffered a loss of some sort when the flames raced through the ravine and climbed the hillside, surprising residents. Most had escaped, as far as he knew, though one couple hadn't been accounted for. One of his goals for the press conference was to broadcast information about the Wilcoxes and hope someone knew their whereabouts.

Bennett parked as close as he could and wove his way past a firetruck and hoses. Firefighters were still inspecting homes and brush to make sure that smoldering embers were extinguished. As a member of the volunteer force, he'd been in the thick of the fire with them last night until Chief Stark had sent him home.

The chief was directing her team when he neared her, and she lifted her chin toward him in acknowledgment. Bennett spoke to several weary firefighters, offering his appreciation for their long night of work.

"Hey, Ben," Paula said when she was free. A former marine, Paula Stark has been a firefighter for twenty-five years, and Summer Beach had been fortunate to get her. Although the local fire department served the community, they were also brought into the larger firefighting efforts in the region when needed.

Although Bennett knew Chief Stark had been on duty all night, she was still a commanding sight. "How's it looking?" he asked.

"Wish we'd been able to save every home, but the brush around the homes we lost was like kindling. Still, we contained the fire last night, and now it appears to be out."

"Great job here." He paused, hoping against the worst. "Anything on the Wilcoxes?" The couple kept to themselves, though they liked to poke around Antique Times or Pages, the local bookstore.

"Nothing yet. We'll continue to search and watch this area." Chief Stark said, her mouth set in a grim line. "Now, the real work begins for the homeowners."

Bennett knew that was true. "Is it safe to go into my house?"

"Sure, it's clear, but probably a mess."

Bennett nodded. "I'm expecting that."

Chief Stark grinned and nodded toward his shirt. "Grateful Dead, huh?"

"It's a long story," he replied, picking at the faded cotton. "Old T-shirt that's been around."

"That's the best kind."

Bennett strolled past a charred black skeleton of a home. The breeze blew through the rubble, kicking up a whirlwind of ashes and the acrid smell of soot. With a start, he realized it had been Imani's home, where she lived with her son Jamir. Yet the house next door had received little damage beyond burnt trees and shrubs.

Bennett ached with empathy for Imani. She'd once told him she'd bought the home and paid cash for it after retiring from her law practice to open the flower stall. She'd wanted to keep her expenses low so that after years of struggle, she could finally do what she loved for once in her life. This was a tough blow to her and her son. She had to be wondering why her house had been hit, and not others. Celia and Tyler's home suffered little damage.

A wildfire was like that. Winds could shift, and embers could take flight or become lodged under rafters. Once there, the roof would ignite, and the entire home would be lost in a short time. Other homeowners got lucky, and the fire seemed to skip and dance around them, taunting them before moving on.

Seeing Summer Beach residents that he'd grown to know and love suffer misfortune was the hardest part of his job. Some residents left the community for work or to live with other family members, while others, like his wife, were buried in the cemetery on the next hilltop. But everyone was missed and still talked about. That was the way of life in this town.

And then there was the wave of summer residents who came for vacation. Some returned every summer, like migratory birds with homing instincts. He enjoyed welcoming the new residents the most—the fresh influx of Summer Beach villagers like Ivy and Shelly. Each person added a new twist to the local culture, just as Mitch had when he landed there and started selling coffee and pastries on the beach, the year before he opened Java Beach.

Yet in all the years he'd lived here after Jackie's death, Ivy was the only woman who'd stirred his emotions like this. Still, he'd respect her decision —that wouldn't be easy—but he'd keep his distance. If there were to be anything between them, Ivy would have to make a move.

He stroked his chin as ideas formed in his mind. Didn't mean he couldn't make the option of a relationship irresistibly appealing. Or was she the type who responded to men who played hard to get?

Shaking his head, he threw out that idea. He'd never been good at relationship games. He was more of a WYSIWYG kind of guy—what you see is what you get. The *truth*, that's what he preferred. He liked to know where he stood with people.

Bennett slowed in front of his home of fifteen years. He and Jackie had bought it when they'd married. It wasn't the largest home on the block, but the bungalow had one of the best views of Summer Beach and the sparkling bay. Unless there was ocean haze or a marine layer, he could see clear from Catalina Island to the Mexican border.

The detached garage was a complete loss. His family mementos, old photos, childhood toys, yearbooks, holiday decorations, car accessories— all gone. Even his old surfboard. Sure, he'd miss his familiar things, but after losing someone he loved, that experience put other losses in perspective. His sister had insisted they digitize family photos so they could share them, so at least he had his photos of Jackie.

He swung back to his house.

The fire had blazed up to his deck and hot tub, where he'd often relaxed with a glass of wine and gazed up at the stars, or watched ships at sea or helicopters patrolling the coastline. When Jackie was alive, they'd watch the sunset, unwinding together after stressful days.

He stepped through the ashen heap that had been his deck. Then, with a heavy heart, he saw that the fire had also destroyed the back part of his home—the kitchen and an extra bedroom that was to have been the baby's room, but he used as his office. That damage must have happened after he'd left last night.

Covering his nose and mouth with the edge of his T-shirt against the drifting ashes, he fished out a photo of Jackie from the charred remains. She'd had such joy decorating the house after they'd bought it. Seeing this would have crushed her, but he supposed that didn't matter anymore. Bennett coughed into the soft, worn cotton fabric.

The house would require more work than he'd imagined. He certainly wouldn't be able to return for some time.

Poking through the debris with a stick, he collected a few odd items—an old tin snuff-box that had belonged to his grandfather, a wrought iron skillet, kitchen knives.

Almost everything smelled and looked sooty or had been drenched with water. The heat of the fire had melted everything that was plastic and warped even the sturdier stuff.

He'd have to file an insurance claim and get in line, just like everyone else.

Bennett gathered a few items and paused to look out over the village of Summer Beach. At least the majority of the community had been spared. For that, he was thankful. He started back to where he'd parked.

As he passed Paula, she raised her hand. "See you at the press conference."

"Sure thing." He swung into his SUV, which was now dusted with ash as soft and fluffy as snow.

The press conference. It sounded grander than it was. But it was essential to get the news out on the radio and local television for older residents who weren't connected online, as well as to the surrounding communities.

When Bennett returned to the office, he heard Nan bustling around inside.

"Jeffrey just left, but he said to call him if you need anything else," Nan said. She was arranging several changes of clothes in his office. He'd texted her his sizes before he'd left the City Hall parking lot to see Chief Stark.

"I'm amazed," Bennett said. Jeffrey knew his preferred standbys—lightweight slacks or chinos with knit shirts. He'd even brought a pair of jeans, flip-flops, and board shorts.

"Jeffrey had to return to open his shop, but once his assistant arrives, he can bring anything else you need."

"Looks like the two of you thought of everything." It was all here, right down to the socks and underwear and shoes.

Bennett had shopped at Jeffrey's for years, preferring to patronize Summer Beach shops when he could to keep the locally owned stores in business. Even a giant online store couldn't match the service level Jeffrey offered. Jeffrey also offered house credit to his customers, just like his father before him had. Shopping couldn't be easier.

Nan beamed. "I'll leave you to it." She closed the door behind her.

Bennett pulled off the Grateful Dead T-shirt, dusted ash from his hair, and slipped into chinos and a polo shirt. He was glad that Summer Beach was casual, so he didn't have to shape up in a suit except for official occasions. Still, he liked to dress up, especially when he went to San Francisco or New York, although he hadn't done much of that since Jackie died.

Pulling on new socks, he thought about how he could think of her now without being broken up, but it had taken him a couple of years to get to that point. Even now, her birthday and their anniversary were still difficult days.

As much as he'd hated hearing Ivy say she wasn't ready this morning, he understood. How long would it take her? And how long could he suppress his feeling for her? She was the first woman he'd really developed feelings for. Something about her lit his desire. She had a rare combination of sweetness with a fiery, determined spirit he admired. Nice legs, too.

He slid his feet into the shoes Jeffrey had left and rested his hands on his knees. All he and Ivy had to do was get through the summer. By then, he imagined his home would be put back together, and he could move on—with or without her.

From what he'd seen in life, timing was everything. And he was realistic enough to know that their timing might not ever mesh.

A knock sounded at the door, and he heard Boz call out to him. "You decent?"

"Come in," Bennett said, standing up.

Boz walked into the office. Putting his hands on his hips, he said, "This morning I received word of a problem at the old Las Brisas estate."

"Heard you went over there."

"Ivy has taken in a lot of people," Boz said. "Had to check it out."

"That's what Summer Beach is all about— neighbors helping each other."

Boz nodded. "But the zoning—"

"In full disclosure, you should know I'm staying there, too," Bennett said. "I booked my room through iBnB."

"Nothing wrong with that." Boz stroked the salt-and-pepper stubble on his chin. "Plenty of people here rent out rooms. And those guests spend more money at village shops, which is good for the community. But Darla was waiting for me when I arrived at the office this morning."

"She had a busy morning." Bennett thought about Darla's sunrise attack on Ivy. He figured she'd seen cars parked around the property and assumed Ivy had a full house. "Ivy and her family took in a lot of displaced people last night after the open house and the fire. Volunteers set up cots and sleeping bags at the high school gym, but you can't blame people for taking Ivy and Shelly up on their hospitality. That was a huge help, too." His phone buzzed with a text, and he glanced at it before shoving it into his pocket.

Boz nodded. "To appease Darla, I had to visit to see if Ivy was in compliance with the zoning."

"And what did you find?" Bennett asked, keeping his tone level.

"Not much. Ivy's sister asked me in for coffee, and I had a chance to speak to quite a few folks. What I found was a person who's helping her neighbors. Except for one couple who'd booked through iBnB—and you—everyone else was welcomed there as neighbors and friends. Mitch had brought breakfast in, too."

"So where's the problem?"

Boz shook his head. "As far as I'm concerned, if Ivy's houseguests want to express their appreciation by doing something nice for her—whether there's a monetary value attached or not—that's okay, too."

"But you're aware of her financial situation." Bennett hated to mention it, but he had a duty to be forward-looking for the community.

"As I said, nothing wrong with iBnB guests. Doesn't mean residents might complain or ask that restrictions be applied in the future, but right now, what Ivy is doing is acceptable."

"My only concern is that she might not be

able to make a going concern of this based on an iBnB model," Bennett said. "She's already behind on her taxes. The property could end up back in a tax sale situation. With its beachfront location, we'll probably be spending city funds to fight developers again."

"Sounds like you're arguing for Ivy's success."

Bennett liked to see people succeed against the odds. "I represent Summer Beach constituents. What would benefit the community is to have access to the house as a community meeting place, as we did when Amelia Erickson's estate owned it and leased it out for events."

"Which was technically against the zoning," Boz said, lifting an eyebrow. "Although the former mayor overlooked that point for his personal benefit."

The mayor before him had owned a catering company, which catered all the charitable events that were held there. "I don't want to get into that," Bennett said. "Times have changed, and now we abide by the law."

Bennett stuffed his sooty clothes into a bag from Jeffrey's Menswear. He could see that trying to balance his position as mayor with the community's needs—and Ivy's—might prove to be a dilemma. And staying at Ivy's house was compounding issues.

"Just wanted you to be aware of the situation,

boss. Darla's pretty vocal. I imagine the Java Beach crowd has already gotten an earful."

Bennett shrugged. "Of what? Ivy's personal houseguests trampling Darla's flowers as they saved her house from swirling embers? That's all they've got, Boz." Bennett rifled through his messages. "And don't call me boss."

Boz grinned. "Just reporting in."

"Got it."

As Boz turned to leave, Nan slipped into Bennett's office. "Wanted to see how the clothes worked out. Jeffrey was wondering if everything fit."

"Perfect. Thanks, Nan. That was a good idea."

"I wanted to tell you that the Wilcoxes have been located," Nan said. "They were staying at a friend's home."

"That's good news," Bennett said, greatly relieved. He'd feared that they hadn't gotten out of the path of the fire.

"Anything else I can do?" Nan swept a blaze of red curls from her forehead.

Bennett heaved a sigh. "Could you find another place for me to stay in Summer Beach?"

"Aren't you comfortable at the Seabreeze Inn?"

"We don't call it that, and that's part of the problem." It's not that he wanted to move. In fact, he'd hoped to get to know Ivy better.

"That zoning issue?"

Bennett nodded. "Just see what you can find."

"Not that many places in Summer Beach. I heard the Seal Cove Inn is full. But there might be a cot at the gymnasium."

"Please check. I need something for at least a couple of months."

"Summer is high season," Nan said. "Won't be easy."

Bennett picked up the phone to start returning calls. "Maybe you'll find a cancellation."

Nan shook her head. "It's just not right about the Seabreeze Inn, you know. Those women need a break. Can't you rezone the property and let them do what they need to do to make a living here?"

"Ivy has filed for rezoning, and the residents will have their say. It's up to them, the city council, and Boz's department."

"But this is an emergency. By taking in all those folks after the fire, Ivy's doing a service to the community. She's just got to find a way to pay that tax bill and stay here."

"And I hope she does," Bennett said, trying to sound impartial, but he was secretly pulling for her success, too. This issue was new territory to him as mayor, but more than that, it was becoming a deeply personal issue. Part of him even hoped Nan wouldn't find another place.

Nan crossed her arms and huffed. "I'll look for other accommodations, but like I said, it's—"

"High season," Bennett finished, nodding. This is when Summer Beach burst with visitors, and merchants made their money for the year. The fire couldn't have happened at a worse time. He didn't care where he slept, other than under Ivy's roof.

Professionally speaking, of course.

4

While Poppy and Shelly took care of guest needs, Ivy took the Jeep to load up on supplies.

Standing at a giant big box store on the outskirts of Summer Beach, she wondered how to calculate how much of everything she would need. The paper supplies alone would practically fill up the old Jeep. She'd get the necessities—laundry detergent, toilet paper, tissues. And sponges, dish soap, and coffee. She ticked off her list as she went.

After pushing the cart through checkout and loading the old Jeep, Ivy started back. She'd used a bungee cord to strap bulky items to the roof. When she pulled up to the house, Poppy ran out to meet her. Her niece began laughing and pulled out her phone to snap a photo.

Ivy stepped out of the Jeep. "Do you have to take a picture of everything?"

"Come on, Auntie, this is hilarious," Poppy said, laughing. "Who drives around with toilet paper on the roof? People love funny behind-the-scenes shots like this."

Ivy struck a pose, then made a face and tossed a bundle of napkins at her. "Here, find another way to help." She was glad that Poppy was around to lighten the mood.

Still chuckling, Poppy caught it. "Okay, I got it. By the way, Imani is looking for you. She's in the library."

After carting detergent and fabric softener to the laundry room off the kitchen, Ivy nudged open the door and dropped the giant containers. She brushed off her hands and made her way to the library.

Imani was sitting at a small table where she'd set up a mobile office with her laptop, tablet, and phone. She wore a bright tie-dyed sundress, and a broad-brimmed hat sat next to her. She frowned at the screen in front of her.

"Hi Imani," Ivy said, sitting at the table across from her. "I see you found a quiet place to work."

"The internet reception is better here than upstairs," Imani said. "I sent Jamir off to handle the flower buying this morning because I wanted to put in a call to my insurance agent." Imani sighed and ran her hands over her face. "I'll be straight with you. I've got a problem, and I'm hoping we can work together on it."

"I'll do what I can."

"It's like this," Imani began. "I know you're not running a charity here, and I don't expect you to, but I've got to submit receipts for lodging reimbursements to my insurance company. They warned me it will take time to handle the claim and process expenses before I begin to receive reimbursement." Imani paused, blinking hard when her eyes filled with tears.

Ivy reached across the table and took her hand. "I know it's hard. Go on. I'm listening."

Imani continued. "Although I have a sister in L.A., she's at the far northern edge of the county. With morning traffic, it would take me hours to get here and hours to drive home. Not to mention the gas. I really can't afford it."

"But you're insured, right?"

"I am, but I was underinsured to rebuild the house as it was." Imani grimaced. "Not that I need much. But even though Jamir's tuition is covered in the fall he still has books and other expenses. So I'm trying to find other solutions."

Ivy nodded. She knew Imani was devastated at the loss of her home and was trying to do her best. She recalled how shocked she'd been at Jeremy's death and how her entire life had changed in a matter of weeks. When the mortgage came due, without Jeremy's monthly income, she had to move fast or risk foreclosure. And yet, she faced the same problem now.

"We're stronger together," Ivy said. "What can I do to help?"

"Besides running the flower shop, I have skills. I'm an attorney, and since your business is new, I thought you might need some help setting up your corporation, shielding yourself from liability, and making sure your limitations of liability are correct with your insurance company."

Ivy blinked. She hadn't even thought of all that. "You know, I have some challenges, too. Let me explain, and maybe you could help." Ivy told her about her situation with the city and the zoning problems.

"Can't Bennett help you with that?" Imani asked when she finished.

Ivy shook her head. "Appears it's a conflict of interest or something like that."

"Sounds like Ben. There was a scandal surrounding the last mayor and his catering company, so he's playing by the book."

"That's what I want, too."

Imani tapped her fingers on the table, thinking. "I can help to get that zoning passed. And you need it as soon as possible if you're going to save this property. I could help you with the paperwork you'll need for the zoning and to stave off a tax sale. I'm not suggesting an exchange of services either. I'll still pay for the room, but as I said, I need time. And I'm thinking you might be short of funds for legal fees."

"Not the least because I just spent a small fortune on toilet paper."

Imani chuckled. "Maybe you can crowdsource that."

"Crowdsource, that's it." Ideas began bubbling in Ivy's brain.

"That was a joke."

"I'm serious. Since insurance won't cover everything, what if we run a crowdsourcing campaign for funds to help people—like you and Jamir—get back in their homes. Friends and family often want to help, but they think their assistance will be turned down, or the other party will feel like they owe them something. With crowdsourcing, people can donate anonymously if they want so their friends can rebuild their lives without feeling like they need to pay it back."

"That's brilliant." Imani's eyes glittered. "A portion of that could go to lodging expenses until they can move back in. So you get what you need, too." She thought for a moment. "I could put Jamir on that."

Ivy appreciated Imani's way of thinking. It wasn't what she'd intended, but she was grateful the other woman thought of her needs, too.

Thinking in business terms was new for Ivy. Except for her private art students, she'd never managed a business, but she had run a household.

She was an expert on managing expenses, though her business development—that's what Jeremy had called it—needed practice.

Ivy summoned her courage and touched Imani's hand. "Shelly mentioned that you might be able to refer business to us."

"That's right," Imani said. "See, I deal in cut flowers. I love visiting the flower mart in the early morning and inhaling those beautiful scents. The colors and variety are spectacular, and this is an ideal climate for flower growers. I buy direct, too, especially my poinsettias. Did you know the Ecke family ranch down the way was the largest producer of poinsettias for years? Old Paul Ecke is the one who was behind the concept of poinsettias as a Christmas tradition."

Ivy grinned. "We used to visit the farms as kids."

"Well, I sell cut flowers and create simple bouquets for people. Sometimes my regular customers ask me to provide floral arrangements for weddings and parties."

"That must be good business."

"Sure, except I can't design arrangements like that. Nor do I want that kind of stress. I've seen Shelly's creations online. She's super talented. And you have plenty of space here for events."

"I understand that people used to love coming here for parties."

"Maybe you could get away with the occasional party this summer."

"I don't want to risk it until we have the proper zoning." Ivy appreciated how quickly Imani was grasping her situation. "But I think we women need to stick together and help each other." She held out her hands to Imani, who clasped them. "You and Jamir are welcome to stay and pitch in."

A smile bloomed on Imani's face. "My son is pretty handy, too. He helped fix up our old bungalow—painting, laying tile, yardwork."

"Shelly and I haven't had time to put the old maid's quarters in the rear of the house in shape, so Jamir could start on that. More rooms give us more inventory to rent out. I'll take you up on that, but I'll insist on paying Jamir."

"We'll agree to disagree on that later," Imani said, as joyful tears spilled onto her cheeks.

Ivy stood and hugged her. "I have a feeling we're going to become good friends through all this."

"I think so," Imani said. "You'll meet some nice folks here. Maybe even meet someone special."

"I've got to focus on my business first," Ivy said, smiling. She'd been worried about rezoning and the property tax issues, so she was grateful for Imani's assistance.

Jamir would be a valuable addition to the

Seabreeze Inn team, too. Ivy and Shelly had the newly discovered lower level to think about as well, but Ivy knew that area would require a lot more renovation. For now, they were still using it for storage of the older furnishings they'd discovered but decided not to use.

After leaving Imani, Ivy climbed the stairs to her room to put away a couple of packages of coat hangers she'd purchased at the store. When she'd packed her clothes to ship from Boston, she hadn't bothered to include bulky hangers.

After depositing the hangers in the closet, she tapped the loose floorboard she'd snagged her slippers on earlier. It sounded hollow, just like the small opening in the rear of the closet. She tapped around the slat; the sound was different.

Retrieving a metal nail file, she slid it in one side and lifted. The old wood creaked against the effort, but after a few tries, the slat sprang free, sending up a small spray of dust. Inside was a folded piece of paper and a small, dusty box. Sitting cross-legged, Ivy scooped out the items.

"Ivy, are you in here?" Shelly's voice rang out at her door.

"In the closet."

"Come on, I need your help," Shelly called out, clearly perturbed about something.

Dusting off her jeans, Ivy stood up. "I've found something," she said, emerging from the closet.

"What's that?"

When Ivy opened the box, both of them exclaimed. A small diamond ring rimmed with rubies and tiny seed pearls was nestled in the box.

"That's vintage," Shelly said. "Nineteenth-century, I'll bet. I saw a lot of old family jewelry at auctions in New York."

"It's sweet," said Ivy, slipping the small ring onto her pinky finger, where it fit perfectly. "Though it seems small for the wealth that the Erickson's had."

Shelly shrugged. "Maybe it wasn't hers. Where'd you find it?"

"In the closet under a floorboard."

Shelly blinked. "How many hiding places did that woman have in this house?"

"No idea." Ivy held up the paper, which was yellow around the edges and the crease. "This was in there, too." She began to unfold it, but Shelly clasped her hand over hers.

"We don't have time for this. Remember what happened the last time we opened Pandora's Box?"

Ivy stared at the paper. Shelly had a point—their lives had been upended when they'd found Amelia Erickson's secret stash of stolen masterpieces, even though Ivy still refused to believe that Amelia was doing nothing more than protecting them for posterity. The woman had been suffering from Alzheimer's. Of course she would hide things and forget about them.

"Maybe this is nothing," Ivy said, turning the ring on her finger. "Just a keepsake she'd tucked away."

"That's right. Come on." Shelly tugged on her arm. "I need you downstairs now."

Ivy stared at the folded notepaper. She still wondered what had been so important about this ring to Amelia Erickson that she'd hidden it under a floorboard.

Shelly blew out a breath of exasperation.

"Okay, I'm coming." With a sigh of regret, Ivy tucked everything into a drawer in her vanity. "What's so urgent downstairs?"

"Our neighbor must have some disconnected brain cells." Shelly motioned for her to follow. "Seriously. You've got to see this."

Shelly raced down the stairs, and Ivy hurried after her. When Shelly opened the door, Ivy's mouth fell open.

"How dare Darla stoop this low," she said and charged out the front door.

5

"You can't do this!" Ivy marched down the front stone steps toward Darla, who was standing on their lawn holding a hand-lettered sign that read *Neighbors against the Seabreeze Inn.*

"Free speech is my civil right," Darla said, waving the giant red letters in her face.

"You're out of control."

Darla ignored her. When a car drove by, Darla raised two fingers to her mouth, let out a screeching whistle, and waved the sign.

The high-pitched whistle brought Poppy and Imani to the front door.

"This is rich," Poppy said, flicking on the video on her phone.

"I call it harassment," Imani said. "I'll see what I can do."

"Darla, I respect your privacy, but no one here is bothering you today," Ivy said. "Can't you leave these poor people alone? Imani and her son lost their home last night, and Celia and Tyler and others were evacuated. Can't you have some compassion?"

"Gotta nip this in the bud," Darla replied. "The high school gymnasium shelter is open. They can go there."

"Is that what you'd want in their position?" Ivy put her hands on her hips. "Better yet, why don't you offer your spare bedrooms to some people? You have room. Why not help your neighbors?"

Poppy stepped closer and zoomed in on Darla, who seemed to be at a loss for words.

Imani strode forth. "Miss Darla, do you want me to call Chief Clarkson and report you? I can't get you out this time because I'm representing Ivy now. And old Hal won't take your frivolous cases anymore."

Ivy widened her eyes in surprise. Sounded like more Summer Beach gossip she was sure she'd hear later.

"They weren't frivolous," Darla shot back.

Imani crossed her arms. "The judge didn't agree. Come on, you haven't been to Java Beach yet, have you? Your folks there are probably missing you."

Darla cast another narrow-eyed look at Ivy. "I'll be watching you and your sister."

"You can watch all you want," Ivy said. "Just don't set another foot in my yard unless you have something nice to say." She turned to go back inside the house.

"Just like her husband," Darla muttered as she lowered her sign.

Ivy whirled around. "I am *nothing* like Jeremy was."

Shelly stepped to her defense, instantly shedding her cheerful yoga girl persona and jabbing her finger in the air, New York-style, in Darla's face.

"If you think that, then you don't know Ivy at all," Shelly said. "And that's your loss, lady. *Big* loss. She's the kindest woman you could ever want as a neighbor. She's not the one you have to worry about. That would be *me*," she finished, jerking a thumb toward her chest.

"Down, tiger," Imani said, stepping between Shelly and Darla. "Neighbors, neighbors, get ahold of yourselves. Things were hot enough around here last night. Don't you go pouring gasoline on tempers in town, now, you hear?"

Shelly and Darla stood glaring at each other before Darla stepped back.

"Got my eye on you two," Darla said, creeping back toward her property.

"Yeah, yeah," Shelly called out. "Same here."

Ivy placed her hand on Shelly's arm. "Thanks, but that's enough."

"And I got it all on video," Poppy said. "Wow, neighborhood fights in sleepy Summer Beach. Who knew?"

"Calm down, ladies." Imani spread her hands in a conciliatory manner. "Darla's had some emotional difficulties in the past."

Ivy pushed a hand through her hair. "You think?" Her phone jingled in her pocket, and she glanced at it. A photo of her daughter Sunny flashed on the screen.

"She had a nervous breakdown." Imani shook her head. "She doesn't handle change well." She paused. "Do you need to get that?"

Nodding, Ivy answered her phone. "Hey, sweetie, can I call you back?"

Tyler appeared at the doorway. "What's all the yelling about?"

"It's over," Ivy called out. "We're terribly sorry."

Sunny's voice crackled through the phone. "Mom, are you there? I'm in Belgium."

"Uh, yeah, sweetie, that's nice."

Tyler spit out a few choice words, and bellowed, "Can't a man sleep around here?"

Celia raced behind him and put her hand on his shoulder. "Tyler, just relax, babe. Everyone's on edge today."

Just then, a snarling Chihuahua shot between

their legs, out the front door, and hurtled down the steps, its toenails clattering like firecrackers on the stone steps.

"Mom? What's going on?"

"Can't really talk."

"Pixie!" A pink-haired woman in a bamboo green bathrobe pressing a cell phone to her ear wedged her way between Celia and Tyler, knocking him into the wall. She raced after the rocketing little dog. "Pixie's loose. I have to call you back. Pix-eeeee!"

"That's it," Tyler said, shrugging off his wife's hand and regaining his balance. "This place is insane. I'm sleeping on the boat. Join me if you want to."

"Mom, I'm calling from *Belgium!*"

Ivy shielded the phone's microphone and whispered. "I know, sweetie. I'll call you back."

Sunny wailed, "But, Mom—"

"I told you, I'm not moving." Celia's dark eyes flashed with anger, and she spun around to march upstairs.

Frantically, Ivy tapped off the phone. *Of all times…*

Tyler strode across the property to his car and flung open the door. As he did, he slipped on the ground that had been hosed down to excess the night before. With his lanky limbs akimbo, Tyler's feet slid out from under him and he fell, splayed in the mud. Cursing, he stood up, covered in a gritty

74

mixture of sand and dirt. He ripped off his shirt and threw it on the ground in disgust before jumping in his convertible and spinning his tires as he fled the scene.

Pixie's parent—*Gilda*, Ivy recalled—scooped her up, admonishing the little dog, who was panting with delight. She flounced back inside the house.

"Got that, too," Poppy said, squealing. "Our first marital break-up and rabid runaway pooch. This is better than a reality show."

Ivy flung up her hands. "Delete it. We don't have their permission." Turning to Imani, she said, "Has everyone gone mad?"

"It's a small town. Sometimes we get on each other's nerves. Especially during Santa Ana winds —the devil winds." Imani jerked her thumb in Darla's direction, who'd already slammed the door to her house. "You'll have to work on that one."

"I'm not catering to her," Ivy said, lifting her chin.

"Cheaper than fighting it out in court," Imani said. "She's one of those sue-happy types."

Rolling her eyes, Ivy said, "Oh, for Pete's sake. I'll find a way to deal with her."

"She's got a thing for Mitch's pastries, if that helps," Imani said.

Poppy burst out laughing. "Is that what you call them?"

Shelly grinned. "He does have sweet buns."

Ivy whipped around. "Poppy! Shelly!"

"Sorry, Auntie." Poppy stifled a laugh.

"Oh, my!" Imani laughed and fanned herself. "Getting steamy here."

Ivy threw up her hands. "What am I going to do with all of you?" She was only half-way through their first day with a full house, and with this cast of characters, she already needed something. A glass of wine, a bath, chocolate, a nap. She pressed her hands to her temples.

"Picketing neighbors, couples breaking up, runaway dogs, even the mayor—" Ivy stopped short. "I don't know if I can do this."

Shelly slung her arm over her shoulder. "Sure you can, sis. I got your back."

"And she's impressive," Imani added.

"I didn't mean to laugh, Aunt Ivy," Poppy said, falling in behind them.

Shelly took Ivy's hand. "Come on, everyone. I'm making Sea Breezes. With or without the extra kick?"

"Definitely with," Imani said.

Once in the kitchen, Shelly lined up blue-rimmed Mexican bubble-glass tumblers. Poppy cranked open the antique ice trays and filled the glasses, while Shelly poured chilled cranberry juice followed by pink grapefruit juice.

"Ivy, would you slice the limes?" Shelly asked.

"On it." Ivy plucked a couple of fresh limes

from a shelf in Gertie. The other fridge, Gert, seemed to be working fine so far. She'd find time to clean it later, but for now, she shoved a couple of boxes of baking soda inside.

Ivy quickly sliced the limes to use as garnish.

Shelly glanced at Poppy and Imani, who were perched on stools chatting about Darla and Tyler and Pixie. "Virgin or fully loaded?"

Poppy giggled. "I still have to drive back to L.A., so make mine a virgin."

Shelly made a face. "Why would you go back when we're having so much fun here?"

"Where am I going to stay here?" Poppy lifted her hands. "You've got a full house."

"Stay in my room," Shelly said. "There's an extra, short little bed with wheels underneath mine you can use."

Ivy smiled. "That's called a trundle bed."

"Whatever it is, it's handy. And you're already wearing my clothes—regrettably better than I do —so you might as well stay, girl."

"We could sure use you," Ivy added.

"I'd like that." Raising a shoulder, Poppy said, "I'll go with half a splash."

Imani shook out her hair. "Fully loaded for me, hon. This has been one helluva 24 hours. Not even that, actually."

Shelly poured vodka into Imani's juice cocktail and a tiny splash into Poppy's. "How about you, sis?"

Ivy blew wisps of hair from her face. "Much as I'd like to kick back and relax, I've got a long to-do list." And she had to call Sunny back. The hair on the back of her neck bristled. Sunny *never* called unless she needed something. She hoped Sunny was okay.

"When have I ever known you not to have at least one list?" Shelly handed her a virgin Sea Breeze. "But ditto for me."

Ivy raised her glass and hooked her arm with Shelly's. "Ladies, we've survived windstorm and fire, Darla and marital meltdowns, attack Chihuahuas and—well, all the rest. Here's to us—the early survivors of the Seabreeze Inn. And to Imani, who might have lost the most, but laughs the loudest. Bless you, sweetie."

"Amen, sunshine," Imani said, giving her a knowing look. "You've discovered my secret."

They all clinked glasses and drank down the refreshing juice cocktails.

Ivy looked from one woman to the next, thinking about the role they were playing in transforming the old Las Brisas estate into the new Seabreeze Inn. She was thankful that each woman was in her life. A little more than a month ago, she could never have imagined any of this.

Ivy looked around their circle and smiled. "This is quite the team. Shelly is our master groundskeeper, floral designer, decorator, and event planner. Poppy is handling the website, reservations, publicity, and marketing. Imani has volunteered to guide our legal affairs, zoning application, and insurance matters. And her son Jamir will help us spruce up the maid's quarters in the back. What an incredible team we make."

"And here's to our uber-organized leader," Shelly said. "Ivy is the one who had the vision and put us all together."

After relaxing for a while and regaining her equilibrium, Ivy's mind began whirring again. "Poppy, let's put together a Welcome letter to give to every guest, or slide under their door. We'll let them know what services to expect while they're here."

"Will do, Aunt Ivy."

Imani leaned in. "You need to let these people know how to pay you and the terms if they decide to stay on."

"In the spirit of neighborly assistance, I'm comping last night and tonight for everyone," Ivy said. "Our guests need a chance to decide what to do. Many will probably be able to return home." She turned to Poppy. "Let's give them our iBnB link so they can book if they want."

"Will do," Poppy said.

Ivy turned to her sister. "And Shelly, you and I need to tidy and stock the guestrooms." She checked her phone. "I also need to call Sunny back."

"I'm down for a long nap," Imani said.

"Which means I'm kicking Jamir out of the room. You can show him what to do."

"We will, and you deserve a rest," Ivy told her. She could see in Imani's eyes that the emotional impact of losing her home was just beginning to hit her. The poor woman needed to take care of herself. Jamir might be just as weary, too.

Poppy sprang into action with her laptop, while Ivy followed Shelly to the supply closet.

Ivy was dead tired from last night, too, but as she was beginning to understand, the life of an innkeeper was complicated and full.

The ruby ring and old note Ivy had found crossed her mind for a moment, but she dismissed them, mentally filing that task on her strict Not-To-Do-Today list. There would be plenty of time to explore Amelia Erickson's hidden treasure. And this one, Ivy hoped, would not involve summoning the FBI again.

Perhaps the ring and note might help Megan in her research for the documentary. She made a mental note to tell her.

Later that week, after their guests had settled into their new routines, Ivy asked Imani to help draft a strategy to gain the change in zoning needed to ensure the future of the Seabreeze Inn. Time was of the essence, Ivy thought, to ensure that they could host the events needed to turn the old house into a profitable venture.

Now, Ivy pulled her chair closer to the round table in the library where she had started holding short coordination meetings with Shelly and Poppy every morning before they went about their day tending to guests and renovations. She opened her laptop computer.

"I'll make this quick, because I know we all have a lot to do today," Ivy said, consulting the notes she'd taken during the meeting with Boz at City Hall. "Imani advised me to talk with Jim Boz at the planning department about our bid for re-zoning. So I met with him yesterday."

"Did he offer any guidance?" Shelly asked, tapping her fingers on the polished wood surface.

Ivy knew Shelly was awaiting a delivery of fresh dirt that she planned to use to mound flower beds, but this was important, too. "He did, and what's more, he seems supportive," Ivy said.

Shelly arched an eyebrow. "That's surprising. I thought the City was against the rezoning of this property."

"Boz and the Summer Beach City Council were against Jeremy's grandiose plan," Ivy said. "But our plan for an inn actually has an advantage. From Boz's perspective, our action would establish new zoning for an inn…" She trailed to a stop, unsure of how to choose her words without upsetting Shelly.

Shelly tilted her head. "Isn't that what we want?"

"The City is in favor of this because it would make the property more attractive, not only to us but also to potential future owners. Just in case." Ivy leveled a gaze at Shelly and Poppy.

"In case of *what?*" Poppy asked.

"Oh, I get it," Shelly said, color rising in her cheeks. She pushed back from the table and sprang up. "The city doesn't have confidence in our ability to perform, so if we crash and burn, then another innkeeper can step in."

"Thus staving off big developers in the future," Ivy finished, gesturing to Shelly.

Shelly paced behind them.

"That's not likely, is it, Aunt Ivy?" Poppy shifted a worried gaze between Ivy and Shelly.

"Not as long as we keep working our business plan and hitting our goals and occupancy levels," Ivy said with conviction, although in her heart, she knew the odds were stacked against them. They needed to schedule more events because the costs of ongoing renovations were rapidly mounting.

Shelly gripped the back of her chair and shook her head in frustration. "I don't know. Do you really think we can make our numbers?"

"If we all pull together, I know we can," Ivy replied with renewed confidence. "I'm entering costs and income and recalculating the cashflow spreadsheet every day." *Just as on the old household budget. Seeing numbers in black-and-white was reassuring.*

When Shelly looked doubtful, Ivy spun her laptop around. "Look at this. We're already doing it." The margin was slim, but the numbers *had* edged into the profit territory—even if only slightly.

Shelly and Poppy peered at the screen.

This wasn't the first time Ivy had overcome adversity in her life—or people not believing she was capable enough. She'd encountered that on the swim team in high school and in her early life-guard training. In this case, it was City Council members.

Ivy tapped her pen on the yellow notepad in front of her. "Imani's suggestion is to use the city's posture to our gain."

"And how do we do that?" Poppy asked, leaning toward her with an eager expression.

"Can you create a report detailing the number of locals currently in residence, and how many of them are employed or have businesses in Summer Beach?" Ivy turned to her sister, who had eased back into her chair and seemed ready to listen again. "And Shelly, can you put together a projection of community events we manage or participate in?"

"Like what?"

"Yoga classes, horticulture tours, beach walks, music events. Write them on a calendar, estimate the number of attendees, and tally the totals for me. I'll handle the art classes and art show events. We want to show the positive impact the inn is having on the community. More services at no cost to the community. If you think any events will bring in tourists or outsiders, note that. Imani has a tourist dollar multiplier figure we'll use to calculate the benefit to Summer Beach." Ivy pursed her lips. "And we need all of this tomorrow."

"You always did like a good challenge," Shelly said.

"I can help you right now," Poppy said, touching her hand. "I bet we can have it done before the dirt for the flower mounds arrives."

"Thank you both," Ivy said, rising. "This zoning decision will be close. Imani briefed me on how the council members usually vote. But since we're housing the evacuees, she thinks the sentiment in our favor is as high as it can be right now. And Boz wants me to present at the next council meeting."

6

"Here are the reports you asked for," Nan said, reaching across Bennett's desk to hand him two thick, bound reports.

"Thanks," Bennett said, taking the feasibility study that Jeremy Marin had submitted to the City of Summer Beach, along with the City's analysis. He'd hoped he'd never have to look at these reports again, but he needed to refresh his memory. A resort developer interested in the Las Brisas del Mar property—now quickly becoming known as the Seabreeze Inn around town—had contacted him this morning. Bennett needed to recall all the salient points to deter him.

A worried look creased Nan's brow. "How did David Peterson find out about the property?"

"Same way they all do. From the tax records.

Ivy's in arrears on the property taxes, and that's prime beachfront property."

Nan chewed on her lip. "She really needs to be successful there, doesn't she?"

Bennett leaned back his chair. "If she wants to stay."

"She and Shelly sure have been doing a lot for the community. Putting all those folks up at the inn, some of them free of charge."

It had been more than a week since the ridgetop wildfire, and Bennett was still ensconced at Ivy's house. "Have you found any other accommodations for me yet?"

Nan's eyes darted to one side, then back again. "Can't find a thing."

Bennett flexed his jaw. Staying there, he felt he was too close to the issue. Yet, he was comfortable. Ivy and Shelly had experienced their share of mishaps—from running out of hot water one morning to a cat's persistent nocturnal yowling—but overall, they were making positive contributions to the community.

He flipped open a report, his eyes scanning the page. "Would you keep looking, please?"

"Aren't you comfortable at Ivy's?"

Ivy. The words on the page blurred as he thought about her. He enjoyed rising early and having coffee with Ivy in the kitchen before other people rose. After a few minutes, she usually found something that required her immediate attention

—rearranging flowers, restocking tissue—so he figured she was trying to keep her distance from him.

However, the internet connection at the house didn't reach upstairs, so that gave him an excuse to go downstairs and find a chair in the library, where he discovered she worked every evening, reviewing pending reservations with Poppy or discussing plans for yoga and horticulture classes with Shelly.

"It's pleasant enough there," Bennett finally said. He glanced up. "Please keep looking."

"I will, but it's the summer vacation rush. And the horse races in July. And well, August is booked out months in advance." She shook her head. "You might as well be asking me to make reservations to the moon, especially since you need long-term lodging."

"Do what you can, please." He'd boarded up the rear of his house that the fire had swallowed and put a tarp over the gaping hole in the roof, but it would be weeks, at least, until the work was done and he could return.

Nan fidgeted her bright pink nails. "Oh, well…"

As she left, Bennett had the distinct impression that Nan was avoiding this task and conspiring to keep him at Ivy's.

However, the reports loomed before him, so he turned his attention back to his work.

An hour later, Bennett heard a tap on the door. Boz poked his head in. "Time for the council meeting."

"So it is." The reports were pretty dry reading, but he had the gist of the arguments down again.

"There's been a change in the agenda," Boz said.

"And what's that?"

Boz came in and stood before him, flexing his fingers as he spoke. "Has to do with an emergency rezoning issue."

"On what property?"

"The old Las Brisas property. Ivy and her attorney are here, and I think you'll be interested in hearing what they have to say."

"Ivy has an attorney?" He hadn't heard Ivy say anything about this. "Let's go." Bennett clenched his jaw and followed Boz into the chamber where the City Council met.

Bennett was surprised to see Ivy and Imani seated in the small audience. "We'll start in just a moment."

With her professional face on, Ivy nodded, as did Imani. Ivy seemed a little nervous, and his heart went out to her. He knew how much the rezoning meant to her—they talked about it over coffee in the morning, but she hadn't mentioned that she'd be here today. But then, wasn't that precisely what he'd told her to do? To follow the guidelines and appeal to the City Council? And she'd come prepared. He was pleased that she'd taken his advice.

Bennett picked up his gavel and struck it on its small wooden platform. "The Summer Beach City Council has now come to order."

The small council—just five members, including himself—decided on general business matters first. A proclamation honoring a retiring teacher was made, and then the council moved on to several issues regarding the recent fire.

The meeting moved along fairly quickly. Bennett consulted the agenda. "Jim Boz, director of planning, is next on the agenda. Mr. Boz, you're up." He laced his fingers in front of him, listening intently.

Boz nodded toward Ivy. "I'd like to introduce Ivy Bay Marin and her attorney, Imani Jones, to discuss a matter regarding emergency housing in Summer Beach."

Ivy stood and faced the council members.

"Ms. Marin, how can we help you?" Bennett asked, trying to keep his tone professional and respectful. Ivy looked especially nice today. He'd seen her in her dark jeans and a white T-shirt before he'd left the Seabreeze this morning, but she'd added a coral necklace and earrings that brought out the highlights in her hair and a nubby white jacket.

Ivy squared her shoulders. "We've been talking to Jim Boz in planning, and he asked us to provide additional details on how we impacted the city during the recent Ridgetop Fire, as well as our plans for the future."

While Ivy paused, Bennett saw Boz nod to her. So Boz was in on this and hadn't told him. Bennett steepled his fingers and motioned for her to go on. Not that Boz needed to keep him informed of every detail. Bennett trusted his staff to manage their departments.

"My house, which was formerly known as Las Brisas here in Summer Beach, has been housing evacuees for the last week." As she spoke, Ivy made eye contact with every council member. "Several of the guests have suffered severe damage to their homes. Due to the high summer season, reservations at nearby hotels have been booked months in advance." She paused and turned to Imani, who handed her a sheaf of papers. "We've taken the liberty of surveying the accommodations in Summer Beach, as well as in the surrounding communities, and we've found that there are no long-term vacancies for these people. We've calculated the number of residents we're serving."

Bennett leaned in. "May we see those numbers?"

Ivy handed the papers to him. She wore a serious, earnest expression on her face. As Bennett took the documents from her, he saw Darla and a couple of her friends slip in the rear door and sit down. This isn't going to be easy, he realized.

Bennett flipped through the document, nodded, and passed it to the next council member. "You've been quite thorough."

A brief smile touched her lips. "I'm concerned that people who have businesses here in Summer Beach would suffer, and we'd lose some of what makes this community unique." She waved her hand toward Imani.

"Imani has a popular flower stand, Blossoms, in the village," Ivy said. "And Celia is a volunteer with the school district and runs an important musical program there. Gilda writes for magazines—frequently about Summer Beach. We can't turn these people away from their community, particularly when they've suffered the worst and lost everything they had in the fire."

Bennett watched his colleagues nodding as Ivy spoke. She made some excellent points.

"And are these people paying for their lodging?" Bennett asked. He had to put this into the record. "In full disclosure, I've been staying there since the fire, and I'm remitting payment through iBnB, an online vacation rental service."

"As a service to the community, we comped everyone for the first two nights, yourself included," Ivy said. "We have other community service plans, too. My sister Shelly is starting a horticulture club and will be giving weekly garden walks for residents and tourists. I'm planning art classes and an annual art exhibit to bring artists and art lovers to Summer Beach, thereby creating a positive economic impact. And we have large rooms—a ballroom and dining rooms and spacious verandas and a terraced pool area where we can host weddings and parties. This will also employ local residents, such as caterers and students, and bring more money to circulate in the community. On the next page, you'll find a complete impact analysis."

As Bennett and the council members reviewed Ivy's reports, one older council member spoke up. "So what is it that you propose, Ms. Marin?"

"I'd like to have my property zoning changed to allow it to be used as an inn, which will benefit the community," Ivy said. "The property already has an important historic designation. Julia Morgan, the first licensed female architect in the state of California, designed it. She also designed the Hearst castle, and architecture students still visit to study her style and techniques. In fact, we found the original house plans, and the university made copies for students to study."

Narrowing his eyes, the older council member tapped the table. "Your husband tried to get an aggressive rezoning, too. Cost our community a lot of money. One has to wonder if you have the same goal, but a different strategy."

The color drained from Ivy's face, but she

stood firm. After a brief word with Imani, she went on. "Some of you might find it hard to believe, but I knew nothing of this property until my husband's death. My goal is to maintain and improve the property in keeping with its historical designation. To make economic sense and provide long-term service to the community, I need the proper zoning. But this is the only zoning change I will ask for."

Bennett thought her response was good, but she hadn't convinced the council member who'd asked the question. He'd been dead set against Jeremy's plan, and he also lived in the neighborhood just a few houses from Darla. Ivy wouldn't get his vote.

A female council member leaned forward. "You've submitted your request for a rezoning?"

Boz nodded. "She has, and we've had it under review."

The council member jotted a note. "What's your opinion?"

Bennett couldn't read this council member's face. She was known for her keep-Summer-Beach exclusive campaign, so it was a toss-up as to which way she would vote.

"We're favorable toward it," Boz said. "My team and I have been monitoring this situation. Because we have a housing shortage for our evacuees—and this house is an asset that the community can utilize—we recommend the zoning change."

In the back of the room, Darla shot up her hand.

"Thank you, Mr. Boz, and Ms. Marin," Bennett said, preparing himself for Darla's arguments. "We'll open the floor to comments from others now."

Darla strode to the podium, her dark blue hair shimmering under the overhead lights. The rhinestones on her visor also captured the light and shot it back out like tiny, multicolored lasers.

Darla grasped the edges of the podium. "I think the council should consider the damage to the neighborhood that an inn will have."

A council member leaned in. "Such as?"

"The increased traffic and noise."

"What kind of noise?" the council member asked. "Anything after 10:00 pm?"

Bennett glanced at his colleague, who was an old friend of Darla's. Bennett could imagine how he'd vote. In fact, Ivy had probably lost his vote before she'd even arrived.

Darla thought for a moment. "One night, one of the guests had a screeching cat. Kept me up half the night."

"I can just imagine how Ms. Marin's guests felt," a council member said.

A chuckle rippled among the council members.

"Well, they've taken some of the street parking," Darla said. "Beach visitors have to park farther away."

A couple of the council members took notes. A new, younger council member asked Darla, "Besides the angry cat and limited parking, which we all struggle with, is there anything else?"

"It ought to remain a private home like all the rest in the neighborhood," Darla said, straining to get her point across. "Strangers running around the neighborhood put an old woman like me at risk."

The young council member merely raised an eyebrow.

Bennett saw Ivy give Darla a compassionate look, and it intrigued him. He'd thought the two of them were locked in disagreement. Celia had told him about a heated encounter on the front lawn of Ivy's house between Darla, Ivy, and Shelly. And Darla had been the instigator.

The young council member tapped her fingers. "In the summer, a lot of people visit our public beach, which is next to the Las Brisas home."

"But they're not traipsing across my property," Darla said, sputtering.

Another council member asked, "Anything else, ma'am?"

"I should think that's enough," Darla said before returning to her seat.

Bennett called for a vote for emergency rezoning, hoping that Ivy would be granted her petition.

Within moments, the rezoning request was approved.

Bennett picked up his gavel. "If there's no other business, then this meeting is adjourned."

"Thank you all so much." A broad smile lit Ivy's face, and she turned to hug Imani, and then Boz. "You have no idea how much this means to me."

Imani laughed. "Oh, I think we do. I'll see you later, I've got to get back to Blossoms."

Bennett longed to take Ivy in his arms and congratulate her on the approval, but he had to maintain his professional demeanor and distance. Instead, Nan congratulated Ivy by throwing her arms around her.

"I'm so happy for you," Nan said. "I've been on your side ever since you arrived in Summer Beach. You were nothing like your husband, God rest his soul, of course."

"Walk you to your car?" Bennett said after Ivy gathered her papers.

She nodded. "Thanks for your vote."

"I could have abstained—and some may argue that I should have—but this was the best choice for the community." If Ivy were ever going to have a real shot at making something of the old house, she had to have this zoning change to offer the services she needed to attract guests. And an inn was far preferable than having to wait for a property tax sale. Realistically, after what the community had spent to defeat her husband's plan, it could ill afford the cost of purchasing the house, even out of a tax sale. No, this was the best path, and that's why he had voted for it. His vote had nothing to do with what he felt for Ivy.

And he was feeling plenty for this woman who stood beside him.

Ivy glanced at the large clock that hung at the back of the room. "Oh, I didn't realize how late it was. I'm supposed to meet Jamir at the hardware store."

"Then I probably can't talk you into lunch, either?" He smiled, wishing he could take off, too.

"Jamir is starting the cleanup on the maid's quarters in the back. Going to need a lot of work."

"That gives you a few more units?"

"Four. Plus another one that was marked chauffeur's quarters on top of the garages. I hope to have them ready soon."

"I'm sure you will." His gaze fell to her lips, and he felt himself aching for her. "See you later then."

"Thanks again," she said.

"Thank the council members who voted for you—and Boz."

"Nan has been helpful, too. She's the one who

put together the occupancy list of other hotels for me. On her own time," Ivy hastened to add.

"I see." Now Nan's earlier odd behavior made sense. He guessed she really had surveyed all the hotels. If one could trust that, of course. He smiled to himself as Ivy hurried off.

Nan hurried toward him on her way back to her post.

"Nice work on the occupancy list," he said as she passed.

She turned with a guilty look on her face.

"Relax. Ivy said you did that on your personal time."

Nan looked relieved.

"And that's all correct, isn't it?"

"Absolutely."

"So you backed the plan for the Seabreeze Inn." Now he was having a little fun with her. "You wouldn't have any other motives, would you?" Nan was well known for her matchmaking efforts around town.

Nan's face turned the brightest shade of red he'd ever seen—it almost matched her bouncy curls.

"I can't imagine what you're talking about," Nan said, her eyes wide with practiced innocence. "I think the world of Ivy and Shelly, that's all."

"Just so long as we're on the same page." Letting his guard down for a moment, he added,

"And I want to thank you for not finding another place. I think I may have already found one."

Surprise washed across Nan's face. "Here in Summer Beach? Where?"

"Not too far." He grinned. No, indeed, not far at all. Maybe a little distance would be a good thing.

7

"We're legal!" Ivy shouted when she walked into the foyer of her house. She'd had to stop at Nailed It to pay for the materials Jamir needed for the back cottages, but she'd been dying to tell Shelly. Fine time for her phone to have run out of battery.

Shelly raced in from the library. "Woo-hoo! You did it!" She grabbed her, and they jumped up and down together like they had when they were kids. "I was waiting for your call. Dead battery again?"

Ivy nodded. "Like Imani said, it was a close vote," she said, still flushed with excitement over the change in zoning. "Thank goodness she helped me prepare some excellent talking points."

Poppy rounded the corner from the library,

waggling her hands overhead. "I'm so happy for you, Auntie."

"Your work paid off, too." Poppy had helped her prepare the community events they were offering by doing the layout and images. "The visuals you prepared are so professional that it swayed the council."

"Was you-know-who there?" Shelly asked.

"Darla spoke out against us, of course, but she didn't really have anything solid. Actually, I felt sorry for her. She talked about strangers putting her at risk. That made me wonder. Anyway, as Imani said, one of the council members was an old friend of hers. But three out of five was enough to pass."

Celia and Megan came in from the living room, where they'd been working on their laptops, and joined the celebration. Although they were guests, they had a stake in Seabreeze Inn's success, too. Megan was writing the documentary script, while Celia was bringing in music students from her school program to practice their performances in the music room. She'd even paid to have the piano tuned. Ivy loved hearing music fill the house.

"Time to celebrate," Shelly said, thrusting an arm in the air. "It's Sea Breeze time, and now it's official. We should have a sign made."

"I've got the website ready to go," Poppy said, twirling Shelly around.

All the women wound up in the kitchen, laughing and talking about future plans. Ivy watched Celia, who seemed happy to have company. Ivy felt terrible for her. On the day Tyler had stormed out, he'd taken the boat and set sail, not telling her where he was going. She'd been tracking his movements on social media, though he wouldn't take her calls. So Ivy had started including her in activities. Celia had even helped Shelly plant flowers.

Shelly mixed pink grapefruit and cranberry juice, while Ivy pulled out a tray of cheese and added crackers and grapes.

Celia glanced around. "I can help. How about I make a salad? I bought fresh vegetables from the Farmers Market."

"That sounds good," Ivy said. After passing the juice spritzers around, she asked Shelly to make one for Jamir. "He's working out back. I'll take it to him."

She left the women in the kitchen to check on Jamir in the rear bungalows. People always gravitated toward the kitchen. She thought about putting a large, rustic dining table there. With the zoning issue settled, she could begin to make more upgrades.

The help's quarters were located in a two-story structure behind the main house. Ivy scrutinized the exterior as she approached. Shelly had a plan to create a storybook setting around the units, and she was in the process of planting jasmine vines and climbing pink roses.

The four units shared a common area and kitchen. Ivy thought it would be ideal for families or groups traveling together.

Ivy tapped on the open door to a lower unit. "Hello?"

Jamir had headphones on, and he was swaying while he was removing the old wallpaper from the bathrooms. With his youth and energy—not to mention height—he could finish the job in a fraction of the time it would've taken her.

"Hey," she said, waving at him.

"Hang on." Jamir slipped off his headphones. "Thanks for getting supplies. Going much faster now."

"It's looking good." She offered the juice drink to him. "Here, have our house specialty."

He took the glass and drank. "Had it at the open house. It's terrific. A lot sure has happened since that night."

"It's been busy, that's for sure." Ivy liked Jamir. He always had a quick grin and seemed easy going. He and Poppy were often bantering. She was trying to scare him about how hard university courses were, but Jamir's confidence couldn't be cracked.

"I feel like I'm wasting your intelligence by asking you to do this."

"Nah, it's relaxing. Reminds me of what Mom

and I used to do in the old house when we first moved in."

"She'll rebuild soon."

"Oh, yeah. Nothing stands in Mom's way."

"I'll say."

They were laughing when Bennett came around the corner, and Ivy almost choked at the sight of him.

"Are you okay?" Bennett asked, rubbing her back.

"Yeah, I just—wait, what are you doing here? Shouldn't you be mayoring?"

"Even mayors have lunch." Bennett nodded toward Jamir. "I had a look upstairs, and you're right. That unit has a lot more light."

"You should look at the old chauffeur's unit," Jamir said. "Pretty spacious."

"I don't need much," Bennett said, chuckling. "Haven't got much anymore."

"Yeah, I hear you," Jamir said. "That's the upside, isn't it? That's what my mom said. Easy to get loaded down with stuff—and stuff often holds you back from making important decisions."

Ivy nodded. How well she knew that. "Why are you looking at these units back here? Isn't your room comfortable?"

"Sure, I just thought if I'm going to be here awhile until my house is repaired, then it might be better for me to be out here. You know, put a distance between—" he stopped short and glanced at Jamir.

"You can say it, man," Jamir said, shrugging. "I've seen the way you two avoid each other. That only means one thing."

"Jamir!" Ivy couldn't believe the kid had picked up on her feelings for Bennett. She felt the old familiar heat rise in her cheeks that gave her away.

Bennett just chuckled. "With your powers of observation, you'll make a good medical diagnostician someday. But as for Ivy, well, we're just friends, right?"

"That's right," Ivy said. Why did she feel like she was trying to talk Jamir out of the obvious?

Bennett put a hand on his hip. "Would it be okay if I moved into one of these units? I can help fix it up, too."

"That's fine," Ivy managed to say. Knowing that Bennett was sleeping in the room next to hers was comforting. That was the companionship part of marriage that she missed. Still, it also kept her awake some nights as she relived the kiss they'd shared and how it felt to be in his arms, knowing that he was still so close and—

"If you have time, of course," Bennett was saying.

"Sorry, what?" With a jolt, Ivy looked up at him.

"I asked if we can look at the units now," he

said grinning. "One was open, but the others are locked."

"Oh. Sure." Ivy fished in her jeans pocket for the master key she carried and then led him into the next unit. It was identical to the one Jamir was working in.

They walked into the next unit. "Same as the last one, only reversed," she said.

"Any of these would be fine."

"I want you to look at the chauffeur's apartment. I think it's more you."

"Save that for your deluxe guests. A full apartment on the beach? You can get a lot for that."

Ivy made a face and walked up the stairs to the unit over the garages. "Here you are." If he was going to extend his stay, he needed to be comfortable. She'd already decided to give Jamir the room next door to his mother that was opening up and get mini-refrigerators for the long-term guests. She'd offered them larger accommodations, but Imani had declined. Ivy wanted people to be comfortable. And they still had the lower level to tackle.

She swung open the door to a full apartment with a living area, kitchen, and bath. It even had a wide balcony with an ocean view.

"I love this balcony," she said, opening a set of the French doors to let fresh air in. Leaning over the railing, she could imagine setting up an easel here.

Bennett rested his forearms on the railing next to her. "Bet the sunsets are spectacular from this vantage point."

After a few moments, they went back inside. Their heels made hollow sounds against the smooth hardwood floor. A fireplace anchored one end of the spacious living room. In the kitchen, tiny black-and-white hexagonal tiles covered the kitchen counters and backsplash, while larger ones covered the floor. "This would look nice with pops of red," she said.

Bennett stepped into the bathroom and looked around. The wallpaper was ancient, too, but it had been preserved in remarkably good shape. "A little glue here and there, and it will be fine." He turned on the tap. The water gurgled and hiccupped as it struggled to flow, but it finally leveled out. "Water looks good."

"The estate kept it in good repair, or that's what my real estate agent said." Ivy cast a suspicious glance his way. "Didn't you look at these rear units?"

"Just once. I had a hard enough time getting anyone to look at the main house, remember? Honestly, I'd forgotten what these looked like."

She folded her arms. "Really. Are you playing with me?"

A smile danced on Bennett's lips. "What makes you say that?"

"I seem to recall that you sent photographs of the entire house to me."

"Which you didn't look at."

Ivy waved her hand. "But if I did, would I find photos of these quarters?"

"That was quite a while back. Not sure if I can remember."

"I don't think you forget much of anything."

Bennett stepped closer and tucked a strand of hair behind her ear. "I'll never forget what happened between us the night of the fire."

Ivy's heart hammered as she thought of it again, too. If she took just a step closer...hadn't he said it was up to her?

Instead, she stared at him for a long moment, weighing the consequences of her actions. While the ocean roared, a shorebird landed on the balcony to peek in at them. Still, she did nothing. She wasn't ready.

Finally, Bennett said, "You know what I'd really like?"

"I-I can't imagine."

He touched her hand, sending an electric shock along her nerves.

"When I was a teenager, I lived for two things. Surfing and working on cars. My father was always tinkering in the garage, and I learned everything I know about cars from him. Today's cars are complicated, run by computers. But that old red Chevy in the garage beneath us was one sweet ride. Imagine cruising along the coast in that, feeling the wind in your hair."

"Amelia and Gustav probably had a lot of fun in that."

"Bet I can get it running again."

"Really?"

"I need a hobby, and I find working on cars relaxing. Mind if I give it a try? It would give you another car to drive."

"Wow, I've never driven anything like that," Ivy said, imagining how much fun it would be to put the convertible top down and feel the ocean breeze on her shoulders. It was such a classic. "My father would love that. I think his father had one like this at one time."

"Imagine taking your parents for a spin."

Ivy folded her arms. "You'd do that for me? Why?" Jeremy had changed cars every year or so. Everything had to be new.

"For the fun of it. Have you forgotten about that?"

Ivy grew quiet. Bennett had struck a chord. Sure, she'd had a few laughs with Shelly the past month since they'd embarked on this crazy adventure, but it had been a long time since she'd done anything for the sheer fun of it. "I guess I have," she said softly.

Instantly, a look of remorse swept over Bennett's face. "I'm so sorry. It hasn't been long for you. I didn't mean to—"

Ivy pressed a finger against his lips. "It's okay. You're right." She rested her head against his chest, needing to feel the touch of another. She closed her eyes, mesmerized by the strong, steady thump of his heart.

Tentatively, Bennett brought his arms up and around her, encircling her with the most gentle embrace she'd ever felt. She heard a soft moan and realized it was hers.

Could she trust Bennett? If she were honest with herself, she missed the touch of another person, the embrace of a man she loved. For the entire time that she and Jeremy had been married, she'd trusted him. Even now, she didn't have definitive proof that he'd strayed, only gossip from people she hadn't known that long. And yet, Ivy couldn't ignore it. Jeremy had been seen in public showing affection for another woman. How far had it gone? She didn't know, but she knew now that her husband had been hiding a lot from her.

Like this house.

Late at night in bed, she still vacillated between sadness and anger when she thought of Jeremy. For her sanity, she had to get to the point where she could choose to remember only the good, though that didn't mean she would forget what he had done. Now that her eyes had been opened, she had to make sure she didn't regret a decision about Bennett.

She and Bennett stood together for a long

time, swaying slightly. Ivy enjoyed the feel of his body against hers. A cool, steady ocean breeze from the balcony cooled the heat of her skin against his.

After a while, Ivy pulled away. "I'd like for you to stay here," she said softly. "We're friends, and it would be good to have you here."

Bennett nodded. "Old friends. At the very least."

"I guess we are."

Bennett pointed toward a section of the beach on the other side of the point where the waves crashed in stronger sets than on the main village side. "Right over there—that's where I first saw you. All those years ago. I bet you don't even remember."

She smiled up at him. How many times had she thought of those summer nights? "We were gathered around a campfire, and you were playing the guitar.

He gazed at the spot. "Good times."

Briefly, Ivy wondered about what might have been if they'd started dating then. How different her life might have been.

"I hate to leave," Bennett said, running his hand along her cheek. "But I have to go back to the office."

"The city doesn't run itself," she said, taking his hands in hers. The warmth of his touch sent thrills through her. "I'm glad you're staying."

"Me, too," he replied. "I'll have to thank Nan. And pick up supplies for the old car."

He leaned forward and brushed her forehead with his lips. "See you later, and remember, it's okay to put fun back into your life. Think about what you'd like to do. I want to hear it later."

"I'll make a list," she said, laughing, although it wasn't a bad idea. How much of that list, she wondered, might include Bennett?

8

$\mathcal{S}$itting in the library, Ivy clutched the phone. "The wedding is the weekend after the Fourth of July holiday? Yes, I think we can manage that."

Imani had referred one of her floral customers to Shelly for wedding flower arrangements. The couple had planned to marry in the bride's parent's backyard, but their palatial home had suffered extensive damage in the Ridgetop Fire. Construction repairs would take far too long. With the wedding so close at hand, Caroline and Hal Jefferson were scrambling to find a new wedding venue for their daughter, Victoria.

As Ivy listened, Caroline reeled off her list of requirements. Ivy repeated them back as she made notes. "A ceremony outside with the ocean in view. By the pool? Oh, yes, it's a lovely area.

Followed by a formal dinner. And dancing in the ballroom? Of course, we can accommodate you. No problem at all." They spoke a little more, and Ivy suggested a time to meet.

After hanging up, Ivy raced to find Shelly to share the news. Her sister was outside tilling the soil near the rear guest quarters, preparing the ground for planting.

"I just booked our first event," Ivy said, nearly breathless with excitement.

Shelly put down her garden tools and brushed dirt from her hands. "You spoke with Caroline?"

"Yes, and it's all settled. The ceremony will be by the pool." Ivy told her about the plans while they strolled to the pool area. "Let's see what we need to do to prepare the pool area."

"What if it rains?"

"We can move the party indoors, or we can rent a pop-up to cover the area. Little chance, though. The summers here are fairly dry."

Ivy and Shelly paused. The dry, dusty pool stretched out before them, a relic of an earlier gilded era.

Designed by Julia Morgan, the pool was similar to the Neptune pool she had designed for newspaper magnate William Randolph Hearst for his castle in central California. It was smaller, though just as exquisite. A Greco-Roman, temple-like structure with tall colonnades anchored one end of the pool, while four carved Italian marble statues graced the perimeter. Marine blue and black tiles arranged in a Greco-Roman design rimmed the pool.

"We'll have to fill the pool for the wedding," Shelly said, standing outside next to the gaping hole. "Wonder if it will still hold water?"

"Hope so." Ivy circled the old pool. "Caroline Jefferson insisted that the ceremony be held outside. They have a pastel theme. Sherbet shades of soft pink, yellow, and coral."

Shelly tapped her chin in thought. "I could plant pink and white roses by the temple—that would be a pretty backdrop for their wedding photographs. White gardenias with glossy green leaves, too." Shelly peered at the pool. "So do we just turn on the hose and fill the pool?"

"There has to be more to it than that." Ivy sighed. "First, we have to clean it." A job this size would take all of them. "We should have a professional look at it. Fortunately, the family is paying the facility fee upfront. With the wedding so close, they were so anxious to lock in the venue. Others are booked up."

"So what if the pool leaks?" Shelly asked. "The ground just dried out from the soaking we gave the landscape and house the night of the fire. If that pool leaks, I can imagine us floating away like an ark. We'd wake up in the middle of the Pacific, halfway to Hawaii."

Ivy grinned at her sister's imagination. "More likely marooned on Catalina Island."

"Sounds like a new reality show." Shelly's eyes glistened at the thought.

"Sure, I'll tell Megan," Ivy said. "Seriously, maybe Mitch knows someone who could look at the pool. He was pretty handy at installing the door to the lower level, and everyone seems to pass through Java Beach." Shelly had been keeping her distance from Mitch, but Ivy still thought he was a good guy.

"Yeah, maybe." Shelly dragged her toe along the stone that surrounded the pool.

"Or I can check. But since you're managing the exterior grounds—"

"I know. I should call him."

Shelly looked resigned, and Ivy wondered if anything else had happened between them.

"Can you reach out to him today? We don't have any time to waste. No telling how long this might take." Ivy paused. "Everything okay between you two?"

"Not great." Shelly waved her hand. "I've been avoiding him."

Ivy understood why Shelly was cautious, yet her sister was naturally spontaneous. This caution grated against Shelly's nature, even though it was probably for the best. Ivy slung an arm around her shoulder. "Everyone makes mistakes in life. Give Mitch a chance."

When Shelly didn't reply, Ivy stared out at the waves rushing into the beach and racing out again. A couple of little girls holding hands jumped and screamed, running away from the waves and then chasing them back. They reminded her of herself and Shelly. Rushing in, yet afraid to get too close, then changing their minds and craving excitement when the danger was just out of reach.

Rocking on her heels, Ivy said, "Remember the first day we arrived in Summer Beach? We sat outside at Java Beach, drinking coffee, watching the waves, and digging our toes into the sand."

"That was nice," Shelly said, lifting a shoulder.

"I don't know about you, but I sure could use an iced vanilla latte right now."

At the thought of Ivy going with her, Shelly smiled. "I'd like that, too. Going together is more fun anyway."

9

"On three," Bennett said. "One, two, three —push."

With a concerted shove, Bennett, Mitch, and Flint pushed the vintage Chevrolet out of the garage until it rolled to a stop in the car court behind the main house. A cheer went up among them.

"Wow, looks even better in the sunlight," Mitch said to Bennett. "Can't believe you had the real estate listing all that time and never pulled this baby out to look at it."

"Didn't have time, and I didn't want to get too attached." Bennett ran his hand over the curved fenders. The car was dusty, but still a beauty. "Have to replace all the hoses, sparkplugs, and tires. Change the oil and liquids. These engines are fairly straightforward. With just a little work, she might fire right up. The estate manager used to take her out for an occasional spin just to keep it operating."

Bennett had met his friend Flint for coffee at Java Beach this Saturday morning, and when they began talking about the vintage car and what Bennett planned to do with it, Flint couldn't wait to see it.

"What a great project car," Flint said. "Awfully good of you to want to get this running for my sister. That Jeep Ivy and Shelly are sharing was passed through all the kids. Forrest and I had to share it, of course."

"If I were you, I'd have a hard time letting this baby go after doing all the work it's going to need." Mitch circled the cherry red car, which had a creamy white convertible top, a wide chrome grille and bumpers, and wide whitewall tires.

"I like to tinker with cars," Bennett said. "Takes me back to a simpler time with my Dad." He didn't want to share his real motivation for working on the car, not even with friends as good as Mitch and Flint—especially Flint. Maybe later, but not yet. He and Ivy still had a long runway to traverse.

"Forrest was always better at cars and building things than I was," Flint said. "While I was off on any boat I could find to watch the whales and dolphins, Forrest was always engineering something in the garage."

"Not me," Mitch said. "I was catching the waves every morning I could."

"And you still are." Bennett gave him a fist bump. "I'm right there with you—in spirit."

"Getting older is tough." Flint chuckled. "Course, I'm way behind you."

Bennett gave him a playful cuff on the head and knocked his Padres baseball cap off. "Look who's talking, old man. When was the last time you were up on a board?"

Laughing, Flint scooped up his cap. "Too long, my friend. But if you go, I'll go."

"You guys should join me in the morning," Mitch said. "When that sun rises, it's just you and the sea. Great way to clear your head, keep your perspective, and form your intentions for the day." He gestured to the house next door. "After I've been surfing, not even Darla can rattle me."

Bennett gazed at his younger friend. That's exactly what he needed to sort out his complicated feelings. "You're on. Flint—are you in?"

"Hey, I'm in just to watch you," Flint said, knocking Bennett's cap off.

"Deal. Summer Beach at sunrise," Bennett said, scooping up his hat and pulling it back on over his messy hair.

Flint opened the car door and let out a whistle. "Get a load of this interior. Enormous steering wheel, round dials, and more chrome. They really knew how to style cars back then."

"A pretty sweet ride." Mitch said.

"Going to look even better soon." Bennett ran his hand over the cherry red dash and steering wheel. Even the door panels were painted red and covered with red padded leather. The red leather bench seats were in good condition, too. A little leather conditioner and they'd shine.

"Ivy is going to look great in this," Flint said.

"It's so retro," Mitch added, stepping back to look take it all in. "Really sporty for its time."

"I hope she likes it," Bennett said, perhaps a little too softly, but neither of his friends noticed.

Flint had gone around to the rear of the car. "Look at the size of this trunk. You could stash a body or two in there." He jiggled the trunk, but it was locked. "Ben, do you have a key for this?"

"Course I do." Bennett shoved a hand into his pockets. "Had a couple, actually."

Mitch chuckled. "If there's a body in there, it's probably petrified by now."

Flint ran his hands around the lower edge of the trunk, looking for a latch. "You never know what's in these old places. I mean, stolen master-pieces? Never saw that coming. What else did the woman stash around here?"

"Ivy found a couple of things," Bennett said, checking another pocket. "A letter and a journal, though the journal didn't have much in it. The lower level is where most everything was stored."

As they were talking, a flash of gauzy white

caught his eye, and he glanced up. Ivy was walking around the pool area. She wore a flowing white dress that rippled around her legs in the ocean breeze. Her hair was pulled back from her face and piled high on her head. Standing near the miniature temple at the end of the pool, she looked like a goddess. Like Venus come to Earth. He smiled to himself.

Flint leaned on the trunk of the car. "Found the keys yet?"

"Hang on, I'm looking for them." Bennett brought his attention back to his search. "Maybe I left them upstairs." He'd already moved into the little apartment over the garage that Ivy had shown him. It hadn't taken him but a few minutes to gather up his belongings. And Jamir had helped him move up furniture from the lower level that Ivy and Shelly wanted there.

"Maybe you left them over there by the pool," Mitch said, a grin tugging at a corner of his mouth. "Because that's where you're looking."

"I need to talk to Ivy, that's all. Would you go look in the kitchen, Mitch? There are several keys on a ring we can try. Be right back."

While Mitch climbed the stairs over the garage that led to Bennett's apartment, Bennett wove through the hedges that Shelly had cleaned and clipped down to size.

"Good morning," Bennett called out.

Ivy turned, and as she did, the sun hit her just

right, illuminating the golden streaks in her honey brown hair. Her emerald eyes blazed in the sunshine. She raised her hand in a wave.

"Checking out the pool?" As soon as the words left his mouth, she smiled. And he winced. "That's obvious, I guess."

"I need to call someone to inspect the pool before we fill it. We were going to ask Mitch for a recommendation, but we missed him at Java Beach yesterday. Or maybe you know of someone." She nodded toward the car. "I see you've brought out the old Chevy. What an amazing find."

"Mitch is upstairs. He'll be right back. I think he knows someone." Bennett paused for a moment. For all his professional self-control, the sight of her this morning nearly took his breath away. "Would you like to sit in it? Mitch is just getting the keys for the trunk."

"Sure, I'd love to see it." She grasped a pinch of her long dress between her thumb and forefinger and lifted it as she climbed a short set of stairs to the temple. "But I want to show you something first." She put a finger to her lips and gestured for him to follow her.

Bennett walked behind her, admiring her grace as she climbed the stairs on silent feet.

"Look, there." Ivy motioned up toward a bird's nest that had been built in the temple's stone rafters. "A mother found the perfect place for her babies. Listen, they're calling for her."

Bennett craned his neck to see the tiny chicks, which were poking their heads from the nest in search of their mother and peeping for more food.

As cute as the baby chicks were, he let his gaze slide back toward Ivy, who was transfixed by the scene above them. The curve of her cheek, the arch of her brow, the fullness of her lips. He ached to take her in his arms again. The other day when they were looking at the chauffeur's apartment, she had filled him with fresh longing. She seemed to have no idea the effect she had on him, and that's the way he wanted to keep it for now. He understood her situation. Still, he was a normal man with normal desires that she'd awakened in him.

"We'd better go," she whispered, backing away from the chicks.

He held out his hand for her to take, and she rested her hand in his for a moment, as if it were the most natural thing to do. As if they'd done that a thousand times. Ivy was at once thrillingly new to him, and as familiar as the beach girl he'd carried in his heart for years.

"Have time to look at the car?" he asked when she let go of his hand.

"A few minutes. I'm so excited to see it."

They strolled back to the car court, where

Mitch and Flint were waiting. Flint opened his arms as Ivy grew closer.

"Hey, sis, how're you doing?" Flint gave Ivy a hug.

"Guess you heard we got approved for the new zoning," Ivy said. "Thankfully, I got this guy's vote."

"Mom called to tell me," Flint said. "I hear you've had a full house."

"One room in the main house has opened up," she said, inclining her head toward Bennett. "We're working on the old maid's quarters. And we booked a wedding, so we have to spruce up the pool area. We'll need it for the summer crowd anyway." She asked Mitch if he knew of any local pool repair services.

"Ask Jen or George at Nailed It," Mitch said.

Ivy stepped back to admire the vintage car. Though it had a layer of dust on it, she seemed to appreciate the beauty beneath the grime. "It's gorgeous."

"Can you imagine driving down the 101 Highway in this?" Bennett was looking forward to taking out the car with her once he got it running. This was his gift to her, and he hoped she'd be excited about it.

"I'd love that," she said, running her hand along the red leather seats. "Keep track of what you spend on it because I'd like to reimburse you. Can you put the top down?"

"You bet," Bennett said. No way would he ask her for money for the repairs, but they could argue about that later. "Careful not to get your dress dirty. Flint, Mitch, can you guys give me a hand with this?"

They unlatched the top and eased it back with care.

"Wow," Ivy said. "It's gorgeous."

The cherry red interior, though dusty, still shone under the summer sun.

"It's pretty musty," Flint said.

"Easy to take care of that," Bennett said. He brushed off the driver's seat with his hand and turned to Ivy. "Would you like to get in?" Again he offered her his hand, and she rested her fingertips in his palm as she slid in.

Bennett caught his breath. She looked perfect seated there. Her shoulders shimmered under the sun's rays, and her white dress contrasted with the red interior. She glanced around.

"This is an amazing car," she said. "I absolutely love it." She ran her fingers across the dash and the chrome-accented instruments, and then she opened the glove box. "Look what's in here," she said, her eyes brightening. She pulled out a pair of dark vintage sunglasses and slipped them on. "Cat's eye, these were called."

"Great shades," Bennett said. The over-sized, dark-tinted lens glasses were straight out of the 1950s. Tiny rhinestones sparkled at the corners.

With the sunglasses on and framed by the beach, Ivy looked like a glamorous movie star in a vintage auto ad.

"You look amazing, sis," Flint said. "Like you were born for this."

She laughed, returned the sunglasses to the glove box, and slid out. "I love vintage cars, and I can't wait to drive it. We'll have to take it along the coast."

Bennett grinned. "We can park it and watch the sunsets."

"So let's get this trunk opened," Flint said. "Might be separate keys for the ignition and trunk." Mitch tossed the keys to him. Flint caught them and slid a key into the keyhole on the trunk. *Nothing.* As he sorted through the keys, he said, "I'm taking bets on if there's a body in here."

Ivy frowned. "That's awfully morbid. Amelia Erickson might have hidden a lot of things—though I prefer to think of her as sheltering masterpieces for art lovers. But a murderer, I'm sure she was not."

"Can't be completely sure about anyone," Mitch said, shifting a glance toward Bennett.

Bennett caught Mitch's meaning. He didn't need to say any more. Trusting the wrong people had changed the course of Mitch's life, very nearly derailing it forever. No, if you were someone like Mitch, he supposed you might not be surprised about much anymore.

"My bet's on empty," Mitch said.

"Definitely a body," Bennett said, teasing Ivy with a wink.

She smiled back, picking up on the game. "I'm going with artwork. How about you, Flint?"

"Vintage jumper cables." Flint tried a different key and turned it. *Click.* He lifted the trunk lid.

Leaning closer, the four of them peered inside. Sunlight flashed against the chrome on the trunk, momentarily blinding Bennett's view. He blinked.

Inside the cavernous trunk, a pair of dead eyes stared back at him. As Ivy cried out, he leapt forward.

10

"*S*he's a little creepy," IVY said, letting out a breath at the sight of a large, vintage doll in the trunk of the car. Her heart pounded, but then, she'd always been a sucker for ghost stories and scary things. The moment she'd seen those lifeless eyes, she'd lost it. *How embarrassing.*

Ivy pressed a hand against her chest. Flint and Forrest had been relentless in their shenanigans when they were young, especially toward Shelly, who was younger and more gullible. Ivy had been her sister's protector, admonishing the twins. Even though the boys meant no harm—it was all in fun —their scary stories still kept Shelly up at night, and it was her or her older sister Honey's responsibility to put Shelly to bed when their parents were away.

Flint reached in and brought out the doll,

whose dark blue eyes stared out at a new world. "Wonder how long she's been in there?" He handed the old doll to Ivy.

Ivy smoothed the doll's hair back. "My guess from the fifties, based on the age of the car. But I think this doll is older than that." She inspected the sweet, porcelain-faced doll, which reminded her of one her mother had and her own daughters had played with when they visited from Boston over summer holidays—when they weren't on Nantucket.

The doll had a halo of golden hair and wore a white, lace-trimmed pinafore over a print cotton dress. At her ears were tiny golden earrings, and her feet were clad in lace-up booties. Ivy ran her finger over dainty, mother-of-pearl buttons. "Poor baby, in the dark all these years when you should have been loved by a little girl somewhere."

"Still looks new," Flint said. "Maybe it was a gift that Mrs. Erickson forgot about. When we were kids, Mom and Dad used to hide birthday and Christmas gifts in the trunks of their cars because we'd tear apart the house searching. Wasn't until my kids were born that Mom and Dad shared that secret."

"What else is in there?" Bennett reached into the trunk and lifted out a red-and-white plaid wool blanket. "They probably used this on cool evenings. Driving with the top down and the heater on, just like we do." He handed the blanket to Mitch. "Hold this, would you?"

Ivy watched as Bennett leaned into the trunk again, appreciating how his shoulder muscles moved beneath the thin T-shirt. He was in good shape. And then she recalled how he looked the morning after the fire without his shirt on. She blinked, enjoying the view.

A woman can look, Ivy told herself. She was a mature, modern woman with full agency—not like her grandmother's generation whose life choices were fewer.

Bennett stretched farther into the trunk. "Found your jumper cables, Flint. Looks like you're the winner, old man." He nudged his friend.

Mitch inspected the nubby wool blanket that was a perfect color match to the car. "This is like a time capsule."

"Just like the lower level was," Ivy said. "The whole house, really. You've seen our kitchen, but you should see the claw-foot tubs in all the baths. They were the most luxurious in their day."

"Still are." Bennett grinned. "A six-foot man can easily recline in them."

His words formed a pleasant picture in Ivy's mind. "What else is in there?"

Turning back to the trunk, Bennett brought out another red wool blanket. And under that was a small trunk. He opened it, revealing a cache of doll accessories and clothing.

Ivy shook her head. "Some little girl didn't get her gifts. I wonder what happened." So much of Amelia Erickson's life was a mystery that would probably never be fully pieced together. She stepped closer to Bennett to inspect the contents of the doll's traveling trunk. The leather top of the trunk bore a name: Anna.

"I wonder if that's the name of the doll or the little girl?" Ivy ran her fingers across the cursive letters. Picking up the doll, she said, "I think I'll call you Anna."

An array of dresses and accessories filled the trunk, which was wrapped with dark grey, floral-stamped leather. Wooden strips arched over the top of the trunk. Inside, in the upper tray, bonnets, shoes, brushes, muffs, and purses were carefully arranged. The doll even had a little tiara.

Beneath the tray were expertly made doll clothes. There were more dresses, along with a brocade coat, evening dress, cotton nightgown, fur tippet, and woven wool sweater. She ran her hands over the fine fabric. The evening dress was finished with what looked like seed pearls and a faux emerald necklace. She picked up a riding jacket and examined the workmanship. Under that was a small doll-sized violin.

"These aren't just any doll clothes," Ivy said. "They're made like real clothes, with piping and bound buttonholes. The inside seams are finished, and the dresses have deep hems. I've never seen anything like this. They should be in a museum or a collection to be fully appreciated." She peered into the vast car trunk again. "Anything else?"

"Not that I can see," Bennett said, running his hand over the carpeted mat. He stepped back to close the trunk.

"Wait," Ivy said. She lifted up the front edge of the mat. "Amelia hid things in the oddest places." But there was nothing.

"Let's lift it out for a better look," Flint said.

Bennett grasped the other side. Together they lifted it from the car and laid it on the ground.

Even the interior of the trunk was finished in polished cherry red paint. Here they could see the brilliance of the original paint.

"Once the car is washed, buffed, and waxed, it will look just like this," Bennett said. "It's been garaged and covered all these years, so the paint is in excellent condition."

The men were admiring the paint and discussing what kind of products they would use when Ivy spied the edge of something tucked in a crevice farther back. She'd have to climb in the trunk to reach it. "Bennett, can you reach that? Be careful, it's probably delicate."

"Could be a bill of sale," Flint said, his face lighting up with interest. "I'd love to see the old records on this. Wonder what she cost when she was new?"

"Probably what my utilities run for a month," Mitch remarked.

As Flint and Mitch chatted, Bennett carefully worked an envelope out of the crevice and passed it back to Ivy.

The spidery writing on the front was too small for her to read, and the envelope was sealed. "Is there anything else?" She couldn't wait to open it and read it.

Bennett checked a few other crevices. "Not that I can see." He straightened.

"I'll take this inside," Ivy said. "I want Shelly to see these things, too. And I'm going to need a magnifying glass or some reading glasses. Anyone hungry? Shelly's trying her hand at making bread."

"We ate at Mitch's, but I could go for a slice." Bennett closed the trunk.

"Count me in," Flint said. "We'll push this baby out of the way and put the top up."

Carrying the doll and the trunk, Ivy left the men outside and made her way back into the house.

"Look what we found in the trunk," Ivy called out to Shelly, who was wiping down the counters and humming a Taylor Swift song. The most enticing aroma was wafting from one of the old turquoise ovens. A tripod was set up on the center work area, and Shelly's phone was mounted to it. A remote lay beside it. Clearly, she'd been filming a new vlog.

Shelly turned around. With a swipe of flour across her face, Shelly looked as happy as Ivy had seen her in a while. "Wow, what's that?"

"A vintage doll and a complete wardrobe." Ivy smiled. "I think her name is Anna."

"Where did you find her?"

"In the old red Chevy in the garage." Ivy placed the doll's trunk on the table and propped up the doll beside it. "I've never seen a doll quite like this." Her face and hands were painted porcelain, but her limbs were made of soft, stuffed fabric.

"Mom had one sort of like this from her mother," Shelly said. "But it had been well loved by many girls in the family. This one looks almost new."

After Shelly wiped off her hands, she approached the treasures and looked at them. "Many people collect antique dolls. You might be able to match her to a vintage doll manufacturer. I'd love to film a short segment on this. My viewers might have information."

Ivy put her elbows on the table and rested her chin in her hands. Her intuition was crackling as if she were trying to find the right frequency to dial in the mystery. "Think there's anything unusual about this doll?"

"What do you mean?"

"One, this is Amelia Erickson's home, and she had a lot of unusual behavior, and two, why did she store her in the trunk?" She reached into her pocket. "And three, what's in this letter?"

"Where'd you find that?"

"In the trunk." Ivy pressed her fingers against her temple. "I forgot about that note upstairs, too. The one with the ring."

"You've had a lot on your mind." Shelly retrieved a sharp paring knife from a wooden block. "Let's open this one." Her eyes glittered with excitement.

Just then, the rear door opened, and Bennett, Mitch, and Flint trooped into the kitchen. They were still talking about their favorite car care products and debating the merits of one wax over another.

Shelly said hello to Bennett, while Flint gave her a brotherly bear hug.

Ivy noticed that Shelly was cordial to Mitch—nothing more—although Ivy could feel the restraint in her sister's usually bubbly personality. Shelly still liked Mitch, she decided.

"Looks like the flour attacked you." Mitch reached out and brushed flour from Shelly's cheek. "The bread smells delicious. Rosemary?"

"Good nose," Shelly said, her face brightening a little.

"I didn't know you liked to bake," Mitch said.

"I'm experimenting. I filmed a homemade bread segment for my vlog." She showed him a pair of loaves that were cooling on a rack.

"Those look good." Mitch nodded. "And this is a great kitchen for filming. Lots of natural light, high ceilings, and plenty of space to get the right camera angles. If you ever want to come over and watch me make the pastries, you're welcome to film it. My kitchen is smaller, though."

"I think my viewers would like that," Shelly replied, growing more excited. "Your kitchen has more authenticity. It's a real working kitchen."

"Though this one has a great retro vibe," Mitch said, moving closer as they spoke.

In Mitch's presence, Shelly had forgotten about exploring the new treasures. Ivy got up and poured water for Flint and Bennett, who had finally decided on the right wax product before moving on to products for leather interiors.

Shelly hooked her thumbs in her jeans. "Would you teach me how to make your cream cheese Danish?"

Mitch's eyes lit at the prospect. "I'll teach you how to make anything you want. Come over tomorrow morning. Bring your camera."

"I will. I'd like that." Shelly pulled her phone from the tripod. "This is all I need right here. But I do have lights if your kitchen is on the dark side. Ready to try the bread?"

As Shelly picked up a knife to cut the bread, Mitch and Flint and Bennett gathered around.

Ivy brought out Irish butter from Gertie and helped slather butter on thick slices of warm bread. The scent of rosemary was utterly tantalizing, and the flavor was delicious.

Mitch moaned with pleasure. "This is fabulous," he said, beaming at Shelly.

Good for her, Ivy thought as she saw how focused Shelly and Mitch were on each other.

After finishing her slice of bread, Ivy plucked a pair of reading glasses from the counter before she made her way back to the table.

Seated at the table, she turned over the envelope. It was made of thin paper—the kind used for airmail letters back then—and was addressed to a museum in Germany. The return address was from Mrs. Gustav Erickson. Ivy slipped on her reading glasses.

Picking up the paring knife, Ivy sliced open the envelope. The envelope and the paper were thin and crinkly, so she took care unfolding the letter inside.

As the words came into view, she was perplexed. The writing was in German. Yet she could make out a few words. *Vater*, for father, and *museum*. *Direktor*, which she assumed meant director. *Puppe*—puppy? She was guessing now. Maybe it meant *doll*. She couldn't make out much more.

Bennett noticed her sitting quietly and pondering the letter.

"What's it say?" he asked, finishing a slice of bread.

"I can't read most of it, but I think Amelia's father might have been a museum director. You know what that could mean," she said pointedly.

"The FBI again?"

"This could be helpful to them."

11

*E*arly the next morning before guests rose, Ivy pushed back the drapes in her bedroom to let in the morning sun. A shaft of sunlight illuminated the doll she'd propped on a chair next to her vanity. She shifted Anna out of the direct sunlight and positioned the trunk beside her. Stepping back, she admired the doll's quaint charm.

Recalling the modest, ruby-and-diamond ring and note she'd found under a floorboard in the closet, she sat at the vanity, slid open the drawer, and lifted the items out. On closer inspection, she saw a tiny inscription inside the ring. Again, she couldn't make out the words except for the word *liebe*. Love. A gift to a beloved woman, probably to a wife.

She unfolded the notepaper, where only one

line was scrawled in the familiar feathery script that Ivy assumed belonged to Amelia Erickson.

This belonged to my natural mother.

Ivy lowered the notes, thinking about what it meant. Undoubtedly, her birth mother. The phrase was simple enough, but its straightforward nature piqued her thoughts. Natural mother… birth mother. Why wouldn't she simply say *mother*? Was Amelia raised by another woman, an adoptive mother? And if so, how did Amelia come by this modest ring?

Ivy slipped the ring onto her pinky finger. It was sweet, and it matched the red-and-white checked jersey top she'd put on over her white jeans. She added a navy scarf and loafers, along with a soft denim jean jacket.

Next, she picked up the letter they'd found in the trunk. She snapped a photo and put a call through to Ari, one of the FBI agents who had come to the house to collect the paintings. Ari picked up on the first ring, and Ivy told him what she'd found.

"Send it right over," he said, giving her instructions to upload the photo to a secure internet portal. "I will look for it."

She thanked him and hung up. She'd thought Ari would be more excited, but he'd always been hard to read. Ari was the type, she imagined, that if he won the lottery, he'd calmly make an appointment with a financial advisor and then re-turn to work. And tell no one else.

As fascinating as this mystery was, Ivy had to focus on the day ahead. She had a full schedule brought on by the wedding preparations. Taking a piece of paper from a heart-shaped notepad her mother had given her, she jotted down her day's to-do list.

Before she went downstairs, she smoothed her hair and added a touch of lipstick. She'd learned her lesson the first morning after the fire when she'd run into Bennett, bedhead and all. She was actually running a proper inn now, and it wasn't only Bennett, she rationalized, that she had to look decent for.

This was Ivy's new life, and she had to dress the part. No more schlepping out of bed into jeans and a paint-spattered T-shirt to give art lessons to youngsters. She and Shelly were part of the fabric of Summer Beach now. Here, she real-ized, gossip rolled through the town like a tsunami, and Java Beach seemed to be the morning gossip headquarters.

Ivy walked softly through the hallway so as not to wake the guests. Fortunately, they'd found a runner carpet on the lower level that muffled foot-steps on the herringbone-patterned wooden floors, which made all the difference. She paused by Shelly's door and tapped on it, then poked her head inside. "Are you two up?"

"Come on in," Shelly said.

"Morning, Aunt Ivy," Poppy added.

The pair were in their yoga outfits, and Shelly was spotting Poppy in a yoga position. Poppy's legs were extended straight up, and she was balancing on her back and elbows.

"This looks like summer camp," Ivy said. "How's the trundle bed? Comfortable?"

"Totally," Poppy managed to say, though her voice sounded scrunched in that position. Ivy couldn't remember the last time she'd done that.

Shelly let go of Poppy's legs. "Now hold that. And breathe."

Poppy wavered a little, but held the position, breathing through it as instructed.

Turning to Ivy, Shelly said, "Want to go next?"

"I'll loosen up with beach walks first," Ivy said, brushing a strand of hair from her eyes. As she did, her ring caught Shelly's eye.

"That looks beautiful on you," Shelly said, taking Ivy's hand to look closer.

"The note said it belonged to Amelia's natural mother."

"Natural. Then she was adopted."

"I don't know. The letter didn't say anything else." She paused. "I don't know if I should be wearing it."

"Why not? You're entitled. It was here, and there are no other heirs."

"It feels very personal." Ivy glanced at Poppy,

who was holding the pose an awfully long time. "Someday I'll do that," she said to Shelly.

"I'm holding you to that," Shelly said, her eyes sparkling with excitement. "In fact, I'm going to post an exercise schedule—we should have an activity board—and alternate beach walks and yoga classes in the mornings. Everyone will be welcome to join us."

"I'm sure guests would like that," Ivy said. "That will get them up and out early with a healthy start to the day."

"We'll have the late sleepers, too," Shelly said. "Maybe a sunset walk and wine on the beach would appeal to them."

"Poppy could make up a schedule for us," Ivy said.

"Hey..." Poppy's breathing sounded labored. "Can I come down yet?"

"Oh, sure," Shelly said. "Didn't mean to forget you. Actually, we'll work up to longer holds."

Poppy flopped onto the mat. "I think I just did."

Ivy and Shelly grinned.

"Why don't you move your yoga class into the sunroom?" Ivy suggested. "You'll have an ocean view, too."

They pulled Poppy to her feet, and the three of them made their way downstairs. As they walked through a hallway, Ivy spied a bit of foam stuffing.

"That's odd," she said, stooping to pick it up.

"Here's another piece," Shelly said, scooping up another piece.

Poppy hurried along. "There's more. It's a trail."

Ivy looked at Shelly. "Are you thinking what I'm thinking?"

Shelly raced ahead into the main reception room. "Pixie!" She grabbed a pillow and tugged it from the Chihuahua's mouth. "Wrong!"

Ivy and Poppy rushed in to find Shelly and Pixie locked in a tussle over one of the new marine blue pillows Ivy had bought.

"Where's her puppy parent?" Ivy said, whirling around. "She shouldn't be left alone."

"That's Gilda." Poppy charged back upstairs. Moments later, they could hear the commotion upstairs, and Poppy reappeared with Gilda.

"Oh, my goodness," Gilda, said, frowning and running a hand through her short pink hair. "I've never seen Pixie do such a thing." She scooped the long-haired Chihuahua into her arms. "How did my little sweetums get out?"

Ivy dangled the mangled pillow from her fingers. "Sweetums has an inappropriate appetite." At least the dog hadn't attacked one of the antique pieces. Still, Pixie might get around to that unless this behavior was checked.

"She never did this at home," Gilda said, stroking Pixie's fur and kissing her on the nose.

"Didn't you just get her?" Ivy asked. "You don't really know what her bad habits are yet."

"Three weeks ago," Gilda said, nuzzling the little dog. "But I know dogs."

"Um, I'm no dog trainer," Shelly said, watching Gilda. "But isn't what you're doing like rewarding her for good behavior?"

"I guess you're right," Gilda said. "Bad dog," she cooed. "Are you hungry? Maybe she's hungry. I have some dog biscuits in my room."

Pixie licked Gilda's cheek.

"Or you could punish her, so she doesn't do this again," Shelly said.

"Oh, I'll pay for the pillow," Gilda said. "That's no problem."

Ivy could see they weren't getting anywhere with this.

Holding Pixie, Gilda scurried back upstairs.

Poppy folded her arms. "I'll get a bulletin board so we can post the activity schedule—and the pet rules." She knelt to pick up the remains of the pillow stuffing.

Ivy sniffed. "I smell coffee. Wonder who's up?"

"Bennett usually is," Shelly said.

"But he has his own little apartment now." Ivy made her way into the kitchen.

Sure enough, Bennett sat at the counter, sipping his coffee and perusing his email. "Morning," he said, glancing up. He was wearing board shorts, flip flops, and the old Grateful Dead T-shirt.

"Why aren't you in your own kitchen?" Ivy asked.

"Is there a rule about that?" he replied.

"No, I just thought…"

"Guess I like having company around," he said. "You three are always up to something. I don't want to miss anything." He spied the torn pillow. "What's that?"

"Pixie," Ivy said, tossing it into the trash. The slobbery mess was beyond repair.

"We're going to start beach walks and yoga in the morning," Shelly said. "You won't want to miss that."

"Then why don't you join me now?" Bennett asked, shoving himself off the stool. "I'm on my way out to meet Mitch and Flint. We're surfing this morning."

Shelly brightened. "This I've got to see."

"Let's go," Poppy said.

Before Ivy could beg off, Shelly quickly poured to-go cups of coffee for them, and they set out with Bennett. The last thing Ivy needed to see was Bennett without his shirt again, but then, this was the beach life. She'd just have to get used to seeing scantily clad men running around, including Bennett.

She smiled to herself.

Actually, that wasn't too bad. Her friends in Boston would surely be jealous.

Ivy rolled up the legs of her white jeans, shed her loafers, and slipped into the flip-flops she kept by the back door. "Ready."

Poppy and Shelly shoved their feet into theirs, too. "*Vamanos*," Shelly said, holding her cup high over her head like a torch to light the way.

The four of them crossed the veranda and strolled onto the sandy beach. They wound around to the other side of the point where the waves were larger.

This morning, the waves were rushing to the shore in steady sets. Ivy brushed her hair back in the cool breeze and breathed in the fresh scents of salt air and warm sand. The sun sparkled on the beach, catching tiny crystalline bits of fine sand. Ivy slipped off her flip flops and dug her toes in the sand. *What a morning.*

"I can hardly believe this is our life now," Ivy said. "What did we do to deserve this?"

"You gave birth and raised two girls, wiping their noses, reading bedtime stories, struggling through calculus homework." Shelly laughed. "You had laundry duty for the past twenty years. Me? I'm just along for the ride."

"Not so," Ivy replied, poking her sister in the ribs. "You helped keep my sanity."

"Ha, fooled you!" Shelly flung out her arms,

threw her head back, and whirled around, dancing on the sand.

Bennett laughed. "You three sure have livened up Summer Beach."

"Oh, you haven't seen anything yet." Shelly thrust up a hand, waving at Mitch, who lit up at the sight of her.

Mitch and Flint ambled toward them. Mitch had a surfboard under each arm. "This is a surprise."

"Yeah, I brought my crew," Bennett said, playfully shrugging. "Thanks for bringing me a board."

"Can't wait to see you guys get up on those." Ivy knew he'd lost his surfboard in the fire.

Flint chuckled. "Don't know about them, but I'll settle for clinging to mine for dear life."

With the sun behind and warm on her shoulders, Ivy took off her jacket and watched as the three men paddled out to sea to catch the waves. With Shelly and Poppy beside her, they watched them, laughing at Bennett's and Flint's attempts to stay on their surfboards.

This was the part of the beach lifestyle she'd missed—playing in the water, chilling on the beach. She had a full day ahead of her—Jen at Nailed it had given her the name of a pool restoration company. The owner was stopping by this afternoon to inspect the pool and give her a quote.

Fortunately, the man also had a pool service company, and he told her that he'd been retained to care for the pool by the estate manager until Jeremy had bought the house. So the equipment was probably in fairly good repair, not decades-old as she had thought. Still, a property this age could go downhill quickly in a couple of years of neglect.

"Whoa, look at Bennett go," Shelly shouted.

Years ago, this is where surfing had really taken off as a popular sport in southern California. Ivy walked closer to the edge of the water, peering out. Bennett was riding a good-sized wave and managing to stay in control. She was impressed. Surfing was coming back to him.

"And there's Uncle Flint," Poppy said, standing beside her. "Wow, they've still got it. Impressive." Her voice held a note of awe. "Mitch is the smoothest, though."

"He sure is," Shelly said, a smile dancing on her lips.

Ivy felt like she was back in high school, watching the guys on their boards. Only then, she would've paddled out and joined them. Shelly, too. All the kids in the Bay family had grown up at the beach, surfing, swimming, and boating.

"Bennett and Flint are getting the hang of this again," Ivy said, staring out. "Oh, look. Is that a whale on the horizon?" She pointed. "It's over there at two o'clock."

All three women were intently focused on the sea and didn't see the large wave gathering strength until it rolled onto the shore and crashed into them, soaking them up to the waist.

"Ow!" Ivy screamed at the icy blast, while Shelly howled with laughter, and Poppy sputtered from a direct hit in the face. The three women grabbed each other, struggling to stay upright as the waves rushed back, but the undertow was too strong, and it knocked them from their feet.

Gulping cold saltwater, Ivy grasped Poppy's shirt and caught Shelly's outstretched hand. "Hang on," Ivy cried out, but her words garbled in the surf.

Tumbling in the frothy rush of waves tugging them back to sea, Ivy finally struggled to her feet and helped Poppy and Shelly. "Get back," she cried, eyeing another set of waves that was bearing down on them.

"Run," Shelly yelled as she clambered back to the safety of the dry beach.

"Where's Poppy?" Ivy whirled around. She'd lost her grip on her niece.

"There she goes," Shelly pointed at the sea, where Poppy was bobbing in the water, her hands outstretched toward them.

Poppy had been swept out in the wave, and the next set was rolling in, and it was even more massive than the one that had taken them down.

Instantly alert to the danger, Ivy dove into the

surf and swam toward Poppy, who was sputtering in the strong, icy-cold waves that were overpowering her. She knew Poppy wasn't a strong swimmer, and she'd never forgive herself if anything happened to her.

She couldn't think about that.

The frigid water numbed her limbs, yet Ivy increased her pace, lengthening her stroke. She was desperate to reach her niece, yet the motion of the sea yanked her back.

Squelching the panic that seized her chest, Ivy swam on through the incessant waves.

"Poppy, hang on!"

12

*S*teeling herself against each icy blast, Ivy pulled hard against the powerful waves with each stroke, determined to reach Poppy, who was slipping beneath the surface. Although the water wasn't deep on this shore, a person could be swept away and drown in a few feet of water due to the powerful undertow.

Ivy stretched out her arms toward her niece. This time, her fingers grasped Poppy's stretchy yoga top. Ivy looped her hand through the back T-strap.

"Got you," Ivy cried out. "Just relax." She paddled back with Poppy, moving with the waves and using their force to catapult them back to the beach.

Just then, a pair of strong arms scooped Poppy

from the water. "I've got her," Bennett called. "Hang on to me, Ivy. We're almost there."

Ivy clutched his shirt, and together the three of them braced themselves against the raging onslaught until they reached the soft, dry sand. There they collapsed, panting and coughing.

Shelly raced over and fell to her knees beside them. "Everyone okay?"

Poppy nodded, and after a great, heaving cough, she dissolved into laughter. "Oh, my gosh! That was incredible!"

"Incredibly close to drowning," Ivy said. "We were too close and not paying attention."

"Acting like a bunch of tourists," Shelly added. "Have we been gone that long?"

"Evidently," Bennett said. "But thanks for getting me out of surfing."

"You looked pretty good out there," Ivy said, pushing back her tangled hair.

"I was taking a beating, too." Bennett grinned. "And Flint will be lying if he says he wasn't." He turned to Poppy. "Glad you're okay, Pops."

"Aunt Ivy had me," Poppy said, looking tired yet exhilarated. "But thanks for carting me in."

Shelly beamed at Ivy. "Ives was a lifeguard one summer at the neighborhood pool. She saved a few kids and a couple of older people, too. Did she ever tell you that?"

Poppy squeezed water from her hair. "You two

haven't been around long enough for me to hear all the old stories."

"Sorry I stole your thunder." Bennett nodded toward Flint and Mitch. "Looks like they're coming in."

The pair hopped off their boards and jogged toward them.

Flint knelt by Ivy and Poppy. "We saw that, but we were pretty far out. Are you two okay?"

Ivy nodded. "A wave caught us off guard. We were watching you."

"And a whale that was passing by," Shelly said. "That wave flattened us." Soaked to the skin, she flung herself back on to the sand and began swinging her arms and legs in the sand to make a sand angel.

Beside her, Poppy laughed. "Wow. That was exhilarating, though."

"This side of the point can be dangerous, so watch yourselves." Bennett grinned. "The City can't afford the bad press."

Ivy shot him a playfully perturbed look. "Is that all you care about?"

"I'm just glad you're all okay," Bennett said. "But if we need another lifeguard, I'll let them know you're qualified. You were pretty quick."

"We shouldn't have been washed out in the first place," Ivy said. She knew better than that, but she'd been away a long time. She clasped her knees and drew them in, shuddering from the icy water and the cool morning breeze.

Flint jogged to his car and brought back towels for all of them. "We should get you all inside into hot baths."

Ivy was drenched with sticky saltwater and covered in a fine coat of sand. She'd never come so close to losing anyone in the water, and it scared her, even though she'd reached Poppy in time. A few seconds under the surface and water in the lungs could spell disaster. She shuddered against the cold morning wind.

Bennett wrapped a towel around her. "Come on, let's get you inside." He put his arm around her and helped her to her feet. Ivy clutched the towel around her, and they started back to the house.

"S-sorry to break up the surfing party," she said through chattering teeth.

"I was almost done anyway," Bennett replied. "I caught a few good waves. That's enough for me."

Ivy turned back and saw Mitch pulled Shelly to her feet. He was taking good care of her. Flint unfurled a towel around Poppy, and they followed, too.

As they climbed the steps to the house, Shelly touched Ivy's hand. "Your ring," she cried. It's gone."

Ivy sighed. "I must have lost it in the surf."

Strangely, she felt a real sense of loss. In barely the space of an hour, Ivy had lost the beloved ring that Amelia had kept safe for so many years. She'd been irresponsible. If she'd know she was going in the water, she never would have worn it. But it couldn't be helped. She shrugged. "People are more important than things. Imagine if we'd lost Poppy."

"I can't even," Shelly said. "I'm so glad you caught her. You were always the stronger swimmer. That's a plus for our guests."

"I hope that's the last time." Ivy shivered again. Had she been just a few seconds too late, her dear Poppy might have suffered an irreversible fate. Ivy bit her lip. She'd rather give her own life than see her sister Honey suffer such a loss.

"Here we are," Bennett said, opening the door and whisking her inside the kitchen. "You're all minutes away from hot baths." He led Ivy up the rear servant's stairs, while Shelly and Poppy followed.

At her door, Ivy hesitated. She touched Bennett's chest with fingers that were still tingling from the frigid water and icy shock. "I can manage this."

Bennett gazed down at her. "Let me help you." He pushed the door open and led her through her bedroom and into the bathroom. "Sit here on the side of the tub, and I'll run warm water through your hair to get rid of the sand before I fill your bath."

Ivy followed his instructions, reveling in the warm water and the feel of his gentle touch on her scalp. When the sand was rinsed out, he wrapped a towel around her head, turban-style.

"Just another moment." He washed the sand down the drain, then ran a warm bath, adding a dollop of rose-scented bath oil she had on a small table next to the tub. She watched in awe. He really knew how to take care of a woman, and it touched her heart.

"It's ready for you," he said. He pulled her to her feet and kissed her forehead. "Relax. I'll rustle up some breakfast while you soak."

She smiled. "A woman could get used to this, you know." How easy it would be to fall under his spell.

Bennett paused by the door. "It's what you deserve," he said, before closing the door behind him.

Ivy peeled off her clothes and left them in a heap by the tub. She slid in, welcoming the warmth and the scented bubbles that rose around her.

Ivy leaned her head back and closed her eyes. Was Bennett too good to be true? Did he have a dark side that he was concealing? Having been married to one man most of her adult life, she was relatively inexperienced with dating—not that *that* was what they were doing.

She'd heard horror stories of women who had been taken advantage of and lost their life savings to unscrupulous men—some lovers, some money managers, such as Bernie Madoff, who'd stolen millions.

She opened her eyes. She *had* to be careful.

Ivy gazed at the high-ceilinged roof and the carved Romanesque statue of a lady draped in a cloth that stood near the bath. She'd positioned a dusty rose, one-armed recliner—a fainting couch she'd heard it called—at the end of the bath area, which she'd seen in the old photographs in Nan and Arthur's compiled history of the house.

This house was all she had in the world. This was the retirement that Jeremy had committed to putting aside for them while she cared for the girls and the house and his health and well-being.

And he'd never meant for her to have this. Or even know anything about it. How could he have been so heartless? And she'd thought they had a good marriage. Or maybe their relationship seemed that way because it was on autopilot.

Another thought struck her.

Somewhere out there, another woman was probably lamenting the fact that she hadn't received this house on Jeremy's death or an interest in whatever they had planned to build here.

Even though the bath was warm, she shivered at the thought.

She resolved that no matter how kind Bennett seemed to be, she had to protect herself. And any man who truly loved her would understand that.

Ivy swirled her hand among bubbles. She'd talk to her parents about contacting the attorney they'd used to set up their estate. She would place this house in a trust so that no matter what happened, she would not lose it.

That is, *if* she could manage to pay the outstanding property taxes by the end of the year.

The wedding fees would make a big dent in that bill, but it was only a beginning. She and Shelly needed to run the inn at full capacity all summer. Could they manage? Whatever was left over after the taxes and expenses were paid, along with payments to Poppy and Jamir, they'd decided to split.

Ensconced in unexpected luxury, Ivy closed her eyes again, determined to enjoy this moment. She was beginning to understand that life was a series of moments. And one moment could change the direction of life. She had to be careful with Bennett, or she'd find herself on a path she wasn't sure she was ready for.

After Ivy had bathed and dressed in a flowing, coral-colored sundress with a print scarf draped around her bare shoulders, she made her way downstairs.

The smell of bacon greeted her, along with the sight of Bennett and Mitch cooking brunch. Flint was preparing a salad. They'd clearly showered, too. In Bennett's apartment, she figured. Poppy and Shelly had beat her downstairs and were perched on stools at the tile counters.

"Good morning, again," Ivy said. "I feel like we're starting this day over."

"This time with a good breakfast," Bennett said. He took a tray of rosemary bread that Shelly had made from the oven and spread butter on the toasted slices. "Almost ready," he said to Mitch, placing a thick piece of toast on each plate. He topped the slices with crisp bacon.

Ivy hugged Poppy. "How are you feeling now?"

Poppy gave her a sheepish grin. "I'm so sorry I needed rescuing. I'll have to put myself back in swimming lessons."

Ivy smoothed her niece's hair and held her tightly. "That's an excellent idea. Once the pool is filled, I can help you here. It's never too late to improve your skills on anything."

Ivy turned back to the breakfast that Bennett and Mitch were preparing. "Looks like an assembly line."

"Only way to run a professional kitchen." Mitch slid poached eggs onto each slice. After whisking a creamy mixture, he drizzled it over each creation.

"Hollandaise?" Ivy asked.

"That's right." Mitch reached into a large stainless steel bowl and scooped a handful of salad onto each plate. "Along with romaine and baby spinach, strawberries, slivered almonds, and a mango dressing."

Ivy looked on in awe. "I didn't know we had all this in the kitchen."

"We didn't," Shelly said. "Bennett brought it from his kitchen."

And he cooks. Ivy shook her head. Was she crazy for hesitating, even for a second? She caught Shelly's eye and was sure that she was thinking the same thing.

"There we are," Mitch said, smiling at Shelly. "A simple brunch."

"Outside okay?" Shelly asked. "It's warmed up on the terrace."

Everyone agreed and picked up items to carry outside. Shelly brought plates while Poppy followed with a pitcher of virgin Sea Breezes and a stack of glasses.

Ivy brought out utensils and napkins, while the men followed with more plates. She unfurled an antique, cream-colored Battenburg lace tablecloth over the table that she had brought from the butler's pantry.

"This looks like something out of a magazine

spread," Ivy said, pleased at how beautifully the outdoor brunch was coming together. *This is my life now.* Again, she marveled at how during the darkest time of her life, her luck had turned, even though she still had much work to do. "We have to live in the moment and appreciate this."

Shelly's eyes flashed. "Hold that thought. She trotted back into the house. Moments later, she returned with a vase of flowers for the center of the table. "Megan's coming to photograph this. We can use it in our marketing."

Mitch touched Shelly's hand and smiled. "You always have the best ideas."

Ivy watched the two of them. Shelly and Mitch seemed like a good pairing, even though he was much younger. From the corner of her eye, though, she caught a glimpse of Bennett, who was also watching them. However, Ivy was startled to see that he looked less enthusiastic, and she wondered why. She would talk to Bennett, she decided. Maybe he knew more about Mitch than he was sharing.

While Poppy poured the drinks, Megan bounded out with her camera, which was a professional digital camera and video recorder. "Oh, this is lovely," she exclaimed as she took a few shots and a short video of the table before they sat down.

Gathering around the table, they sat on antique iron chairs for which Ivy and Shelly had bought new marine blue cushions. The outdoor furnishings had been stored in a shed off the garage before Shelly and Jamir had liberated the set and cleaned it. They'd seen more pieces that they planned to clean and arrange around the pool before the wedding.

Shelly raised her glass. "To our chefs. And to surviving the big waves. All of us!"

They all raised their glasses to toast, and Megan said, "Hold that," as she caught the action. She moved around the table to photograph and video various angles. "Got it. Great shots. Act like I'm not even here."

Flint laughed. "So you can catch us chewing?"

As they began eating, the conversation turned to the wedding preparations. The pool professional would stop by later in the afternoon.

"So who's getting married?" Flint asked.

"I'm dealing with Caroline Jefferson," Ivy said. "It's her daughter Victoria. And the groom's name is Orlando. She's been anxious to organize every detail. They'd planned the wedding at their home, but since the fire wreaked such havoc, the house won't be ready."

Flint's eyes widened. "Wait. *The* Caroline Jefferson?"

"That's her name," Ivy said. "Why?"

Flint shot a look at Bennett and Mitch. "You know, right?"

They nodded, and Bennett said, "You're planning on having security?"

"For a simple wedding?" Ivy shrugged. "I don't see why we should."

Flint widened his eyes. "You might want to reconsider that."

"If you think we'll need security, one of you had better fill me in," Ivy said, glaring at the men.

Bennett raised his eyebrows. "Caroline Jefferson is her married name. You probably know her as Carol Reston."

While Ivy tried to digest the fact that she'd been talking to one of the world's most legendary, reclusive singers that rivaled Celine Dion and Barbra Streisand in sheer vocal power and finesse, Shelly and Poppy turned to each other and high-fived.

"Woo-hoo!" Shelly cried. "Imagine the press we can get for this."

"No, no, no," Ivy said. "Caroline made a point of saying no media, but I thought she was talking about the attention we got from the paintings we found. Of course, I assured her there would be no media. 'No problem,' I said."

"You'll need security," Bennett said. "Make sure you're not responsible for that."

Though it was exciting, Ivy groaned. She'd even promised they would take care of security. She'd had no idea what that meant, or on what scale. No, this wasn't something they could handle, nor should they be expected to. "Then I'll need to change that in the contract."

"Have you sent it to her yet?" Shelly asked.

"Not yet," Ivy said. "Maybe Imani can help me draft the agreement."

All at once, Poppy jumped up with her phone in her hand. "Oh, my *gosh*, you *do* know who her daughter is marrying, right?" She whipped the phone around. "Rowan Zachary's son!"

"Why didn't anyone tell me?" Ivy said, pressing her fingers against her temples. Now she felt even more pressure to make sure everything was perfect. Undoubtedly, photographs would be widely disseminated.

"Carol Reston is one of our most famous residents," Bennett said.

"There are others?" Shelly asked.

"A few," Bennett said. "High-profile people like Summer Beach because it's a small town and no one bothers them most of the time. Sometimes tourists spot them in the summer—our celebs are fairly good natured about posing for pictures with fans—but most of the year they can walk around like everyone else."

Ivy stabbed a piece of romaine lettuce. "I feel like such an idiot for not knowing who she was."

"Caroline's a quiet person when she's in residence," Mitch said. "She comes into Java Beach and hangs out on the beach like everyone else, even though it's hard to miss her flaming red hair.

Some people take her for Bette Midler behind those enormous sunglasses."

Poppy's fingers were flying over her phone as she pulled up social media. "People are calling this the wedding of the year."

Flint speared a strawberry. "Mom and Dad might be going. They've done business with Caroline's husband for years, and I know they've had them to the house for dinner."

"Why am I the last to know about all of this?" Ivy asked.

Flint shrugged as he sliced into the eggs Benedict. "You weren't here, Ives. You and Shells missed a lot."

"Clearly," Shelly said.

Rowan Zachary. Ivy could hardly believe it. Her teen idol.

Shelly turned to her. "Weren't you crazy about Rowan Zachary when you were in high school?" Before Ivy could answer, Shelly snapped her finger. "I remember now. You had giant posters of him plastered onto the walls of your bedroom." She giggled, her eyes growing wide.

"That was a long time ago," Ivy said, dismissing her sister's comments. Aside from her crush on Bennett, she'd also had one on Rowan, but he'd been so far out of reach that it was just a fantasy.

And now her fantasy crush would be here at the Seabreeze Inn.

"What a wedding party," Megan said. "Try to get written permission to use some photography. That would be amazing for your portfolio."

"I respect people's privacy," Ivy said. "I won't ask, but—"

"Listen to this!" Poppy was still tapping away on her phone. "Rowan lives in L.A. And he's *single*," she announced in triumph as if she were Mrs. Bennet in *Pride and Prejudice* and anxious to marry off Ivy and Shelly.

"And *only* interested in seeing his son get married," Ivy added. She was a grown woman now and fully capable of keeping things in perspective. She glanced across at Bennett.

Rowan Zachary was only a fantasy, nothing more. She only hoped this wedding would be worth the extra trouble.

13

*A*s the morning sun cast a pinkish hue across Summer Beach, Bennett stretched his legs and loosened his muscles for his morning run. Three miles up the coastline, and three miles back. Then a shower, a power shake, and off to the office. His weekday morning routine rarely varied.

Breathing in the crisp morning air, he began trotting near the water's edge. As his muscles warmed up, he increased his speed, keeping pace with the music piped through his earbuds.

On his way back, he slowed as he approached Ivy and Shelly with a group of guests on a brisk walk. Imani, Poppy, and Megan strode with Ivy, while his neighbor Celia hung back with Gilda, who led Pixie on a leash. The dog carried an old beach toy in its mouth. An older couple he had yet to meet brought up the rear.

Celia looked distraught, and he wondered if she'd heard from Tyler. Bennett couldn't believe that guy had taken off on his boat like a spoiled brat, just when his wife needed him the most.

After what Bennett had been through with Jackie and her illness, he took a different view of marriage as a partnership now. He thought about the senseless squabbles he and Jackie had once had. In retrospect, he chalked those infrequent quarrels up to their immaturity and self-centered-ness. In the grand scheme of life, those disagree-ments had been minor irritations.

Now, looking back, these incidences were still in his head and part of the fabric of their history, even though he chose to focus on their best times. For the most part, they had been happily married and looking forward to creating a family together. If only he'd known enough to appreciate every moment. Not that he hadn't been grateful, but he'd give anything to have a second chance to re-place those less-than-ideal days—days when he was tired or irritable—with the opportunity to show his wife how much she'd meant to him. *Every day of his life.*

Had he known then how precious little time they would have together, he wouldn't have wasted it. Still, he was fortunate to have many moments he cherished and celebrated in remembrance.

Bennett wondered why it took a lifetime for many—if not most—people to figure out that life was meant to be celebrated.

He had Tyler's cell number. Observing Celia —her slumped shoulders, her withdrawn appearance—Bennett decided to check in with Tyler. If the man would take his call.

"Good morning," Ivy called out.

"Ladies," Bennett said, jogging past. "Morning, Celia. Gilda."

Celia gave him a wan smile, which quickly disappeared.

Bennett nodded at the older couple. Retired, perhaps. Maybe visiting their grandchildren in Summer Beach. With the children out of school for summer break, local families were taking off for vacations, while others were pouring into Summer Beach to soak up the sun. The horse races in the nearby village of Del Mar would begin in a couple of weeks, and the horse racing community would crowd into Summer Beach restaurants.

The morning fitness program Ivy and Shelly had organized looked like it was off to a good start. He smiled to himself as he slowed before bounding up the steps to his apartment. Maybe he'd try yoga tomorrow morning with Shelly. Breathing in, he turned to face the ocean, thankful for his life in Summer Beach. This was an exhilarating way to start the day.

When Bennett arrived at the office, Nan waved him down. She wore a dour expression.

"What's the problem, Nan?"

"We've been served," she replied. She handed him a sheaf of papers. "Darla is suing the city for infringing on her right to the peaceful enjoyment of her home."

"Is anyone bothering her?"

"She claims it's due to the rezoning of Ivy's home."

The first challenge of the day. Bennett put on his mayor's game face. "We'll deal with it." He took the documents. He'd sure like to sit down and talk to Darla, but now she'd gotten her attorney friend involved. "Would you contact the City Attorney on the phone for me, please?"

Bennett strode into his office. Maybe he could sort this out before it went farther. In his experience, he'd learned that some lawsuits were filed because people didn't feel like anyone was listening to them or addressing their concerns. He wondered what made Darla the way she was.

A large part of running a city like Summer Beach was understanding the people who lived there. Some just didn't like newcomers. They were there first and felt like the city belonged to them. But newcomers brought with them fresh perspectives and new ideas to share.

Bennett thought about Celia, who'd started an

enhanced music program in the Summer Beach school system. Many children were eagerly learning to read and play music.

Or Ivy and Shelly, who were sheltering some of the community's most beloved residents who'd suffered severe damage to their homes.

Bennett tended to a few phone calls and emails, had coffee with Boz, and then returned to his desk. Near noon, Nan buzzed him on the phone.

"Do you have time to speak to Ivy Bay, Mr. Mayor?"

"Send her right in." Bennett wondered what business she had that she couldn't discuss with him at the house.

Ivy opened the door. She was wearing a knee-length, swingy cobalt blue dress that showed off her shapely calves. At the sight of her, Bennett's mood instantly improved.

"Good morning," she said, smiling. "I stopped by to see if we need a permit for an art show."

"Come in." He rose to greet her, a little sur-prised at himself by how pleased he was to see her. "Sounds interesting. At the house?" he asked, leaning on the edge of his desk. She took a couple of steps closer but kept a professional distance. He understood; she *was* in the mayor's office.

"On the grounds." Ivy unfolded a paper she'd pulled from her purse. "Shelly and Poppy and I created an entire summer's worth of events. You're welcome to look at our tentative schedule. I'd appreciate it if you'd let us know if we need approvals for anything."

As he ran a finger down the list, Bennett nodded, impressed at their thoroughness. "I'll look into this for you. May I make a copy of this?"

She nodded, seemingly pleased at his interest. Or maybe she was imagining that.

"When do you plan on having the art show?" he asked.

"In August. That's the height of the season, and all the vacationers and horse racing community will be here. We're hoping that will drive attendance." Ivy paused. "And we're planning a big winetasting to kick it off."

"Residents and visitors will love that. I'm happy you came in." He hesitated, watching her body language. "It's almost noon," he began, intending to ask her out for lunch, but she suddenly seemed fidgety.

Looking flustered, Ivy said, "Is it noon already? Oh dear, I have to be someplace in a few minutes." She whirled around to leave. "Thanks for looking into that for me."

"Sure, that's what I'm here for." *What was she running from?*

"I'll see you later then," Ivy said awkwardly.

"May I walk you out?"

She lifted her eyebrows in a sweet-looking apology. "I really have to run."

Next time, he told himself. All he wanted was a little time alone with her, without Shelly or Poppy or Flint or Imani—or any of the other guests around them.

After Ivy left, Bennett looked at the list she'd made and then at the lawsuit that Darla had filed. If only he could bring these two women together. Much like Celia and Tyler. At times, he felt more like a counselor than a mayor, but then, he supposed that's what being the mayor of a small town was often about. Settling differences. Mending fences—sometimes literally. Above all, being of service. With Jackie gone, Summer Beach had become the family he missed out on having, aside from his sister Kendra and her husband Dave and their son Logan.

Next time. But then, he had already put a plan in motion.

Later that evening, after Bennett had returned from work and had dinner with the mayor of a neighboring town to discuss a big-box retailer store proposal that would negatively impact their resident shopkeepers, he made his way to the garage underneath his apartment. Flint and Jamir had helped him wash and wax the Chevrolet, and now the vintage car had a brilliant shine.

Bennett opened the garage door and admired the car. He'd cleaned and reconditioned the red leather interior and polished the chrome. The car looked beautiful, but he still had a lot of work to do on the engine. He'd also found an online store that specialized in vintage tires, and he had ordered new wide whitewall tires for the car.

He'd spoken to the prior estate manager, who had been overseeing the property for years, and learned that far from being neglected for decades, the car had actually been kept up just as the house had been. The property manager had started the car every month and had driven it around the neighborhood. Only since Jeremy had owned the property had the vehicle been neglected.

Bennett ran his hand across the red leather seat. Jeremy seemed like a man who neglected much in his life, from this house and car to his wife. Bennett would not make the same mistake.

He opened the hood, pulled a notepad from his pocket, and began making a list of things he would need for the car. This weekend he planned to do a lot of work, and he was anxious to get the car in top shape for Ivy.

Through the windows in the kitchen, he could see Ivy working on her laptop computer. He watched her pause and stretch her arms out in front of her and then overhead. She took her glasses off and laid them on the table.

Tucking his notepad into his jeans, he climbed

the stairs to his apartment to retrieve a bottle of wine, and then he started across the car court toward the kitchen and opened the door.

Bennett stepped inside and smiled at Ivy. "Hey, you look like you could use a break from whatever you're doing."

She sighed. "I've been working on the budget for the wedding. Although I've managed a household budget, this is the first time I've created a budget for a client event, and I hope I'm not leaving anything out."

Bennett glanced at the round clock on one of the antique stovetops. "It's 9 o'clock. Why don't you leave that for tomorrow?"

Ivy closed her laptop. "That's a good idea." She gestured toward the wine bottle he was holding. "What do you plan on doing with that?"

"Thought I'd find a spot on the beach, have a sip, and clear my mind. But I seem to have lost my wine glasses in the fire."

Ivy pushed back from the table. "We have plenty to choose from in the butler's pantry." She gestured for him to follow her. "How many do you need?"

"That depends."

"On what?"

"On if you want to join me."

Ivy let out a soft chuckle. "I don't know, it's been a rough day."

"Every day is what you make it." Bennett

paused, knowing he was venturing into sensitive territory. "Did you hear from Darla today?"

"How did you know?"

"Because the City was served with a lawsuit, too." Bennett gave her a sympathetic smile.

"I don't have the money to deal with a lawsuit. And we've been exceedingly cordial to her. Why does she hate us so much?"

Bennett held up the bottle of wine. "Subjects such as these are usually best discussed with a good libation."

"You're on," she said, reaching for two wine goblets and a corkscrew.

Bennett and Ivy walked across the veranda and onto the soft sand. The tide was out, and the moon cast a silvery glow on the waves. Bennett led her toward the water and slipped off his flip-flops. "Here, I'll take your shoes."

She handed him her flip-flops, and together they walked through the foamy surf until Bennett pointed to a large flat rock. "That's a good spot."

They eased themselves onto the rock.

As Bennett opened the bottle and poured two glasses, the steady roar of the ocean filled the silence between them. Watching the red wine swirl into the glasses, he said, "This is a good Cabernet Sauvignon from Napa Valley that a client gave me after we closed on their new home. I hadn't taken it out of the car yet."

"That was fortunate."

"Indeed, it was." Bennett held up his glass to the moonlight. "Exquisite goblet." The bowl was etched with vines and grapes, and the green stems had a wide foot with graduated coils.

"European, I'm sure," Ivy said. "I like them because they're unusual, and they don't tip over easily."

"Spoken like a true connoisseur. Actually, these are Römer glasses from the Rhein wine region." He cradled the glass in his hand and touched his glass to hers. "Here's to a good future ahead."

"Thanks," she said, touching his glass. "Have you been to Germany?"

"I have," he said, swirling his wine before sipping it.

Ivy did the same, gracefully tilting her hand. "Recently?"

"Quite some time ago. With my wife." He and Jackie had spent their honeymoon in Europe.

He and Ivy gazed out over the waves in companionable silence.

Bennett thought about the trip he and Jackie had taken. It had been a month of visiting all the places she'd read about and longed to see. A month of doing nothing but indulging in the sheer joy of life and living for the moment.

At the time, he'd thought the trip was wasteful

—they could've spent the money on home repairs, but in the end, he'd been glad they had gone. Especially now. And those old cabinets he'd wanted to replace? They were gone now, so what did it matter? He was happy he had the experience and the memories.

He glanced at Ivy, who was deep in thought beside him.

Finally, Ivy asked, "Why does Darla want to ruin my life? Will that really make hers so much better? And what does she really hope to gain?"

"That's a lot of questions."

"Start anywhere."

"Perhaps she wants to exert her dominance because she was here first," Bennett said thoughtfully. He had the same questions. "Maybe she feels left out."

"We invited her to the open house, and we helped protect her house from flying embers. Shelly even replanted her flower garden."

"A judge will take all of that under consideration. You've been a good neighbor to Darla."

"Even if the judge finds in my favor, I'm still out the cost of defense. And I don't have that kind of money." Ivy's eyes filled with tears of frustration. She quickly drew a hand across her face.

"Have Imani look at the documents. Maybe you can trade her for the cost of her room."

Ivy nodded and leaned into him, shivering

slightly. "We already have a working arrangement."

The breeze off the ocean was refreshing, prickling Bennett's skin, yet he enjoyed the warmth of her body beside him. He slid his arm up around her shoulders. "Is this okay?"

She closed her eyes and nodded. "It's been a long time."

"I understand." His heart was pounding as rapidly as hers was.

"I like having someone to talk to besides Shelly." Ivy was quiet for a moment before she added, "I'm concerned about Shelly, too. Or rather, Shelly is worried about Mitch. And that's the problem."

Bennett liked that Ivy was confiding in him, but this surprised him. "Why is that?"

As though she were thoughtfully choosing her words, Ivy sipped her wine. "Shelly cares a lot for Mitch."

"And I think he cares for her, too. What's the problem with that?"

As she turned toward him, moonlight illuminated her face, revealing worry lines on her brow. "You remember what the FBI agents told us."

Bennett did, but he didn't want to talk about it. Ivy looked lovely in the moon's soft glow, though he knew she'd had a stressful day and had a lot on her mind. He would try to figure out a way to appease Darla. Leaning in, Bennett ran his thumb along her cheek. "Things aren't always as they seem."

Ivy looked directly at Bennett. "Wouldn't you agree that Shelly deserves to know the truth about someone she's falling in love with?"

This conversation wasn't going as Bennett had hoped. "That's between Mitch and Shelly. If she's worried, she should talk to Mitch about his past." This is why Mitch never told anyone about the time he'd spent in prison. People would want to know details, and they'd have a hard time trusting him again.

"But you know about it, don't you? You know what Mitch is hiding."

"He's not hiding it; he's exercising discretion, which is his right." Bennett blew out an exasperated breath. "Besides, it's not my place to talk about it. If Mitch wants other people to know, he can tell them. I will not gossip about a friend, and I hope you don't either. The FBI shared that information in confidence."

"I'm only trying to protect my sister."

"Shelly can solve this entire issue by simply asking for the truth from Mitch."

"But will he tell her?"

Bennett threw up a hand. "Ivy, I don't know what you want from me. I've told you I won't get into this. All I wanted was for us to take a walk on the beach, unwind after the difficult day we both had, and simply enjoy each other's company. Was that too much to ask?" As soon as the words were out of his mouth, he regretted his sharp tone. He was tired, and the lawsuit was weighing on his mind, too. "I'm sorry," he added.

Ivy fell silent. After appearing to consider his words, Ivy said, "You're right. They're adults, and they should manage their own affairs. I'm just the protective older sister." She slid her hand over his and held it there.

"I appreciate that," he said. The warmth of Ivy's hand on his touched his heart. Bennett brought her hand to his lips and grazed the back of her hand with a kiss.

Ivy inched closer to him and lifted her face to his.

Just then, a buzzing noise vibrated between them.

Ivy quickly pulled away from him. "I have to take this, Bennett. It's Sunny. She's in Europe, and she might need something." She pulled out her phone and tapped it. "Hi, sweetie. Are you okay?"

A whiny voice floated from the phone. "Mom, I've been trying to reach you. You said you would call me back, and I really need to talk to you."

"I'm sorry. What's wrong?" As Ivy listened to her daughter, she made a walking motion with her fingers and pointed toward the house. She wagged her fingers in a little wave and mouthed *thank you*.

Bennett raised his glass to her and took hers.

Frustrated, yet trying to be understanding, he watched Ivy go.

Of course, she should talk to her daughter, but he couldn't help wondering if they were ever meant to be—or if their lives were destined to be a series of misses. And could he handle that?

14

"*H*ow much longer do you want to stay?" Ivy raked her teeth across her lower lip. She didn't want to turn down her daughter's request, but she was running low on money herself.

Sunny's voice crackled over the phone. "Until the end of summer. That's when all the best parties are. I *can't* miss that."

Parties. Sunny was suffering from her father's death as they all were, but she was in denial about their situation. Ivy needed to get through to her. She rubbed her hand across her forehead, calculating the number of weeks. "I can't afford to keep sending you money. It's time you came back to the States to find work or make plans to go back to school. We agreed on one month, but it's been—"

"I *can't* leave yet. Besides, you said you didn't

have the money for my last year of tuition," Sunny charged.

That was true, and it still hurt. Ivy exhaled a long breath and counted to herself. *One. Two. Three.* "That's right. And I don't have the money to support your European lifestyle. Misty said you can stay at her apartment and sleep on the couch. Or you can come here and help me run the inn. Stay here and finish school at one of the state colleges."

"*State* colleges? Mom, you *really* don't understand. Dad would not have wanted me to graduate from a state college. Misty didn't have to."

That was true then, but now, she had adjusted her outlook to reflect her new reality. Sunny needed to do the same. "I understand very well. And Misty graduated before your father died. But this is now, and it's time for you to make a decision on your future. You can apply for financial aid and take out loans to finish your education."

"*Financial aid?*" Sunny's voice hit an irritating high note.

Wincing, Ivy held the phone from her ear. *Four. Five. Six.* "That's how I went through school. A part-time job, student loans, scholarships. I'll help you when I can."

"You've really let me down, Mom, and I know Dad wouldn't have liked this." Sunny's tone was sharp and biting. "Why can't you help me now?"

"Because I'm working to make the money to

keep this inn running and pay the taxes before it's sold at auction," Ivy said, a little harsher than she'd intended. She did not appreciate Sunny using her father to shame her. *Seven. Eight. Nine.*

Ivy ran a hand through her hair. "I'm not going to keep arguing with you, Sunny. I love you, but those are the options. What I've said is final."

"Dad never asked me to work," Sunny spat out. "If I have to, I'll find work here, but I'm staying."

"You're twenty-two. You're an adult. If that's what you want, you can do that—"

Click.

Ivy glanced back at Bennett, who was still sitting alone on the flat rock, sipping wine and watching the waves. Though she regretted cutting the evening short, she wasn't very good company anymore.

She reached the kitchen door, flung it open, and tossed her phone onto the counter.

Shelly looked up from a notepad she was writing on. "Uh-oh. Your energy is so negative your aura is turning black. Who was on the phone?"

"Sunny. She's decided to stay in Europe and find a job."

Shelly's eyes widened. "Won't she need a work visa?"

"I don't think she's thought that far ahead. She's still blaming me for derailing her life, and she wants to make me pay for it. But I know that it's the pain she's feeling over her father's death that's making her lash out at me. She's looking for someone to blame, and I'm the easiest target. Plus, it's not easy to accept grown-up responsibilities when you've never had to." Ivy plopped down on the stool next to Shelly. "Remember when we were that age?"

"And that impetuous?" Shelly grinned. "Yeah, I do. And she'll figure it out, just like we did. Even though she is pretty spoiled."

"Will she? The world was different back then. I worry about her. I'm afraid that she trusts the wrong people."

Shelly arched an eyebrow. "So you mean…she takes after me?"

"I didn't mean for it to sound like that. And I think you're doing just fine." Ivy caught a glimpse of her sister's notepad. "What's that you're working on?"

"Some promotional ideas for the inn. I'm starting the Horticulture Chats next week. I'll let everyone know we have room for special events."

"I appreciate that."

"Why don't you go soak in the bath and relax?"

"Maybe I will," Ivy replied. Though she still felt bad about leaving Bennett, the idea was appealing. So was finishing the book that she'd started for the book club Imani had organized.

As she made her way through the hallway up-stairs, she noticed some tufts of cotton. Stooping, she picked up a piece. It looked...*old*. As it dawned on her what it might be, she cried, "No, no, no." She took off running toward her room.

Sure enough, her door stood ajar, just wide enough for a small dog to wriggle through. She must not have closed it well earlier; she'd forgotten the *click*. She had to pull the door closed until she heard that.

Flinging the door open, she spied the target of Pixie's evil transgression.

The exquisite vintage doll lay on the floor, its seams gaping like gashes in her soft skin. Anna's eyes stared in shock at the ceiling; her limbs lay akimbo.

"Pixie!" Ivy charged down the hall and rapped on Gilda's door. She fought to compose herself, but she was shaking inside.

Gilda opened the door. "Yes?" She held Pixie in her arms, and the little dog was trembling and peering at Ivy with round eyes, as though Pixie knew exactly why Ivy was upset.

As calmly as Ivy could, she asked, "Would you come with me, please? I believe Pixie may have been in my room."

"I don't know why you'd say that. She's been with me all night." Gilda followed her, still clutching Pixie. When they reached Ivy's room,

Gilda gasped. Then her face turned bright pink, nearly matching her hair.

"Why, I don't think Pixie could have possibly done that." However, as soon as the words left Gilda's mouth, Pixie leapt from her arms and attacked the doll, growling and shaking a leg in its mouth.

"Pixie, stop it right this minute," Gilda cried, lunging after the little dog. "You know better than that. How *could* you?"

"Can't you please keep a close eye on her?" Ivy loved dogs, but this one was trying her patience. Gilda liked to keep her door open because Pixie scratched on it, but that left Pixie free to roam.

"I'll buy another doll for you." Gilda stooped and held Pixie's face between her hands. "You've been a bad, bad girl." Gilda crushed Pixie to her chest and stood. Raising her eyebrows in an apology, she said, "She's ruined some of my shoes, too, but I just love her to death."

Pixie would *not* be ruining anyone else's shoes here. "I don't need another doll," Ivy said. "This is an antique, but it can probably be repaired."

"I'll call my seamstress tomorrow. You could take it there. Then everything will be okay again."

Gilda was missing the point. Ivy picked up the doll and inspected it. "I can stitch it up, but please watch Pixie while you're working on your computer. If she goes after another guest's belongings,

I can't protect you. Or her. I might have to ask you to leave, though I don't want to do that."

"I do want to stay," Gilda said, pleading. "I'll take her to obedience training. I promise. I could even write an article about that." Clutching Pixie, Gilda hurried back to her room.

Watching her guest leave, Ivy wrestled with conflicting feelings. She loved dogs, and she was glad that she could give Gilda a place to stay while her home was rebuilt.

But unless Gilda could watch her dog, Ivy could imagine the fight that would ensue if Pixie got into a guest's personal effects and destroyed something valuable. *Pillows, dolls, shoes.* Pixie wasn't particular, and that was a problem. Other guests had brought cherished items from their homes that they'd saved from the ashes. Ivy sighed. Such was the innkeeper's dilemma.

She turned the Murano glass knob on the door. A lock would solve the Pixie problem. It was odd that this was the only bedroom door that didn't have a lock. She added that to her *Absolutely-Must-Do* list.

Bending down, Ivy gathered the stuffing that Pixie had torn from the doll and placed it in a crystal bowl. She lifted Anna from the floor with care. Opening the cavity on the doll's back, she began to replace the missing tufts.

As she pushed in the stuffing, Anna's body seemed curiously misshapen. Working to shift the stuffing, she slid in her fingers and touched something hard. Metallic. Intricate.

She grasped the item and pulled it out. More stuffing fell around her feet.

Ivy held up a necklace encrusted with jewels. Not tiny, modest stones as in the ring she'd found —and then lost.

The faces of these gemstones were the sizes of small coins.

Behind her, footsteps sounded in the hallway. As the door opened, she whirled around.

"I brought you some lavender bath oil for— whoa, what the heck is *that*?" Shelly's eyes grew wide at the sight of the necklace.

"Pixie tore open the doll. I was stuffing it back together when I found this in its torso." She held the glittering necklace out to Shelly. "Do you think it's real?"

"Who would go to the trouble of hiding costume jewelry in a doll?" Shelly examined the piece. "Diamonds, emeralds, rubies. This is the real deal, Ives."

Ivy pressed the palm of her hand against her forehead. "Here we go again." Finding the artwork in the basement had been exhilarating, though the experience had taken time away from the inn. Even so, she'd been thrilled at the discovery and the chance to return stolen goods to their rightful owners.

"That letter you found in the car," Shelly said. "Maybe it has something to do with this."

"I emailed a copy to Ari."

"Think he'll tell you what it said?" When Ivy shook her head, Shelly added, "Let's run it through a translation program online. Bet we can come close."

"If we can make out the writing."

Shelly moved closer. "Anything else in there?"

Ivy felt around the inside, then turned the doll over and shook her. A large canary-colored ring bounced out onto the floor.

Shelly picked it up and whistled. "This alone could pay your back taxes."

"Is it a diamond?"

Shelly held it up to the light and inspected it. "Judging from the precision cut, excellent color, and fine setting, I'd say probably. Canary diamonds the size of rocks are popular in New York and the Hamptons, but this one blows them all away." Shelly slipped it onto her finger.

"Stunning." Ivy felt the doll's soft limbs. "I think there's something in the leg."

"We need to do major surgery on Anna. Scissors?"

Ivy gazed at the doll's looming eyes and sweet smile. "She's still so precious, and I don't want to ruin her. I have a seam ripper, and I'll go slowly on her." Ivy opened a drawer in her vanity and reached inside for her sewing kit. She'd pared down her sewing equipment from what she'd had before, but she'd saved her best tools. "Here it is."

Shelly spread a couple of large towels on the bed, and they both sat crossed legged, bending over the doll like surgeons. "Okay, Anna, this won't hurt much."

Using extreme care, Ivy slid the seam ripper along the old cotton thread, shredding it. The seams gave way, exposing discolored tufts of stuffing. Ivy reached inside and felt around. After a moment, she withdrew two pieces. "Matching bracelet and another ring."

They continued, gently opening the seams and removing jewelry so stunning they gasped at each new piece.

"These are the most amazing jewels I've ever seen," Ivy said. "This is custom work.

Shelly gazed down at the jewelry with eyes as bright as the gemstones. "Remember what Bennett said about things left on the property? These are part of the sale of the house, not like the masterpieces we found downstairs. We can keep these, like the car."

As Ivy surveyed the intricate pieces, an odd feeling came over her. These pieces were also rare works of art. Perhaps they'd been given to commemorate the most special times of a person's life. "If these were yours, wouldn't you miss them?"

"Well, yeah, but it's been so many years." Shelly clasped her arms around her legs and rocked back and forth. Finally, she stopped and clenched her fist toward the ceiling. "Why do we always have to find great stuff that belongs to other people?"

Ivy chuckled softly. "I don't think we could sell these anyway. Jewelry like this is bound to raise a lot of questions."

Shelly picked up a bracelet and held it to her wrist. Diamonds dazzled in the light, sparking rainbow prisms that flashed across Ivy's white duvet. "When Ezzra and I went to London, we went to see the Crown Jewels exhibit." Shelly's lips parted. "These are the kind of jewels that families pass down from one generation to the next."

"Do you think?" Ivy was almost afraid to say it. "We have to call Ari. We should look in Anna's traveling chest, too." She lifted it and brought it back to the bed.

Ivy and Shelly removed the articles of clothing, one at a time, feeling the seams.

Slipping her fingers into a little purse, Ivy said, "Bingo." She withdrew a tissue-wrapped package. Inside were several large, loose diamonds.

"And something in the lining of this coat," Shelly said.

When they reached the bottom of the trunk, Ivy measured the interior with her fingers and compared it to the exterior. "This seems shallow. I think there's a false bottom."

"I can slice the edges with a knife," Shelly said. "I have a paring knife in my room."

"Get it." Jumping up, Ivy headed for the bathroom, and then returned with her metal nail file. When Shelly returned, Ivy held out her file. "This might help dislodge the shelf."

Shelly sliced the interior paper from the trunk walls. Working carefully, they dislodged the wooden bottom and lifted it up.

Ivy caught her breath.

Nestled in the bottom of the trunk within folds of ivory linen yellowed with age was a sight that took their breath away.

Inside sparkled a tiara laced with diamonds and pearls the size of the top of Ivy's pinkie finger. Teardrop-shaped aquamarines rose above the base.

Stunned, the two sisters looked at each other.

"This is a very important piece," Ivy said. "Someone went to a lot of trouble to transport these items. Probably between countries, past customs agents, and authorities."

"But who, and why?"

Ivy shook her head. "And why was she abandoned in the trunk of an old car?"

Shelly held up the lacy tiara. "Did no one, in all those years, ever look in the trunk?"

"Maybe they didn't have any reason to, or weren't interested in a doll." Taking the precious tiara from Shelly, she placed it on the crown of her head and turned to look in the vanity. Instinctively, she knew that Amelia had been involved. "Amelia clearly cherished the finest art."

"And the finest jewelry." Shelly drew together her eyebrows. "These might be hot rocks, as in stolen. Like the paintings."

"Then I wonder," Ivy said, removing the tiara. "Where was Anna in her journey? Was she coming or going?"

And how did Amelia Erickson figure in this? Ivy still wanted to believe her innocence, but with each discovery, evidence was mounting against the wealthy collector. More than that, how many other secrets did this house have?

As Ivy and Shelly stared at the sparkling array of jewelry and gemstones laid out before them, a knock sounded on Ivy's door.

"Ivy," Bennett called out, "I brought you something I thought you might like."

The two sisters stared at each other.

"Might as well let him in on the secret," Ivy said, making her way toward the door. "He knew about the last one." She opened the door a few inches. Behind Bennett, she saw Imani and her friends chatting in the hallway. From the conversation, it sounded like they'd been out for dinner and drinks.

"Hey," Bennett said. "I know it's late, but after that phone call, I thought you might like the rest of your wine. I couldn't help but overhear some of your conversation."

Glancing behind him, Ivy said. "Come in. I need to show you something." When Bennett looked surprised, she quickly added, "Shelly's inside, too. We found something."

Behind Bennett, Ivy also saw the top of Gilda's pink hair bobbing down the hallway. As she neared, Ivy saw Gilda's attention was focused on Pixie.

"Hurry," Ivy said. She opened the door just enough for Bennett to squeeze through and yanked him inside. As she closed the door behind him—just in time to avoid Gilda and Pixie—she saw Imani grin and give her a thumbs up.

Not the news she wanted spread around town. Ivy shook her head and pressed a finger to her lips. Luckily, it was Imani, who could keep a confidence, and not another guest, like Gilda, who Ivy knew gossiped at Java Beach every chance she got. She liked Gilda—even Pixie—but she also valued her privacy. Ivy was beginning to realize privacy would be a rare commodity as an innkeeper with guests living down the hall.

"What's up?" Bennett stopped with the wine glass aloft. His eyes grew wide at the jewelry spread out on the bed. "Geez Louise, where did all this loot come from?"

15

*I*vy leaned against the door. "I'll definitely take the rest of that wine."

Bennett handed her the glass and furrowed his brow at the jewelry. "I think I should have brought the rest of the bottle. Is all that real?" He waved a hand toward the bed as Ivy nodded.

"We got it from Anna," Shelly said.

Bennett looked between the sisters. "Wait —who?"

"The doll," Ivy said. "That's the name on the trunk. We did surgery on her."

"I'm not following—oh, I see." Bennett approached the limp doll and picked it up. "All that was in here?"

Ivy nodded.

"But how did you know to look?"

"We didn't," Ivy said. "At least, not until Pixie

got into my room and went after the doll. She tore apart poor Anna, and when I was re-stuffing her, I felt something inside."

"This," Shelly said, handing the necklace to Bennett.

"So we kept looking." Ivy tapped the doll's trunk. "We found more here. But the false bottom held the most amazing piece. A tiara." Ivy watched as shock and wonderment registered on Bennett's face.

"After the paintings, I hardly know what to say," Bennett said. "Technically, this was on the property."

"But you think these might be stolen goods, too?" Ivy sighed. "These are incredible pieces—heirloom quality. The size of the diamonds, the pearls—all the stones. And the artistry." She touched the teardrop aquamarines in the tiara with reverence. "They are very important jewels. I'm planning to take photos and send them to Ari."

Bennett put his hands on his hips. "If there's no hit on a stolen goods list, then you're one lucky woman."

Ivy pushed her beach-blown hair from her face. "These must belong to an important owner. Because someone went to an awful lot of trouble to avoid detection in transport."

"Is it possible that our Amelia was taking her own jewelry back to Europe?" Shelly pulled her

phone from her pocket and began snapping photos. She paused and waved her hand. "I mean,
look at this house."

Ivy sank onto the edge of the bed and sipped
her wine in thought. "Wealthy people carry jewelry all the time. But not like this. Or do they?"

"If it were right after the war, it might have
been more dangerous," Bennett said, easing down
next to her. "A lot was going on. Instability,
bribery, shifting political factions."

Bennett was so close that Ivy could feel his
breath on her cheek. Shelly noticed his proximity
but carried on as if it were nothing unusual.
"That would have been several years later. Anna
was in the Chevy."

Bennett turned to Shelly with a questioning
expression.

"Don't look at me," Shelly said. "I've got nothing. For all we know, Amelia and Gustav dealt in
stolen goods, though Ivy doesn't want to believe
that. I'm a New Yorker. Nothing surprises me
after Bernie Madoff."

Bennett's fingers grazed hers. "You could start
with Clark. He can check records for you."

Shelly lowered her phone. "Who's Clark?"

"Chief Clarkson," Bennett said.

"I don't have time for this," Ivy said, wearily
closing her eyes. "Not with our first wedding to
plan, a pool to repair, and guests and attack dogs
to see to."

Bennett's hand smoothed over hers. "He'll come to you this time."

Ivy stared at his hand over hers. It was such a simple action, and yet it thrilled her to her core—more so than any of the sparkling jewels before her. She slid a quick glance at Shelly, who pretended not to notice.

Ivy pressed the wine glass to her lips, grateful for Bennett's thoughtfulness. Between the crazy rush of feeling she had for him, the insane stash of jewels, Sunny's temper tantrum, and a looming celebrity wedding and contract to negotiate, thoughts were ricocheting through her mind like ping-pong balls.

Her beloved old clock on the nightstand glowed the late hour. She no longer had the luxury of staying awake half the night with a whirring mind, grappling with ever-mounting problems. Perhaps a few more sips of wine would relax her tonight. She leaned toward Bennett, recalling how his arm had felt around her as they'd sat on the rock listening to the rhythmic waves of the ocean. A shoulder rub sure would relax her…

Where did that come from? Ivy snapped her thoughts back from her dreamy abyss. When she and Jeremy were dating, he used to rub her shoulders when she was stressed out over an exam, but he'd stopped doing that sometime after the children were born. And certainly, no one had touched her shoulders in the past year, except to offer a condolence embrace. Sadly, she had too much to do to let Bennett distract her.

"I'll call the police chief in the morning." Ivy reached for the edge of the towel that Shelly placed on the bed and rolled up the precious jewelry inside of it. No one would look inside rolled-up towels, and she had to make sure the jewelry was secure.

"What shall we do with the tiara?" Shelly asked.

"Put it back where we found it for now." Ivy lowered the diamond-encrusted tiara into its familiar nest of aged linen. "We can finish this tomorrow."

"It's late," Bennett said, rising from the bed. "If you want me to be here when Clark arrives—"

"Thanks, but I'm experienced now." Ivy smiled at his offer. "Before you go, I'll check the hallway. Our local guests might talk."

Bennett jerked a thumb toward the window. "I could sneak out that way."

"That I'd like to see," Shelly said.

Making a face, Ivy crossed to the door and eased it open. The hallway was empty. She motioned toward Bennett. "Hurry, it's clear."

Bennett slipped out, then turned and kissed Ivy on the cheek. "See you later, sweetheart," he said, affecting a smooth Cary Grant accent.

"Shh." Ivy swatted him on the arm, perturbed that he wasn't taking this seriously.

"People could hear you." She shut the door behind him.

Shelly chuckled. "Bennett really likes you," she said, her voice holding a note of awe.

"And why is that so unbelievable?"

"It's not. I was watching, and he was more interested in you than all the glittery goods on the bed." She passed a hand over the gemstones. "I have no doubt that Ezzra would have been transfixed by these. I could've ridden through the room on a horse, bare as Lady Godiva, and I assure you that he would not have noticed."

"Don't be ridiculous. There's no way we could get a horse in here."

Shelly's mouth opened in surprise, then she burst out laughing and flung herself onto the bed. Ivy flopped next to her and clasped her hand.

"Can you believe all this?" Shelly said, staring at the high ceiling. "It's almost as if the ghost of Amelia is prodding us to discover her secrets. I wonder what else she hid around here."

"I wish she'd wait until our summer is over," Ivy said. "We have so much work to do."

"If we kept just a few of the loose stones—hey, *ouch!*"

Ivy squeezed her sister's hand. "We're not going there. None of this belongs to us. Seriously."

"You're infuriatingly moral, you know that?"

"I like to sleep at night."

"Me, too. Preferably with a roof over my head."

How could she explain her thought process to Shelly? "We can make this inn work on our own. Trust me."

Shelly let out a long sigh. "I usually do, big sis."

Ivy jabbed her sister in the ribs. "Usually, but not always. And that's where you get in trouble."

"Hey," Shelly cried, dissolving into laughter and poking Ivy back. She attacked Ivy with tickles under the arms, then leapt from the bed and slammed the door behind her.

Grinning, Ivy shook her head in disbelief. Her life was sheer madness now.

Thank heavens for Shelly. What would she do without her?

Ivy drained the last sip of wine and placed the glass on the nightstand. She started to replace the trunk's faux bottom over the tiara, but its fiery brilliance caught her eye. Reaching in, she brought out the tiara and sank onto the bed. She plucked her reading glasses from the table and positioned them on her nose to bring the detailed work into focus.

Turning the platinum tiara in her hands, she inspected its artistry, appreciating the intricacies of the jeweler's work. A highly skilled artisan had clearly crafted this piece, and it would've taken a long time. Somewhere records of this piece probably existed.

Didn't jewelers keep logs of their finest work? Didn't they sketch out ideas as artists did before embarking on important works, particularly if pieces were commissioned by clients? Ivy thought she'd recalled seeing such drafts.

She traced her jawline in thought.

Hallmarks. Wasn't that how silversmiths identified pieces? By stamping marks on their work. Scrutinizing the edges, she found some faint, depressed figures marked on the platinum, but she couldn't make them out.

She padded to her vanity and rummaged in her sewing tray. She brought out a small magnifying glass that had a tiny hinge and stand on one side that made it easy to prop up to thread needles.

Squinting through the glass, she tried to make out the figures, but they were still too small. She lowered the magnifying glass. *What do jewelers use?*

A loupe, she recalled. A small magnifier that allowed jewelers to inspect the most detailed jewelry. Larger magnifiers enabled them to craft fine designs or set even the tiniest slivers of stones. Like her, they were artists.

Where could she get a loupe? That is, without taking in the astounding piece she held and broadcasting their discovery. Another idea popped into her mind. She snapped a photo of the hallmark and then blew it up on her phone.

It worked. If only she knew how to read it.

"For the wedding, we'll need strings of white lights —fairy lights—to illuminate the landscaping and trees around the pool," Ivy said, tapping her fingers on the table in the library.

Poppy nodded, taking notes. "Any other types of lighting?"

"Better coordinate with Shelly on that. She's in charge of landscape and exterior, and she has more event experience than I do. Have you seen her this morning?"

"Yoga class ran over, but I left early. I didn't stay for Savasana, the last asana." When Ivy looked blank, Poppy added, "The relaxing pose. Also called the corpse pose."

"That's my favorite," Ivy said. She lived for that flat-on-the-back pose at the end. Sometimes she even drifted to sleep.

Poppy smiled. "Well, Gilda can be chatty afterward."

"Speaking of Gilda, let's get some chew toys for Pixie," Ivy said. "Maybe the poor pup is just bored."

"Why?"

Ivy hadn't told Poppy about the jewels she and Shelly had just found, though she trusted her niece. "We've found something," she began, but before she could continue, the front door chimes rang.

Poppy hurried to answer the door. When she returned, her eyes sparkled with curiosity.

"Chief Clarkson is here for you," Poppy said, standing at the entry to the library.

"Come in. And close the door, Poppy. But you should stay." Ivy held her hand out to the chief. "I'm glad you could come so quickly." When he shook her hand, her fingers nearly disappeared in his beefy hand.

"Bennett mentioned you've uncovered another one of the Erickson's secret stashes," he said, his deep voice filling the library.

"This one is different." Ivy reached for her phone to share photos of the jewelry that she and Shelly had taken last night. "I'll email these to you."

The chief studied the photos. "These items are here?"

"In my room."

Poppy watched the exchange with wide eyes, straining to see the images on the phone.

The chief squinted at the hallmark photos. "Are they secure?"

"I think so." *Rolled up in towels.* Ivy bit her lip. She'd have to do better than that. She'd check with her bank about a safety deposit box.

"Since these items might be related to the

paintings, I'll pass this on to Ari at the FBI," Chief Clarkson said. "He might wish to visit again."

Ivy nodded. She hoped he would come before the wedding. Their client wanted everything to be perfect, and so did Ivy and Shelly. This was their first event, and Caroline Jefferson knew an awful lot of VIPs.

"Would you like to see the pieces?" Ivy asked.

"I'll need to for the report," the chief replied.

As they left the library, they ran into Gilda, who was meandering through the hallway. "Hi, Chief. What brings you here today? Anything wrong?"

Ivy knew they should have taken the rear staircase. Her heart sank. Within the hour, Gilda and the Java Beach crowd would be speculating on what the chief of police was doing at Seabreeze Inn. And that would give Darla more ammunition for her lawsuit.

"Just paying a friendly visit," he said.

"We like to make sure our guests are safe," Ivy said, fumbling for an answer. "A simple inspection."

Ivy pulled Poppy aside. "Not a word of this to anyone. And please find Shelly. Bring her to my room."

Poppy's curiosity was almost palpable. She hurried away.

"Ma'am," the chief said, as he walked past Gilda.

Ivy led him upstairs to her bedroom. In the hallway, they passed Imani, who exchanged greetings with the chief. Ivy watched the two of them chat with warmth and ease, and a thought struck her. Was Imani interested in Clark? Or vice versa? She'd ask Bennett.

"See you around, Clark," Imani said, as she started off to her flower stand to begin the morning. Her pink tie-dyed sundress swirled around her legs, and Ivy noticed that the chief did a small, nearly imperceptible double-take on Imani before turning back to her.

As Ivy watched, she wondered if there might have been a relationship there, or maybe a possibility of one in the future. But that thought was for another day. Today, she had a cache of jewels to attend to.

"This way," Ivy said, opening her door. Once inside, Ivy unrolled the towels. She was just starting to share the story when Poppy and Shelly slipped into the room. Shelly was still wearing her black yoga wear.

The chief was visibly impressed. "This is quite the collection. What makes you think these are part of the art collection?"

"I don't know," Ivy said. "But they could be."

Shelly brought out the doll trunk, and when Ivy lifted out the tiara, Poppy took her phone and began tapping away.

"That's quite a piece," Chief Clarkson said. "Real, do you suppose?"

"It has hallmarks on it," Ivy said, turning the piece. "I've photographed them. I imagine the metal is, but I don't know about the stones. They *look* real."

The chief nodded thoughtfully. "As with the paintings, unless these turn up on a stolen property report or list, there isn't much we can do. However, I would advise you to find another method of storage." He stood. "I'll make a record of this and forward details to the FBI."

"Wow," Poppy said, her eyes trained on her tiny phone screen. All heads swiveled toward her.

"What is it?" Shelly asked.

Poppy's eyebrows shot up. "Have any of you searched for stolen tiaras on the internet?"

Ivy and Shelly shook their heads.

"It could be from any number of places. Germany, Russia, France, Italy. It's probably of royal lineage, so it won't be that hard to track down." She passed her phone around.

"The era of some of these would fit with Amelia Erickson's lifespan—or before," Ivy said. "These items have historical value to entire nations, not only individuals."

Shelly groaned. "Then maybe there's a reward."

Ivy shot her sister a pointed look. "National art treasures should be preserved. Remember when you went to see the crown jewels in London?"

"You saw those?" Poppy asked. "Oh, look, a tiara was recently stolen in England." She gazed at the photo. "Not this one, though." She looked up. "It shouldn't be too hard to match this one with images on the internet of other pieces."

The chief grinned. "Young lady, you may have found your calling."

"She's a real sleuth," Shelly said, flinging her arm around her niece.

"I'll be sure to call you for every jewelry heist we have in Summer Beach."

"Do you have many?" Ivy asked, suddenly concerned.

"Not even one," the chief assured her. "This is Summer Beach. One year a surfboard disappeared, but the guy had forgotten where he'd left it after a few beers. Now, if there's nothing else, I've got to be on my way."

Shelly showed him out while Poppy scooted to Ivy's side, her focus still on her phone and the details she was finding.

Poppy tapped the screen. "It says here that a lot of crown jewels have disappeared during war or government overthrows. Looting was common. War trophies, it was often called." She lowered the screen. "What was Amelia doing with all of this?"

"That's still the question, isn't it," Ivy said. "The note in her journal I found in the closet indicated that she thought she'd kept a journal before. I wish I could find it."

Poppy was quiet for a moment. "That poor woman. To have lived such a life and not been able to remember it."

"Many people suffer from Alzheimer's, like our grandfather Alec did," Ivy said. "He died before you were born, and I was pretty little, but I remember how sad my grandmother seemed all the time." She paused, remembering the heartbreak her father had suffered, too. It was the only time she remembered seeing her father cry. "At least the scientific and medical communities have identified it and are searching for cures."

"I feel so bad for Amelia." Poppy gazed over the array of jewelry. "We could always auction this jewelry and donate the money to help find a cure for Alzheimer's in the Erickson's name.

"I love the way you think." Ivy hugged Poppy. "Even though these are stunning pieces, we don't need them. Wouldn't it be nice if we helped find a cure for that dreadful disease? I think Amelia would've liked that, too."

Poppy glanced shyly at the tiara. "Before we do that, would you mind if I…"

"Try it on?" Ivy smiled. "Do you remember that I gave you a play tiara set when you were little? Doesn't seem that long ago. Sunny and Misty picked it out for you. It was part of their favorite princess costume."

"I wore that forever. My mom still has it."

"Sit in front of the vanity."

Poppy did, and Ivy placed the tiara over Poppy's sleek blond hair. "Every inch the princess, with or without the title." Taking Poppy's phone, she snapped a few photos for her.

Shelly opened the door. "Gorgeous. A perfect fit, too."

Poppy grinned. "Want to try it on, Aunt Shelly?"

Shaking her head, Shelly said, "You wear it best."

"Ivy is thinking about auctioning everything for charity."

Shelly pressed a hand against her chest. "You what?"

"For Alzheimer's. It's not a bad idea."

"Have you lost your mind?"

"Shelly, this isn't ours," Ivy said. "Based on what Poppy found online, I'm fairly certain these pieces have historic value. We don't need any of this in Summer Beach."

"But this is like winning the lottery. You're going to turn that down?"

"It's the right thing to do," Ivy said. "Either there are rightful owners out there, or this can be used for a better cause that could possibly benefit millions of people. Remember Papa Alec?"

"Not much. I'm younger than you." Shelly

dragged a toe across the wooden floor. "What about us?"

Ivy waved her hand at the walls around them. "We're fortunate to have the income from this house, which is paid for. Jeremy worked for that, and you're my partner. Nothing will ever change that. I like knowing that I've earned my way."

Shelly seemed unconvinced. "What if Darla wins that lawsuit, and we have to close the inn?"

"Then we'll sell this place and find another business." Ivy saw the look of desperation in Shelly's eyes. "We've been underestimating ourselves for too long. As I look back, Jeremy did and said a lot of things that undermined my confidence, and I think Ezzra did the same to you."

Poppy looked from one aunt to the other. "I think you're both amazing. I always have, but especially now. I want to be like you two when I'm older."

Shelly laughed. "We're not *that* much older."

Just then, a commotion erupted in the hallway. Gilda's voice rang out. "Pixie, Pixie, where are you?"

The voice of an older man in a nearby room rang out. "She's tearing up a rug in our room. Get your little monster out of here."

"Disaster strikes again." Ivy shot a look at the clock. "And Caroline Jefferson will be here shortly for a tour of the pool and ballroom."

"I'm on it," Poppy said, removing the tiara

and placing it on the antique vanity. "I thought Pixie was in obedience training."

"Clearly, it takes a while," Ivy said, scooping up the jewelry.

"Maybe she needs a doggie psychologist instead." Shelly finished rolling up the jewelry in the soft towels. "Go. I'll put all this away."

Ivy raced to see how much damage Pixie had done. They had to gain control of Pixie and calm the other guest. Summer Beach was a small town, and they couldn't afford derogatory gossip, even about another guest's dog.

And Ivy needed a lock on her door right away. She'd visit Nailed It this afternoon. Jen would probably know a good locksmith, and Ivy needed to pick up more supplies for Jamir.

Ivy rushed toward the latest Pixie disaster. The chief was right. Rolled-up towels as a storage device weren't such a good idea.

16

"*P*lease come in, Mrs. Jefferson," Ivy said, trying to sound composed after hurriedly picking up after the latest Pixie disaster.

"Call me Carol, everyone does," the petite, red-haired woman said. She stepped inside, taking in every detail of the house. "What an amazing job you've done with this old place. I've always loved it."

Like many singers and actors who had larger-than-life personas, the legendary singer was much smaller than she seemed on screen. Yet she carried herself with regal self-assurance. She clearly took good care of herself, too. Her glowing skin was so remarkable that she appeared not much older than her daughter, who was getting married.

"You've been here before?" Ivy asked.

Carol strode into the reception area. "A few

charity events over the years. I've always loved these chandeliers."

Ivy made a mental note of that. She'd brought in a tidy sum from the sale of the chandelier in the foyer, though that one had been a rare collectible. "Is your daughter with you?"

"Victoria has a fitting in the city, so it's just me today."

"In Los Angeles?"

"Oh no, dear. New York. She selected the most incredible Claude Morelli dress—couture, of course—and personally designed by Claude for my Victoria."

Ivy smiled. She had created her own wedding dress from one she'd found in a vintage thrift shop in Boston. The fabric was beautiful, so she'd bought it and redesigned it—and received so many compliments. However, the wealthy lived a different reality, Ivy realized.

Ivy led her into the various rooms they could use, from the large dining room and parlor into the ballroom. "The dining room will seat fifty, so if you'd like to invite more to the reception, I'd suggest you move into the ballroom."

Carol tried to frown, although her forehead barely moved. "Did I say fifty? The number keeps growing. We're at about a hundred now, but I do expect that to grow by fifty more people or so. Rowan keeps sending extra names."

"We'll have to know the actual number so we

can plan the correct amount of tables, chairs, floral arrangements, and place settings." Ivy had to take control. She hadn't thought a guest list would be that difficult, but then, her wedding had been only family and a few close friends.

Carol managed to partially arch an eyebrow. "Single men are so disorganized when it comes to planning. Rowan's ex-wife used to do everything for him. Still, he's such an amazing talent that everyone forgives him. You know how it is."

Ivy didn't, but she quickly adjusted the plan. "The formal dining room will be too small. However, we can arrange tables in the ballroom, leaving a dance floor in the middle and putting the musicians at that end. We can spill out into the adjoining room if we have to."

"What a good idea," Carol said, her face lighting up. "We'll supply a raised dais for a solo artist in the center of the room." She winked. "I have a few songs to perform, but let's keep that a secret. It's a surprise for Victoria."

"Of course." Ivy led her through the butler's pantry into the kitchen, where Shelly and Poppy joined them. After introducing them, she said, "We have plenty of room for your catering team in the kitchen."

Shelly stepped forward. "Who is your caterer?"

"Alain George," Carol said. "He said he'd arrange a team of servers as well."

Ivy swallowed her surprise, though Shelly maintained her cool. Alain George was a famous television chef and had exclusive restaurants in New York, Los Angeles, and London that booked reservations months in advance—unless you were a celebrity, Ivy supposed. "Well, he's welcome to visit before the wedding if he'd like to see the kitchen."

"He's cooked in my kitchen many times," Carol said with nonchalance. "I'm sure he could cook over a campfire, and it would be fabulous. My assistant will contact you if he needs to. His name is Blair."

"Have him call me," Poppy said, whipping out a card. "I'm Ivy's assistant."

"Of course," Carol said pleasantly. Eyeing Poppy, she said, "You look awfully familiar. Are you an actress or musician?"

Poppy giggled and shook her head. "I graduated from USC with a master's degree in communications. I manage our public relations and marketing."

"If you ever decide to change careers, call me. You have the *look*." Soon Carol was telling them all about when Victoria had attended the university. "She'd failed all her classes and stopped attending school but we hadn't known it for months and months because I had been away on tour in Europe and Blair never said a word and I could have just *strangled* him for that."

By the time Carol finished, Ivy was practically gasping for breath, but Carol hadn't taken a single one. *Must be her vocal training,* Ivy mused.

What a different world Carol lived in from most Summer Beach residents, Ivy thought. Carol and her husband had an enclave on the ridgetop, where Bennett said buyers had been eagerly tearing down cottages on adjoining lots to build larger homes that took full advantage of the astounding views—until the city declared a moratorium on new building in an effort to preserve its small-town charm.

"Shall we see the pool now?" Ivy led Carol across the veranda to the majestic pool, which was slowly filling with water. She and Shelly had finally engaged a contractor through Jen at Nailed It to make sure the pool was sound. Meanwhile, Shelly had been transforming the surrounding patios and landscape.

"What a lovely setting," Carol said. She framed the setting with her hands like a director and swung back and forth. "That spot right there, with the ocean in the background. It's perfect."

It was exactly the spot that Ivy and Shelly had planned. The two sisters traded small smiles.

Ivy indicated an area to set up chairs. "Not too close to the pool. We don't want to have any accidents. The pool will be lit, too, for safety."

"Marvelous," Carol said with a wave of her

hand. "But do keep the lights low. The moon will be full, so it should be a magical evening."

"We can also provide soft fairy lights surrounding the area," Shelly said. "I assure you, it will be utterly magical."

Carol grasped her hands. "I can't tell you how thrilled I am that you two are taking care of every little detail to such perfection. Blair will be delighted, too."

After seeing Carol off, Ivy hurried to the hardware store. She waved at Jen, who was creating a new summer barbecue window display with an outdoor grill and grilling gear. She'd set a picnic table with pink-and-green flamingo tablecloths and pink outdoor dishes. A heat lamp in the shape of a palm tree towered over a whimsical pink flamingo blow-up pool toy.

As Ivy pushed the door open, a tinkling bell announced her arrival. "Love it," she said, greeting Jen.

The shopkeeper stepped out of the window. "It's the vacationer's idea of what a summer cookout should look like. We often sell the entire window display. What can I help you with today?"

Ivy told her about her need for a lock on her door, as well as the need to keep Pixie under control.

"I've seen that feisty little Chihuahua around town," Jen said. "How about an expandable doggie fence? Gilda can keep her door open for ventilation, but Pixie can't escape."

"I'd rather not because it could disturb other guests. Pixie is quite a yapper. We also have a guest with pet dander allergies who loves animals, but then her sneezing and coughing keeps others awake, so they complain. Our long-term guests have different needs than weekenders and vacationers."

Ivy had already decided to talk to Gilda about moving into one of the newly refurbished quarters in the rear, which Poppy had christened the Sunset rooms. Shelly had created a magical walkway from the house leading to the units with a series of stepping stones and arches. Over the arches, she was training jasmine and climbing roses. Shelly had even included a special pet lawn for biological necessities. Away from the main house, guests could bring pets yet not disturb other guests.

"I can recommend an excellent locksmith," Jen said. "Gus has been in Summer Beach for years. He lives on his boat in the marina." She handed Ivy a card from a wooden rack entitled *Handy Folks*.

"Thanks," Ivy said. "I'll call him right away."

"Use our phone," Jen said, handing her the receiver of an old rotary phone. Square and black, it sat solidly on the counter, a testament to the quality workmanship of that era.

"Wow, I haven't seen one of these in ages."

Jen laughed. "It's a real conversation piece. My father refused to replace working equipment. After he died, I couldn't bring myself to part with it."

"I know what you mean," Ivy said. "You should see the old appliances we have in the kitchen. Turquoise refrigerators and O'Keefe and Merritt ovens. We've named the matching refrigerators Gert and Gertie, and now they're part of the family."

"Sounds like they're from the 1950s. People pay a lot for those now."

"I'd love for you and George to come over for brunch this weekend," Ivy said. "The veranda has incredible views. We have some fairly good resident cooks, and everyone pitches in. You could too, if you want." Ivy thought about the brunch that Bennett and Mitch had prepared with Shelly's rosemary bread.

"That sounds like fun," Jen said. "I'll ask George."

As Ivy made her call to Gus, Jen wrapped up her purchase.

"Tomorrow?" Ivy asked. "Sure, that's fine. See you then." She handed the receiver back to Jen.

"Do you have plans for the Light Parade yet?" Jen asked. "It's a big holiday here in Summer Beach over the Independence Day weekend. I'll change the window display again for that."

"I haven't thought much about it," Ivy said, although she knew Poppy had been making plans.

Ivy thought back to when she and Jeremy were younger. They used to go to the Boston Pops concert, enjoying the fair weather and the jubilant crowd. Once the children came along, they settled for watching fireworks from the shore so their active girls could play. Later, as the girls grew older, Jeremy often traveled for clients and opted to stay over in Florida or California, saying it was too short of a holiday to return home for. Now she wondered if that had been the truth. She would probably never know.

Nor did it matter anymore, she told herself. She could choose to dwell on the shortcomings of their marriage—or recall only the best of times. She brought her attention back to Jen.

Jen leaned across the counter. "The big event in Summer Beach is the floating light parade. Everyone decorates their boats and takes them out on the water. It's quite a sight to see. Main beach and the entire marina turn into one big party, and people on the ridge invite friends to watch from their balconies. You have a perfect view from the inn."

"Then we'll have to plan something special," Ivy said. "Maybe a party on the veranda for guests."

"We have all the supplies you could want, except for the food."

After Ivy left, she walked along the main street, past a hairstylist, a menswear shop, and a beach fashion boutique. She didn't have much time to explore today, but she was looking forward to when she could. When she came to Antique Times, she opened the door. Arthur was at the desk repairing a vintage necklace.

"Ivy, what a pleasure," Arthur said, rising to greet her with a broad grin.

Although she had only been here for a couple of months now, she already felt more at home and welcome than she'd felt living in a large city. She'd had her favorite neighborhood shops in Back Bay, but the pace there was different. In the winter, cold weather kept people inside. In the summer, when people emerged from the winter hibernations, Boston was a beautiful city full of activity, but it was still a big city. While she missed the culture in Boston, she was warming to the simplicity of Summer Beach.

"I didn't know you repaired jewelry," Ivy said.

Arthur held up the gold necklace, which had an amethyst pendant in a lacy filigree setting.

"I've learned to be a jack of all trades here. Not everything that comes in is in top condition." He opened a jewelry case and positioned the necklace on a display.

"I didn't realize you had vintage jewelry here," Ivy said.

"We buy a lot of estate jewelry."

"How do you know what you're buying?"

"I have a friend who is a fine jeweler. He takes the best pieces for his clientele, then passes the less expensive pieces to us. That way, we always know what we're selling is authentic. We refer customers to each other, too."

Ivy wished she could take him into her confidence. Even the jeweler, whom he seemed to trust. But she couldn't. Not yet. She needed to hear back from Chief Clarkson and Ari, then she would decide what to do.

"How do people establish the provenance of jewelry?" she asked.

"Much the same way they do with art. And you know all about that," he added with a grin.

"People keep records?"

"They do with the most important pieces. Auction houses, jewelry designers. Many mark their pieces."

"Hallmarks."

"In Europe, marks are called an *assay*, which may differ from one country to the next. The marks will often include maker and the metal grade—that's usually required, and it's just good business."

Taking her phone from her pocket, Ivy tapped her photo folder. She turned the phone around. "What do you make of this?"

Arthur took the phone and studied the image. "This is definitely European. That's the mark for platinum. And this one…" His voice trailed off, and he looked up, his lips parted. "Where is this from?"

"It's an old piece," she said, side-stepping his question.

He gave the phone back to her and placed his palms on the countertop. "That's a maker's mark," he said quietly. "AH."

"What does AH stand for?"

"That will usually refer to the actual maker of the piece. Initials of the first and last names. Companies also mark pieces with trademarks."

"How do I find out more about this?"

"Start by searching on the internet, or by contacting a reputable auction house. They have experts on staff for this type of piece." He glanced toward the back of the shop where a customer was browsing. "A rare and valuable piece, I would say."

Ivy sucked in a breath. From the bright look in Arthur's eyes, she realized that he had quickly ascertained the truth. "Could you not mention this?"

"Whatever you share with me is confidential. No one else needs to know."

She breathed a little easier. Still, she knew Nan was one to talk. Would he tell his wife?

He must have seen the question in her eyes because Arthur added, "Not even Nan."

"I wouldn't have asked…"

"You didn't have to. I know my wife. Love her to pieces, but every human being has shortcomings. Better if you know what they are and plan around them. Like the old saying…" He pointed to an old sign on the wall of a pig with a microphone. "Never teach a pig to sing…"

"…it wastes your time and annoys the pig," Ivy finished, reading the hand-lettered quotation. She and Arthur had an understanding. For now, at least. But could she trust him? She wanted to believe she could.

Arthur slid a small loupe across the counter. "Take this with you. I think you're going to need it."

"I'll bring this back." Ivy thanked him again and left.

As Ivy hurried back to the inn, she thought about Jeremy's shortcomings. She hadn't thought he'd had many, but with distance, she'd gained clarity. When they'd met, she had talked herself into the fairytale and the happily-ever-after ending. For the most part, they had been happy. But had their happiness only been possible because she chose to make it that way?

Looking back, Ivy had come to realize that she could have questioned Jeremy more about why he didn't answer his phone in the evenings or why he couldn't fly back to Boston more weekends. In fact, she *had* brought up these questions, and he had given her plausible, acceptable answers. Yet even then, she knew in her heart that if she continued to dig, what she might find could destroy their marriage and their family.

If she were honest with herself now, which she was determined to be, it was that fear that immobilized her.

The thought was sobering and not at all how she liked to view herself. If she had demanded more of her husband, would he have complied or would their marriage have ended? It was all too easy to hear a story about a friend or neighbor and pass judgment on what they should or shouldn't do in their marriage. And she'd had the children to think of, too.

As she neared her home, she lifted her chin and strode with renewed purpose. Her future did *not* have to be a reflection of her past. Since Jeremy's death, she had changed and grown. Any man who came into her life now would have to meet a far higher standard than Jeremy.

So many serious, life-defining decisions were made when one was so young and inexperienced. If ever she had needed parental guidance, it was then. Yet, she'd been stubborn, and had not taken advantage of her parents' experience or wisdom.

Had her parents seen through Jeremy? She recalled the night she had called her mother to tell her about Jeremy.

"Mom, I have the most amazing news!" Ivy

didn't wait for her mother to reply. Instead, she blurted out, "I'm getting married!"

The line went silent for a moment, and Ivy wondered if their telephone connection had been lost. "Mom? Are you still there?"

"This is such a surprise. Who?" Carlotta's voice sounded strange, with a sort of guarded happiness edge to it.

"His name is Jeremy, and he's the most amazing, romantic man I've ever met. He's from *France*," she added as if that explained everything.

"We'd love to meet him," Carlotta said.

Ivy squealed. "And you will, sooner than you think. We've decided to get married next month when we have a break from school. His parents are going to be in town. You have to come, too."

Although she and Jeremy had been dating for a while, she hadn't told her parents. And now she was busy shopping for a wedding gown. She had wanted to wait, but Jeremy insisted that this was better. *Why wait?* he asked her. *Aren't you as confident as I am, my love? If you're not, maybe we should call this off.*

Of course, I'm sure. I'm as committed as you are, darling.

She had been so anxious to keep what they had. As Ivy thought about it now, she hadn't given her parents a real opportunity to approve or disapprove of Jeremy before their marriage.

Once, when she had asked her mother what

she thought about Jeremy, Carlotta had said, "All marriages are compromises, even down to the daily choice for dinner. No man is perfect, and no woman is perfect. How well they compromise— and accept and agree to those compromises—determines their level of happiness. As does the equitable share of power. If the balance is off, then the partner with more power must be more considerate. Otherwise, that partner may take advantage of the position."

Ivy hadn't fully understood her mother at the time, but she did now that she had lived it. When Ivy had pressed her mother, Carlotta had only hugged her and said, "I trust you to always make the best decision for your life."

Ivy reflected on her marriage. Had it been a truly happy union? As happy as she made it, she realized. Was it unbalanced and complicated? She nodded to herself. Yet she'd had no idea to what extent until after Jeremy's death.

And next time—if there were a next time— Ivy would take more time to get to know a man.

She was rebuilding her life. And this time, she was determined to rebuild her life *her* way.

17

$\mathcal{B}$ennett parked near Blossoms and stepped from his SUV. He'd just been with the City Attorney for an afternoon-long meeting, and legal terms were swirling painfully in his brain. Depositions, discovery, evidence. Part of the job, but not the part he liked. He'd been through enough litigation with Jeremy on the Seabreeze Inn property. And now from Darla, of all people.

As Imani was finishing with another customer, she lifted her chin toward him. "Have you met the mayor of Summer Beach?" Imani introduced a new summer resident who had just arrived for the horse races in nearby Del Mar. The man had manicured nails and expensive, dark sunglasses.

"Welcome to Summer Beach," Bennett said, shaking the man's hand. "Where are you staying?"

"We bought a home in the old section. My wife loves old, Craftsman-style homes. Going to be a busy summer between the races and the big wedding."

"Wedding?"

"Carol Reston's daughter. A lot of our friends are driving down from L.A. for it. Our guest rooms are already booked."

They spoke a little more while Imani wrapped up several bouquets for the man.

"Thanks," the man said to Imani. "You'll see me every week. My wife loves fresh flowers."

"Want me to deliver them to your home?" Imani asked.

The man winked. "I like to have an excuse to get out of the house and enjoy this view. Can't get this in downtown L.A."

After the man left, Bennett turned to Imani. "Looks like you picked up a good customer."

"I'll need it to rebuild my house and put Jamir in college. I'm haggling with my insurance company right now." She shrugged. "What can I do for you today?"

"Having dinner with my sister and her family," Bennett said. "What do you suggest for her?"

She smiled. "Kendra loves orchids, even though Dave always buys her roses."

"Maybe he loves roses." He paused. "You know a lot about the local residents, don't you?"

"Java Beach isn't the only place folks wag their

tongues. Between me, Mitch, and the hair salon, we've got the gossip dialed in. I listen, but I don't talk much." From her inventory, she plucked a tall orchid plant that had a brilliant burst of purple flowers arching from a long stem. "Kendra likes vivid colors. This one has a lot of blooms yet to open, so she can enjoy it for a couple of months. She'll know what to do with it."

Bennett took the plant and paid for it. "What do you think about Darla's case?"

"You know I'm representing Ivy."

"And I've just been with the City Attorney. Seems to me we're on the same side. What does Darla really want from this case? In your personal opinion?"

Imani glanced around and lowered her voice. "From what I hear, she just wants to make a point."

"Why?"

Imani brushed her long sisterlocks over her shoulder. "I think she's feeling left out. You know, she used to have a full life. After her daughter passed, she's got no one except a distant sister. And her mother's been ill, too. I think Darla's angry at the world about all that. Even if she doesn't want to talk about it. Sometimes what folks don't say is more powerful than what they do say."

Bennett nodded thoughtfully. That made a lot of sense. "Maybe we can diffuse the situation."

Imani plucked a few wilted leaves from long lily stems. "I'm not in it to make money. I only want to help out a friend."

"You and Ivy seem to have gotten pretty close."

"She's a good egg." Imani grinned. "But I think you've got that figured out already."

Bennett lifted his shoulders and let them drop. "Maybe I have. Anyone you have your eye on in Summer Beach?"

"Some things I don't talk about," Imani said with a wink. "Though I'm happy to listen to offers."

Bennett chuckled. "See you around, Imani."

"You bet, Mr. Mayor. You're right in my backyard these days."

Bennett picked up the orchid and secured it in his SUV. He swung into the car, and instead of turning on the air conditioner, he rolled down his windows to let the sun-warmed ocean breezes blow through his mind.

Whenever he had a problem, he found that being near the water put things in perspective. The ocean was a vast cradle of life, a source of endless energy. Some talked about the negative ions that had the power to enhance moods. He just knew he always felt better near the beach. Always had, even as a kid.

A vision of Ivy as a young girl floated into his mind. He was remembering more and more about his late teenage years. Was it because he was looking back more, or because Ivy had stirred long-forgotten memories? Whatever it was, he closed his eyes for a moment, breathing in the fresh salt air and reminiscing. He hadn't played his guitar in years, and he wondered where it was. If it were in the garage or the extra room, it was toast. Burnt toast. Maybe it was stuffed in the back of his bedroom closet or the hall closet.

He glanced at his watch. He still had time to swing by for a look. Breathing in again, he told himself, *just a minute more.*

His thoughts drifted back to Darla. The other morning as he was getting ready for work, he'd heard her yelling at Shelly about trimming her large eucalyptus tree, which was hanging over on the side of the Seabreeze property. Branches were brushing against the maid's quarters that Jamir was working on.

He felt sorry for Darla and her loss, but that was no excuse for lashing out against Ivy and the community. He'd make a point to include her, but he wondered how much latitude he would have now since she was suing Summer Beach. Still, with the right approach—call it diplomacy—there was a chance that Darla might drop the suit.

He started the car and headed toward his sister's house, mulling over a plan.

Once he got to Kendra's house, he saw her husband Dave outside with their son Logan. The two were bent over a tangled strand of holiday lights. Dave was tall and broad with a perpetual tan. He'd played on the golf team in high school, found his calling, and now worked for a company that distributed golf clubs and other gear. Kendra had worked as a medical science researcher before Logan was born, and she was planning to return once he was a little older. She'd always been the one who'd played with his science sets while he was out surfing or jamming with friends on his guitar.

Bennett brought the orchid from the car. "You're either a few months early or late with those."

Logan ran to him and threw his arms around him. "Dad's repurposing them. Want to come out to the boat after dinner and see what we're doing?"

Dave parted a string of lights with care. "For the Light Parade. Thought we'd light up the boat and take it out in the water parade this year." He looked up. "Nice orchid. You know Kendra prefers roses, right?"

"Must have forgotten," Bennett said. "Roses are for lovers, though."

Dave grinned. "Come on in. Kendra's making a big summer salad. We could take it out to the boat and eat on the water."

"Sounds good. I'll take this inside." He

stepped into the cozy bungalow and found Kendra in the kitchen slicing tomatoes.

"So you're taking the boat out on the water in the Light Parade." He gave his sister a hug.

"Logan is so excited about it. And he's old enough to help now. Sure you won't come with us?"

"I'm thinking of something else."

"Oh?" Kendra raised an eyebrow.

Bennett knew what that meant. It was Kendra's way of asking him if he had a date. A smile tugged at his lips. He'd let her guess.

When he didn't answer, Kendra tossed the tomatoes into a large bowl with lettuce, cucumbers, and other vegetables. "Want to slice the strawberries?"

"Sure."

She handed him a strainer full of freshly washed berries and a knife. "Feta cheese and pine nuts okay?"

"Sounds good. You're making Mom's summer salad?"

Kendra wiped her hands on a lemon-printed apron. "You remembered."

"A lot of memories are coming back to me these days." He chuckled. "I've been thinking about the summers we used to spend at the beach. Mom would send us out and tell us not to come back until dinner."

Kendra crumbled feta cheese into the bowl. "Times have changed since then."

"Not as much in Summer Beach."

"That's why we live here." She gazed from the kitchen window and nodded toward the ocean. "Logan loves the water and ocean life. Your friend Flint made quite an impression on him. He wants to study marine biology now that he knows he can follow dolphins."

"Actually, Flint's a marine mammologist. One of the top in San Diego."

"Logan sure liked him." Kendra paused, her eyes gleaming. "His sister is the one who owns the inn?"

"That's right."

"Small town. I've been hearing a lot about her," Kendra said, tossing a handful of pine nuts into the salad. "She's leading morning beach walks and holding painting classes. And she and her sister are planning an art show. Not to mention hosting the Reston-Zachary wedding."

"Sounds like you've been hanging out at Java Beach."

Kendra laughed. "I get all my intel from my hairstylist. Word has it that Ivy is getting chummy with Carol Reston." She threw him a challenging look. "Wonder if she'll be going all Hollywood on us?"

"Not Ivy," he said, perhaps a little too quickly. "She's pretty level-headed. Her sister is another story, though. Shelly makes videos about gardening."

"Carol might introduce them to some hot celebrities. Maybe the father-of-the-groom, Rowan Zachary. He's about Ivy's age. Did you know his son Orlando is an actor, too?"

Bennett frowned. *Rowan Zachary? What an outlandish thought.* He couldn't imagine Ivy falling for someone as Hollywood as that. "Wasn't his last girlfriend twenty years younger than him?"

"Ah, so you do keep up with the gossip," Kendra said, laughing.

He tossed a strawberry at her. "Just what I hear at the inn. I have to keep up with my constituents." He knew what Kendra was doing. She was egging him on about Ivy.

Kendra bit into the berry. "I've seen her around town. She's pretty cute."

"Rowan's ex?" Bennett feigned ignorance.

She poked him in the ribs. "No, silly. Ivy."

"Hadn't noticed."

"Right." Kendra slid a glance his way. "Don't forget, I know you."

Indeed, she did. Was he that obvious?

Maybe only to his sister.

Bennett slid sliced strawberries off the plate and into the bowl. "Anything else?"

"Grab the sourdough baguette. I'll put a lid on the bowl, and then we're good to go."

He followed his sister out to the car. Logan and Dave were loading lights into the car.

"Climb in," Dave said.

A little while later, Dave parked at the marina, and they made their way to their boat.

As they walked, Kendra turned to Bennett. "You should decorate your boat and take it out, too."

"My decorations went up in the fire."

"So? Get more. It would be fun. You could take Flint and his wife. And Ivy." She grinned.

"If I didn't know better, I'd think you were trying to set me up."

She elbowed him. "Just giving you a nudge, bro."

He grinned. "I can take care of myself." Though it was a good idea. "Have any extra lights?"

Dave turned around. "As long as you help untangle them."

They ate onboard in the marina, waving at friends who walked by, while others stopped to talk. After they were finished, they took the boat out for a sunset cruise. Enjoying the wind in his hair and the sea spray that cooled his face, Bennett watched the sky change colors as the sun slipped to the horizon.

Summer Beach was a unique community of personalities, and that's what he liked about it.

18

The damp marine layer that shrouded Summer Beach in a damp morning mist was burning off early under the warmth of the summer sun. As Ivy approached the Starfish Café, Megan waved. The filmmaker was already seated at a table midway down the hillside that sloped to the beach. The cafe had once been a private residence—probably built in the 1930s, Ivy thought, judging from the Victorian fretwork and cupola that overlooked the ocean. She breathed in the sweet scent of jasmine as she made her way toward Megan

Ivy followed a garden path through a riot of bougainvillea and rose gardens that dotted the hillside. She had always loved the gardens and ambiance, though it had been years since she'd been here. Her parents had brought her and her siblings here when she was a child.

Megan stood to embrace her. "Thanks for joining me here. This place has the best açaí bowls and croissants for breakfast, along with salads and fresh Mexican-style seafood for lunch and dinner."

"It's a beautiful setting, too," Ivy said, admiring her surroundings. Orange umbrellas shaded the outdoor tables. Around them, silvery-green succulents spilled from deep blue Mexican pottery situated on low white-washed walls.

"Isn't it?" Megan took her seat and tucked her short, wavy blond hair behind her ears, revealing a tiny rose tattoo. "Josh can't wait to return. We have a contract pending on our house in Seattle, and Josh has one more project to finish. We'll have to look for a place here soon."

"We'll miss you at the inn, but I can't wait to welcome you as neighbors."

Megan motioned toward a server. "Although I love the inn, I wanted to get away so we could really talk about the Amelia Erickson project. I've been doing research, and I've turned up some interesting material."

"I'd love to hear it."

The two women ordered coffee, and Ivy opted for a fresh fruit platter with yogurt. It was mid-morning and remnants of the early morning crowd were lingering, though it was still early for lunch. Vacationers in shorts and flip-flops were languidly sipping Bloody Marys and mimosas and pondering what to do while they waited for the sun to fully emerge from behind the clouds.

Megan began. "I was going through film archives in L.A. for another project when I came across some notes that a filmmaker had made. There was a mention of Amelia and Gustav Erickson. They were avid supporters of the arts. Not only of paintings, which they collected, but of other artists and artisans, as well as emerging technologies."

"What kind of technology?"

"Film. Silent films first, and then the new talkies."

When Ivy smiled, Megan added, "That sounds quaint now, but it was hotly contested at the time. The move to talkies destroyed some careers and made others."

Ivy's instincts bristled. "What other types of artisans did the Ericksons contribute to?"

Megan reached into her stylish black backpack and withdrew a small moleskin notebook. She flipped to a page. "Here it is. Filmmakers, fashion designers in Paris, jewelers, sculptors—so many in the arts and artistic commerce."

Ivy sipped her coffee. "Amelia referred to someone with the initials AH once. Anyone connected to her with those initials?"

Megan ran her finger down her notes. "Not

that I recall, but if I see anything, I'll let you know." She added a note.

"Are there any names I'd recognize?" After her conversation with Arthur, Ivy realized she needed to be careful about revealing information about the jewelry. She was expecting a call from Chief Clarkson or Ari any day. Although Gus the locksmith had come over as promised and installed a lock on her door, the thought of having such precious jewelry in her room was unnerving. This afternoon she would visit the local bank and inquire about safety deposit boxes.

Megan turned a page. "The Ericksons financed several European filmmakers, including the important female director, Alice Guy-Blaché, who was the first person to create a story for film." Megan smiled. "Alice was also the first film director, and others, such as Alfred Hitchcock, learned from her. Besides underwriting projects, the Ericksons also introduced talented people. They held salons with creative people and financiers at their homes in San Francisco and at Las Brisas del Mar."

Megan read off a few more names that Ivy recognized. "They also knew Peter Carl Fabergé, the jeweler. He fled Russia after the Bolshevik Revolution. His sons reestablished the business after his death in Paris. Peter Carl was close to the Imperial family in Russia, and many thought he died of a broken heart after they were executed."

"Fabergé," Ivy repeated softly. "Anything else about them, or their clients?"

Megan rested an index finger along her temple. "I once saw a documentary on Fabergé and his creations. He was such a visionary artist, and royal houses and wealthy families collected his pieces. He was known for his imperial eggs, of course, but his jewelry suites—*parures*—and tiaras were stunning."

Choosing her words with care, Ivy went on. "I wonder if any serious jewelry collections disappeared during the war."

Megan's eyes lit up. "There was a movie made about one. Three American military officers pilfered the jewels of a German royal family, who was also related to the British monarchy. They sold some jewels in Europe and smuggled others into the States."

"Military officers *stole* the crown jewels?" Ivy was aghast at the thought. *But, could it be?*

"Unfathomable, I know." Megan shook her head. "The thieves were caught and convicted of the crime, but only a fraction of the jewels were ever recovered. However, I don't think the movie was an accurate representation." She rolled her eyes. "Hollywood never lets history stand in the way of a good story. That's why I'm in documentaries, especially for historical works."

Ivy mentally filed away this information. She

could enlist Poppy to help her research later. Surely they could find more details online.

Their brunch arrived, and the two women ate while they talked. Ivy nibbled on pineapple spears and strawberries as she listened to Megan.

"Amelia was also friends with Marlene Dietrich," Megan said. "Did you know they were both born in Berlin?"

Ivy shook her head. "Actually, I know little about her, other than her interest in art."

"The more I research, the more I'm fascinated with the Ericksons, and Amelia in particular," Megan said. "While Gustav was an investor, it was Amelia who guided their investments in the arts."

"She definitely had the eye for quality and creativity," Ivy said.

Megan looked up. "She understood art, and she had deep connections in the art world."

"I'd like to know more about her." Ivy wondered what other secrets the old house might hold.

Resting her chin in her hand, Megan said, "I've been through the book that Arthur and Nan put together, but what's missing is Amelia's personality. While her works are chronicled, we know very little about the kind of person she was."

"The journal I found was incomplete." Ivy drummed her fingers on the table. "She lived out her final years in Switzerland. Can you find anything there?"

"I've tried." Megan wagged her head slowly.

"The facility where Amelia lived suffered a fire, so all patient records from that time were lost. I hit a dead end on physicians and nursing staff, too. I have a colleague in Switzerland who is doing some research. However, patients and staff from that era have passed away—and many of their children, too. We're talking about people's grandchildren now. They really don't recall anything."

Ivy gazed out over the ocean, watching the incessant waves roll toward the shore and out again. The perpetual motion was mesmerizing. As she watched, an idea formed in her mind. "The Ericksons made their mark here in the States, but who were they before they came here?"

"I can start in Berlin," Megan said.

"And I'll keep an eye out for other artifacts." Ivy wished she could tell Megan about her find now, but she needed to talk to Chief Clarkson or Ari again.

Later, after leaving Megan, Ivy strolled to the beach. Perching on a bench, she checked her phone. The only messages were from Shelly suggesting she pick up more supplies, and from Poppy alerting her to a new guest arriving later today.

Acting on a whim, Ivy tapped Ari's number.

"Ari here."

Ivy quickly explained the situation. "Did Chief Clarkson forward the photos to you?"

"He did, and I've had a look. The pieces look

quite collectible, but we don't have any open cases."

"What about in other countries?"

"We've checked Interpol. Isn't it possible that was part of Amelia Erickson's personal jewelry collection?"

"Maybe, but that doesn't explain why the pieces were sewn into the doll. Don't you find that strange?"

He hesitated. "Mrs. Erickson was quite ill toward the end of her life. She may have been acting erratically. Paranoid, even."

"I hadn't thought of that."

"We see a lot of unusual behavior, Ivy. Even though we try to get into people's mind, you'd be surprised at their justifications."

"And the photo of the letter I sent you? About the museum?"

"It stated that Amelia Erickson was sending a doll that might be of interest for a museum collection."

"That's it?"

"It was quite short. And of course, neither the letter nor the doll reached their destination."

"Can you continue searching? I really think there's more to this discovery than we realize."

"When we can. Unfortunately, this will take quite a bit of research, and my team is still working on establishing the provenance of the paintings and contacting heirs and organizations that may have a claim to them."

Ari and Cecile had explained that it would take time for a determination of ownership. A judge would make the final order that would allow the distribution of the artwork.

Ivy thanked him and hung up. She would have to let Ari and team do their jobs, but she and Poppy could also conduct their own search.

On the way back to the house, she stopped by First Summer Beach Bank and rented a safety deposit box, and then went to a pet shop and bought a couple of dog toys for Pixie to keep her busy.

Making her way toward the house, Ivy noticed Shelly in the garden talking to someone. Her sister waved when she saw her, and as Ivy approached, Mitch came into view.

"Hey, Mitch," Ivy called out.

Shelly's eyes sparkled with excitement. "Mitch was just telling me about the lighted water parade. Have you heard about it?"

"Jen over at Nailed It mentioned it," Ivy replied. "I was thinking of having a party here for the guests so they could watch from the veranda."

Shelly's smile fell. "Mitch has asked me to go out on the boat with him."

Although she could have used Shelly's help, Ivy was pleased to hear that. "Go, have a good time. It's supposed to be spectacular."

"Are you sure?" Shelly asked, frowning. "Maybe Poppy can help you with the party."

"She might have other plans." Ivy glanced at Mitch. Beneath his chill exterior, she could tell that he was pleased Shelly had agreed to go. "Don't worry, I've got this. Believe it or not, I've thrown a lot of parties in my life. Maybe I'll invite Mom and Dad."

Of course, most of the parties she'd thrown had been children's birthday parties, but if she could manage fifteen sugar-crazed six-year-olds high on birthday cake and party games, she could handle a relatively sedate party of adults.

The wedding, however, might be a different story. Ivy wasn't sure why she'd been feeling uneasy about the event—beyond the usual anxiety to make sure all the details were addressed. Still, she hadn't been able to shake the feeling that this wedding would be one to remember, though not necessarily for the obvious reason.

19

"*T*ry searching for the words *maker's mark*," Ivy said, leaning toward the laptop to watch Poppy's online search. They were huddled in the library. At midday, the house was reasonably quiet, though a few people were meandering through the hallways.

Poppy's eyes widened. "Look at all these," she said.

Last night, Ivy had read about the marks that jewelry makers put on their pieces to denote metal quality, producer, location, or company.

"This is more complex than I'd imagined. Look at these lists." Poppy scrolled through a list from the United Kingdom that had a variety of marks. "And different countries have different marks."

Ivy thought about what Megan had said about

associates and friends of the Ericksons. "Can you find what marks Fabergé might have used?"

Poppy's fingers flew over the keyboard, and she pulled up a new screen. "Here it is. Russia. Peter Carl Fabergé."

Ivy and Poppy perused the history. "Fabergé made jewelry for many of the royal houses of Europe," Ivy said, pointing at the screen. "Wait, look at this. Fabergé engaged other workshops run by master workers, who often put their marks on pieces."

"You're looking for AH, Aunt Ivy?" Poppy pointed to the screen. "How about August Holmström?"

Ivy jumped from her chair with excitement. "Maybe AH is his mark. What can you find on him?"

Poppy's fingers raced across the keys. "Born in 1829 in Finland, died in 1903 in Russia. Seems to have been a family business. His son Albert used the same mark. And his daughter and granddaughter were also jewelry designers." She paged over to one of the world's top auction houses. "Here are some of his pieces for sale." Poppy scrolled down.

When an image of a delicate tiara appeared on the screen, Ivy cried out. "It's not the same, but look at that craftsmanship." She traced a series of delicate flowers and ribbons rendered in diamonds and crowned with teardrop aquamarines. "It's clearly the same designer."

"And look at that price," Poppy said. "Wow, if only you could sell it, or any of the other pieces."

"I don't think they're mine to sell. I only want to find the rightful owners."

Poppy pulled up another image of the maker's marks. One was clearly AH. "Do any of these marks match the ones on the tiara?"

Ivy pulled out her phone to check. "The AH seems the same, but the others aren't as clear. I'll go get the tiara."

"And traipse around here with a half-million-dollar tiara?" Poppy whispered. She picked up her laptop. "Let's go to your room."

The pair climbed the stairs and stopped at Ivy's door.

"Wait, it's locked." Ivy fished the key from her pocket and slid it in. With a deft turn, she opened the door.

While Poppy set up her laptop at a writing desk, Ivy retrieved the rolled-up towels from the bottom of the closet, where she'd stashed them under some linens.

"We'll check everything else, too." Ivy deposited the towels on the bed, and then she opened the doll's trunk. She lifted out the false bottom and reached in to lift out the tiara.

Empty.

"It's gone!" Ivy cried, her pulse doubling at the discovery. "Didn't you put it back?"

"I thought Shelly put it back." Poppy pointed to the antique vanity. "I left it right there on that side."

"You're sure?"

"Absolutely," Poppy said with a sharp nod. "You and I ran out to tend to Pixie and the rug and the other guest."

"We need Shelly." Ivy pulled out her phone and pressed her sister's number. "Shelly, can you come up to my bedroom right now? We've lost something."

"What?"

"Something very *precious*."

"Oh, no," Shelly exclaimed over the phone. "I'm in the kitchen. I'll be right up."

Immediately, Ivy heard Shelly pounding up the stairs.

Shelly raced into the room. "What happened?" she cried.

"The tiara," Ivy said, pointing toward the empty doll trunk. "Did you put it back?"

"I thought *you* did."

"We ran out to deal with Pixie." Ivy felt a knot forming in the pit of her stomach.

Shelly shook her head. "I'm sorry. I rolled up the other jewelry, stashed it, and hurried after you. When did *you* see it last?"

"That was it," Ivy said.

"So who else knew about this?" Poppy asked.

Shelly shifted her gaze between Ivy and Poppy. "Bennett, Chief Clarkson, Ari. That's all, am I right?"

Ivy fidgeted with her sleeve. "And Arthur. Kind of."

"Arthur at Antique Times?" Shelly asked, incredulous. "Why would you tell *him*?"

"I didn't. Not exactly." Ivy drew her hands over her face. "I showed him the picture of the maker's mark, and Arthur guessed that we'd found something of value. He doesn't know about any of *that*," she said, motioning to the towels.

"Or maybe the tiara *is* in there," Shelly said, sounding hopeful. "I *was* rushing."

Quickly, Shelly unfurled the towel. Jewelry and gemstones tumbled onto the bed in a rainbow arc of color. She unrolled the second one, but there was no tiara. "Who else has been in here?" she asked.

Groaning, Ivy said, "Anyone could have been. Gus only just put the lock on the door."

"Who's Gus?" Shelly asked.

"The locksmith that Jen referred," Ivy replied. *Could Gus have pocketed the tiara?* A sick feeling gathered in the pit of her stomach.

Shelly pressed her hands against her temples. "Did you tell Jen, too?"

"Of course not." Ivy slid her gaze toward the

vanity, which was next to the door. *Would have been awfully tempting.*

"Can you reach Gus?" Poppy asked.

"He lives on his boat in the marina," Ivy replied. "Jen said he's lived in Summer Beach forever."

Shelly raked her teeth over her lower lip. "Maybe we should call Chief Clarkson."

A man's footsteps sounded outside the door, which Shelly had left ajar in her rush. "Why do you need to call Clark?" Bennett said as he tapped on the door. "Everyone decent?"

Ivy pulled him inside and slammed the door behind him, making sure to lock it. "The tiara is gone."

"Gone?" Bennett looked nonplussed. "Did you give it to Clark?"

"It's missing from the vanity where I left it," Poppy said.

Feeling her head throb, Ivy rubbed her forehead. "Today I'd planned to take the entire lot to the bank to lock in a safety deposit box in the vault."

Bennett touched her hand. "Who had access?"

"Everyone, but Gus the locksmith was here a couple of days ago," Ivy said. "Do you know which boat is his?"

"Slow down," Bennett said. "You do need to call Clark. And you should know that Gus just left. He always takes off this time of year. Says there are too many people at the marina, and the light parade bothers him."

"Where does he go?" Ivy asked.

"Mexico," Bennett said. "But before you go accusing Gus, you need to look at everyone who's been here at the inn."

Ivy slid her hand down to her neck, which was also aching from the stress. "The chief will undoubtedly want to question all of them. That won't go over well with the guests. Before we do that, we have to make absolutely certain that it hasn't been misplaced."

"My vote's on Gus," Shelly said, putting her fists on her hips. "Your tiara is probably making land on Baja right about now."

"It's not *my* tiara," Ivy snapped, flinging her hand toward the loot on the bed. "All of that was meant for someone else years ago. I don't need it, I don't want it. This is what happens when you have those kinds of valuables lying around. It's too much responsibility."

Ivy could feel her blood pressure rising and knew her face was probably turning an unseemly shade of red, but she couldn't help it. With a celebrity-studded, wedding-of-the-summer to prepare for, the last thing she needed was a full-scale investigation of the resident guests.

Shelly advanced toward Ivy. "My advice? Turn all of this into cash. Problem solved."

"It's *not* ours," Ivy shot back.

"Wait a minute, you two," Bennett said, sliding his hands over Ivy's shoulders. "There's a solution to this problem that doesn't involve a fight."

"I'd like to know what that is," Ivy said. "Miss New York is always spoiling for a fight."

"Calm down, aunties," Poppy pleaded. "I was the one who left it out. If anyone is at fault, it's me."

Shelly hugged Poppy. "No, you're not. I should've seen it."

"And I should have put a lock on my door sooner." Ivy felt bad for Poppy. It wasn't her fault at all. "Bennett's right. So what's the solution?"

Kneading Ivy's shoulders, he said, "First, secure all of that somewhere."

"I'm on my way to the bank right away," Ivy said. His hands were warm and welcome on her shoulders. She rotated her stiff neck. "I rented a safety deposit box."

"Good. Next, call Chief Clarkson," Bennett said. "He can put the word out to local dealers. If a tiara turns up, they'll be in touch. If a person wants to fence stolen goods, they usually don't go too far to do it."

"Why wouldn't they?" Poppy inclined her head. "If it were me, I'd get as far away as I could to sell it. Not that it was me."

Shelly slung her arm around Poppy. "Most thieves aren't as smart as you. Come on, let's make a list of who's been here and give that to the chief."

"On it." Poppy grabbed a pen and pad from the desk.

"Gilda, Megan, Celia, Imani, and Jamir," Ivy began. "Although I can't imagine any of them would do that."

Shelly pointed at the pad. "Put Gus at the top. Mark my word, you don't need to go any farther."

Bennett shook his head. "He's not the type, but okay. He was here."

Poppy wrote his name down, then looked up. "Mitch?"

Ivy shot a glance at Shelly, who nodded with reluctance. Ivy didn't want to think about that either, especially given his record, whatever it was for.

Bennett sighed. "He was here, too, so put his name down, Poppy."

Poppy scribbled his name, then she added another one.

"Who'd you add?" Shelly asked, looking over her shoulder. "*Darla* was here?"

"I invited her over," Poppy said, looking sheepish.

Shelly folded her arms. "What for? She's our enemy."

"Not exactly our enemy," Bennett said. "Let's call her our challenge. We have to figure out how to diffuse her."

"It's a frivolous lawsuit," Shelly shot back.

"So why was she here?" Ivy pressed.

"It was the day that Mitch brought in some pastries. He said he'd made extra, but I think he just wanted to see Shelly. Anyway, you were both gone, so I put them out, and Mitch asked if we'd seen Darla because she hadn't been into Java Beach that morning. He was worried about her. So I told him to call her, and he did. She came over and fawned over Mitch like she always does, and then she left."

"Did you leave her alone at any time?" Shelly drew her lips into a thin line.

Poppy thought for a moment. "I took a call in the library. And Mitch had to go. But other guests were around. Gilda came down, and that other couple who were here for a couple of days. Oh, I need to add them to the list, too."

Bennett shook his head. "Not Darla. And definitely not Imani or Jamir. Or Gilda or Celia. I've known these people for a long time."

While Ivy didn't care for Darla, she didn't strike her as the type, but she couldn't rule her out, either. "Check our guest list, too, Poppy."

"Right away," Poppy said, hurrying out the door.

Ivy stepped away from Bennett to get a bag from the closet. "This is all going away right now." She began to place the jewelry inside, taking care with the delicate pieces.

"Here, I'll help." Shelly brought a clean hand towel from the linen closet. "We can use this to wrap the necklaces and bracelets in." She began to help Ivy.

"Thanks," Ivy said. "Sorry if I went off on you."

Shelly touched her hand. "Me, too." She tilted up one side of her mouth. "I hope it wasn't Mitch."

"I'm sure he had nothing to do with it." But could Ivy be sure? None of them wanted to think about that. Chief Clarkson would probably want to talk to him, given Mitch's record. Which they still didn't know anything about.

"I have a little bag you can put the stones and rings in," Poppy added. "Be right back."

Bennett's phone buzzed. He pulled it from his pocket and frowned. "I need to take this. Glad we're getting this sorted out though." He took Ivy's hand and kissed it before stepping out into the hallway.

Ivy watched him go. He was good at helping diffuse disagreements, and she hoped he could do the same with Darla. Maybe she should try, too.

As she and Shelly worked to organize the jewelry, Ivy gently asked, "Have you talked to Mitch yet? About you-know-what?"

Shelly angled her head. "Suppose this proves that I should. How many times will a situation like this occur? Probably not often, but what if he went to prison for something entirely unrelated. Some victimless crime…like too many parking tickets?"

Ivy smoothed a hand over Shelly's. "You know you're making excuses for him, right? People make mistakes, but look at him now. Don't you want to know more about him before it's…too late?" Ivy hesitated, but given the look in Shelly's eyes, it was already too late. Her sister had really fallen for Mitch. Better Mitch than Ezzra, but still, Shelly needed to know the truth.

Shelly sighed. "At what point in a relationship do you ask about someone's prison record?"

Ivy's phone rang, and she paused to check it. Her elder daughter's name and photo popped up on the screen. "It's Misty."

"Tell her hi for me."

Ivy tapped out a message. *What's up, sweetie? Aunt Shelly says hi. Show going well?*

Great! Going anywhere for the 4th?

"She wants to know if I'm going anywhere for the holiday." Ivy shook her head. Not as an innkeeper.

"There are two of us," Shelly said. "If you want to fly out for a visit, go. I can cover for you."

"Thanks, but not yet. The wedding is too soon. I'll wait until Sunny is back from Europe so I can see them both at once." Ivy tapped a reply to Misty. *Can't leave our guests. Wish I could join you in Boston. Will visit when Sunny returns.*

That's okay. Just checking in. Love you, bye!

Ivy slipped her phone into her jeans pocket and eased onto the edge of the bed. "Have you heard from Sunny?" With an aunt closer in age than her mother, her younger daughter often reached out to Shelly.

"Occasionally she sends a photo." Shelly shrugged. "She's a good kid. Looks like she's having fun."

That was the problem with Sunny. She couldn't seem to prioritize the important things in her life. "Do you know if she found a job?"

Shelly shook her head. "I know you're worried about her, but remember when we were young? We did okay. She will, too."

"I hope you're right." Still, Ivy couldn't help worrying about Sunny. Misty had adjusted to her father's death, but Sunny was still lashing out at the world in anger. Ivy hoped she wouldn't be driven to make an irrevocable mistake.

20

*B*ennett was lying flat under the vintage Chevrolet working when he saw a pair of flip-flops approaching the car. "With toes that ugly, it can only be one person." He slid out from under the car on a rolling creeper. Shading his eyes from the sun, he grinned up at Mitch, glad to see his friend.

"What a sweet ride," Mitch said. "Looking pretty good. When do you think you'll be taking it out?"

"Not long," Bennett said as he sat up and wiped his hands on a rag. "Just finished the oil change. Still need to give it a tune-up, and I'm waiting on a part. I'd hoped to have it ready this weekend, but I'll need a little more time." Between his mayoral duties and the occasional real estate clients, his days were quite full. "Weekends are my only time to work on it, and even then I'm often booked. I'm not like you, you old beach bum."

Mitch chuckled. "Hey, I'm not old." He held out a hand and helped Bennett to his feet.

Bennett gave him a bro hug. "And you're the hardest working beach bum around. What's going on?"

"Checking in with you about the holiday. I invited Shelly onto the boat for the light parade. Want to come?"

"Sure. Taking my boat or yours?" Mitch had a sizeable sport fishing boat that he'd converted for whale watching charters, while Bennett had a smaller yacht.

"Mine if we have a crowd. Yours if we have to decorate."

"Or if we keep the group small." Bennett picked up a microfiber cloth and wiped down a smudge on the fender.

"Are you asking Ivy?"

Bennett shook his head. "I would have, but she said something about putting on a party here for the guests."

Mitch pushed a hand through his spiky, bleached hair. "Won't be many people here. Imani's going out with friends, and so is Gilda. Megan's flying back to be with her husband in Seattle. Their house sold, so he's staying in an IBnB up there while he finishes a work assignment before relocating here. And Celia's hoping Tyler comes back."

"Do you keep a log on everyone?" Bennett chuckled.

"I hear things at Java Beach," Mitch said, rubbing the stubble on his chin. "You'd be surprised. People never think the help is listening."

Bennett glanced around. They were alone. Shelly had gone inside the house, and Jamir was working on the new units outside of earshot. He was sure he could trust Mitch. "Have you heard anything about a theft? A small piece, but one with a lot of history."

Mitch stiffened. "Theft of what? From where?"

Bennett squatted down to wipe the hubcap. "From here. Something of value." Though he spoke nonchalantly, he watched Mitch closely from the corner of his eye.

"I can't believe you'd ask me that." Mitch narrowed his eyes and shook his head. Looking away, he puffed out a breath of disgust.

Bennett stood up and placed his hand on Mitch's arm. "Hey, I'm not attacking you, I'm just wondering if you've overheard anything. If you do, you'll let me know?"

"Yeah, but I stay clear of those people now," Mitch said with a conciliatory nod.

"Proud of you for that." He clapped a hand on his shoulder. "Now, about that holiday. Dave gave me some decorations, so we can get to work. How about we take my boat?"

"You're on," Mitch said, relaxing again into his usual easy grin.

"Well, don't just stand there," Bennett said, tossing him a soft cloth. "The leather conditioner is on the floorboard. Passenger side."

Mitch caught the cloth, then poured a small dollop of creamy liquid onto it. "Didn't know these old cars had leather interior."

"This was probably a custom order, or customized after purchase. This was the Erickson's playground, their beach house, so everything here was designed for fun, guests, and large parties. " Bennett watched what Mitch was doing. "That's good. Use circular motions." He leaned into the open hood to check the dipstick.

Mitch rubbed the leather conditioner into the red and white bench seats. "I can just imagine this tearing down the Pacific Coast Highway back then. Top down, wind in the hair, Elvis blaring on the radio." He paused. "Ah, sweet."

"Sure is," Bennett said.

Mitch jerked his chin toward the house. "No. Shelly. She's brought us something."

Bennett glanced up. Shelly was walking toward them. In her hands, she held two tall drinks. She wore sleek black yoga pants and a fluttery black top that hung off one shoulder. He supposed that was on purpose. She'd looped a bunch of colorful necklaces over that, and her hair was piled up in a messy bun. He smiled to himself. Shelly and Ivy couldn't be more different in their style, but Shelly fit Mitch pretty well.

"Hi, guys," she said. "Thought you could use a couple of Sea Breezes. Virgin, of course. Don't want to impede your progress on this beauty."

Bennett took one of the icy drinks. "Just what we needed." As he cooled his throat, he watched Mitch and Shelly together. They looked at each other the way he and Jackie once had.

Bennett hoped they wouldn't break each other's hearts. He knew how that felt and how long it took to piece a heart back together.

For years he'd had a hollow ache in his heart that never seemed to go away. He'd learned how to get through the days, and even how to talk about his wife without going into a depressed state. But that had taken a long time. Mitch was young, and he could handle it, though Bennett hoped that this evolving relationship had a good chance of success. Mitch had come a long way, and he was probably ready for a relationship or close to it.

Bennett watched Mitch drink Shelly in like a man thirsty for a beautiful woman. When the ocean breeze blew an errant strand of hair around her dangly earring, he untangled it for her while she checked him out.

New love was sweet to watch. Bennett couldn't help but smile.

Ivy had mentioned that Shelly had just broken up with a long-term boyfriend in New York. He had to wonder if Shelly was ready for love again. Bennett honestly couldn't tell. He'd never asked how old Shelly was, and he wondered if she wanted children.

None of that was any of his business, of course, but Mitch was a good friend, and Bennett felt protective of him. He'd seen Mitch at his worst and had given him a chance. Mitch was a smart kid; that was all he'd needed. And now, with Mitch's success, the last thing Bennett wanted was to see the guy derailed at this critical time in his life. He'd seen too many of his friends jump into the wrong relationships, and pay for it with broken homes, broken hearts, and part-time kids. He wouldn't wish that on anyone.

To give Mitch and Shelly some privacy, Bennett turned back to the engine. He checked the belts, making notes about which ones he'd need to replace.

As for himself, Bennett felt he'd missed the chance for a family of his own. He wasn't interested in dating women young enough to be his daughter. He liked women his own age who didn't laugh when he listened to the old music he'd grown up with. The songs didn't seem all that old to him.

As for relationships, Bennett was only interested in the real deal now. Yet revealing the depth of his feelings for a woman such as Ivy could be risky. It was still so soon after the death of her husband. *Just a year.* That might sound like enough time, and maybe it was for some people, but it hadn't been for him. Maybe it wasn't for Ivy either. Even if Jeremy hadn't been the most loyal husband, was Ivy ready to risk love again?

Or maybe, *especially* if Jeremy hadn't been faithful. Between his death and his shattering of her trust—even if it had been post-mortem—Ivy had a lot to get past.

If she wasn't ready, Ivy could break his heart without even realizing it. She was worth the risk, he thought, though he couldn't be sure if she would be receptive. From the warm look in her eyes to her occasional touch that sent him reeling, she seemed interested—even though she also concealed her feelings—but it might still prove too early for her.

Go slow. That was the answer. But could he stand it?

21

*I*vy was folding linens in the laundry room and still ruminating over the missing tiara when her phone rang. Seeing that it was Caroline, she rushed out of earshot of the washer and dryer.

Ivy had engaged a couple who lived nearby to begin coming in to do the cleaning and laundry, but they wouldn't start for a few more days. She was exhausted trying to do everything, even with Shelly and Poppy's help. With the wedding drawing closer, the event was demanding more of their attention, and Poppy was already booking more events. Ivy was learning to delegate as much as possible.

Swiftly switching tracks in her mind, she answered Caroline's call.

"Darling!" Caroline's voice burst from the

phone. "You'll never guess who I have with me right now. Chef Alain and the father-of-the-groom. Aren't I the lucky woman to have these two handsome men on either side of me? Anyway, we're just leaving the Starfish Café, and we can be there in less than five minutes. Alain is dying to see the kitchen."

As Caroline's words registered, Ivy glanced at her grubby laundry-day outfit of an old T-shirt and stretch pants. *Rowan Zachary. Coming here.* She knew she would see him at the wedding, but now?

Thinking fast, Ivy said, "I'm with a guest right now. Can you give me ten minutes? Poppy can show them the ballroom." Ivy was halfway up the rear stairs by the time Caroline hung up.

Ivy dashed off a text to Poppy while she shed her clothes. She whipped through a bath with quick splashes of water, sleeked her hair into a ponytail, and threw a long floral, scarf-edged sundress over her still damp body.

Her phone buzzed again. It was Poppy. *They're here.*

Ivy slipped on flats and fairly sprinted down the stairs. *Rowan Zachary. In the house.* Her heart was pounding, so she paused on the last stair, pressed her hand against her chest, and tried to compose herself. A handsome actor that millions of women would die to have in their arms was in her kitchen, along with one of the most famous chefs in the world.

No problem. Just another day at the inn.

Collecting herself, Ivy opened the door to the kitchen. Poppy stared at her with wide eyes.

"Hello, Caroline," Ivy said calmly, trying not to act starstruck by the incredibly handsome man who stood before her, even though her nerves were sizzling in awe.

Ivy took a step forward—and immediately stumbled—right in front of Rowan Zachary, who'd aged from a floppy-haired teen idol and into an elegant Cary Grant of a man. Acting quickly, Rowan caught her arm to keep her from falling.

She looked up into the expressive, chocolate brown eyes she'd seen in movies and on television for so many years. His were a little more lined around the edges like hers, but still warm and...sexy.

"Thanks," Ivy managed to say. She knew her face must be a lovely shade of red, but she had to carry on. Glancing down, she saw that she'd stepped on a pointed scarf edge of her sundress, which she'd bought to wear with heels, not flats. She pinched up a bit of the skirt with one hand and shook hands with the other. "Gentlemen, welcome."

After the introductions, Alain turned to inspect the kitchen. He was a large, barrel-chested man with a commanding presence and a beefy pink face.

"Plenty of counter space, good," Alain said. When he turned to the twin turquoise refrigerators, he took a step back as if in shock. "What are *these?*"

"Those two were here when we moved in," Ivy said, though she didn't introduce them by their given names. She glanced at Poppy, who was stifling a grin.

"Obviously," Alain said, sniffing. "Do they *work?*"

"Quite well," Ivy said with confidence. "We love them." Alain might be a world-class chef, but she refused to be belittled—or even her appliances—due to her circumstances.

Money and possessions did not determine her worth. Ivy had already been through an emotional adjustment when she'd moved into the professor's extra room in Boston. Besides, she thought, look at where she was now. Maybe not worth squillions, but doing just fine.

Smiling sweetly, Ivy said, "And if you like those, you'll love the matching ovens behind you."

Rowan spun around. "Oh, I *love* them," he said, his dark eyes flashing with mischief. "So different, so unique. I know people who would pay a fortune for these—*if* you ever let them go."

"Which I won't," Ivy said, picking up on Rowan's little game.

Alain's face settled into a mask of petulant acceptance. "It's only one dinner. We will make it work, yes?" He clapped his hands. "We will see the outside now."

Ivy led them outside to the veranda and pool, which was now gleaming in the sunshine. Facing the ocean, she indicated where the ceremony would take place.

"The ceremony can take place just after sunset," Ivy said. "The sky will transform into a brilliant watercolor, framing the couple as it evolves into a deep purple, starlit sky. Your photographer will have incredible shots."

"Absolutely mesmerizing," Rowan said, training his eyes on her.

Rowan's gaze made Ivy feel a little self-conscious. No other man had looked at her with such intensity in quite a few years. As she thought about it, his gaze reminded her of how Jeremy had once looked at her. Her husband told her that French men didn't hide their appreciation. *Why should they?* he'd said. Idly, Ivy wondered if Rowan had spent much time in France.

Caroline looked out over the scene. "While we won't have the view that we would have had from our home, the ocean is closer. I suppose it will do."

"We're lucky to have such a lovely venue on such short notice," Rowan said. Turning to Ivy, he added. "This setting is sublime. I'm surprised you weren't already booked."

"We've just opened as an inn," Ivy said.

Alain paced the length of the veranda, and

then paced off the pool. "We will put the *après* ceremony appetizer assortment there by the pool." He rattled off the assortment.

Caroline shook her perfectly coiffed head, although not a hair moved. "Darling, we talked about this. Remember what I said about the Roquefort. I will not have blue cheese in my sight. If I see it, I'm throwing it into the pool."

Ivy gulped. She'd confiscate the Roquefort herself if she had to. But it was not going in her clean pool.

Alain scowled, but ultimately he gave in. "Only for you, Carol, darling."

They looked around for a few more minutes, and then Caroline announced that they must leave.

"I'll see you out," Ivy said, walking to the front door with them.

In the foyer, Rowan paused and took Ivy's hand. "It's been an absolute pleasure," he said, never taking his eyes off hers as he brushed his lips across the back of her hand. "Your eyes light the shadowed pathway to my soul."

If Ivy were butter, she would have melted right there.

Caroline winked at her. "Ask which film that line is from."

Rowan gave Caroline a playful scowl. "Don't give away all my secrets." He kissed Ivy's cheek. "So refreshing, my dear."

After they left, Ivy turned back to Poppy and Shelly, who'd appeared on the stairway.

"Woo-hoo," Shelly said, doing a slow clap. "You have a new admirer. Way to sweep a man off his feet with an unforgettable entry."

"I thought I'd try something new," Ivy said, laughing. She waved off Shelly's comment. "Rowan is an actor. Clearly, he's used to occupying center stage." Still, he certainly knew how to fan the flames of a woman's heart.

"This wedding will create huge demand," Poppy said. "I love how you described the sunset wedding as a watercolor. I wrote it down, but can you check it? I'd like to use it on the website and in our marketing brochures."

"Sure," Ivy said. After a tumultuous start, she finally felt that she was easing into the role of an innkeeper. The wedding would be the ultimate test. Looking at Shelly and Poppy, she said, "I want you both to know how grateful I am to you."

"Well, you are paying us the big bucks," Shelly said, teasing. "At least in food, lodging, and location."

They'd all been forgoing the majority of the salaries they'd projected with their bookkeeper, who they'd engaged when it became clear that setting up even the simple accounting system wasn't in any of their wheelhouses.

"Soon, my lovelies, soon," Ivy said, throwing her arms around both of them. "There's no one

I'd rather have by my side on this wild adventure." Taking only what they needed, they were managing to keep the inn running. With most of the renovations behind them—except for the lower level—the rest of the summer's profits would chip away at the tax bill.

Shelly laughed. "Speaking of wild adventures, you should come out with us on the boat for the Light Parade."

"What about the party for the guests? I'm sure they'd be disappointed."

Shelly shrugged and turned up her palms. "Everyone has plans, Ives. Come with us. Mitch and Bennett need help decorating the boat."

Bennett hadn't said a word about that to her. But it wasn't as if they were dating. "Sure, if it's okay."

"Seriously?" Shelly gave her a look. "I'm sure it will be."

Poppy picked up a new dog treat on the entry table. "This must be Pixie's."

"I left it there earlier," Ivy said, taking it from her. "And yes, I'm resorting to bribery. I'll drop it off."

Poppy drew her eyebrows together. "Anything more on the..." she lowered her voice and glanced around. "Missing item?"

"Nothing, but I'm determined to find it," Ivy said, punctuating her words with the chew toy.

"That piece has a history, and it's important to someone. I feel like it's here somewhere."

Shelly squinted her eyes. "You think someone here has it? Or do you mean, misplaced?"

"I have no idea," Ivy said. "It's just a funny feeling I have." She didn't know how to explain the feelings that sent chills down her spine, but she'd learned to take note of them.

Lifting her pointy-scarf skirt, Ivy started up the stairs to deliver the chew toy. At least this had been an interesting break from washing and folding.

As she made her way down the hallway, Ivy could hear muted voices floating behind the doors she passed. The house had come alive around them, transformed from a cold, drafty place into an inn that was bubbling with laughter and vitality —and the occasional drama.

She paused in front of Gilda's door. Ivy understood how important Pixie was to Gilda. The poor woman seemed adrift and would be lonely without her little long-haired Chihuahua, but Ivy had to figure out how to gain control of the Pixie situation.

Ivy raised her hand to knock on Gilda's door.

"Come in," Gilda called out.

"I brought a chew toy for Pixie," Ivy said. "She's really been good lately. Where is she?"

Gilda pushed back from a writing desk where

she was working. "I put Pixie's bed and blanket behind the screen. She likes her privacy."

When Pixie emerged from behind the lacquered screen, Ivy held out the chew toy. The little Chihuahua sniffed it before eagerly grabbing it and racing back to her hideaway. Her little toenails tapped on the wooden floor, sounding like castanets.

"That was thoughtful," Gilda said. "Pixie is such good company. Losing everything has been overwhelming. I know she misbehaves, but I don't know what I would've done without her."

"I know how hard it is to have to part with cherished possessions," Ivy said. Even though possessions were mere objects, these items held memories for some and defined life for others. Perhaps for the latter kind of people, the loss from the fire had the greatest emotional impact.

"I've never *not* had anything," Gilda said. "It's been devastating. Imani's doing better than I am, but I think that's because she has Jamir."

"Shelly and Poppy and I are here for you," Ivy said. "So are others in Summer Beach." She hoped they could help ease Gilda's loss and others like her who'd lived on the ridgetop.

Ivy thought about how Bennett was taking his loss in stride. Perhaps because he'd once suffered the loss of a loved one, he had a different perspective.

From what Ivy had seen among her circle of

friends, people reacted to challenges and tragedies in their own way. Some who'd gone through difficulties turned bitter, while others gained a new, balanced perspective on the vagaries of life. She wasn't a counselor, but she knew that friends and human interaction helped.

"Would you like to join us by the pool this evening for a glass of wine or a cup of tea?" Ivy asked.

"That's kind of you. I usually hide up here and watch TV or read. Though maybe I will," Gilda said, smiling.

"The offer is always there. It's nice to gather at the end of the day with those you know or meet new people." Though Gilda was reclusive, she liked knowing other people were nearby. Ivy thought about a hotel in London that she and Jeremy had visited. Guests gathered in the parlor at the end of the day. She had an idea that she wanted to discuss with Shelly.

"Are you coming to the party this weekend?" Ivy asked. She hoped Gilda would attend.

Gilda's eyes lit up. "My brother has asked me to spend the weekend with them. I'm leaving in the morning."

"I'm happy for you," Ivy said. As she left Gilda and started toward the library, Ivy thought about how the guestlist for the party had rapidly dwindled. Everyone seemed to have plans.

With Independence Day nearly here, Ivy wondered what she would do. Although Shelly's invitation was there, Ivy was old school. Bennett should be the one extending the invitation. Or was that hopelessly old-fashioned today?

Still, what if Ivy went on board the boat with Shelly—only to find that Bennett had asked another woman along? Maybe that's why he hadn't mentioned anything. As Ivy thought about it, she really didn't know if he was dating anyone.

22

"I hope you have a relaxing weekend, and we look forward to welcoming you back," Ivy said to Celia, who was on her way to see her parents in San Francisco. She held the front door open for her. Outside, the sun was hovering low on the horizon as the day was drawing to a close.

"My mother wants me to stay in San Francisco," Celia said, swinging her long dark hair over her shoulder. "I have cousins visiting from China, so I'm tempted, but the children in Summer Beach would miss the summer music program. They're doing so well. And what if Tyler returns and I'm not here?"

"Do what's in your heart," Ivy said, though she wanted to say that it might serve him right— or at least wake him up. "This is between the two of you. But make sure you tell him how you feel—and what you expect of him in the future."

"Thanks. I'm giving this a lot of thought." Celia slung her designer canvas bag over her shoulder and stepped onto the front terrace.

Celia's husband still hadn't returned to Summer Beach, and Ivy could see the worry in her eyes. Ivy hoped he would be okay. With a small boat on the water, anything could happen, especially when the seas were rough. Ivy stepped outside beside her. "Are you worried about him?"

Celia nodded. "But Tyler finally checked in with his brother, so at least I know he's alive and still out on the boat. Or he was as of last week. Whatever he decides, I'm going to be okay. Really I will." With a shrug, Celia descended the stairs. "I'll see you soon." She rolled her matching bag beside her on the front path where they'd last seen Tyler.

Ivy watched Celia climb into an idling ride-share car and waved. Another older couple had already departed. As soon as some guests left, others were arriving.

Poppy had posted their new room availability online, and they had quickly filled the rooms for the long weekend. Jamir had finished painting the units in the servant's quarters—the Sunset rooms, they were now calling them—and Poppy had added those to their inventory. Ivy was surprised that two of those four rooms had already been booked.

As Ivy watched Celia depart, Shelly ambled up the path carrying an armful of creamy white flowers and greenery. Shelly waved, too. "Hope Celia has a good weekend and finds a big party up in San Francisco," Shelly said. "She needs to blow off some steam over that lousy Tyler."

"I kind of agree, but we should try to stay out of guest's personal business," Ivy said, even though it was hard to stand by and watch.

Shelly quirked up a side of her mouth. "I get that. It's not like we're sterling examples either, is it?"

"I think we're both doing much better," Ivy said, admiring the tall stalks of fragrant tuberose Shelly carried. She leaned in to inhale their sweet, heady aroma. "Gorgeous, but I know these didn't come from our garden."

"I stopped by Blossoms to say hello to Imani." Shelly went inside and began filling in the center table arrangement in the foyer with flowers. "Isn't the scent intoxicating? One stalk can perfume an entire room."

"Some of my favorites, too," Ivy said, following her inside.

Shelly fluffed the flowers. "When I admired the tuberose, Imani insisted I take them. Wouldn't allow me to pay for them. Maybe I'll grow some next year."

"Imani's very generous," Ivy said. She and Shelly had taken good care of Imani and Jamir, too. With his tall frame, Jamir was always hungry, so Shelly and Ivy made extra food for him when they cooked so he wouldn't have to go out to eat. Bennett often made sandwiches for him in his upstairs apartment in the rear. Jamir was like everyone's kid brother.

Shelly stepped back to check the bouquet and adjust the tuberose stalks. "Say, have you seen a rogue gardening glove around?"

"Did you leave it outside?" Ivy asked.

"One is right where I left them in the kitchen, on top of my gardening boots by the back door." Shelly ran a knuckle along her jawline. "But one is gone."

"Maybe you dropped it on the way in." Ivy scooped up a couple of leaves that dropped.

"You're probably right. Maybe a squirrel ran off with it. Or the ghost of Amelia Erickson is playing tricks on us."

Ivy shivered at the thought. "Don't let the guests hear you say that."

"Poppy lost a USC T-shirt," Shelly said. "Maybe we do have a ghost."

The thought had crossed Ivy's mind. She'd missed a couple of small items that weren't really important. A hair clasp, a favorite bookmark. Surely they'd turn up. Still, it made her wonder.

She pulled off another yellowed leaf. "I'm sure Poppy's T-shirt is in the laundry."

Shelly let the ghost topic go. "So are you coming out on the boat with us tomorrow?"

Ivy shrugged a shoulder. "I haven't received an invitation."

Bennett's rich, gravelly voice rang out behind them. "Do you want that engraved, or will a verbal invitation do?"

Ivy whirled around. "How dare you sneak up on me like that?" He'd caught her off guard, and she didn't know if it was that or the magical sound of his voice that sent her pulse pounding in her ears.

Bennett held his hands out. "You haven't answered my question."

"Depends on who is going," Ivy said, challenging him. If he'd invited another woman, how would she feel about that? She held her breath, waiting. And hoping she was wrong.

"Mitch and Shelly. Me. And I hope you, too." Bennett nodded his head in an apology. "I just heard that you canceled the party. With Shelly going, I thought you knew you were welcome." He took another step toward her.

Shelly perked up. "That's what I told her."

"I didn't want to assume," Ivy said lightly. "How did you know I'd canceled the party?"

Bennett gestured over his shoulder. "Poppy posted it on the activity board. Along with the news of the new honor bar in the music room. That's a nice touch."

"Thanks," Ivy said, easily accepting his compliment. With each passing day, she was growing more confident of her decisions at the inn. "And I would like to join you. I love being on the water." *It's so romantic*, she almost added, but she stopped herself.

"This will be an amazing night." A smile played on Bennett's lips as he held her gaze. "I have some special things planned."

Bennett's eyes sparked a feeling of pleasure that rippled through her body. "What shall we bring?" Though she tried to keep her composure, there was no denying the connection with Bennett. Did he feel it, too?

"Only yourself," he said, his words conveying more than was said.

"Told you." Shelly smothered a grin and focused on the flowers.

Behind them, Poppy cleared her throat, breaking the spell between Ivy and Bennett. "You won't believe the call that just came in."

With reluctance, Ivy turned toward Poppy. "Problem?"

"I hope not." Poppy glanced down at a pad she held. "A woman named Debra is checking in soon. You'll never guess who referred her."

"Darla," Shelly said, chuckling.

Poppy's eyes grew wide. "How did you know?"

"Actually, I was kidding." Shelly clamped a hand over her mouth.

"Is this a set-up?" Ivy frowned.

"That's Darla's sister." Bennett stroked his chin. "I've met Debra, but it was a long time ago. She didn't strike me as that type. Maybe she just needs a room."

Ivy frowned. "But why wouldn't she stay at Darla's home?"

"I got the impression they're pretty different," Bennett replied.

"You're awfully diplomatic." Shelly jabbed her hands onto her hips. "Maybe because Darla is a b—"

"Shh," Ivy said, lowering her voice. Guests were making their way into the music room, where Poppy had set up a table with complimentary tea and coffee, apples and grapes, and cheese and crackers and cookies. Ivy and Shelly had stocked a cabinet with wine and spirits, along with a modest suggested price list for those and a bowl for people to leave whatever cash they wanted.

"I think your idea is going over well," Poppy said.

"Let's go welcome everyone and mingle," Ivy said, noticing that people were beginning to chat and introduce themselves. Between the yoga and painting class, beach walks, and Celia's student musicians, the Seabreeze Inn atmosphere was feeling more and more like a welcoming haven to relax and rejuvenate. The sound of soothing piano music from one of Celia's protégées, a teenaged boy who lived in the neighborhood, was already filling the house.

"May I escort the proprietor?" Bennett offered Ivy the crook of his arm.

"One of them," Ivy said, smiling at Shelly. She appreciated this lovely gesture. Ivy slid her hand over his arm, enjoying being close to him. Local residents might notice, but she figured this might be a subtle beginning.

Shelly and Poppy followed them into the music room, which also opened onto the terrace. Soon guests were sipping wine or sparkling water, chatting, and sharing their holiday plans. The cool evening breeze and the beautiful music seemed to put everyone at ease.

After saying a few words of welcome and making suggestions for restaurants and places to visit, Ivy watched as locals circled Bennett to talk about city issues. Ivy stepped aside. He was their mayor, after all, and they had important business to discuss. She went outside on the terrace to join Shelly. The setting sun cast a pinkish glow over the small gathering that was spilling outside around the pool.

"Look at this happy crowd," Shelly said, sipping a glass of wine. "You've done an amazing job with this place."

Ivy nudged Shelly's shoulder. "Couldn't have done it without you and Poppy."

Shelly took in their surroundings—the grand old house, the pool, the ocean. "Think we're going to make it here?"

"I *know* we will." Ivy spoke with confidence. However, though the summer was well underway, Ivy also knew that a lot could still happen. Yet she was determined that they would not be deterred.

"As long as Carol Reston's wedding party goes well, we'll be on track," Ivy said. *To pay the back property taxes and have a little left over for the winter.* Although she didn't say it, Shelly caught her meaning.

"We'll come through this," Shelly whispered.

"I'll do everything in my power to make sure we do."

"Even if it means cavorting with the mayor?"

"I am hardly *cavorting* with the mayor." Ivy laughed at her sister's use of the word.

"Speaking of that, I kind of miss New York, this time of year," Shelly said, sounding homesick for the city. "I know we'll have a good time tomorrow, but New York this time of year was always special. There's nothing like being among thousands of people watching the most amazing fireworks over the East River." She waved a hand across the skyline as she spoke. "Last year, a 1,600-foot-long waterfall of fireworks burst between the towers of the Brooklyn Bridge. It was spectacular."

"Sounds incredible," Ivy said. "Summer Beach can't compare with that." Shelly had always been drawn to the excitement of New York, but she hadn't been happy there for a while. "Your life is better here, don't you think?"

"Is it?" Shelly seemed to mull this point over as she watched their guests becoming more animated. Nodding inside, she added, "I just hope that none of our guests snatched the crown jewel."

"Me, too," Ivy said softly. What if one of them had?

23

The next morning, Ivy and Shelly prepared a red, white, and blue Independence Day brunch with their signature Sea Breeze cocktails. They also served blueberry and cranberry muffins from Java Beach, along with vanilla and cherry yogurt with granola. The guests soon left in a flurry of flip-flops and beach hats to go to the beach or visit friends and have barbecues.

Although Bennett and Mitch hadn't asked them to bring anything, Ivy and Shelly still packed a picnic basket for the boat. Ivy tucked in an assortment of cheeses, along with homemade rosemary crisps Shelly had mastered.

"I'm adding strawberries, mandarin oranges, grapes, avocados, and cherry tomatoes," Ivy said, making room for the fruits and vegetables. She'd been shopping at the weekly farmer's market, where she was enjoying getting to know the local vendors who had farms near Summer Beach. "Anything else?"

"Honestly, as long as we have sunscreen, wine, and a corkscrew, I'm happy," Shelly said.

Just then, Bennett opened the back door to the kitchen. "That looks incredible. And a lot better than the sandwiches Mitch said he's bringing."

"Better to have plenty to share," Ivy said.

"In case we drift off and get stranded on a desert isle." Shelly grinned as she rolled up napkins.

"I'll take that for you," Bennett said, lifting the wicker basket with ease. He cast an appreciative glance at them. "You both look great."

"Thanks," Ivy said. She had worn a navy-and-white striped French T-shirt with navy clam digger pants and deck shoes, while Shelly had opted for a bright blue sundress with a flowing ruffled skirt and rubber-soled sandals. "You look ready to get on the water yourself."

Bennett wore a loose white shirt and light blue shorts with well-worn deck shoes. Nothing fancy, just relaxed and comfortable. His cropped hair had light sun streaks.

Ivy smiled to herself. She liked his look.

Gathering their essentials, along with sun visors, Ivy and Shelly followed Bennett to the SUV.

As they climbed into the car, Ivy admired how

Shelly's strappy dress showed off her toned arms, which Ivy still hoped for. *Or maybe not*, she thought. She and her sister really were built differently. The older Ivy became, the more accepting of her body she had become. She'd never be tall and model thin, but as long as she was healthy and reasonably fit, she decided she'd be fine with that. After all she'd been through, comfortable was good enough for her now.

When they reached the marina, they parked. Mitch waved them down and helped Shelly from the back seat of the SUV. "Wow," he said, admiring Shelly's outfit—or more accurately, the way she wore it. "You look gorgeous," he said, giving her a quick kiss on the cheek.

"Oh, thanks." Shelly looked surprised and even blushed a little.

Bennett brought out the picnic basket and carried it with one hand, while he took Ivy's hand with the other. He leaned toward her. "Is this okay?"

"It's nice," Ivy said. "As long as you don't mind all the people around."

"I don't if you don't," Bennett said, glancing around. "This is the busiest holiday of the year here."

Ivy squeezed his hand in answer. It was as if he were making an announcement that they were together.

The marina was crowded, at least for Summer

Beach. Lots of locals—Ivy was beginning to recognize more people—milled around greeting out-of-town guests and family members who'd come to Summer Beach for the Light Parade on the water.

As they started down the walkway to the boat, people stopped to speak to Bennett and Mitch. It took them quite a while to walk the short distance, but they were with the mayor and the owner of one of Summer Beach's most popular hangouts.

Arthur and Nan waved from the deck of one decorated boat, while Jen and George waved from another one, along with Imani and Jamir. Red, white, and blue ribbons festooned the boats, and flags waved in the breeze. The party atmosphere was infectious.

"Seems like everyone in town is here," Ivy said. She saw more than one person do a double-take upon seeing her and Bennett together.

"Word that the mayor is holding hands with a new woman is bound to travel fast," Bennett said, squeezing her hand.

"Kind of a big step, isn't it?"

Bennett brushed a stray strand of hair from her eyes. "I couldn't be prouder. I'm the luckiest guy here."

Ivy nodded at Shelly and Mitch in front of them. "Mitch might argue that point."

"We're both lucky." The light in his eyes

matched the brilliance of the afternoon sun. With their flecks of green and amber, Ivy thought he had the most magnetic hazel eyes she'd ever seen.

"Here we are." Bennett stopped by a large cabin cruiser. Teakwood accents gleamed against pristine white. Lights were stretched from bow to stern and from port to starboard. "Wait until the sun sets. The lights are amazing. We'll join the water parade then. It starts near a neighboring yacht club, and we'll cruise the coastline."

They all made themselves comfortable. Bennett took the wheel, and soon they were underway, heading out to open waters.

Ivy lifted her face to the breeze, loving the feeling of the light salty spray misting her face. "This reminds me of when we used to go out with our parents when we were kids."

"Growing up by the ocean sure had its advantages," Bennett said. "My sister Kendra and I did the same. We learned to sail when we were pretty young."

Ivy turned around to look at Shelly and saw her sister nestled in the crook of Mitch's arm. They were both laughing and seemed incredibly happy, and Ivy was pleased for them.

At once, a vision of the future opened in Ivy's mind. Bennett and Mitch, spending weekends on the boat. *This could be our new lives.*

But it was too soon to have such thoughts. Ivy

blinked, banishing the thought from her mind. *Enjoy the day*, she told herself. *Just enjoy the moment.*

Ivy tipped her head up again and breathed in the fresh salt air.

"Dolphin pod at two o'clock," Mitch called out.

Bennett eased off the throttle. They bobbed in the water as they watched the magnificent creatures. "Let's drop anchor here."

Ivy and Shelly brought out the picnic they'd packed, and Mitch brought out the sandwiches he'd made.

"What are these?" Shelly asked. "They look yummy."

Mitch grinned. "I used your bread recipe. Spread slices with olive oil and pesto, added tomatoes, scallions, and thin-sliced, seared albacore tuna. Then I put the sandwiches into a Panini grill."

"Impressive," Bennett said, grinning. He put on music, and they all kicked off their shoes and sat on the deck eating, basking in the sun, and watching the dolphins and whales swimming past. The water lapped against the hull, gently rocking the boat.

"I could stay out here and watch for hours," Mitch said. "Out here, all the issues and problems of the day vanish, at least for a while. When you return, you see everything with a better perspective."

Shelly leaned against Mitch, and he kissed the top of her forehead.

Ivy gave Shelly a smile. She hadn't seen her sister this happy in ages, and she was delighted for her. Maybe this relationship would work out well for her. Mitch seemed absolutely smitten with Shelly. He was watching every movement she made.

Bennett touched Ivy's hand. "How're you doing?"

"Never better," she said.

"Want to go up on the bow?"

"Sure," she said, taking his hand, which felt steady and firm in hers.

After they sat next to each other, Bennett reached into his pocket. A smile tugged at his lips. "I was running on the beach the other day, and I saw something sparkling in the sand."

"What's that?"

Bennett brought out a small ruby and diamond ring encrusted with tiny seed pearls.

Ivy's lips parted in surprise. "Amelia's ring. You found it!"

"I couldn't believe it. But there it was—as if it were waiting for me to find it and take it home." He slipped it onto her pinkie finger.

"This ring must have meant a lot to her," Ivy said, admiring it. "I'm so glad to see it again."

They reclined and held hands, listening to music and the lapping water and watching gulls soar overhead. Occasionally one of them pointed out another boat, or fish jumping through the waves, but mostly they were simply comfortable together. Bennett asked her about Misty and Sunny, and Ivy told him how proud she was of them—even Sunny, who was having a hard time adjusting to her father's death. And Bennett told her all about Kendra and Dave and Logan.

As the sun began sinking toward the horizon, Bennett turned the boat back toward the coastline.

Soon Bennett waved at friends in nearby boats, and they fell in line together. The sun set, casting a burnished brilliance across the waves.

"I'd like to capture this image," Ivy said, watching the boats. "It's an interesting perspective."

"You want to paint it?" Bennett asked.

"That's right," she said, appreciating his perceptiveness. She pulled out her phone to take a few snaps before settling back to enjoy it all.

As dusk encroached, Mitch plugged in the strands of light, surrounding them with the sweet enchantment of fairy lights. Lights on nearby boats flickered on, too. Some were blazing with brilliance, while others merely twinkled in the night.

"What fun," Shelly said as she gazed back at the line of boats behind them.

"I just love this." Standing next to Bennett, Ivy waved as they cruised by Summer Beach. They were close enough to the shore to see people waving back at them. Bonfires dotted the beaches, and the lights from houses shone like stars. Laughter rippled across the waves from other boats.

Ivy admired the beauty of the lights wavering on the water. *I'll paint this,* she decided, snapping a few more photos with her phone.

All at once, fireworks whizzed straight up into the night sky from the beach and exploded over them. Ivy tipped her head back, mesmerized. The canopy of sky overhead dazzled with sparkling explosions of red, white, and blue. As fireworks popped in the night, a sweet burning smell filled the air. Ivy watched as tiny embers disintegrated before reaching the water.

"This is truly magical." Ivy was enjoying every moment, even if she was shivering slightly in the cool evening breeze.

Bennett draped his jacket across her shoulders. "Better?"

"Much," she said. "Do you remember the first time you ever gave me your jacket?"

Chuckling, he said, "I sure do. It was when you were looking at the house for the first time, and when we walked into Amelia's bedroom where it always seems cooler, you shivered. For days I could detect your perfume on the collar of that jacket."

Bennett put his arm around her, and she leaned into the warmth of his torso, still watching the fireworks around them.

"I'm impressed you remember that." Ivy recalled every moment of that day, too, only she had been anxious to get away from him. How her feelings toward him had changed in just a few weeks. Now, this felt so right. "But that's not the time I was referring to."

"No? When?"

"Years ago. We were sitting around a bonfire, just like those people on the beach—a lot of them are probably teenagers, just like we were. I was cold, and you gave me your hoodie. And then you began playing your guitar. I've never forgotten that. You almost didn't get your sweatshirt back."

Bennett stared at her with amazement. "I can't believe you remember that night. That was one of my favorite memories, too. But for some reason, I remembered you as a blond. That's why I had a hard time placing you at first."

"You're right." She laughed. "That was my ultra-blond summer. I had a deep tan, too. I looked like a Hawaiian Tropic model, or I thought I did." She didn't mention the twenty-five fewer pounds.

"I like the way you look now." Bennett fell

silent for a moment, and then he added, "Think about how much time we let slip by."

"We had other lives to live," Ivy said, thinking about Jeremy and the girls. She figured he was thinking about Jackie.

"And now it's our turn again." He brought up her hand and kissed her palm as brilliant fireworks lit the night sky around them with dazzling jewels of color. "Let's not let anything get in the way of us again."

"That's a beautiful sentiment," she said, pressing his hand to her heart. "Let's just see how we go. This time, we have all the time in the world. Let's not rush it."

If Bennett were disappointed, he hid it well. "As you wish," he said, kissing her cheek. "I'm not going anywhere."

When they reached the end of the water parade, and the fireworks ended, Bennett turned back toward Summer Beach and tucked her hand into his. They took their time cruising back, watching the beach bonfires dying down as people wrapped up their parties. Smoke from the fireworks smudged the night sky. The moon illuminated the velvet expanse, which was pinpricked with a blanket of stars.

Ivy looked over at Shelly and Mitch, who were deeply ensconced in conversation. When Shelly saw her glance their way, she led Mitch to where Bennett and Ivy were.

"This is so awesome," Shelly said, excitement bubbling in her voice. "I captured a lot on video for a special vlog. Mitch gave me some fresh angles and insights, too."

By the time they returned to the marina, other people ahead of them had already pulled into their boat slips. The party atmosphere was dying down.

Bennett steered the boat into his slip, and Mitch stepped out to tie it up.

Mitch helped Shelly off, and then he picked up the picnic basket. "We'll get rid of the trash on the way back." With their arms draped around each other, Mitch and Shelly strolled off into the night.

Ivy watched them meander along the dock and smiled. "I'm really happy for them."

"So am I," Bennett said. "Seems like they both deserve someone good in their life."

The lights on the boat next to them still glowed, casting a soft light over them. Bennett turned to Ivy and slid his arm around her waist. "Being with you today meant a lot to me. I want you to know that."

"I enjoyed it, too," Ivy replied, looping her arms around his neck for balance as the boat swayed with the gently lapping waves. She rested her head against him, feeling the steady rise and fall of his chest. *This feels so right.* A little shiver coursed through her, though she was plenty warm in his arms.

Stroking her back, Bennett said, "We can come out on the boat any time you'd like with or without Mitch and Shelly. It's such a feeling of freedom, being away from everyone, away from Summer Beach gossip." He pulled back and lifted her chin. "Which, after tonight, you *will* hear. Are you ready for that?"

In his eyes, she saw strength and compassion…and something more. "Bring it on," she said chuckling.

Bennett bent down and grazed her forehead with his lips. "You set the pace, Ivy. I'll be here."

"Thank you for understanding," she said, feathering her lips across his for a brief moment before pulling away with reluctance. "Let's catch up with Shelly and Mitch."

Bennett helped her off the boat, and they strolled across the weathered wooden deck. At the end of the walkway stood Shelly and Mitch, along with two familiar figures. Poppy…and—

Ivy broke into a run. "Misty!" She wrapped her arms around her eldest daughter and rocked her back and forth. "I'm so glad to see you! Why didn't you let me know you were coming?"

"I wanted it to be a surprise," Misty said. "I thought I'd get in earlier, but my flight connection was delayed. I called Poppy, and she picked me up."

Poppy trailed her cousin. "I was on my way to L.A. when Misty called. She made me promise not to tell you."

"This is so exciting. But what about the play?" Ivy asked. "Is it still on?"

"Of course, and the run has been extended," Misty replied. "We just had a break for the holiday. Since I had an extra day off, I thought I'd come to see you." A curious expression crossed her face as her attention shifted toward Bennett.

Ivy could almost feel the questions that Misty had for her bursting from her mind. Ivy turned toward Bennett and held out a hand to him.

"I want you to meet a friend of mine, Bennett Dylan. The mayor of Summer Beach." Ivy smiled. "He takes a keen interest in everything here in town, and he's been such a help to us."

"I can see that," Misty said, greeting him with a quick smile and heightened curiosity. "I mean, the Summer Beach Light Parade, the bonfires and beach party—everything was such fun. Poppy showed me around."

Ivy realized Misty must have seen them on the boat or strolling hand in hand along the walkway. Her pulse quickened. She hadn't planned to share this relationship, as new as it was, with her daughters yet. But there would be no denying it to Misty.

Her daughter looked pleasantly surprised, not at all as taken aback by this unexpected development as Ivy would have thought. However, if it had been Sunny standing at the end of the dock instead, Ivy was sure there would have been an explosion to rival the fireworks, but Misty was simply surprised and intrigued.

Or as a trained actress, was Misty merely hiding her feelings well?

24

*E*arly the next morning, Bennett rose with the sun, feeling great. As he laced up his running shoes, he thought about Ivy. Being with her yesterday had been a rare treat. Out on the open water, away from the inn and the community. She filled his heart with such hope and light. That was how he saw her smile—like a beam of sunshine warming the cold, darkened corners of his heart. A heart that had lain dormant for so many years.

After a brisk run on the beach, he joined the rest of the guests in the dining room, although he could've had breakfast in his apartment over the garage. He liked being part of the surrogate family that was developing at the inn. The vacationers came and went—and they were interesting, too—but the core group of neighbors who'd landed here after the fire had become even closer.

Having an extra day off felt like an eternity to him, but City Hall was closed, and he didn't have any real estate clients this weekend. Everyone had taken off for the holiday.

He sauntered into the dining room, which Ivy and Shelly had set up for breakfast. Mitch supplied fresh muffins, which were tucked into linen-lined baskets next to coffee and tea. Yogurt sat on ice, and fruit filled another basket.

"Morning, Mayor," Imani said as she poured a cup of coffee. She had on one of her brightly colored tie-dyed sundresses that she favored. "Quite the fireworks show last night. Have a good evening?"

"Best Fourth of July I've had in years." Bennett picked out a cup of cherry yogurt.

"So it seems." Imani gave him a wink and lowered her voice. "Just so you know, I think it's great."

"What's that?" Bennett acted like he had no idea what she was talking about, just to play with her.

She nudged him. "Come on, Ben. How long have we been friends?" She angled her chin toward the arched doorway to the dining room, where Ivy had just appeared with her daughter.

Bennett grinned. "Word travels fast in

Summer Beach. Join me?" Grabbing an orange, he slid into a chair at a table.

Balancing her coffee, Imani eased into a chair next to him. "Saw you and Ivy holding hands at the marina. Didn't take a rocket scientist to figure it out."

"Think anyone else noticed?" He raised his eyebrows in an innocent look. He'd purposefully planned it that way. If he were dedicating himself to Ivy for a long-term courtship—*what an old-fashioned word*, he thought, *but it fits*—he didn't want any competition. He was willing to take it slow, but he was insuring his position. Maybe that was a strategic move, but strategy and long-term planning were also what made him a good mayor.

Imani sputtered in her coffee. "You might as well have announced it on the steps of City Hall. But I think it's sweet." She glanced at Ivy again. "Is that a new guest with her?"

"It's her daughter. Misty. She's an actress in Boston."

"Does she know about you two?" Imani whispered.

He grinned. "Hate to disappoint you, but there isn't much to know about."

She rolled her eyes. "Oh, this is going to get interesting." Imani chuckled. "I'll keep watching. We have our own little reality show right here in Summer Beach."

"Stop," he said, nudging her back. They had

long-running jokes between them. "Shouldn't you be out selling flowers?"

"They'll keep. Everyone sleeps in the day after a holiday." Imani paused. "Did you know that Darla's sister checked into the inn last night?"

"Ivy mentioned it. Have you met her?"

"I haven't, but I'll try to," Imani said. "Maybe she could influence Darla to back off on her lawsuits."

"I met her on a prior visit. She and Darla seem to have different temperaments."

Imani sipped her coffee, taking in the information. "Debra isn't staying with Darla, so that might be a sign. I'll talk to Ivy and Shelly to see what I can find out."

Bennett watched Ivy as she took Misty around the dining room to meet other guests. Misty was a younger version of her mother, though she stood a little taller. With her large, expressive eyes and air of confidence, it was easy to imagine her being on stage. When Misty saw Bennett, her face lit up and she waved.

Bennett lifted his hand in a wave back to her.

After returning to the inn last night, they'd all gathered around the fire pit and talked. He and Ivy, Mitch and Shelly, and Poppy and Misty. Misty had spoken with enthusiasm about the new theater production, and she seemed to take to him. Though he'd made sure to keep his distance from Ivy, and Ivy didn't make any moves toward him in front of Misty. *Plenty of time for that.* He and Mitch had turned in early to give Ivy and Shelly time to catch up with Misty in private.

Ivy's professional demeanor was firmly in place this morning around all the guests. She nodded at him with a slight smile as she approached the table beside her daughter.

"Good morning," Ivy said. She introduced Misty to Imani. "If you need flowers or legal advice, Imani can help you. You'll meet her son Jamir soon, too. Dr. Jamir, one day." They chatted for a few minutes before Imani rose from the table.

"I'm off to open Blossoms," Imani said. "Say, has anyone seen a purple silk scarf? I thought I left it downstairs in the music room yesterday."

"Poppy probably picked it up," Ivy said. "I'll ask her."

"Well, I'd better be off," Imani said. "Those flowers can't ring themselves up." She grinned at Bennett again before she left.

Bennett turned to Ivy and Misty. "Hate to leave you, but I've got errands today. And an old Chevy to finish putting together."

"You've done so much work on that car," Ivy said. "I can't tell you how much I appreciate that. Can I at least pay you for parts?"

Misty looked between them. "What old Chevy?"

Ivy told her about the vintage car, and Misty's

eyes grew even larger. "I would love to check that out later."

Bennett promised to show it to Misty. The car wasn't ready yet, and he wanted Ivy to have the first ride in it. "It will be ready soon. Another couple of weeks, I'd say." He caught Ivy's eye, and they shared a brief, private moment.

Poppy made her way to the table and touched Misty's arm. "Ready when you are."

Misty swung around to her mother. "Mom, we'll be at the main beach. Come out with us."

Ivy hugged her daughter. "I might, but I have a lot of work to catch up on today. You two go. Have a good time. And no hassling the cute life-guard. I hear he's got a girlfriend."

"Thanks, Mom, loves ya." Misty kissed Ivy's cheek and dashed off arm in arm with Poppy.

"Would you like to join me?" Bennett asked.

"I need another coffee," Ivy said. "Misty kept me up late last night talking."

"I'll get it," Bennett said. "Cream, right?"

Ivy nodded and eased into a chair.

When Bennett returned, she was checking her phone.

"Oh, my goodness," she exclaimed, pressing her hand against her chest.

Placing the coffee in front of her, he asked, "What's up?"

She lowered the phone. "I've got a message from Ari. He got a hit on—well, you know what."

She glanced around. "I need to tell Shelly about this. You have to hear it, too. Come with me?" She sprang from the chair and picked up her coffee cup.

"Sure." His curiosity piqued, he followed her from the dining room. He loved watching Ivy, and he was so proud of her for the job she was doing here at the inn. Though he'd been skeptical that she and Shelly could pull it off, they had fortunately proven him wrong. In just a few weeks, the Seabreeze Inn was securing its place in the fabric of Summer Beach—and Ivy was stealing his heart.

They found Shelly in the kitchen clipping flowers for arrangements.

Ivy closed the door behind them. "Shelly, I just heard from Ari about our discovery."

Shelly swung around. "You mean, about the *jewels*?"

"Shh, yes."

"Listen to this." Ivy perched on a stool at the counter and read from her phone. "The FBI case had been closed, but he believes these are part of a vast jewel collection that was stolen in 1946." She looked up at Shelly. "Remember what I told you about Megan?"

Shelly started bouncing at the counter, and flower petals burst like a shower around her.

Ivy turned to Bennett. "Three U.S. military personnel were imprisoned for a major jewel theft in Germany right after World War II. They discovered a cache of jewels that a royal family had hidden for safekeeping."

"And you think this is part of that?" Bennett asked.

"I'd mentioned the possible connection to Ari, and he investigated. Megan found some details about the Ericksons. Amelia was born in Berlin but married and moved away after the First World War. She also knew Peter Carl Fabergé and Marlene Dietrich. Anyway, I'd asked Megan if she knew of any high profile jewel thefts—just in conversation—and she mentioned one. Ari followed the trail, and here we are." She held out her phone. "He sent old photos and paintings of the Hesse family members wearing certain pieces."

Shelly and Bennett peered at the small screen as Ivy scrolled through them.

As Ivy came to one, she and Shelly both exclaimed. "That's it," Ivy said.

"The tiara," Shelly added. "The *missing* tiara."

"How are we going to explain that," Ivy said, passing a hand over her face. "You do know how this looks, don't you?"

Bennett did. But he wasn't as worried about Ivy and Shelly as he was about Mitch. They didn't have a criminal record that was closely tied to this type of theft. He let out a long sigh. He wanted to believe Mitch, and everything he'd seen his younger friend accomplish since he'd landed in

Summer Beach indicated that he was on the straight path now, but any law enforcement officer would look at Mitch with suspicion if he were anywhere close to such a theft or disappearance. Did he know Mitch as well as he thought? He believed he did.

"Has anything else gone missing around here?" Bennett asked. "Except for Imani's missing scarf, that is." She'd probably misplaced it, or another guest would turn it in. Still, he remembered it, and it was probably an expensive scarf.

Ivy shook her head. "Nothing besides the odd tennis ball or dryer sock. Well, unless you count a hair clasp or bookmark. Nothing of value."

"Couple of my running socks disappeared." Bennett grinned. "Guess they ran off with different mates."

Shelly tapped her chin in thought. "I think it's the ghost of Amelia Erickson, tidying up her house. I've heard that can really happen."

"No," Ivy said. "I told you we can't let that rumor out or have guests thinking this place is haunted. They'd be too scared to sleep."

Shelly nodded. "Okay, so if the case is closed, then what do we do with the jewelry?"

"The case will have to be reopened, I suppose," Ivy said. "Those jewels are not ours to keep."

Shelly threw up her hands in frustration. "Just

one of those pieces could remove that boulder of debt from your shoulder."

Ivy shook her head. "Once we have this inn with positive cash flow—more coming in than going out—I can probably get a loan to pay it off."

Bennett shook his head. "If you're in arrears and in danger of losing the property to a tax fore-closure sale, getting any kind of loan will be tough. It's high risk, and taxes take priority. No one wants a mess to sort out if they can lend on another property instead."

Ivy sat up and glared at Shelly. "We *will* make this inn successful. Look at it," she said, waving an arm around the kitchen. "We're doing it now. I've run the cash flow out and estimated the operating expenses. We're going to make it, and there is no reason to take what's not ours."

Shelly sank her head into her hands. "You're always right. It's just so tempting to solve our problems all at once."

"Ivy's right. Have some patience, Shelly." It wasn't really his position to intervene, but he wanted to show Ivy support. Not that she needed it. She was standing up to Shelly just fine.

Bennett knew how much Ivy could use the help, and he admired her all the more for her po-sition. Many people would take the easy way out.

Ivy picked up her phone again. "Unfortunately, we still don't know how Amelia was involved."

"Ha. Up to her neck, I'd say." Shelly made a face. "She was clearly dealing in stolen goods. That heist made huge headlines at the time. Of course Amelia knew what she had." She jabbed a finger in the air. "And that will make Megan's documentary even better. People love to hear about bad guys—a lot more than good guys. Maybe we could sell the movie rights for a big blockbuster."

"I don't believe Amelia was buying stolen property," Ivy said, flattening her hands on the counter. "At least not for herself. My guess is that she was holding valuables for other people, and in this case, we know exactly who she might been buying it for. We have to prove she was innocent."

"We don't *have* to do anything," Shelly said, her eyes flashing. "What we *need* to do is tear this place apart and see what else she might have hidden."

"What a waste of time," Ivy said. "What we need to do is make this inn successful. *That's* our business, not treasure hunting."

"That still leaves the tiara unaccounted for." Shelly shook her hands in another attempt. "Come on, who's to know?"

Ivy glared at Shelly. "I've already sent *all* the photos to Ari."

"Then you better find that tiara," Shelly said, folding her arms.

A sudden thought struck Bennett. Was he suspecting the wrong person? What if it weren't Mitch, but Shelly who had conveniently misplaced the tiara? Ivy wouldn't want to hear that, of course. On the other hand, if that were the case, could Shelly have taken Mitch into her confidence? The two of them had grown awfully close. Was Mitch in danger?

Bennett slid his hand over Ivy's, and she turned her lovely smile his way, making his heart ache. As mayor, he couldn't allow himself to be exposed to any illegal or underhanded activities. Although he cared for Ivy, a scandal could tarnish his reputation, career, and standing in the community—and even implicate him as an accessory. Was Ivy worth this risk?

25

The next morning, Ivy walked along the water's edge with Misty, enjoying time with her daughter before the Reston wedding later in the day. Misty was telling her all about the theater play and the excellent reviews she'd received. Occasionally they paused to pick up an unusual shell or watch a gull dive into the surf for a fish.

"Have you checked in for your flight back to Boston tomorrow?" Ivy asked.

"Just before we left the house." Misty placed her arm over her mother's shoulder. "Wish I could stay longer, but now that I have a lead, I have a big responsibility."

"You're welcome anytime for as long as you want to stay," Ivy said, hugging her daughter. "This is our home now, even though we share it with others. Maybe it's not what we imagined, but this house has opened a new chapter in my life."

"I really came to see how you were doing, Mom, and I'm happy this is working out for you. You always loved organizing our summer holidays on Nantucket, and this is sort of like that. And it's been great to see Nana and Gramps and all the cousins."

The day before, Ivy had called her parents to tell them about Misty's visit, so Carlotta and Sterling threw together an impromptu family lunch at the house, inviting Flint and Forrest and all their children to see Misty. Ivy's parents were also preparing for their long ocean voyage in the spring, and Misty had been fascinated by their level of detail. Plus, she'd had the chance to hang out with Poppy's sisters, Summer and Coral, and her brothers Reed and Rocky. Flint and Tabitha were there with their children: Skyler, Blue, Jewel, and Sierra. Even Honey's daughter Elena took the train from Los Angles to see her.

Ivy kept her arm around Misty as they walked. "I'm really proud of the way you're handling your career. Acting can be tough."

"I'm determined." Misty slid a glance toward her mother. "So what's the deal with the mayor, Mom?"

Ivy had been waiting for Misty to ask this question. They'd been so busy since her arrival that they hadn't had a chance to talk.

"At this point, Bennett is just a friend." Which was true, but Ivy was treading carefully. She wanted to hear her daughter's feelings first.

"Looked like a little more than that. You were holding hands, and I saw you in each other's arms on the boat."

"Well, we like each other. And that holding hands bit is new. We're taking it very slowly."

Misty took a few moments to digest this. "Do you think you might marry again?"

Ivy stopped and turned to her daughter, taking her hands. "You know I loved your father very much, and it's been hard adjusting to his absence. While I'm not avidly looking for his replacement, Bennett just happened along. I'd met him briefly years ago when I was younger than you are. He's a good man, but I'm not rushing into anything."

"It's hard to picture you with anyone else," Misty said. "Even though I've seen the house now, I still can't believe you've really moved for good. It seems like you're away on vacation, and you'll be back in Boston sometime soon."

Ivy glanced back at the inn. "As you can see, I'm here to stay."

"I understand, I really do. But Sunny..." Misty shook her head. "She says you have a new life here, and it doesn't include us anymore."

Sunny's words tore at Ivy's heart. First and foremost, she was a mother, and her life would always include her children. "Running an inn in

Summer Beach isn't what I'd ever planned on," she said gently. "But life doesn't always comply with our plans."

"I get it. And what Dad did wasn't right. Not telling you about the house. He was my dad, but if I were married and my husband ever did that with our money, I'd be plenty upset." She took a breath. "I still loved him, though."

"And so did I. He will always have a piece of our hearts. No one will ever replace him." As conflicted as she was over Jeremy, he had been a loving father to the girls, even if he had spoiled them a little too much. But his exuberance was part of who he had been. And another woman had found that attractive, too. Ivy could hold a grudge, which would serve no purpose whatsoever now, or let it all go.

"Not even Bennett?"

"Darling, we have the capacity to love more than one person in our lifetime. I can't foresee the future with Bennett, but I am still a young woman. Forty-five might seem old to you now, but I promise you it isn't. I'm not yet half as old as my grandmother was when she passed away. I hope I still have a lot of living to do."

"That's an interesting way of looking at it." Misty nodded in thought. "I was just surprised when I saw you with Bennett."

"What do you think of him?"

"He's cool, I guess. He really listens to people.

And he has total goo-goo eyes for you. Without being all mushy about it." Misty grinned. "And he doesn't dress *too* bad for a guy his age."

Ivy laughed at Misty's assessment. "I appreciate your input."

"Think you'll date other guys, too?"

"I haven't thought that far ahead, but I suppose I wouldn't rule out the idea." As much as she liked Bennett, a lot could happen. And there was plenty she didn't know about him. She'd never seen him angry or frustrated. Did he have bad habits? Was he a closet gambler? She didn't think so, but after trusting Jeremy for so many years only to find that he'd led a double life, she was hesitant now.

And certainly more discriminating.

Misty hugged her. "Dad's death was hard on you, but look at you now. I never thought I'd see you running a business. And if you want to date, I think that's okay, too. Just don't tell us the *details*, okay?"

"Thanks, sweetie." Misty's words meant a lot to her. "This last year, I've had to paint an entirely new picture for myself."

Misty fell in step beside her again. "Do you ever get scared, Mom?"

"Sometimes," Ivy answered truthfully. "But I have a lot of people in my corner. You and Sunny, Shelly and Poppy, my mother and father, Flint and Forrest and Honey." She paused. "And all the friends I'm making here in Summer Beach. I don't ever want you to think that you're alone in Boston." Ivy pressed a hand against her chest. "You are always in my heart, and you are always welcome here."

"And I have a pretty cool room, too. Totally vintage. What a tub. You could get two people in there."

"You have Jamir to thank for cleaning and painting those rooms." Ivy and Shelly had decided to keep one of their newly renovated Sunset rooms open for family and friends that popped in.

"He's nice, too." Misty was quiet for a moment. "It's good to know I could come home. I felt so bad for you when you moved into the professor's spare room. You didn't belong there."

"We do what we have to do sometimes. No need to be ashamed about it." Carlotta's words echoed in Ivy's mind. "My mother always told me that you start from where you are. Every day can be a new beginning if you decide it is."

Misty inclined her head and grinned. "Good advice."

"Now, you're welcome to stay for the wedding, or you can go meet your cousins somewhere."

Misty's eyes twinkled. "Could I stay? Carol Reston is a legend, and I'd love to see her. I'll help if you need me to."

"I will take you up on that. We have a lot to do."

As if on cue, Ivy's phone buzzed with a text. When she looked at it, she saw that it was Carol, adding yet another couple to the guest list. And did she have an extra room for them at the inn for them to change in? From that comment, Ivy knew Carol must be overwhelmed because they'd already discussed that, and Ivy had a suite reserved for them.

With a smile, Ivy turned her phone around to Misty. "Actually, it looks like you can start right now."

Later that afternoon, after making sure that all the tables and chairs and supplies had arrived and everything was on track, Ivy slipped into a quick bath. Now she sat at her vanity and brushed her hair back into a sleek, efficient bun.

For the wedding, she had to appear understated, not fussy. Carol had invited Bennett, and he'd asked Ivy to be his plus-one date. Ivy had laughed and told him she would be working, but they agreed that she'd sit with him at the ceremony.

She added discreet pearl earrings and nestled a single strand of pearls into the soft collar of her taupe knit dress. The success of this wedding would be invaluable publicity for booking similar events at the inn. As Ivy nodded with approval at her modest reflection in the mirror, her phone buzzed with a message.

It was another emergency text from the mother-of-the-bride.

Even though the wedding details had seemed endless, with Poppy's help, Ivy had finally crossed off each task from the list. The past few weeks, Carol Reston had contacted them each time an idea, no matter how small, had popped into her head—even though she engaged a wedding planner to handle details. It seemed the nervous mother-of-the-bride was having pre-wedding jitters, too.

Fortunately, Poppy would have Misty's help tonight. Ivy was grateful for the extra person on her team.

Ivy tapped a reply to Carol, reassuring her. She tried to call Shelly, but her phone went to voice mail. With a sigh, she called Poppy.

"Hi, Aunt Ivy. What's up?"

"Carol just sent another request. She's worried about the deep blue flowers that Shelly planted around the perimeter clashing with the pastel wedding colors. Not sure which flowers she means, but can you or Misty track down Shelly and ask her to remove them? Or snip the flowers and bring them inside."

"Either way, I'll take care of it," Poppy said, laughing.

"I'm so glad you still have your sense of humor. Soon this wedding will be over."

"And then we'll have more," Poppy replied. "That's our goal."

"This first wedding has been a real learning curve. Just think how easy others will be after this," Ivy said, laughing.

In search of the egregious blossoms, Ivy hung up and stood by the window to look out over the pool. Shelly had planted creamy white gardenias and blush pink roses in planters around the pool. Sure enough, brilliant blue-violet lobelia flowers spilled along a pathway to the pool.

The view was so serene, and Ivy imagined painting the pool scene just as it was. The afternoon sun illuminated the still pool, turning it into a shimmering hue of aquamarine blue. She clicked a photo on her phone to save it for later study.

While she watched, Celia stepped to the edge of the pool and dove in with a clean splash, her long black hair fanning behind her and balancing the sleek one-piece suit she wore. She'd asked to swim her laps before the wedding guests arrived.

Stunning. Click.

Ivy would share that with Celia, too. Celia had just returned from her trip to San Francisco, saying that while she enjoyed the time with her parents, she didn't want to miss the wedding. San

Francisco was a short plane trip away, and Celia visited often.

The quiet scene reminded Ivy of artist David Hockney's series of pool works that he had painted in Los Angeles. Her trained eye took in the colors and shapes. *Naples yellow on the chaise lounges and umbrellas.* Even though the bottom and sides of the pool were white with black Romanesque grids, the water shimmered with blue hues.

The sun passed behind a cloud, so without the sun's brilliant light, the water deepened in color. *Cobalt blue now.* Considering the shades, Ivy thought about the intrinsic hue of water and the selective, weak absorption of red in the visible color spectrum. White light scattered, and the resulting visible color was blue.

She took another shot before turning from the window. That was a project for another day—perhaps for the art class she'd been teaching. Of all people, their new guest Debra—Darla's sister—had shown up in the class. Debra was quiet and thoughtful; the polar opposite of Darla.

Yesterday after Ivy and Misty had returned from the long family lunch, they had run into Debra at the honor bar in the music room, where she was having a cup of tea. Debra told Ivy that she was there to discuss the settlement of the estate left by their father. Ivy hadn't known that Darla's father had died, but then, she knew little of Darla. The woman had too many prickly thorns to get past, and Ivy wondered if she ever would. The judge had ordered mediation, and Imani was helping her prepare.

If only there were a simple solution.

Ivy stepped into a pair of low-heeled pumps. As she did, she paused, gazing at the interior of her closet. She turned slowly, taking in the closets and drawers, the molding, the parquet floor. As outlandish as Shelly's idea to tear apart the house might have been, there was a kernel of possibility in it.

Based on the partial journal entry Ivy had found a few weeks ago, Ivy believed that Amelia had kept a journal. Had she taken it with her? Did it still exist somewhere? Perhaps Amelia's personal effects had been given to a friend. Or maybe the journal was still here, hidden for safekeeping, as Amelia seemed to do.

All Ivy had to do was learn to think as Amelia had. Yet the poor woman's memory had been slipping, even when she lived here.

But Ivy couldn't think about that today. The wedding party would be arriving soon.

As Ivy walked through the hallway, Pixie scurried back into Gilda's room. Her little toenails tapped on the parquet floor.

Ivy stopped by the door. "Gilda, you might want to keep Pixie inside with all the people we're having downstairs."

"I like hearing what's going on in the house," Gilda said, pushing away from her computer on the desk to pick up Pixie. "I get claustrophobic with the door closed." She kissed Pixie's nose. "The obedience training is really helping, don't you think? She hasn't chewed anything in a while."

"She's turning into quite a good girl," Ivy said. She hoped the training would stick. Gilda hadn't wanted to move into the rear Sunset units, saying she liked being among people in the main house.

Ivy made her way downstairs to the ballroom, where Shelly and Poppy had been working on decorations and floral arrangements since morning. Shelly had also brought Jamir onto the job, and he was now ferrying arrangements to the tables while Poppy folded napkins.

"Is Alain's team here yet?" Ivy asked.

"They're outside," Shelly said, jerking her thumb toward a palladium window. "Just arrived. I think they got stuck in traffic."

"Well, I'm sure they'll make up the time."

"The kitchen is cleared and ready for them." Working with brisk efficiency, Shelly snipped a bent leaf from an artistic arrangement of pink peonies, white lilies, and blush pink roses that were wound around curly willow twirled into in fanciful shapes. Against pristine white tablecloths and soft coral accents, the floral arrangements were natural focal points.

The door chimes sounded. Glancing through the tall windows, Ivy saw a white Bentley and two large SUVs easing to a stop in front of the house.

"That must be Carol with the wedding party. Jamir, could you give us a hand?" Ivy made her way to the foyer and opened the door to welcome them.

"Hello, darling," Carol cooed as she entered with her husband Hal, who was also an accomplished producer in the music industry. She looked radiant, but her daughter's eyes were rimmed with red. "Isn't it the most glorious day for a wedding?"

"Thank goodness for weather cooperation," Ivy said. "I'm sure you're anxious to see how the venue has turned out." Ivy led them through the ballroom and out to the veranda and pool area, which looked spectacular and was brimming with Shelly's artistic floral arrangements.

Celia had just finished her laps. Wrapped in a terry robe, she waved as she slipped back inside.

Carol and her husband were pleased, though Victoria was subdued. While Carol was exclaiming over the view for photography, Victoria cut in. "Where can I change?"

"I have a suite ready for you." Ivy showed them upstairs, and Jamir quickly brought in their luggage, taking special care with the wedding dress. Carol's wedding organizer arrived with a team of assistants clad in sherbet wedding colors, while a makeup artist and a hairstylist bustled upstairs to assist Carol and Victoria. Meanwhile, Chef Alain and his team took up their posts in the kitchen.

After making the wedding party comfortable in the guest suite, Ivy joined Shelly and Poppy and Misty in the kitchen where they were folding linen napkins at the table. "Everything seems to be going well up there," Ivy said.

"Here, too," Shelly said.

"Except for the bride," Jamir said quietly. "She looked like she'd been crying. Think the wedding is still a go?"

"A lot of women cry on their wedding days," Ivy said, assuring him. "It's an emotional time, but Victoria will rally, I'm sure."

The rear kitchen door squeaked, and Bennett and Mitch ambled in, taking in the flowers and decorations as they did. For the wedding, Bennett was dressed in a charcoal suit with a crisp white shirt and a burgundy tie. He looked incredibly handsome. Ivy tried not to stare, even though her heart seemed to flutter.

Ivy smiled at him and nodded her approval. Although she was working, she looked forward to watching the ceremony with him. And her parents would be here, too.

"What an amazing job you've done," Mitch said, his eyes widening at the sight. He gave Shelly a hug, and she beamed up at him.

"This is Shelly's work," Ivy said, anxious for

Shelly to receive credit for her stunning achievement. And it was. She'd conceptualized and executed the flowers and decorations to perfection.

"Need a hand with anything?" Bennett asked.

Ivy quickly took him up on his offer. "The chairs by the pool—can you make sure they're aligned? I noticed the rental company left them a little askew on one side." She turned back to Shelly as Bennett and Mitch headed outside.

"You're way ahead of schedule," Ivy said, admiring Shelly's organization. Her sister was clearly in her element. The floral arrangements were as exquisite—actually, even more so—than those she saw in magazines. Shelly had often sent her photos of her work or posted images on social media, but seeing the flowers close up was splendid. And the scent was sweetly enticing. "Your flowers are magnificent."

Shelly gave her a funny little smile. "You do know this is what I did in New York."

Ivy got her point. "I never saw your work in person. It's even more stunning."

"Do you miss what you did in New York?" Poppy asked.

"Sometimes," Shelly replied. "I had the chance to design a lot of glamorous events there. In comparison, Summer Beach is pretty laid back. But here I am."

Ivy detected a note of regret in Shelly's voice. Suddenly, Ivy wondered if her sister missed her old life more than she'd imagined she would. Shelly had always liked being on-trend, and while Summer Beach was turning out to be all that Ivy could have dreamed of, perhaps Shelly wasn't as content—or as driven to making the inn successful—as Ivy was. Maybe they could talk tomorrow after the wedding.

After a while, Carol reappeared downstairs on her husband's arm. Hal was a tall, elegant man with just the right amount of distinguished gray at the temples. Though small in stature, Carol was a stunning presence in a deep coral-colored dress with diamonds draped at her neck and wrists. Her trademark red hair was coiffed to perfection, and her makeup was expertly applied, taking years off her face. She lifted a hand to Ivy.

"My wedding planner will oversee everything from here on. She and her assistants will welcome guests—she knows many of our friends, of course. From there, guests will be escorted to the veranda where Chef Alain's team will serve."

"We'll be here if you need us," Ivy said.

"And I can't wait to see your dear mother and father again," Carol said, her eyes brightening. "They are true connoisseurs of the arts—I have a fabulous collection of South American art and craft pieces they recommended. I had no idea you were related."

Ivy smiled. People who had lived here for years in the small towns and enclaves that hugged the

California coastline were often deeply connected. Ivy realized how much she had missed that.

"And look who's arrived," Carol exclaimed.

Rowan Zachary was making his way toward them, and it was all Ivy could do to maintain her even-keeled demeanor. As in high school, Rowan still lit a fire in her, and her heartbeat quickened. He was even more handsome up close, she thought, as he closed the space between them. A brilliant aura seemed to surround him like a spotlight. *Yes, that's the way I would paint him.* Ivy blinked away her imagination. *If* she were going to paint him, but she had no intention of doing that. None at all. But what a portrait that would be...

"There's my fresh-faced beauty again," Rowan said, greeting Ivy with a kiss on each cheek.

"Hello, Rowan," Ivy forced herself to say calmly. Keenly aware of her likely burning pink cheeks, she took a half step back from Mr. Adonis. Rowan had been a fantasy crush, nothing more. From the corner of her eye, she caught sight of Bennett, who was watching her intently.

"Now where can a man get a libation?" Rowan asked. "With my only son getting married, we've been celebrating all day."

"I heard it's been several days," Carol said, arching an eyebrow. "Victoria has been trying to reach Orlando since yesterday." She took a step closer and leaned toward Rowan's ear. "So help me, if your son doesn't show up, there will be hell to pay," she hissed. "So I suggest you find him now. And if you don't wipe that stupid grin off your face, I'll do it for you."

Ivy gulped and glanced away.

"I promise he'll be here," Rowan said, his voice subdued. "Excuse me, ladies."

Ivy watched Rowan cut through the crowd of well-wishers for the bar. While he waited for a cocktail, he checked his phone. After getting a cocktail, Rowan slipped outside to take a call. Surely Victoria and Orlando would work it out, Ivy thought. But she couldn't worry about that. Some events were simply out of her control.

Soon the wedding party was well underway. Musicians set up near the pool, and servers began circulating with *hors d'oeurves.*

Ivy made the rounds to make sure everything was going well. As she neared the kitchen, she could hear Alain barking orders at his team. She peered in. For the duration of the wedding, the kitchen was his domain. Servers were hoisting trays to carry them outside to an *hors d'oeurves* table.

As one picked up a tray, Ivy noticed a blue-veined cheese. Remembering Carol's admonishment, Ivy followed the server out and motioned to Poppy and Misty, who had been circulating and talking to Carol and Rowan and others in entertainment.

Whispering to them, Ivy said, "Carol will go nuts if she sees Roquefort or Gorgonzola or Stilton cheese. She hates it, but for some reason, Alain is serving it anyway. Please take all the blue cheeses off the platters. Rearrange the presentation, or put a flower there or something. Carol threatened to throw it in the pool if she saw any."

Poppy's eyes flew open. "Not our clean pool!"

Bennett stepped up beside Ivy and put his hand on her shoulder. "Is there a problem?" he asked softly.

"Carol banned blue cheese, but there it is."

Misty picked up an extra platter and balanced it on her forearm. "I'll handle it. No one ever notices servers." She winked at her mother. "Just another part to play."

Staring after her, Ivy and Bennett and Poppy chuckled.

"She sure reminds me of her mother," Bennett said before he was pulled away by another guest. *I'll be back*, he mouthed.

Ivy understood. Bennett knew a lot of people, and she needed to keep watch on the party. When Ivy saw her parents arrive, she made her way toward them.

"What a gorgeous wedding," Carlotta said, who was dressed in a striking summer dress of shimmering lavender silk that flowed with every step. Teardrop amethyst earrings brushed her neck, and a chunky amethyst necklace set off her dress to perfection. Carlotta nodded toward the flowers. "Those are world-class floral arrangements. Shelly's work?"

"All of it," Ivy said. "I knew she was talented, but I didn't realize *how* talented." Had she underestimated Shelly's abilities? Perhaps bringing her sister out here *had* hindered her career in New York. And yet, Ivy loved having her here.

"Creativity runs in our family," Sterling said. "You're all visionaries in your respective fields. Your mother and I have always seen this very clearly."

Moving onto the veranda, where strains of keyboards, a harp, cellos, and violins filled the air —accompanied by the mesmerizing sound of the ocean—they chatted a little more. As people began to take their seats for the ceremony, Ivy sat with her parents and saved a place next to her for Bennett. She asked her parents more about their plans to sail around the world.

Her father slid his arm around her mother. "We've just decided to wait until spring for better weather. In the meantime, we can get the house sorted out and get our medical checkups."

"Is there anything I should know about?" Ivy still thought about her parents' health.

"Oh, *mija*, stop worrying," Carlotta said, laughing. "We're in excellent health."

"Sailors have to be in tip-top shape," Sterling said.

"You both look like you have that covered," Bennett said as he took a seat beside Ivy.

They all continued chatting as other guests sat around them. Ivy enjoyed sitting between Bennett and her parents, who seemed to like him, too.

The sun slanted a rosy glow across Carlotta's face. She turned toward the ocean, where the sun was casting gossamer threads across the water. "Such a lovely setting for a wedding. But if they're going to marry at sunset, they'd better hurry."

Ivy frowned and checked her phone. Her mother was right. Talking to them, she'd lost track of time. She glanced around.

All the guests were seated and waiting. Gilda, Celia, and other inn guests were standing on an upper balcony, while Misty, Poppy, Shelly, and Mitch had gathered to one side of the terrace in a prime viewing spot, though Ivy knew they were ready to assist if needed.

Framed by a pink-and-coral backdrop of the setting sun, Poppy and Misty were perched on a carved stone balustrade and bent together in whispered conversation. Mitch had his arm around Shelly's shoulder, and she was resting her head on his. Ivy was happy for Shelly, but she needed her help.

"Excuse me," Ivy said, sliding from her seat. Bennett stood and stepped aside.

"Anything I can do to help?"

She squeezed his hand. "Shelly bought lanterns to light after the ceremony. But I think we might need them lit sooner rather than later." The lighting, however, was the least of wedding problems. She hurried toward Shelly.

Shelly tapped her wrist and held her palms up. "Where are they?" she whispered.

"On their way, I hope," Ivy said. "But they're going to miss the sunset. Can you light the lanterns now before the ceremony?"

"We're on it," Shelly said, motioning to her team.

Nearby, the wedding planner was jabbing her cell phone, and Hal was nervously checking his watch. The photographer looked antsy, adjusting his camera and eyeing the waning light. Carol was absent, though she was probably with her daughter. The wedding planner rushed inside.

Where was the groom? Orlando Zachary was nowhere to be found. And where was Rowan? They were at least half an hour—no, more now— behind schedule. Ivy sighed, preparing herself. This wedding was on the verge of unraveling.

a s the last of the lanterns flicked to life in
the blue-hued twilight, and the scent of
gardenia filled the air, Ivy saw the harried wedding planner return and take up her post near the
rear of the house to manage the processional
party. The woman looked vastly relieved and gave
Ivy a quick nod. Ivy returned to her seat between
Bennett and her parents.

"Crisis averted," Ivy whispered to her
mother.

"Thank heavens," Carlotta replied.

Bennett twined his fingers with Ivy's, and she
savored the warmth of his touch in the cooling
evening air. With lanterns flickering around them
and the enthralling sound of the ocean rising behind the strings and keyboard, Ivy thought it was
one of the most romantic scenes she'd ever seen.

A sigh of relief escaped her lips, and Bennett squeezed her hand.

Being here with Bennett, along with her parents, her daughter, her sister, and her niece meant so much to Ivy. She was among family, but more than that, they had all worked together to create this night for Carol and her family. Glancing up at the grand old home, Ivy smiled. Shelly had positioned spotlights that illuminated architectural features and towering palm trees. Even the house seemed to glimmer with renewed life.

Soon the ceremony was underway. As music soared through the twilight and waves broke on the shore, attendants in diaphanous silk of sherbet hues gathered around the floral-draped arch on the terrace. Every young woman hit the mark that the wedding planner had rehearsed with them. The scene was so lovely and executed to such perfection that Ivy thought it looked like a professional theater scene.

Thankfully, the bleary-eyed groom also appeared, along with his cadre of sheepish-looking groomsmen. Running his hand over his thick, dark hair that was so much like his father's, Orlando took his place beside them, front and center.

A young nephew escorted Carol to her seat. The music rose, and Hal emerged with his daughter on his arm. Victoria looked resplendent in her custom-designed Claude Morelli wedding gown, which was an exquisitely romantic creation of shimmering candlelight silk, Belgian lace, and tiny seed pearls. With expert makeup that hid her recent trauma, Victoria glowed in the lantern light as she arrived at Orlando's side and clasped his hand.

Ivy pressed a hand to her heart as the couple exchanged vows. When the couple exchanged a kiss, Bennett brought Ivy's hand to his lips and feathered a kiss on her fingers. A lump formed in her throat as she thought of the commitments each of them had made to others they'd loved—Jeremy and Jackie.

Ivy couldn't help but wonder what the future held for her and Bennett, though she was trying not to think too far ahead. It was still too soon for them, although every passing day brought them closer.

Ivy saw a smile flicker on her mother's face as she touched the edge of Ivy's dress. Carlotta had seen Bennett's motion, she realized, and it seemed to please her. Maybe this was the beginning of Ivy's new future after all. Bennett, the inn, Summer Beach. Having her family nearby, her daughters visiting.

She liked this new life, she decided, though after the tragedy of the last year, she could hardly believe that her life was actually righting itself after a horrendous storm. It were as if she were in a lifeboat blown off course that had finally found smooth waters again. A vessel filled with family and new friends.

Ivy and Bennett stood as the guests closed in on the newly married couple, hugging and congratulating them. The fog of uncertainty surrounding the wedding had lifted, and Ivy saw Carol and Hal beaming with pride and relief.

Ivy let out a breath. Surely the party would be a breeze now. Glancing to one side, she saw Shelly giving her a thumbs-up. *Success, at last.*

Rowan slapped his son on the back and kissed Victoria on the cheek. As he did, Ivy noticed that he seemed unsteady on his feet. Likely he'd lingered too long near the drinks table, but it was a grand celebration with a full dinner and more entertainment ahead. When Carol glared at Rowan, he returned her irritation with a rakish grin.

"Looks like there's an argument brewing," Bennett said, *sotto voce*, nodding toward Carol and Rowan.

Ivy shivered. "I'd hate to be on the receiving end of her wrath."

Behind the wedding party, the pool shimmered with deep blue hues. Soft lights illuminated the pool, as well as nearby carved statues and floral arrangements. The effect was utterly magical.

Ivy knew guests would mill about here for a while before going into the ballroom for the seated dinner.

Bennett leaned in, his breath warm on her neck. "You'll be okay for a moment? Seems Mitch wants me."

"Go on," Ivy said. "I'm going to check in with Carol and Hal."

He kissed her on the cheek. "Did I tell you how beautiful you look this evening? I think you're the most elegant woman here."

She laughed softly. Her taupe dress hardly stood out against all the lovely, colorful dresses here. "I'm more Boston than Summer Beach tonight."

"Very sophisticated," he said. "It suits you well."

Ivy watched Bennett leave, admiring the ease with which he moved through the crowd. Another couple greeted her parents, and as they began to talk, Ivy slipped away toward Carol, who also had a group of well-wishers around her.

For some reason, Ivy's intuitive sense was on high alert. Shifting her course, she moved toward the group gathered beside the pool.

Rowan was holding court near the edge of the pool with a group of women, who were hanging on his every word. Watching, Ivy could see that he was in his element with an adoring crowd before him. She caught snippets of the story he was telling about Orlando and the first time Rowan had met his new daughter-in-law. His gestures were growing more pronounced as the story went on.

"Excuse me," Ivy said, making her way toward Rowan. She didn't like where he was standing, or the way he was wavering. His motion was ever so slight, but still…

Above the din of the crowd, Ivy could hear Rowan reaching the end of the story. The women were laughing, and Rowan made a grand gesture with his arm. However, the movement threw him off balance, and he teetered on the edge of the pool, his eyes widening as he struggled to regain his balance.

Too late.

His drink flying from his hand, Rowan plunged into the water. The splash soaked the startled women, whose natural reaction was to move away from it. They roared with laughter at Rowan's antics.

Other guests turned in surprise, and Rowan sank amid gasps. Then he surfaced, holding his hand up.

"I'm okay," came Rowan's garbled call, though he was bobbing vertically in the water and gamely grinning between gasps for air. Using his arms, he tried to push down to keep his nose and mouth above water, but he was slipping farther down.

Oblivious to his distress, friends were cheering him on.

Ivy broke into a sprint. Her lifeguard training quickly took over. *Throw, don't go*, shot through her mind. At the edge of the pool, she hefted a life preserver and tossed it out to him.

"Hang on," Ivy called out to Rowan. "Grab hold of the lifebuoy."

Rowan reached for the life ring but slipped under before he could grasp it.

Without hesitating, Ivy kicked off her pumps and dove into the pool after him. When she reached him, he had turned face down on the surface. *Floating.* Positioning her hands across his shoulder, she flipped him over and swam to the edge, dragging him with her. By then, several men had gathered to help pull Rowan from the water. Ivy checked his breathing and bent over him to perform CPR.

After a little while, she helped Rowan roll onto his side as he began to cough. "That's it," she said, encouraging him. "You're going to be okay."

The crowd burst into applause.

Rowan gazed at her, his eye filled with gratitude. "Saved by an angel," he croaked.

"Dad!" Orlando burst through the gathered throng and knelt by his father's side.

"He's okay, but he should be checked out by a physician," Ivy told Orlando.

Rowan shook water from his hair and waved off her comment. "Don't need a doctor. Need some dry clothes—and another dry martini," he quipped with his famous grin.

"I've got some clothes you can wear, Dad. Come on." Orlando helped him to his feet.

The wedding photographer pushed his way through the crowd and snapped a photo of the groom and his drenched father. The duo grinned and gave each other a high-five for the camera.

Ivy quickly stepped out of the frame. She pushed dripping hair from her face and blinked. Mascara was most likely running down her cheeks, but she didn't care.

Once the photographer was finished memorializing the moment, Ivy said to Orlando. "Take him upstairs to the room where Victoria changed."

Rowan flashed a rakish grin toward Ivy. "Can't imagine being rescued by a more beautiful woman. Doubly lucky, I am."

"Just glad I was watching," Ivy said. "And next time, don't stand so close to the edge. Especially when you've been drinking."

"Aw, life's better on the edge." Rowan reached out to Ivy and grasped her hand. "Come find out with me, my darling."

Snap. Another flash momentarily blinded Ivy.

Snap. Rowan kissed her on the lips. *Snap*.

Ivy was mortified—and furious. How dare he take such liberties?

All at once, the wedding planner swooped in

to save Ivy, clapping her hands for attention. "The show's over out here. Everyone into the ballroom now, where Chef Alain's marvelous dinner will be served. The father-of-the-groom will join you just as soon as he's changed."

As people moved toward the door, Ivy stepped back and immediately felt Bennett's arms around her wet torso.

"You were amazing," Bennett said. "You need some dry clothes, too." To his credit, he said nothing about Rowan's stolen kiss.

"That's a good idea," Ivy said, shivering in the evening air. Bennett whipped off his jacket and wrapped it around her.

Her parents, Shelly, and Misty hurried to her. Moments later, Poppy sprinted out with an arm-load of towels she'd grabbed from the laundry room. Within minutes, Ivy was enveloped in all the towels and love she could ever hope for.

"You were always a first-rate lifeguard," her father said, tucking another towel around her neck.

"Couldn't l-lose the father-of-the-groom," Ivy said through chattering teeth.

"Oh, wow," Poppy said. "Just think of *that* press."

"I'd rather not," Ivy replied.

The wedding photographer stepped in front of her and snapped another photo. "Well done," he said, giving her the thumbs up.

"That's enough," Bennett said, taking command of the situation.

"Let's get her upstairs," Carlotta said.

Bennett cleared the way, while Carlotta guided Ivy toward the house, and Shelly and Misty followed.

Pausing, Ivy glanced back at Bennett. "We sure know how to make a splash here in Summer Beach, don't we?"

"Sure do." He touched his fingers to his mouth in a kiss for her. "Mitch and I will look after things for you. Take your time. I'll be waiting."

After trailing water upstairs to her room, Ivy peeled off her soggy taupe dress and slid into a warm bath that her mother had drawn for her. While she relaxed under the rose-scented bubbles, Shelly, Misty, and Carlotta lounged in her bedroom, reliving the events of the evening.

Closing her eyes and languishing in the warm water for a few minutes, Ivy listened to the sweet sound of their laughter and the music flowing from downstairs. Then the music kicked up a notch, and Carol's bold, soaring soprano spiraled up the staircase with one of her most popular hit love songs that Ivy had heard hundreds of time.

Downstairs in her own home, it was *Carol Reston—live*. And Ivy was in her bathtub. She laughed at the absurdity of it all.

Just then, her mother raced in with a fresh

terry cloth robe Ivy had bought for the guest rooms. "Come with me," she commanded. "You can't miss a Carol Reston performance in your own home. Finish your bath later."

Ivy grinned at her mother. "You have a point," Ivy said, hurrying from the bath.

Carlotta helped her wrap her hair in a turban. Decked out like a terrycloth mummy, Ivy rushed down the hallway with her mother, Misty, and Shelly. They sat on the stairs and peered through the banisters to watch the party.

"Great seats," Ivy said, laughing.

Misty hugged her. "I feel like a kid watching the grown-up party."

With the spotlight shining on her glossy red hair, Carol changed the tempo and belted out another song as if she were on stage before thousands. The acoustics in the house were incredible, surprising Ivy.

Soon the bride and groom were whirling around the dance floor, and the magnificent ballroom was filled with guests dancing and laughing and singing under sparkling chandeliers—just as it had been decades ago.

Ivy squeezed her mother's hand. "Thanks, Mom. Carol is truly amazing."

"Didn't want you to miss this party," Carlotta said.

Shelly hugged her, and Misty cuddled next to

her. "But you gave the most amazing performance of all. Loves you muchly, Mom."

Ivy kissed her daughter's forehead. "Loves you, too, babycakes."

As Carol motioned to the band and kicked up the pop song another notch, Shelly punched the air and called out, "Woo-hoo!"

And before long, Ivy was clapping and singing along with Carol Reston and all the other guests. Ivy couldn't imagine what else the weekend might have in store, but how could anything possibly top this?

27

"Careful with this one," Bennett said, handing Mitch an antique crystal serving bowl etched with delicate flowers.

He'd talked Mitch into forgoing his regular morning surf to help him clean up after the wedding. After making a pot of coffee, the two men had collected dirty dishes and went to work. Bennett submerged his hands into the soapy dishwater to retrieve another piece.

Mitch dried the crystal bowl and placed it on the long center counter, where a grouping of fine china and crystal was nearly overflowing.

"So you and Ivy were looking pretty cozy last night," Mitch said.

"We had a good time." Bennett scraped bits of food from a platter. "I also spent time with her folks, Carlotta and Sterling. They shared their plans to sail around the world—their route, the supplies they're taking, where they plan to stop—although they said they're flexible."

Bennett gazed out the kitchen window toward the ocean, imagining what it would be like to take off like that someday. Maybe even with Ivy. Yet there was still so much he didn't know about her.

After hearing about her efforts last night—he'd been inside when Rowan had fallen into the pool—Bennett learned Ivy was an expert swimmer and adept at life-saving techniques. He'd been impressed with how she'd saved Rowan, but he wished he'd been there to spare her the trouble. Still, she did what was necessary when she had to, and he admired that.

Bennett rinsed soap from the heavy silver serving platter and passed it to Mitch. "I'd sure love to sail off like that someday."

"That would be so cool," Mitch said, taking the platter and toweling it dry.

Bennett thought about what a good time he'd had at the wedding last night. After Ivy had changed into a lilac-colored sundress and pulled her still damp hair back, she'd returned to the party downstairs. She still wore pearls at her ears, but her face was devoid of makeup, except for a little lip gloss. Even so, she was easily the most beautiful woman there in his eyes.

Ivy spent most of the evening making sure all the guests were comfortable, but he'd managed to get her on the dance floor for a couple of dances toward the end of the evening. Since Misty was there, he hadn't wanted to take Ivy away from her daughter too much.

Bennett frowned as he reached for a pair of serving tongs and plunged them into the soapy water. Rowan had also insisted on a dance with Ivy. As Bennett had watched them, he'd felt odd twinges in his chest. Ivy laughed at his jokes, while Rowan held her tighter than Bennett thought was really necessary.

Rowan Zachary could get away with that he supposed.

Still, Bennett thought he saw Ivy step back to keep her distance a couple of times during the song. Or maybe Bennett had imagined that. The dance floor was pretty crowded, and it had been hard to keep his eye on them without staring.

Bennett scrubbed the tongs and rinsed them before passing them off to Mitch. "You and Shelly seemed to be getting along well, too."

"Yeah, I really like her." Mitch toweled off the tongs and added them to the growing stack on the counter.

"You do know she's older than you, right?"

"Age doesn't matter to me," Mitch said. "I like her for who she is. Inside, you know what I mean?" He swiped his hand over his sun-bleached hair. "She's a lot like me, a reformed vagabond."

"You have any regrets about that?" Years ago,

Bennett had found Mitch sleeping in an old pickup truck by the beach. Bennett had taken Mitch to breakfast, thinking that he'd give him a good meal before sending the kid on his way. Instead, Bennett was drawn to Mitch's intelligence and eagerness to make something of himself, so he urged him to stay. From a modest coffee stand on the beach, Mitch had saved his money and opened Java Beach. And Bennett had backed him all the way.

"None. I'm happy and blessed right where I am," Mitch said emphatically. "Doesn't mean I wouldn't like to see some of the world. And the stories Shelly tells about New York—wow. Pretty wild parties. That's not me, though. Give me a beach bonfire with a few good friends, and I'm happy."

"You'd pass up a crack at the Big Apple?"

Mitch laughed. "I might be beach cool, but I'll never be city cool."

"Ever talk about the future with her?"

"Like what?"

Bennett flung his wet fingers toward Mitch, splashing him. "Don't play dense with me."

"Hey!" Mitch popped him back with his damp towel and chuckled. "Man, it's too soon, but yeah. I like her like that."

Bennett slid more dishes into the water and added another squirt of dishwashing liquid with more hot water. "From what Ivy has said, I think

Shelly would like a family pretty soon. You don't want to waste her time. You know, at her age."

Mitch contemplated this for a few moments before he spoke. "Couple of kiddos could be cool. Raise them on the beach, teach them how to surf, right?"

"Unfortunately, I wouldn't know."

"Oh, hey man, I'm really sorry." Mitch hit his forehead with the palm of his hand. "Didn't clear my brain on the water this morning, so I'm a little slow."

"Don't worry about it. Just think about what I said before you get too involved. I'd hate to see either one of you hurt. It's a small town, too. You'll see a lot of each other." Bennett passed a couple of plates to him.

"Don't I know it?" Mitch swiped the towel across the plates and started a new stack on the counter. "When you're a couple, you really have to tell each other everything, don't you? Like, about the past and stuff."

"Works better that way." Bennett shot a look at him. "Haven't told her?"

"It's not the best topic of conversation."

"All that matters is that you've changed." Bennett trusted Mitch. His actions in the years since he'd landed in Summer Beach told Bennett everything he needed to know.

Before Mitch could answer, the kitchen door swung open.

"Hey, you guys didn't have to do all this," Ivy said as she walked in.

She wore a flowing, marine blue cotton blouse with jeans. Perfect for a visit to the beach later, Bennett thought.

"It's nothing," Bennett said.

"Smells so clean in here, too." Surveying the room, Ivy's face lit with delight. "I'm really grateful for the help. I'd planned to spend all day cleaning up after the wedding."

"That's why we're doing this," Bennett said, grinning. The look on her face was what he'd been looking forward to, and she didn't disappoint him. She was a woman who didn't conceal her emotions, even when she thought she was. He knew she cared for him—more than she let on, he hoped. "I thought you might have other plans today."

"You need a cleaning crew," Mitch said. "You know, since you're so busy with superhero moves, saving people and all. Pretty impressive, by the way. Java Beach was buzzing about it this morning."

"Thanks, I can just imagine." Ivy blushed a little. "And more help is definitely on the list. I shouldn't have guests washing dishes."

"I hope I'm not *just* a guest," Bennett said, laughing.

"Of course not." Ivy ran her hand over his

shoulder before plucking a coffee cup from a cupboard.

She didn't have to say it, but Bennett knew she was conserving expenditures until the property tax lien was paid. Her husband had left her in a financial bind, which he sympathized with. After Jackie died, he had a huge hospital bill and burial expenses that took a long time to pay off. He'd thrown himself into work during that time, even though many days he didn't feel like facing the world. But he would've done anything for his wife, so he didn't regret the expenses. He just did what he had to do. And so did Ivy.

"All in good time, I'm sure," Bennett said.

"So what's this about plans I might have?" Ivy smoothed her hands over Bennett's shoulders, lightly kneading them.

Bennett kissed her on the cheek. "You'll see. A man's got to have a few surprises."

"Let me help," she said, picking up a dishcloth printed with blue seashells.

"Get your coffee, then you can put dishes away," Bennett said. "We don't know where everything goes."

"Deal." Ivy set the dishcloth down and poured a cup of coffee. She took a long sip before sliding her hands around a few pieces of crystal stemware and disappearing into the adjoining butler's pantry.

When she returned, she took another sip and

leaned against the counter beside Bennett. "So what's the surprise?" Her green eyes twinkled in the sunlight spilling through the window.

"Well…you'll need sunglasses," Bennett said.

"Come on, tell me," she said. "I have to take Misty to the airport."

Bennett shook his head. "I'll tell you when you return."

Ivy accepted that and returned to work. Half an hour later, Shelly and Poppy joined them as well, though Misty was packing her things and getting ready to return to Boston. With a bevy of workers, the entire inn was soon back to its usual appearance.

When they were all on the veranda sipping lemonade that Shelly had made from fruit she'd harvested on the property, Misty came out with a bag slung over her shoulder. "Hate to break up the party, but it's time for me to get back to my real life."

"This is your real life, too," Ivy said, hugging her daughter. "Think of yourself as bicoastal now."

"Oh, that sounds terribly sophisticated," Misty said, affecting an upper-crust accent.

"You're an actress," Shelly said, laughing. "It's actually fairly common in your crowd, at least in New York and L.A."

"I like that idea." Misty smiled. "And Bennett,

it was great meeting you. And Mitch. I'll see you guys around the holidays."

"That long?" Ivy said, brushing Misty's wavy hair over her shoulder.

Bennett liked watching the two of them together. Ivy was an attentive mother. He hadn't seen this side of her before, and he hoped he'd get to meet Sunny soon, too.

"As long as the show continues to be a success," Misty said. "We'll be dark during the holidays. The theater always brings in *The Nutcracker* ballet then."

"So plan to spend that time here. Or at least, part of your break. Maybe Sunny, too, if she goes back to school." Ivy furrowed her brow. "Have you heard from Sunny?"

"I sent some photos from last night," Misty said. "She's heartbroken that Orlando Zachary got married, but she loved Victoria's dress."

Just then, Ivy's phone buzzed with a message. "Maybe that's Sunny now." She checked her phone, looked surprised, and tapped a quick message.

Misty leaned over and pressed a hand against her lips. "Wow, Rowan Zachary is *texting* you?"

Ivy shrugged. "Just to say thanks for saving his life. He exaggerates, of course."

Indeed, he does, Bennett thought. At least the actor was out of Ivy's life now. He frowned. *Or is he?*

"You keep surprising me, Mom. Wait until I tell Sunny." Laughing, Misty hugged her mother.

Bennett and Mitch walked Ivy and Misty to the old Jeep. Ivy had turned down his offer to take them to the airport, and he guessed it was because it was still a special family time for them. He wasn't a part of that yet, but that was okay with him. He wouldn't force it.

After Bennett promised to look after the guests if they needed anything, Shelly and Poppy piled in, too, and the four women set off. Mother, daughter, sister, cousin—but they could all pass for sisters, he thought.

Tenting his hand over his eyes, Bennett watched until they had disappeared down the street. Turning to Mitch, he said, "Want to help me fire up the old Chevy before she gets back?"

"It's running?"

"Like a dream. I can't wait to surprise her."

"Close your eyes," Bennett said, leading Ivy from the veranda to the car court.

"Where are you taking me?" she asked, laughing.

"Not much longer." Mitch and Shelly had taken off on his boat for the afternoon, and Poppy was trying to find a small coin purse that a guest had lost.

They came to a stop in front of the newly

waxed Chevy. "Here you are," Bennett said. "It's all ready to go."

Ivy opened her eyes. "Oh, I love it!" she exclaimed, running her hand along a curved red fender. "It's really running?"

"Get in. Let's take it for a spin down the coast." He held the driver's side open for her and helped her adjust the bench seat. The white convertible top was down, and the red and white leather seats gleamed in the sun.

Ivy rested her hands on the large steering wheel. "This is so vintage, yet it looks like new."

"That's because it's been garaged and covered for years."

Ivy ran her hand along the dashboard. "These models were old even when I was a kid. I remember my grandparents' old car. A seafoam green Plymouth station wagon with rear fins." She laughed. "It's funny to think of that now."

Bennett loved the sound of her laugh. After he got in the other side, he showed her how to work the dials, although they were all simple. "Radio on, off. Push the buttons to find stations. Heater, lights, windshield wipers." The windshield was an old, split style, with a piece of chrome trim running down the center of it. "You'll get used to that. Let's take it up the Pacific Coast Highway. I have something special planned. Trust me?"

Ivy nodded.

"I'll tell you where to turn."

Ivy eased the Chevy out of the car court and drove slowly through Summer Beach while she was getting used to the car.

"This is fun," she said. "Shelly has more use for the old Jeep anyway with all the plant hauling she does."

Bennett leaned against the leather seats and stretched his arm across the back of the seat. As they drove through Summer Beach, people waved or gave them the thumbs up. Jen and George were standing outside of Nailed It and motioned for them to pull over.

"What a beauty! Where did you find this?" George asked, walking around the car.

"It was in the garage. And Bennett fixed it up for me," Ivy said, linking her arm through Bennett's.

"Wow, this is a keeper," Jen said to Ivy, before throwing a surreptitious wink toward Bennett.

Jen had been encouraging Bennett to ask Ivy out before someone else did. *All in good time*, he'd told her, feeling confident in his plan.

Other people gathered around the car, too, eager to inspect it. Arthur and Nan from Antique Times came out to look at it, along with his friend Jeffrey, who owned the menswear store of the same name. The Chevrolet was quite the car, and Bennett was pleased that Ivy liked it so much.

After they left Summer Beach, they turned onto the PCH, as the road that hugged the California coast was known among locals. Bennett adjusted his sunglasses. The sun was warm on his shoulders, but the sea breeze felt fresh on his skin.

"I love this, and I wish we could keep on driving," Ivy said, the wind whipping a few loose strands of hair back from her forehead that had blown from her ponytail "I haven't seen the Monterrey Peninsula or the Bay area in years. Or the wine country. I've been gone too long."

Ideas flooded Bennett's mind. "With two of you to look after the inn—and Poppy, too—you have some flexibility, don't you?" Already he was thinking about how much he'd like to get away with her sometime. When the time was right, of course.

"Maybe once we have the place running smoothly. Right now, I don't know what I'd do without Shelly, and I'm sure she feels the same way. We still have so much to deal with." She glanced at him. "Between the wedding, Darla's lawsuit, and Ari's visit, I've had a lot on my mind."

Bennett's ears pricked up on that last point. "FBI Ari?"

"I spoke with him about the jewels, and I got an email that said he'll be here tomorrow. With all the excitement of the past few days, I guess I forgot to tell you. Seems they got a hit on the jewelry on an Interpol database, so Ari is coming to collect it."

"That's good news."

"Sort of." She frowned. "Except for that one piece I'm really worried about. And that's the one he seemed the most excited to see. The tiara."

"Still hasn't turned up?" Bennett had a gnawing sense of foreboding in his chest. No doubt, Clark and Ari would want to talk to Mitch about that disappearance.

"No," Ivy said, shaking her head sadly. "We really have to find it."

28

"*I*f you're hungry, turn here," Bennett said, pointing at a side street ahead of them just off the PCH. "Best fish tacos in North Country."

"I'm starving," Ivy said as she turned the shiny red Chevy onto the small lane.

Ivy couldn't remember when she'd had more fun. The Chevrolet drove so smoothly, and the sunshine on her shoulders rejuvenated her spirit. The wedding had been stressful but profitable. And she still had Darla's lawsuit to deal with. Even Darla's sister, Debra, called it ridiculous, but so far, Debra hadn't made any progress with her sister. Nor had Imani, but the mediation was coming up soon.

The taco stand was a small outpost on the beachside of a small community.

Walking toward the brightly painted stand, Bennett said, "These are authentic Baja-style tacos. Grilled tilapia fresh off the boat, sliced avocado and tomatoes, the crunchiest cabbage, and a slightly spicy cream sauce. Handmade tortillas right from the grill, too."

After ordering, they sat at a wooden picnic table on the sand and watched the frothy waves rushing in toward the beach and back out again. A few surfers rode the waves, and Ivy enjoyed just watching. Soon, the owner delivered the piping hot tacos, and Ivy and Bennett squeezed wedges of lime onto the tacos.

"Delicious," Ivy said after she bit into the taco. This was as good as Bennett had promised. "I haven't had fish tacos like this in years."

They took their time, eating and talking. After they finished, Bennett got up.

"I have something else for you to see, too," he said. "Wait here." He walked to the car and opened the trunk.

"You brought your guitar," she cried out, clapping. How many years had it been since that night on the beach when she'd watched the cute surfer playing the guitar? A lifetime ago, and yet, here they were again. She couldn't think of anything more perfect.

Bennett sat next to her and began to strum the guitar.

"I didn't know you still played," she said.

"I just started again. Forgive me if I'm a little rusty." Bennett played a couple songs, and Ivy sang along with him. "Do you like this one?" He began to play *Yesterday*, an old Beatles song.

"I've always loved that song," she said.

He began singing, and Ivy was mesmerized by the gravelly sound of his voice that was as she'd recalled only deeper and more mature. She swayed to the rhythm, letting it carry her back to a simpler time in her life. When he stopped, she rested her head on his shoulder. "That was beautiful."

"Those are the only songs I can remember now," he said, running his hand lovingly over the smooth, lacquered wood. "I got this guitar a few weeks ago, and I've been practicing." He rubbed his fingertips together. "I'd forgotten how you need to build up calluses on your fingers."

"Let me see," she said. After inspecting his fingertips, which were a little red, she kissed them lightly and then raised her eyes to him.

Bennett held her in his gaze, patiently waiting for her to make the next move. They were so close now, but was she ready for the next step? She recalled the passion of their kiss the night after the fire. However, she knew herself well. Once her heart was thoroughly awakened, there would be no turning back for her. And yet, from what she knew of Bennett, he was the closest she'd ever come to finding a man just right for her.

But Misty's visit had reminded Ivy that her decision would also affect the girls. Fortunately, Misty liked Bennett, but Ivy feared that Sunny might have a stronger reaction. Yes, this was Ivy's life, but she wanted all the important pieces and people in her life to mesh together well. And judging by what Misty had said, it was probably too soon for Sunny to accept her mother with another man.

Ivy angled her face and kissed Bennett's cheek. She could feel a sigh of disappointment escape from his chest. That was how she felt, too. She wrapped her arms around him. "This has been a perfect day. From the car to your music—even the best fish tacos—you've made it very special."

Bennett caressed her cheek. "I'm detecting hesitation, though."

"I'm worried about Sunny," she said. "I'm a mother, and the decision I make affects my children, even if they are a few thousand miles away." *There it was.*

He nodded and kissed the tip of her nose. "I understand, but you have to take care of you, too."

Yes, I do. Sliding her hand around the back of his neck, Ivy brought her lips to his and melted into the warmth of his lips. Immediately, she felt her body respond, and a fiery feeling erupted in her chest, spreading through her limbs. Catching her breath, she pulled back and raked her teeth over her lips. She could still desire a man, especially Bennett, but the time wasn't yet right.

"Maybe I shouldn't have done that yet," she murmured.

Bennett put the guitar to one side, enveloped her in his arms, and rocked her back and forth. "Whenever you're ready, I'm here."

His words were warm against her neck, caressing her with such love that she closed her eyes, enjoying the feeling of his body against hers. This was what she missed in her life and what she yearned for again.

They sat there for quite a while, absorbing the power of the ocean and feeling the breeze on their faces, content in each other's company.

Ivy shifted against Bennett, snuggling to his chest. This felt a lot like love to her. In her life, she'd discovered many facets of love. The love for her family, parents, siblings, and children. The love for her husband, for old friends. Even the love for her cherished pets through the years.

Where did the feeling she was developing for Bennett fall on this spectrum of love? And when would she be free to fully express her feelings again? When she knew him better, or when Sunny accepted him? The practical side of her brain seized on those thoughts, and her heart sadly followed her brain's logical path.

She lifted her face to his. "This really has been the most perfect day."

"And I hope there are many more ahead," Bennett said, kissing her forehead.

It was nearly dusk when Ivy and Bennett neared the house. He'd offered to drive, but they didn't have far to go, and she loved driving the vintage Chevrolet. As she turned into the car court, the steady beam of headlights came to rest on a shiny Mercedes sports car with an enormous red bow on top.

"Impressive," Ivy said, pulling alongside it. "Must be a grand gesture for one of the guests."

Bennett leaned forward to check it out. "Which guest, do you think?"

Ivy inclined her head. "Can't imagine. I didn't think we had any new guests, but maybe we had a last-minute check-in."

Bennett got out and helped her from the car. As they approached the house, Rowan Zachary stepped onto the veranda and opened his arms wide. Poppy and Shelly raced behind him.

"My beautiful angel." Rowan's voice boomed across the distance as he strode toward them. "My rescuer, the woman who saved my life, yet stole my heart. How shall I repay her for giving me life once again? Oh, let me count the ways." With a theatrical gesture, he waved his arm toward the sports car. "I thought this would be a magnificent beginning."

Ivy was shocked. Never had she imagined he would do something like this. She could feel Bennett's icy stare beside her. "Oh, Rowan, I—"

Covering the remaining distance in an exuberant leap, Rowan stood before her, and before she could stop him, he picked her up and whirled her around. "And a beginning for us, my lovely woman. I'm absolutely mad about you."

"No," Ivy cried out, struggling against Rowan. "Let go of me."

Bennett clamped a hand onto his shoulder. "Put her down. She didn't ask for that."

When Rowan set her down, Ivy regained her footing, gasping for breath. "Never do that again." She shot a look at the car and shook her head. *What in heaven's name is this man thinking?*

Poppy and Shelly raced across the veranda, clearly excited at the prospect of Ivy's new car.

"Isn't it gorgeous?" Shelly called out.

Rowan swung around. "Your entourage certainly approves."

"And I certainly don't," Ivy said. "While I appreciate the thought, I can't accept it."

"Of course you can," Shelly wailed. "We have to share the old Jeep. You could be driving this incredible car."

Ivy could feel Bennett's barely contained anger emanating from every pore. She turned toward the cherry red Chevrolet convertible. "I already have an incredible car."

"That?" Shelly swung her gaze between Bennett and Rowan. She pressed a hand to her forehead.

Rowan dropped to one knee before Ivy. "You saved my life. You can't turn down my deepest appreciation. Besides, it's already paid for."

Ivy shook her head. "Rowan, your gift is too extravagant, and I can't accept it. Please return it. Or donate it to a good cause—marine life rescue or a children's hospital."

Rowan shook his head. "But I am in your debt. You have to accept my token of gratitude."

"It's more than a small token." Ivy put her hands on her hips. She couldn't help but imagine what her fifteen-year-old self would have thought about her forty-five-year-old self turning down her beloved heartthrob.

Seemingly shattered, Rowan pressed a hand to his heart and rose to his feet. Heaving a sigh, he said, "No woman has ever turned me down like this."

"Go get some rest, Rowan," Ivy said. "You've had an emotional weekend. And go easy on the alcohol. I'm worried about you."

"You are?" His voice held a note of hope.

Bennett took a step toward Rowan. "Ivy's being nice."

"I am concerned about you, but I know you'll find someone else, Rowan. You can give the car to her."

Rowan lifted her hand and kissed it. "I understand, my darling Ivy. But you must know that I'm not one to give up easily."

Pocketing the key fob, Rowan clicked open the car door and got in. With a final wave, he was off.

"I can't believe that just happened," Ivy said.

"And I can't believe you just turned down that gorgeous car," Poppy added.

"I can," Shelly said, her manner subdued. "And Ivy was right to do it. Someday I'll figure out how to do the right things."

"You just did," Ivy said.

Shelly quirked up a corner of her mouth. "I mean, the *first* time around."

"Why don't we take a ride in the Chevy?" Ivy suggested, winking at Bennett. "It's really swell."

"Mitch helped fix it up, too," Bennett said. "Is he around?"

"He dropped me off," Shelly said. "He had to tend to things at Java Beach."

"And we have to get ready for Ari tomorrow," Ivy said to Shelly and Poppy. "Let's keep looking tonight."

How would Ivy explain the missing jewelry? What's worse, she knew how it would look to Ari.

29

*I*vy slid the long safety deposit box from the bank's vault, which must have dated to the 1950s. The First Summer Beach Bank clerk was a trim young man who looked like he'd rather be surfing.

"Not many people use these old relics anymore," the young man said as he removed the double set of keys and returned one to Ivy. "I'm told there used to be a waiting list for them, but many of our customers have their own safes or home security systems now."

It wasn't hard for Ivy to imagine that sophisticated systems in the lavish ridgetop estates might be more effective than the security in this bank, which also seemed like a relic of a bygone era. That probably wasn't the case, but even if it were, she rather liked the old bank. She could just imagine Amelia Erickson sauntering in here to visit her jewelry and clip coupons from her investment bonds as people did before the age of computers. It was quite comforting, this simple security, but these gems and jewelry were likely on their way to a much more fortified residence soon.

"This way, ma'am." The clerk showed Ivy to a small private room.

Ivy placed the long metal box on a small wooden table. First Summer Beach Bank looked like it hadn't been decorated since the middle of the last century. Original mid-century modern furniture made of smooth teakwood with sleek lines sat on the black-and-white marble tiled floor. Two teller windows with old-fashioned grills served the occasional customer, and a concierge sat by the front door at an antique desk. Wood paneling cocooned the bank from the sun's rays. Ivy blinked after coming in from the bright sunshine on Main Street.

"I won't be long," she said to the clerk, who left and shut the door.

Ivy settled into the small room and opened the box. She wanted one last look at the crown jewelry that she believed Amelia had rescued and protected from harm—though Shelly would argue over Amelia's intent.

She arranged the jewelry on the wooden table that was smooth from years of wear. Stepping back, she admired the glittering treasures one last time. These precious works of art were astounding, and Ivy appreciated them not for their value, but for their artistic merit. Everything was here. Well, almost. After she'd sent the photos to Ari, his team had catalogued everything and sent an inventory list back to her.

The police chief, Ari, Shelly, and Bennett were waiting in the bank's small waiting area. Ari had also brought an expert, whom he introduced as Yelena, a forensic gemologist.

Ivy opened the door to the small, secure enclave. "Could you ask the others to come in?" Ivy asked the clerk, though it would be a tight fit in this small room.

Ari and the specialist sat down to examine the jewels while the rest of the party watched through the doorway. Adjusting a sophisticated eyepiece, Yelena peered at the stones and mountings. Diamonds, emeralds, sapphires, rubies, pearls. She took her time, beginning with the most precious pieces.

After completing her examination, Yelena put down her equipment. "The settings have not been tampered with, and the stones appear authentic. From the photos and paintings we have, what you have here appears to be part of a historically important collection that disappeared from a German castle in 1946."

"Thank you, Yelena," Ari said as the woman packed up her equipment.

"How did they get here?" Shelly asked.

"Three people were arrested in the theft," Ari said. "The perpetrators mailed many of the pieces to friends and family in the United States. Although search warrants were issued, it was thought that many pieces had already been sold or remained hidden. These probably fetched quite a sum on the black market."

"Then how did they end up sewn inside of a doll in the trunk of a Chevy?" Ivy asked.

Ari shook his head. "We'll have to do more investigative work, but it's doubtful that we can determine much. It's been so many years. The original parties are deceased."

Ivy spoke up. "My theory is that Amelia had acquired them and was transporting them home."

"Or transporting them to sell," Chief Clarkson interjected.

Ivy wondered if they would ever know the truth about Amelia Erickson. "Would having the doll help?"

"Yes, it might," Yelena replied. "It could yield additional clues."

"We'll double check the inventory," Ari said. "Everything that you photographed and sent to us is here, yes?"

Ivy shot a look at Shelly. "Almost everything."

"You'll have to explain that," Ari said.

"The tiara that had teardrop-shaped aquamarines disappeared. We think it was one crafted by a master worker under Fabergé. According to the maker's mark, that might have been one of the Holmström family."

Yelena snapped her head up. "Was it AH?" she asked. When Ivy nodded, she looked impressed. "You did your homework, so you know the significance of this piece."

"That's why I contacted Ari," Ivy said.

Chief Clarkson frowned. "You didn't report this missing. Any particular reason why you didn't?"

"We thought it would turn up," Shelly said.

"Here we are again," the chief said. "What if your guests' possessions begin disappearing?" He narrowed his eyes. "Or have they already?"

"Only minor things," Shelly said. "A scarf, a coin purse. Though it was a Louis Vuitton."

"Imani's scarf was probably expensive," Ivy added, realizing she should have reported the disappearance of the tiara earlier. She hated to think that a thief lived among them. Scarves and coin purses were one thing—a rare piece of jewelry was quite another.

As Ari and his colleague took possession of the jewelry and began wrapping it up, Ivy, Shelly, and Bennett sat with Chief Clarkson to give him their accounts of what had happened.

When the chief asked if anyone else had

knowledge of the jewelry, Ivy told him that they'd brought Poppy into their confidence. She had also shared the treasures with her parents to get their opinion, and added that Arthur at Antique Times knew they had something, although she hadn't told him exactly what it was.

The chief scribbled notes. "Anyone else?"

Darting her eyes to one side, Shelly chewed her lip. "I might have said something to Mitch."

The next morning, Ivy heard a tap on her door. It was not quite seven. Poppy was on the morning coffee rotation, so this was Ivy's one day of the week without coffee duty, beach walks, or yoga. She'd planned on sleeping in for an extra half hour. Nevertheless, she pulled on a robe and opened the door.

Bennett stood before her. His hair was still damp, though he was unshaven. He looked like he'd raced through a shower and thrown on his clothes in a hurry.

"Anything wrong?" she asked.

"Can I talk to you?"

"Sure, I'll throw on some clothes and be right down."

"There's not enough time. Mitch is here—talking to Shelly—but we haven't much time before we have to leave. Imani offered to come with us to the police station. She's nearly ready. I wanted to let you know what was going on. Can we talk in private?"

"Come in." Hastily belting her robe, Ivy opened the door. They sat on a bench at the end of her rumpled bed, and he took her hand in his.

"It's about the jewelry," Bennett began. "Mitch called me at sunrise to say that Chief Clarkson asked to question him this morning about the theft of the tiara. Mitch had been up all night worrying."

"But I don't think he had anything to do with it."

Bennett ran a hand over his hair. "The chief reached Gus, who remembered seeing the tiara. Described it and everything. But Gus said Mitch was there, too. The way the chief is constructing the timeline, it seems that Mitch might have been the last one to see it, except for you. Doesn't look good for him, Ivy. Especially with his past."

"We just need to look harder. It's probably been misplaced." She couldn't imagine that any of their guests or friends or family members might have taken it. To think that Mitch might have stolen it was unfathomable. What would happen if he were mistakenly accused—or worse—convicted of the crime?

"We'll keep looking," Ivy said. "Maybe it was scooped up in a load of laundry or shuffled away in some papers. I toss things on top of the vanity all the time. Like my robe."

Bennett nodded with understanding. "None of us want to see Mitch accused of this. But the tiara is gone. Apparently, it has special significance, too. Ari said the owners are anxious to have it returned with the rest of the pieces. It's been worn at weddings and state functions, so it has both personal and historical value."

"I understand." When Ivy had sent the photos to Ari, how was she to know that any items would go missing, especially the tiara?

Bennett stroked her hand. "Mitch insisted we stop here on the way so he could talk to Shelly. He wanted to come clean and tell her everything about his past. In particular, about his prison time. That will probably come out, and he wants her to hear it from him first. You know how small this town is."

Ivy nodded. The thought of what this news would do to Shelly was sobering. Mitch's business might also be impacted if Java Beach regulars decided to go elsewhere.

Bennett hesitated before going on. "I hope you'll consider the situation and be supportive of Mitch. I don't want to believe it either, but the evidence is there."

"Maybe this whole thing is a misunderstanding." Clutching Bennett's hand, Ivy leaned earnestly toward him. "I've always liked Mitch, and I think he's good for Shelly. They seem to be a good fit."

"I thought so, too." Bennett rubbed his thumb along her jawline.

As Ivy leaned against him, he curved his arm around her and ran his hand along her shoulder. She could smell the scent of sandalwood soap on his freshly showered skin and still damp hair. His presence was reassuring, though Ivy knew she'd have to brace herself for Shelly's reaction.

"Mitch was pretty nervous about telling Shelly," Bennett said. "Aside from me, he's never told anyone in Summer Beach about the incident. He said he cares so much for Shelly and sees a future for them, so he wants her to know everything about his past." Bennett looked a little remorseful. "Actually, he wanted to share these details a long time ago, but I advised him against it. I know how people can be."

Normally, Ivy would be upset about that, but this was an emergency.

He kissed her forehead before rising. "I'll let you know what happens."

Ivy slid her hand along his forearm, reluctant to let him go. "We'll keep looking here. I know this is a mistake." Yet she couldn't prove it, not without the missing tiara.

Ivy closed the door behind him and leaned against it, wrapping her arms around herself.

On the other hand, what if the chief weren't mistaken?

A few minutes later, Shelly tapped on her door and straggled inside. Her eyes were puffy and rimmed with red. "Guess you know that Mitch came over this morning." Still wearing pajamas, she flopped onto the bed and grabbed a pillow.

Ivy eased onto the white duvet beside her. "Bennett told me what's going on. I'm so sorry."

Shelly burrowed under the cover and wailed. "Why do I always fall for the wrong guy?"

"You don't. I really believe that Mitch is one of the good ones. Look at what he's done with his life, and for the community." Bennett once told her that Mitch often showed up at the youth center with treats and stayed to counsel teens on staying in school and having goals. She pushed the duvet down to stroke her sister's tangled hair. "Mitch cares for you, Shells, and you're good together."

Looking forlorn, Shelly said, "He told me he loves me." She clenched a pillow in her hand and curled it under her chin. "Did Bennett tell you Mitch went to prison and served time for robbery?"

Ivy slid a hand over her cheek. *Robbery.* No wonder the FBI and Chief Clarkson had brought up his record. *And now...what could she say?* "Did Mitch have an explanation?"

"About what you would expect." Shelly sniffled. "His father left the family when Mitch was just a year old, and his mother supported the family by waiting tables. They moved from Portland, Oregon to Las Vegas so she could earn more at the casinos." Shelly stopped, blinking back tears. "Mitch was working, too, and earned enough to buy his first car. But he fell in with the wrong crowd of kids. Small-time thugs."

"That's not uncommon. Did Mitch share details?"

"Here's what he said happened," Shelly said, sniffling and raising herself up on one elbow. "One Saturday night he'd taken his friends out in his car. They wanted him to park in a strip mall and wait for him while they went into a pawn shop. It was hot, and being the desert, he did it to keep the air conditioner running. As it turned out, his friends did a smash-and-grab of mostly jewelry and ran out. Without realizing it, Mitch became the getaway driver. Witnesses got his license plate number."

Ivy clucked her tongue. "Not one of the smartest crimes I've heard."

"So Mitch served a year. He got out early due to good behavior. And now, he could be facing time again. Much more time." Shelly drew her knees up and clasped her pajama-clad legs. "I really care about Mitch, but I'm not as strong as you are. If Mitch is guilty, I don't think I could handle it."

"I don't think he did it." Ivy had no idea what had happened to the valuable piece, but in her heart, she truly felt Mitch was innocent.

Shelly shook her head. "I would like to be there for Mitch, but I have to think of myself for once. What am I doing out here? Dating an ex-con, living off my sister, hiding out at the beach because I couldn't make it in the big city." Her voice caught in her throat. "I'm pathetic, Ives. I want to get married and have a baby, but look at the guys I chose."

Ivy wrapped her arms around Shelly. "Don't blame yourself for promises that Ezzra didn't follow through on. And you're not living off me. You're working hard, too. After the taxes are paid, we'll give ourselves a raise and split everything in half. That's our deal. We're in business *together*."

Pulling away, Shelly said, "Now that the grounds are done, you don't need me."

"Your flowers would be dead in a week without you." Ivy ached for her sister, and for all that Shelly felt she was missing. If only Ivy could make her understand how much she was loved here at Summer Beach. Shelly had a future here. *Couldn't she see that?* "Please don't be so hard on yourself."

Shelly raised her luminous eyes to Ivy. Through shimmering tears, she said, "I'm being realistic. I'm too old to blame others for my mistakes. Or for not achieving my goals in life. That needs to change."

Shelly dragged herself from the bed and padded out the door.

As Ivy watched her go, she had a feeling that she was missing something in this puzzle of the missing tiara—and that it would impact Shelly and Mitch. *But what?*

30

"Great walk this morning," Ivy said as she and her beach walking group climbed the rear steps to the veranda. Chief Clarkson was due shortly, so she'd thought it was crucial for morale to gather the group and start the day with exercise and endorphins. She paused on the terrace level and turned toward the sea, inhaling deeply and raising her arms overhead, leading the group in the final stretch. The sun was already burning off the foggy marine layer.

Gilda put Pixie down. "Now sit, and be a good girl." The little dog obeyed, but as soon as Gilda began her stretches, Pixie bounded off to explore nearby shrubs.

Celia and Megan followed along with the exercises while Debra did a modified version to accommodate an old shoulder injury. Shelly had been guiding her in the yoga class.

"I haven't felt this good in years," Debra said, rotating her neck. "Shelly's been helping me gain more flexibility. Maybe I can get Darla to join us. Would you mind?"

"We'd be happy to have her," Ivy managed to say. Shelly would go ballistic, but what if Debra could talk her sister into dropping her frivolous case?

Imani nodded at Ivy, then shed her jacket and leaned into a runner's stretch on the stone steps. After the group stretch was over, she pulled Ivy aside. "I asked Jamir to cover for me at Blossoms today. Thought you might need me here."

"I'd really like that," Ivy said, stepping out of her shoes.

Everyone at the inn left their sandy beach shoes under a bench Shelly had placed by the rear door to avoid tracking sand inside. The other women left their shoes and padded inside, chatting as they went. Pixie bounded after Gilda and raced inside ahead of the group.

Ivy waited until they'd gone in. "Questioning the guests is going to be awkward. Do you really think this will help Mitch?"

"I don't know," Imani said, shaking her head. "It doesn't look good for him, but I'll help him get the best defense possible. That's not my area of expertise. I practiced civil law, and he needs a criminal defender."

"I just can't imagine that he did it," Ivy said, fidgeting with a fingernail. "Shelly and Poppy and I will keep going through the house today to see if the piece turns up."

Poppy burst through the rear kitchen door. "Aunt Ivy, I've been trying to call you."

"My phone battery was dead, so I left it on the charger upstairs. What's wrong?"

Thrusting out a note, Poppy said, "Shelly left this in the library on your chair. I hope you don't mind that I read it."

Sinking onto the steps, Ivy read the brief note. *Going back to New York to get my old job back and find a new life. Please don't hate for me it.*

"Oh, no, no, no…" Feeling sick at her stomach, Ivy closed her eyes. *Shelly, gone?* She could feel Poppy's worried eyes on her. Standing, Ivy said, "Shelly's upset, but we need to try to stop her." Ivy passed the note to Imani and pushed her hands through her hair, trying to figure out what to do. "Poppy, do you have your phone?"

"She's sending my calls to voice mail," Poppy said. "And we don't have enough time to reach her before her flight leaves for New York." She glanced at the time on her phone. "She's barely going to make it as it is."

"How do you know that?"

"We texted until she stopped responding."

Imani put down the note and wagged her head. "This isn't going to sit well with Clark."

Ivy passed a hand over her forehead. "You don't think he suspects her, do you?"

"Can't say, but it looks bad for her to flee like this," Imani said.

"I'll try to reach her." Ivy bounded inside. As she raced up the steps, she heard the door chimes ring. That was probably Chief Clarkson. Gripping the handrail, she paused.

Poppy and Imani hurried into the foyer. "If that's Clark, we'll take care of him," Imani called up. "I won't tell him about Shelly yet. If she doesn't return, then let me be the one to break it to him."

"Thanks. I'll be right back." Ivy hurried on. When she reached her bedroom, she snatched her phone from the charger and tapped out a message to Shelly. *Please don't leave. Everyone needs you here. We love you. Please, Shells.*

Clutching her phone, Ivy sat on the bed and waited, willing her sister to reply. Panic seized her chest. *Shelly can't leave like this. Without even discussing it.* And then Ivy recalled their last conversation. She covered her face with her hands, thinking about how Shelly thought. Her sister *had* been warning her. But this could be disastrous for Shelly.

Ivy flopped back onto the bed, hot tears streaming from her eyes. When she'd told Shelly that she was going to Summer Beach to take care of the house, Shelly had insisted on coming with her, offering her the moral support she so desperately needed after Jeremy's death. Ivy couldn't have managed without her sister. She wouldn't have had the guts to go through with the idea of turning the house into an inn.

More than that, Shelly had been with her every step on this journey. She was as much a part of the Seabreeze Inn as Ivy was, from transforming the grounds, helping decorate the interior, and leading yoga classes. Shelly had the beachy, bohemian vibe and quirky laugh that guests loved. Nothing would be the same here without her. And together, they were the renegade sisters who had finally returned to their west coast family.

Shelly couldn't just *leave*.

Ivy rolled over and checked her phone again. *Shells? Are you there? Please talk to me.* She stared at the phone, waiting and urging Shelly to reply.

Nothing.

Ivy blew out a breath of frustration. Shelly was probably in the air by now. On her way back east.

And yet, Ivy really did understand. Shelly had always been the more sensitive sibling. She was a people pleaser—maybe even an enabler with Ezzra—though Ivy wasn't well versed in popular psychology. Was Shelly running away from the situation, or finally taking a stand to put her life on track?

Ivy folded her hands over her heart, mentally sending her love to Shelly. Ivy knew that at the center of this situation was Mitch. Shelly must have cared for him more than she'd let on. Once again, Shelly was heartbroken, and Ivy felt a wave of guilt as she thought about how she'd encouraged the relationship with Mitch.

Feeling like she had failed her sister, Ivy stared at the ceiling and let her tears stream along the sides of her face.

After allowing herself about a minute of that, Ivy wiped her tears and brought the phone up again. She called to leave a message, hoping that Shelly would hear it after she touched down in New York.

"I'm not angry with you, just concerned," Ivy replied to Shelly's chirpy recorded greeting. "I love you, and I only want the best for you. Please call when you get to New York."

After hanging up, Ivy closed her hands over her face. She'd had Shelly by her side these last couple of months, and they had almost achieved their goal. Could she manage without her?

She had to. She had to hang on to give Shelly a place to come back to if she changed her mind. And her daughters. This was their new home now, and she would do everything in her power to keep it because she knew the alternative.

Ivy pushed herself up on the bed. Today was another beginning.

She pulled a tissue from the nightstand. Imani and Poppy were downstairs with Chief Clarkson, and soon he would begin the interrogation of certain guests, some of whom might very well leave because of this.

This morning, Ivy had discussed the necessity for this on the walk, and some guests had asked a few questions. Because of this, she stood to lose the guests that were so critical to the inn's cashflow.

This was not the time to shut herself in her bedroom and feel sorry for herself.

Shape up and get out there, she told herself, quickly freshening up. It would be four or five hours before Shelly landed.

And there was nothing more she could do until then.

Hastily, Ivy bathed and pulled on white jeans and a blue shirt with rolled-up sleeves. It was time to go to work. She stepped out into the hallway and shut her door.

Behind her, she heard the sharp, frantic tapping of Pixie's toenails on the hardwood floor. But when she turned around, all she saw was a large straw hat disappearing around a corner.

Ivy pressed her lips together and followed. She really didn't have time for this.

Just then, Bennett appeared at the top of the

stairs. "I came to check on you. Poppy told me Shelly left."

Ivy stopped her pursuit of Pixie to speak to him. After she explained what had happened, Bennett took her in his arms. The warmth of his embrace was soothing, and she clung to him, drawing the comfort she needed.

"I know you miss Shelly," he said, drawing his hand over her cheek. "We all will." Just then, a movement caught his eye, and Bennett pressed a finger to his lips, motioning over her shoulder.

Ivy turned. The straw hat she'd seen was slowly advancing toward Gilda's open door. On the other side, pointed ears poked above the brim, and a tail wagged behind it.

As they watched, Pixie tugged the large hat through the doorway.

"I think that's Celia's hat," Ivy said. "She often leaves it on the bench downstairs."

"Well, Pixie just swiped it," Bennett said.

"She's got big nerve for a little dog. That is, a little thief," she added. Then, a curious thought struck her.

Bennett furrowed his brow. "What'd you call her?"

Taking his hand, she led him to Gilda's room and tapped on the door. "Gilda, may I come in?"

When Gilda didn't reply, she poked her head inside. Gilda's back was to the door. She sat at her desk, tapping furiously on her computer. Her noise-canceling headphones were clamped over her ears, and she was bobbing to music only she could hear. On the walk, Gilda had excitedly told her about a new article on dog obedience training that she was writing for a national pet magazine.

Pixie was nowhere to be seen.

Ivy walked in and touched Gilda on the shoulder.

"Oh, I didn't hear you come in." Gilda took off the headphones and turned her face up to them. She was all smiles and innocence, ignorant that she was harboring a furtive pooch with a purloined straw hat large enough for Pixie to hide under. "What's up?"

"We saw Pixie scurry in here," Ivy said. "She has Celia's hat." All in the day of an innkeeper. Ivy had a fleeting thought, wondering what Shelly would have thought about this. No doubt, she would have laughed and cajoled Pixie from her hiding place. But she couldn't think of her sister now, or she'd start crying all over again. Instead, she reached for Bennett's hand behind her and twined her fingers through his.

"A hat?" Gilda seemed confused. "How could that be?"

"Even though the hat's larger than she is, she was dragging it inside," Bennett said. "Where would she hide it? Maybe under the bed?" He bent down on one knee and lifted a dust ruffle. "Nothing here."

Gilda let out an exasperated sigh. "She's probably in her bed behind the screen. I never go back there. She's pretty territorial."

"Can you?" Ivy asked. "That's Celia's hat. She'll want it back."

Gilda cast a glance toward the screen, frowning as if it were some forbidden territory guarded by giant mastiffs rather than an anxious Chihuahua. "Pixie, bring that out, please."

Silence.

"Pixie? Are you in there? Come to Mommy. Come on." Gilda's voice pitched to a higher octave and turned into a singsong cadence. "Come to Mama, sweetikins." She snapped her fingers toward the screen.

Silence.

"Are you sure she came in here?" Gilda asked.

Bennett shifted. "We both saw her," he said. Though his voice was gentle, Ivy heard the professional, mayoral clip to his words. He meant business.

And Chief Clarkson was waiting downstairs. They didn't have time to wheedle Pixie from her hiding place. Ivy needed to retrieve the hat, return it to Celia, and tend to business with the chief. Now.

Ivy crossed the room to the wooden, four-panel Chinese screen. Painted dragons swirled up the panels like guardians of the lair. While not imposing mastiffs, the two-dimensional dragons were scary enough. She angled the hinged panel on the end toward her and peeked around it.

From the comfort of a thick, lumpy blanket, Pixie charged her with a low growl that erupted into a high-pitched, manic series of ear-piercing yaps. Baring her teeth, Pixie hurtled her wiry frame toward Ivy's shins. Thank goodness she had on jeans, but Ivy was sure those sharp teeth could rip right through the cloth.

Ivy pressed herself against the wall and cried out. "Gilda, help me."

"She gets agitated if you invade her space or try to look at her bed." Gilda approached Pixie with apprehension. "Bring me Celia's hat, babykins."

Pixie stood her ground, barking her ear-splitting commands to drive the intruders away.

Gilda turned up her palms. "You see how she is," she shouted over Pixie's barks. "I'll try to get her to bring it out later. Sometimes she will."

"*Sometimes?*" Ivy was absolutely incredulous. And losing patience by the second. This was an idiotic scene. And yet…a prickly feeling on her neck alerted her to something. *What?* All she knew was they had to break the impasse and explore Pixie's den. "Bennett, can you bring me that blanket on the bed?" It was a new acquisition for cool beach evenings, but it had to be sacrificed for the greater good.

Bennett scooped the marine blue, plaid

blanket from the bed. "Gilda, step aside and let us try."

To Ivy, Bennett said, "On three. I'll disable Pixie while you charge the castle. "One. Two. Three." He swooped the blanket over the snarling Pixie and swaddled her in the thick blanket. "Go!"

Ivy was already in motion, leaping over the angry, wriggling mound that Bennett was shifting toward the wall.

Behind the screen, Ivy spied Celia's hat peaking from under the dog's blanket. Hurriedly, she snatched it.

Pixie was now howling like a wounded animal, sending up a shrill alarm that was sure to wake any guests who were still sleeping.

Pressing her free hand to one ear, Ivy began to back out. "Still have her?"

"Yeah, I got her," Bennett said. "You're safe."

That strange feeling coursed through Ivy again. She nudged the dog's cheery, bone-printed blanket with the toe of her sandal and hit something. Probably a chew-toy, but Pixie was now a proven thief. What else might she have nicked?

Lifting an edge of the fur-pricked blanket, Ivy saw a green tennis ball and a mound of socks. "Found your socks," she called out.

What else was under there?

Ivy tugged back the blanket and reached under. Her fingers touched something soft and silky. She drew it out and a blaze of purple silk unfurled under her touch. "And Imani's scarf," Ivy called out again. She passed it back through the opening in the screen.

Gilda caught it. "Why, I had no idea. Pixie, what a bad girl."

A muffled, agonizing wail erupted from beneath the blanket. Footsteps sounded outside in the hallway.

"What's going on up here?" Chief Clarkson's voice boomed in the room over Pixie's audible distress.

"We've caught the culprit," Bennett said. "Celia's hat. Imani's scarf. A couple of my socks, no doubt."

Exhilaration over the finds burst through Ivy and hope surged in her heart. Maybe…it was a crazy thought…but just maybe…

Gripping one edge of Pixie's blanket, she held her breath and closed her eyes against an imminent flurry of fur. She yanked the blanket from the dog bed.

Pixie's cry reached an unprecedented crescendo at the flagrant violation.

Pressing one hand to her ear again, Ivy let the blanket fall to one side. When she was sure most of the fur had settled, she opened her eyes.

And there, amid balled up tissues, a doll dress that Ivy hadn't missed, and a pair of Shelly's yoga leggings, gleamed the tips of tear-drop shaped, aquamarine stones.

Ivy gasped and cried out, "I've found it!" She lifted the precious tiara from its resting place among Pixie's other ill-gotten treasures.

Emerging from behind the screen, Ivy cradled the jeweled ornament in her hands. "Here it is," she called out in triumph.

All eyes stared at the rare splendor Ivy held in her hands. Bennett and Poppy let out a cheer, while Chief Clarkson, Imani, and Gilda looked on, awestruck. Pixie continued to wriggle and howl.

"This is what you're looking for." Ivy handed the tiara to the chief, who whipped out a handkerchief to accept it. "We'll need to clean out Pixie's treasure trove."

Bennett transferred custody of Pixie to Gilda, who rushed to Pixie's aid and scooped her into her arms. "Why don't you take her for a walk on the beach while we sort out the pilfered property?"

"Poor baby," Gilda cooed to the little dog. "She must have transferred her anxiety outlet from chewing to borrowing. We'll work on that in obedience training."

"And we'll move the screen," Ivy said. "Consider keeping her bed where you can see her."

"But she prefers her privacy," Gilda said, rubbing Pixie's head.

Poppy stepped forward to inspect Pixie's nest, which was full of other people's belongings. "That little dog is a hoarder. Until she shapes up, you'll have to check on her acquisitions every day and return them."

Gilda promised and hurried out with Pixie, who yapped all the way down the hall.

Poppy turned over the purple silk scarf, inspecting for damage before handing it to Imani. "It looks okay, and we'll be sure to reimburse you for dry cleaning."

Ivy opened the screen a little wider, and Poppy ducked behind it. "Here's the Louis Vuitton coin purse. And Shelly's gardening glove, plus a set of keys. Say, is anyone missing a bunch of socks?"

Bennett chuckled. "Pixie's welcome to my smelly socks. Which might be why she stole people's personal stuff. Maybe she felt lonely."

"I'd tried on the tiara," Poppy said. "Maybe it still held my scent or a strand of hair. Poor Pixie, now I feel a little sorry for her."

"Don't feel too bad," Ivy said. "There's your USC T-shirt."

Heaving a sigh of relief in the welcome quietness, Ivy turned to Chief Clarkson. "This will clear Mitch, won't it?"

Chief Clarkson angled his head. "As long as Mitch wasn't Pixie's accomplice or hid the evidence in question here, he'll be released."

"I'm sure you can dust for fingerprints," Imani said. "Let's talk about this," she added with a nod, indicating that they should move downstairs. With her hand on his forearm, she led Clark from the room. On her way out, she winked at Ivy and mouthed, *Don't worry.*

Ivy fell into Bennett's open arms. "We did it," she said.

"That was all you," he replied, wrapping her in his embrace.

Later that evening, Ivy sat on a cushioned chaise lounge on the veranda and tried to reach Shelly, though the call went straight to voice mail again.

At the beep, Ivy said, "Shelly, this is important. We found the tiara. Pixie had snatched it, along with a lot of other missing items, including your gardening glove. This means that Mitch should be cleared. Please think about returning and giving this another try. Or if you feel like you need a break, I understand. I love you, Shells. We're sisters forever."

After Ivy hung up, a sense of loneliness crept over her. Watching the waves, she tried to put everything in perspective. Shelly had a right to make her own decisions. She also knew more about Mitch and his background now, and she must be weighing this, along with other concerns she'd brought up.

Maybe the slow pace of Summer Beach wasn't for Shelly. She'd always liked New York's fast tempo. The inn had been Ivy's idea—her solution to the pressing financial dilemma she'd found herself in. Shelly had happily come along, but she'd had time to decide if this life was right for her. Either way, Ivy had to respect Shelly's decision.

But she still missed her sister. Ivy blinked back tears that gathered in the corners of her eyes.

The lights inside Bennett's apartment above the garage flicked off, and she watched him descend the stairs. She raised her hand to him, and he made his way towards her.

Bennett perched on the edge of the chaise lounge beside her. "Up for a walk on the beach? There's a beautiful full moon out."

"I'd like that." She tucked the phone into her pocket. After sorting out details with Chief Clarkson, Ivy had told Bennett about Shelly's sudden departure.

Bennett offered her his hand, and they made their way to the sandy beach. Moonlight spilled across the water, and strains of piano music from another beachside home sailed across the shoreline on a light breeze.

As they walked hand in hand, the waves rushed to the shore with vigor. With the full moon overhead, the ocean was at high tide, crashing onto the flat rocks where children often scampered and shooting fanlike sprays in its wake.

"Impressive," Ivy said, pausing before the rocks and breathing in. The ocean air never failed to revive and energize her, though tonight that was a more difficult feat than usual.

As if reading her mind, Bennett squeezed her hand, filling her with gratitude for his presence. She loved the comfortable sensation of holding hands with a man again, but if she were honest with herself, when she looked at him, her heart-strings crackled with increasing intensity.

"Impressive, indeed," Bennett intoned, sliding his arm around her shoulder and gazing into her eyes. "You're one extraordinary woman. I know you've had a tumultuous day, but I'm sure you can handle whatever comes your way."

Blinking back a rush of emotions, Ivy met his gaze. Moonlight illuminated his eyes, which reflected the deep, marine-blue shade of the evening sea. His expression surprised her—it held an element she hadn't often seen in her late husband's eyes as the years had worn on.

Admiration. She drew herself up and moved closer into his embrace.

"I miss Shelly so much already," Ivy said. Since she'd seen the note, a persistent ache had settled in her chest.

Folding her hand into his, he pressed it against his chest. She could feel the strong, steady beat of his heart through his cotton T-shirt.

"Of course, you do. We all do. But you'll manage until she returns."

"You sound pretty sure about her return." She laughed softly. "I'm not. I know Shelly."

"Sounds like she needs time to assess her feelings." He ran his thumb along her hand. "Mitch is feeling pretty low over her departure, too."

Maybe Shelly was avoiding his calls, too. "Has he heard from her?"

He rubbed her back. "Nothing but radio silence."

Resting her head against Bennett's chest, Ivy thought of everything that had transpired since she'd arrived in Summer Beach, from the ongoing mystery of Amelia Erickson to the Ridgetop Fire devastation, which had filled the inn with local residents who'd become a surrogate family for each other.

She couldn't have managed it all without Shelly and Poppy, or the others who'd helped her, including Imani and Jamir. Even Misty, who had pitched in with enthusiasm. If only Sunny could visit and experience this, too—perhaps she'd feel like she had a home again.

Ivy had watched each guest—Celia and Tyler, Imani and Jamir, Gilda, Bennett, and others—struggle with their losses after the fire. But during the simple morning beach walks and yoga classes, which Poppy had promised to take over, she'd also seen remarkable healing here by the sea. From all that they had shared, Ivy knew she would count these guests and others in town as friends for the rest of her life—even if she didn't manage to keep the inn or Darla's lawsuit closed her doors.

Banishing that last thought, Ivy blinked against the salty spray. *No.* She would *not* fail. She would find a way to pay the taxes, whether Shelly was here or not. And somehow, she would get through to her neighbor. She *must*.

This was a life Ivy had never dreamed of, but now that she was living it, she couldn't imagine anything else.

And then there was Bennett. She spread her fingers and entwined them in his. He'd been so unexpected in her life. They'd already overcome several hurdles, and together they'd crossed the chasms of her loss and uncertainty. Did she dare hope for more?

His eyes twinkled back at her.

Oh, yes, she could.

Nearby, the piano music deepened into a rich melody that rippled across the beach. Ivy recognized the old tune; it was one of her favorites. She smiled, savoring the beauty of all that surrounded her.

"I love this," Bennett said, humming along and swaying slightly to the music. His chest reverberated against hers, and he pressed his hand against the small of her back.

"It's an older one, but one I've always loved."

A smile played on Bennett's lips, and Ivy felt a

flush course through her. She might have been talking about him. "The *song*, I mean."

He kissed her forehead. "I'll try to hide my disappointment.

Soon they were moving together as one across the sand, their hearts full for each other, dancing and twirling under the moonlight. Ivy lifted her face to his, and Bennett bent toward her, their lips touching, melting into the other, the sensation caressing their very souls.

Ivy smiled up at him. She had a sweet feeling that even now, this was still only the beginning.

The End

AUTHOR'S NOTE

Thank you for reading *Seabreeze Summer*, and I hope you enjoyed it. Continue the Summer Beach saga with the next book in the series, **Seabreeze Sunset**. Find out if Ivy and Shelly will continue to run the inn together, and what happens when the next wave of summer guests come to visit.

If you like historical novels set by the sea, you might like to visit the gorgeous Italian coast of Amalfi, where a newly widowed chocolatier from San Francisco discovers a mysterious secret. Check out **The Chocolatier** now, and get whisked away into a fascinating world. Between chocolate tastings and fabulous 1950s styles and music, this was one of my favorite books to research.

Keep up with my new releases on my website at JanMoran.com. Please join my VIP Reader's

Club there to receive news about special deals and other goodies. Plus, find more fun and join other like-minded readers in my Facebook Reader's Group.

More to Enjoy

If this is your first book in the Seabreeze Inn at Summer Beach series, I invite you to revisit Ivy and Shelly as they renovate a historic beach house in *Seabreeze Inn*, the first book in the original Summer Beach series. In the Coral Cottage series, you'll meet Ivy's friend Marina in *Coral Cottage.*

If you'd like more sunshine and international travel, meet a group of friends in the *Love California* series, beginning with *Flawless* and an exciting trip to Paris.

Finally, I invite you to read my standalone family sagas, including *Hepburn's Necklace* and *The Chocolatier*, 1950s novels set in gorgeous Italy.

Most of my books are available in ebook, paperback or hardcover, audiobooks, and large print. And as always, I wish you happy reading!

ABOUT THE AUTHOR

JAN MORAN is a *USA Today* and a *Wall Street Journal* bestselling author of romantic women's fiction. A few of her favorite things include a fine cup of coffee, dark chocolate, fresh flowers, laughter, and music that touches her soul. She loves to travel, and her favorite places for inspiration are those rich with history and mystery and set against snowy mountains, palm-treed beaches, or sparkly city lights. Jan is originally from Austin, Texas, and a trace of a drawl still survives, although she has lived in Southern California near the beach for years.

Most of her books are available as audiobooks, and her historical fiction is translated into German, Italian, Polish, Dutch, Turkish, Russian, Bulgarian, Portuguese, and Lithuanian, and other languages.

If you enjoyed this book, please consider leaving a brief review online for your fellow readers where you purchased this book or on Goodreads or Bookbub.

To read Jan's other historical and contemporary novels, visit JanMoran.com. Join her VIP Readers Club mailing list and Facebook Readers Group to learn of new releases, sales and contests.